Dedication

To my mother, who taught me the love of words and who read every last word of this book, even before it was a book.

To my sister Brooke, who laughs the loudest at my jokes, and who has the strength of Adair.

To my sister Stephanie, who would wear a t-shirt with my face on it without being asked, just like Ausley. It is for you that I write each day.

To my daddy, who taught me the meaning of integrity, and the love of the Father above.

To Jeremy, because I loved you the first day I saw you and you loved me back.

To my children, when the time comes, never be afraid to walk the hard path and remember you will never be alone.

And finally to the One who created us all…Thank you for ending what we began.

CONTENTS

August Dreams 1
Giants in October 13
Clear as Mud 41
Everything Changes 75
the Great Trees 109
He Arrives 141
Pictures from the Past 171
Called out of the Dark 193
the Phone Call 217
Wade in the Water 235
the Wakeful One 253
Waking Giants 279
Midnight in Montgomery 313
Home Sweet Rome 335
the Council Arrives 367
Ancient Voices 407
Eyes like a Snake 421
the Seer 437
the Edge of Dark 459
Terebinths of Mamre 479
It Begins 515

Simulacrum (sim yə¹ lā krəm): Latin. Image or representation of something that is real; A faithful image, an Image-bearer of the Original Being.

Friguscor (fri'-gus-cor) : Latin. Literally, Cold Heart. A distortion of the simulacrum. A perversion of the original, an unfaithful copy. A race of men who bear a semblance of the original, but lack the essence of it.

Let us make man in our image, according to our likeness, and let them rule over the fish of the sea and over the birds of the sky and over the cattle and over all the earth.' And God created man in His own image, in the image of God, He created him; male and female, He created them.

Genesis 1:26-28

{ 1 }

August Dreams

It begins at the end, for it is the end that begins it all.

There is no moonlight. I run blind in the darkness. Blackness so thick, it devours any scant trace of light. Go! I push myself forward. Creatures' claws scrape against the tree trunks; I hear their screams for blood. My blood. They are coming for me.

My clothes catch on jagged limbs. I jerk in terror, desperate to get loose. Screaming is pointless. My voice is gone. I am the hunted, and they are gaining ground. I am the rabbit and they…they are the wolves. I have to run. I cannot stop here. I have come too far to die here. Searching frantically for a way out of the trap, I find only darkness. I scramble forward not knowing where my feet will land, fearing what's behind me more than what lies ahead. So I run.

The earth groans and cracks as it gives way behind me. The very ground betrays me, racing with the pursuers to catch and swallow me. I must run faster, I must run faster, but the earth is unstable, like running though deep mud. They are gaining ground. Gravity itself shifts with the earth's crumbling, and I feel my center shift with it. My body feels old, each rotation of thigh, knee, leg, foot, thigh, knee, leg, foot, slowing until I am in slow-motion, fighting through an ocean of viscous air that hinders my every step. My breath feels like ice on my lips, tears spill down my cheeks. No, no, no! I shake myself. There is no time to mourn, no time to feel, I must run now, run for my life. Fighting back the rising despair, I cling to the fear and determination that has become my constant companion and my right hand. But I am slowing, and I know it.

And then, like each night before, he is there. Beside me, a man is running. He is dark and beautiful, and somehow familiar, though I do not recognize his face. Perfectly in sync, we race through the forest together. I stumble across a gnarled root. His rough hands steady me. "Veralee, the door...you must get to the door. Remember the door!" he screams against the wind.

Then I see it. A door of light, a beacon in the darkness. I jump, gaining ground ahead of the avalanche behind me. He jumps with me, and we hit the hard earth running. I jump again, and again, my tousled hair whirling with the wind. My stomach knots and curdles. I am so tired, so hungry, so thirsty. I cannot remember the last time I tasted food. My stomach rumbles in anger. "Remember the door," I chant. Remember the door. Remember the door. The door, I must make it to the door.

    I fall and crash hard, my leg twisting and splitting against the jagged edge of an exposed root. My screams shatter the night as I writhe on the forest floor, grasping at my bleeding calf. A small branch penetrates the muscle. I vomit in the grass. Then he is there again. He helps me sit up and touches my face with urgent tenderness. His eyes, emeralds beneath dark lashes, are full of a pain I do not understand, but the determination in them is much stronger. "You cannot stop here, Veralee, you must keep going, you must not give up," he demands, speaking into my ear. I do not know this man, but for some reason, I trust him.

    The groaning of the disintegrating earth behind me, and the screaming dark creatures snap me back to reality. I push myself upright. Pain rolls over me like a wave as I try to step down on my bleeding left leg. Determined, I force down the bile left in my mouth and push myself forward. I look, but I cannot see the door anymore. Pain and frustration blanket my brain and muddle my thoughts. But then something happens. Light flows toward me from the direction of the door, like a hand reaching into the deep to save a drowning woman. As I hobble forward, a million fireflies swirl around me, engulfing me, lighting my way. Their flickering bodies create a trail of light. We run, following the glowing path. But then the man comes to a full stop. The tiny flares have split around a giant oak tree, dividing into two paths. Two ways. The man turns to me, "Which way will you choose, Veralee?" The screeching still pounds in my ears, fear blinds my eyes. "I don't know," I cry out, "I don't know the way!"

    "The way is in your blood," he says as rain begins to

pour and lightning flashes around us. The woods around me begin to spin, as I stand at the crossroads in the pelting rain. The woods spin faster and faster; the screaming echoes ever louder. Then, a still, small sound pricks the air. It is the sound of my heart beating. A trilling sound so low that I'm not sure if I am hearing it or feeling it. I look down at my shaking fingers. A sharp blade appears in my hand. "The way is in your blood," he repeats.

My blood. I scream as I cut my wrist. My blood falls to the ground, and the forest instantly stops spinning. One path goes dark, while the other shines brightly. The man grabs my bleeding wrist, "Run, Veralee. Run. Get to the door. Remember the door!" I see the door again, etched into a giant tree in the distance. I must get to the door.

I must make it to the end; I must finish this. Then just as I reach my hand out to push the door open, the earth gives way and I am flailing, falling into the blackness. And the man is gone.

I sat straight up, banging my head on the reading lamp that I had, once again, left on. I rolled over and looked around. I was back in my bedroom. Every nerve in my body was alive, but the room lay still, dark and silent. The stillness scared me. My breathing came hard and rapid in the humid night air as my heart hammered against my chest. The large, white windows stood wide open, as the rippling of linen curtains blew hauntingly through the room. And I remembered the dream.

Fear reached across the canyon of consciousness, its long

fingers pressing down on my chest and squeezing at my throat. Deliberately, I slowed my breathing down to a crawl, willing the sick panic to pass. I stretched out my cramped legs, which were bent awkwardly beneath me. As usual, my muscles were sore from running, and I watched as the tiny scrapes and cuts from the trees in my dreams began the quick process of healing. Carelessly, I tossed the books that were scattered across my bed onto the floor and flopped back into my pillows. It was the same dream I had had for years, but tonight was different. Tonight I actually made it to the door... and I touched it. This was progress, I mused. But then again, never, ever had I actually opened that door.

The night air smelled thick with rain, and sweat beaded on my forehead. Alabama in August. Curling up on my side I rubbed the soft skin that stretched over my tseeyen, the trait that marked me as Simulacrum. Starting at the base of my right pinky, the tseeyen wrapped to the inside of my wrist, where the design resembled something like a sparrow made of the inner-workings of a clock, with a long tail that curled to the upper side of my hand. Mother said even as a baby I rubbed my tseeyen when I was tired or upset. The low, constant vibration of my mark soothed the last of my shivering. To explain the feeling that the tseeyen gave the body was almost impossible, but once I felt the buzz of electricity pulsing in a wall at an old store, and it instantly reminded me of the comforting vibration of my mark. Though the shape of the tseeyen was unique for each of us, they all vibrated and they all claimed us as Simulacrum. It was comforting to be claimed.

To have irrefutable proof that you belonged burned into the skin.

But the dreams, they had always been fierce. Nightmares of being abandoned to the dark, of being hunted, had claimed my sleep as far back as I could remember. And then, inevitably, came the screaming. My screams would erupt in the stillness of night, forging the gap between waking and sleeping. Mother would come running, wearing that same white flannel nightgown with the little pink roses on the collar. In one fluid motion, she would scoop me into her arms and hold me until my heart stopped racing away with my courage. I would methodically trace my mark over and over with my left fingers, soothing my nerves with the touch of warm skin. "Remember, Veelee, you are never alone; feel the vibration in your tseeyen, the power in it and remember that you are always protected, always being watched over, and never, ever alone." Her mark was circular, with three geometric doves, each touching the other's beak in the center. Separating the birds, were three distinct globes, which held three swirling designs inside. In our Histories the dove stood for many things: atonement, the spirit, and even peace. She was peace enough for me.

On those nights, Mother would lie beside me with her reassuring warmth and presence until the nightmares departed. For when the nightmares were done, when they had used me like a whipping boy night after night, they simply walked away. Then, wrapped in mother's protective arms, sleep would come, deep, peaceful sleep.

But that was long ago. Oh, the dreams still came, but I was nineteen now. This year I was finally old enough to attend the Council meeting in the Terebinths of Mamre, to have a voice among my people... and yet I still trembled in my bed at night when the dreams came. So what did my age really matter if I could not learn to control the dreams... or the fear?

Sleep leaned against my eyes as I gently traced the tiny bird on my wrist over and over. Then something hammered heavily to the ground, and my eyes flew open. *What was that?* I strained to hear more, but my breath thundered in my ears, the loudest noise in the house. The sound came from downstairs. I looked at the clock—4:38. The birds had not yet started singing to the sun. Quietly, I slipped from my bed and out to the hall. Hushed whispers floated through the house. Holding onto the wall, I inched myself forward until I could see the great winding stairs that marched down onto the medallion marble floor of the grand foyer. Daddy's office opened into the foyer. Bending over the solid oak banister, I could just make out the silhouette of mother's robe standing in the doorway to the office. Daddy must have dropped something as he was getting ready to leave for work. I sighed with relief. Pacified that it was just Mother and Daddy, I started to turn back to my bed.

"But Edwin, how long do you think we have until they find us?" Mother's voice caught in her throat, as if she were about to cry. Daddy was slow to answer, weary. He had been working long hours, and his face showed the fatigue more with each passing day.

"Gail, I don't know. I believe they are looking for us now. It's only a matter of time until they figure out it's us they're looking for. Right now they don't know. There have just been reports, rumors at this point." He sighed and pushed back the rolling chair from his great, cherry-wood desk with the floral bands that wrapped round and round the thick, round legs.

"Have you spoken with Austin? You have to tell him that they are watching him, Edwin."

Daddy was standing in front of her now. He leaned down and put his forehead on hers. "Gail, I don't want you to be frightened, I just want you to be aware that things are happening. I don't really know what is happening. Maybe it will all blow over, but...." His voice dropped as he lifted his hands to her face.

I sat down with my back against the banister, uncomfortable watching such a private moment. They spoke for another minute, then I heard the door close. When I looked down, I saw mother standing at the windows watching him leave. Her slender hands were buried deep inside the pockets of her robe.

"How long have you been there, Veralee?" Mother always knew when we were listening. Sheepishly, I slinked down the steps, "I just heard something drop, and it woke me. Then I heard you talking to Daddy."

"So you heard?" she did not turn to me, but kept her

eyes fixed on the window.

"A little. *Who* knows about us? What were you talking about?" Our secrecy was vital to us; it kept us alive.

She turned to me as I stepped onto the cold marble floor. She was debating telling me, I could see that in her face. "Veralee, you have always wanted to know everything, haven't you? And the truth is, you are strong enough now to know it all. Maybe, it is time to tell you." Her voice sounded so far away, even though she was just an arms-length away from me. "I have seen you, Veralee, in my dreams. Something is coming. You... you are stronger than you know....you will have to be. Sometimes we become most free when we have no choice."

She stopped suddenly, and looked so hard at me that it felt like she was looking past me, almost as if she was looking at who I would be, who I could be in the years to come. Her smile touched both of her eyes, "Well, enough of that. We have the 175th in a couple of weeks. I have so much sewing left to do. We might as well start the day." She tried to smile, but this time it didn't reach her eyes. Spinning on her heels, she turned back to the window as if the view of the giant oaks which lined the entrance to Red Oaks called to her. She stood, scanning the horizon like a scout looking for the first of an invading army to crest the hill. Nothing out of the ordinary was outside that window. The great cotton fields that surrounded the plantation blew in the early morning breeze, the gardens sat quietly waiting for the sunrise, the sound of tractors would soon rumble in the distance, and the great oaks trees that dominated the landscape, their lazy arms caressing the ground with their branches, rested serenely on the green grass. All seemed peaceful outside, but inside a haunting shiver ran through the foyer, making the marble feel even colder under my bare feet.

    The 175th celebration would be quite the event. It had been 175 years since the Union Army had marched across Alabama and descended upon Red Oaks in the last days of the Civil War. The Confederate soldiers had caught wind of the Union Army moving in and were lying in wait when the Yankees arrived. It wasn't much of a battle, really. The Confederates were down to mostly old men and young boys with few weapons and less ammunition against a well-trained, well-equipped division of blues. But, the Rebels held the Yanks off for a day and a half before the inevitable happened. So it was here, at Red Oaks, that the tattered Old South in Alabama died alongside its men. Civil War enthusiasts from all over the country would gather here at Red Oaks to commemorate the great battle, and we-- my oldest sister, Adair, really-- would be in charge of running the entire event.

Mother's attempts to change the subject left me undeterred. I looked hard at her and cut easily to the heart of the issue, "Does this have to do with the Friguscor? And why is Uncle Austin involved?"

Mother whirled around in one quick motion, reminding me how agile she still was. Though already in her sixties, she didn't look a day over 40. "Veralee, this is the dance card we have been given. The Friguscor search and we evade, but you know that we cannot stay hidden forever, my sweet child. We live in their world." She closed the space between us and touched my face. She was so beautiful, even in the early hours of the morning.

"What will happen if they find us?" I must have looked like a cornered rabbit, because that is exactly how I felt, though I tried desperately to hide it from her. I didn't want my fear to alarm her. She was always so protective of us.

Reaching down she entwined my right hand with hers so that our tseeyens touched and a small, warm shock of energy flowed between us, the bond of blood. "Do not worry Little Bird, remember we are Simulacrum, and Simulacrum are never alone, for we know the end of the story."

I believed her. Not only because she was there with me, where I could feel her warmth and smell her sweet scent, but also because I was at Red Oaks, where so many of my people had walked before me. Here, where Daddy was the Guardian of the Gate, just like my grandmother before him, and her mother before her... we were safe. And yet, something else tugged at me. I realized that it was the memory of my dream still wrapped around me like a worn blanket. For a moment, it pulled me back, and I felt as though I was among the trees with the terror gaining behind me. *Is this what haunts my dreams? Is this the unknown, the wolves that hunt me while I sleep?*

Mother dropped my hand and absentmindedly walked

toward the large oak doors which led to the front porch. She loved to see the first rays of warm sun reach its fingers over the hills to the east.

Then *he* was there again, stepping out of the fray and into the edges of my mind like a steadying anchor. The smell of him, the touch of his hand and the undeniable truth in his emerald eyes called me back into the dream from last night. Somewhere, on the other side of my dreams, he was reaching for me. I did not know how or when or why....but something told me that the terror from my dreams was coming to Red Oaks. But my heart did not grow cold, because I also knew that *he* was coming as well. *Who are you?* I whispered to the air.

And then, as I heard the groan of the old oak doors closing behind Mother, I heard his voice...

"Remember the door, Veralee."

… { 2 }

Giants in October

Mornings at Red Oaks were my favorite. The scent of coffee drifted up the spiral staircase, compelling a few synapses to fire. My brain slowly churned to action. With eyes still heavy with sleep, I had a hazy awareness that I had dreamt of something important, but what?

All of us, the Simulacrum, had special traits that made us unique. As with any other genetic characteristic, like being tall or having curly hair, these talents ran in families. Like most women in my family, I dreamed dreams that showed me fragments of what was to come. Rarely did I see the entire picture. It was more like seeing sections of a finished puzzle. Often I had trouble discerning what a dream meant until the rest of the picture started to fill in. So usually, until the event came to pass, I could not fully understand the premonition. It was like knowing that something was behind a door, but not knowing what it was. The smell of coffee wafted up from the kitchen in our old plantation house, crowding out, for now, my memory of the dream.

Though it was still early, Red Oaks already buzzed with movement. Brilliant red cardinals and drab gray mockingbirds filled the air outside my windows with song, flitting through the lush garden that surrounded the balcony off my bedroom. The sun warmed the dark hardwood floors, and the sweet scent of hydrangeas and gardenias drifted through the thick, humid air. Still drugged with sleep, I shuffled slowly toward my small green bathroom, which also opened to Ausley's bedroom. Ausley was my younger sister, though she was not so little anymore. The clock on the bathroom counter read 7:30. I had missed my morning run. Usually I arose before the birds, running through the forest labyrinth. Today I had slept through my internal alarm. But class didn't start until 10:00, so maybe I could still run, after some coffee.

I stared at my disheveled reflection in the mirror, my dark brown hair matted and sprouting in all directions, like the Bride of Frankenstein's hair after she was jolted awake. I pushed my hair back and examined my face. Daddy always said that my eyes, like my mother's, were so clear and grey that they shined like a full moon on a velvet black night. My skin, unlike Mother's, was olive, sun-kissed, she would say. Hers was the color of milk and the texture of fine porcelain. I might not have her skin, but those were definitely her silver-grey eyes looking back from the mirror. I liked having that piece of her in me.

Returning to my room, I yelped in pain as my bare foot landed hard on a baby doll's hand. "Mattie!" I groused, as I kicked the doll across the room. Mattox, lovingly known as Mattie, my 4-year-old niece, had already camped in front of the TV watching *Sesame Street*. Otherwise she would have been sticking her fingers in my nose until I woke up. It was a little game she liked to play with me. She would sneak into my room and stand in front of my bed like the child from *The Exorcist*. Then, in the dead of sleep, I would feel something like a fat-legged spider skittering across my nose. I would smack myself in the face, only to wake up with one of Mattie's little toddler fingers jammed up my nostril. She would not jump back when I opened my eyes. Softly, she would giggle mischievously and chirp, "Mornin' Veelee," in her charming, deep southern birdie voice. A tickle ran down my nose as I thought about it, and I twitched like Samantha from *Bewitched*.

"Mornin,' Veelee," Mattie called, not downstairs after all. She sat crisscross applesauce in the middle of my bed staring at the painting of the two trees that covered the entire wall behind my headboard. I regarded the mural and felt the wind that blew across the trees in it ripple through my bones. All of my life I had slept in that room, in that bed, under that painting. And all of my life I had known that the painting was not simply made of oil and pigment. Always I had known that somehow, when my great-grandmother Vera had set her brush to the stark white wall, she had transferred much more than paint into a picture. She had birthed life into it.

"Veelee," Mattie said, her finger pointing at the lifelike trees. "Are these *the trees*? The ones that start the Fwee-gee-corty in the bad people?"

I picked up my hairbrush and ran it through Mattie's silky, blond hair. "Friguscor," I corrected her. Then I thought more about her question, "Yes and No. This," I said, gesturing with the brush to the larger of the two trees, "is the *One Tree*, the tree that began everything, that birthed the world from its branches. It is where the Eiani in our blood comes from." Then I turned and stepped toward the second tree in the painting. Placing my hands on its great, grey canopy, I continued. "And this is the *Tree of Shadows*, where the balance of the world exists together. Good and evil, I mean, good and bad are both in this one." The tree seemed to stir under my hand, as if awakening from the dried paint. Quickly, I pulled my hand back and watched the curious painting, but nothing rose from it.

"So that tree," she said pointing to the Tree of Shadows, "is what makes them bad... what makes them dangerous? And they smell bad, too." Mattie said pinching her nose and bobbing up and down on my bed. She was trying to lift the veil and grasp a bit of the history of our people, but her arms were too small to wrap around the complexity contained in that picture. Not yet. Too much there, and too hard to explain to such a small child.

I touched her arm and let my hand find her tseeyen. She had the fine bones of Adair with the mischievous eyes of her father, Phineas. Mattie stopped bobbing and smiled. All Simulacrum received their tseeyen at birth, though it didn't actually show on the skin until the eighth day. The blood decided its shape. It seemed to say something about us, to describe us in some way. As we grew, it did not change, but it became more defined, more distinct on the skin. Her tiny alabaster wrist held a complex pattern. At first glance it looked like a Celtic motif of lines and angles. But over the past year, I thought I could make out a picture in the lines, which looked very much like a scale, just like Adair's. A scale with a palm branch on its balance. I placed my mark on hers and felt her childlike love.

"We are safe here at Red Oaks, Li'l One," I reminder her. Then, to divert her attention I said, "I think I hear *Sesame Street* starting." Her eyes lit up.

"Veelee...slide me down the hall first! Just one time! Please, please!" Then I heard it. The whispering of wind, ever so faint, ever so far away, blew through my room. The windows were closed, but one glance told me the morning was still. I suspected the sound came from the painting itself. I could almost swear it stirred more and more each day, as if something were bringing it to life slowly, one color at a time.

Mattie was right that these trees had split mankind into two groups, but it was neither easy nor pleasant to explain. From *the One Tree* all of man was created, but the *Tree of*

Shadows caused the divergence. It began the day an Original man ate fruit from its branches and was forever changed. Knowledge from the tree fed pride in the man until he had no use for the One Tree. His growing arrogance eventually arrested the flow of the life source, Eiani, from the Tree into the man. Thus, the cold-hearts, or Friguscor, developed. As the man enticed others to eat the fruit and follow his path, the Friguscor began to spread throughout mankind.

In the beginning, the Original men and the Friguscor tried to coexist peacefully. Tragically, *The Histories* tell us it was malicious envy between two brothers that separated them entirely. These two brothers, one Friguscor and one Original man, lived and worked beside each other. But the Friguscor brother began to covet the Eiani that flowed in his brother's veins. He could smell its sweetness, taste its goodness in the air that stirred around his brother. The longing for it drove him to madness. One day in the field, the Friguscor overwhelmed his brother, and as the blood ran freely onto the virgin ground, he drank deeply of it. The ground screamed and groaned as the crimson pool grew, for it was now tainted, forever stained by the blood of man. When the Friguscor brother rose up over his dead brother's body, a beast was born. The bloodlust had begun. No longer could Original man live in peace among the Friguscor. Eventually, the Friguscor overtook all mankind. No Original men remained - until the first Simulacrum were born.

From that point on, it was "us" and "them;" no longer was

mankind "we." A war had begun between the Friguscor and Simulacrum that would still rage on today... if they ever found us.

The sound of the phantom wind still rushed in my ears. Closing the door to my room, I thought I caught a glimpse of branches moving in the wind.

"I'm ready, Veelee!" Mattie called to me from the hallway. She was lying on her back on the hallway floor kicking her feet wildly in the air. She was trembling with pure excitement. I smiled and granted her wish.

"Get ready to fly!" I said. Putting my hands on her feet, I pushed her quickly down the smooth hallway floor, sending her sliding until she bumped gently against the far wall. She giggled and writhed and squealed, "Again!"

After five rounds of Mattie's sliding down the hall in her smocked dress, I sent her to watch TV and walked down the back stairway that had once been intended for use only by servants. I tromped down to the kitchen. Even before I entered the room, I could feel that Mother was still upstairs. The blood bond we shared made us very aware of each other's presence. And yet, it was not without its limits. I could not feel my sisters' presence with the same acuity. I had only a general idea of when they were nearby. At the kitchen counter by the window overlooking the gardens, Adair stood, already dressed and looking amazing. My older sister had only that one look... amazing. Age did not detract from that truth, but only enhanced it.

The laws of nature did not control us in the same way it did the Friguscor. Their lives had sixty, maybe seventy vital years, after which they quickly grew old and decrepit. But our clocks ran far longer, thanks to the Eiani and the fruit in the Terebinths of Mamre. So, as a precaution, the Simulacrum Council had chosen to set our years in this world to a maximum of 110. It had not always been this way, but as the Friguscor became more aware of their surroundings and people started living in closer proximity, it seemed best to err on the side of prudence and avoid scrutiny. Because time was not an enemy of the Simulacrum, we embraced it. It never ran out, never stopped, never came to collect from us.

Adair looked lovely standing in the morning light. Blond, fair-skinned and with delicate features, she reminded me of silken elves from children's storybooks. Her yellow skirt was wrapped with a brown belt that accented wonderfully with white pearls and crisp white shirt under her navy blue blazer. She had Daddy's eyes, which, like all of the Simulacrum, were brighter and richer than any Friguscor's. Adair's eyes were crystal blue like the waters in Glacier Bay, Alaska, and they seemed to cut right through you. She was the picture of beauty, which felt like the opposite of me.

Growing up, I had been asked on more than one occasion to give a boy the inside scoop on what flowers she liked, or to help another boy get our phone number so that he could call Adair. Selling her diary had been one of my best ideas. Using a diary I had been given for my birthday, I wrote an entry sounding like a love letter for Daniel, one of the local Simulacrum boys who pined for Adair. He bought the single entry in the diary for five dollars, and I thought I was rich. Daniel never seemed to question why my then eighth-grade sister still had a Hello Kitty Diary, or why she wrote like a fifth grader. Adair never knew why Daniel had become so emboldened in his affections for her, but I did. Boys. They were just so...endearing.

Adair stared at her master checklist, clicking her fingernails together absently, as she often did, much to my annoyance. This was her sick pleasure, list-making. Oh, she was a wild one. You know the type: the kind that writes something down that was not previously on her list, *after* she has accomplished it, just so she can draw a dark black line of satisfaction through it. I didn't even consider "list-making" to be an action verb. But to Adair there was nothing more exciting than a good list and a label maker.

Looking at her then, I realized that she could have been the cover model for an organize-your-life magazine. She was perfectly put together, from the intricate braid that wrapped around her head and tucked neatly with a matching flower clip into one of those overly organized "messy" buns, down to her French-tipped fingers and her Pepto-Bismol-colored toes. Actually, she looked like she had dipped her feet in bubblegum or something. I was pretty sure that Mattie had helped paint her toes, a hazard of having kids, I guessed. With her label maker in one hand and her coffee in the other, she searched for the one part of the list that might rebel against her precise schedule of events.

Her label maker reminded me that it was going to be a busy week, and I sighed. The 175th anniversary of the Battle at Red Oaks was upon us. This would be a big one, which meant there was no avoiding getting firmly roped into it. It wasn't that I minded helping; we had always done the re-enactment as a family. But Adair and her endless to-do lists, Mother and Daddy running themselves ragged with all the preparations, and Ausley and me trying to keep up with it all was a lot to balance on top of work and school. Then, that weekend, there would be the countless conversations with people I had never met, who came simply to get a glimpse of the odd Harper family and even odder still, The Red Oaks Plantation. Of course most everyone in town knew our family, but we were still the center of folklore and gossip, even if they respected us.

Actually I sort of loved the whole thing, I guess. But this year, the 175th anniversary, would be all that and more, and maybe I was over it. The 175th would mean that every Civil War enthusiast from across Alabama, Georgia, Mississippi, Louisiana, Florida, Tennessee, and Kentucky would come flooding through the fields dressed in Confederate and Union uniforms. The re-enactors staged the battle as close to history as possible. So several of the units would bring their restored cannons, and most would carry flintlock guns with bayonets.

the Oaks Remain

Women in period civilian dresses would fill in as cooks, wives, nurses, and widows of the day. Men who weren't soldiers would blacksmith, build fires, pitch tents, and tend to the wounded. The 6th Regimental Band of Alabama always competed in a battle of the bands against the 28th Infantry Band from Georgia. The winner would square off against one of the Union bands from Kentucky. It would be a full show.

I had participated in this event every year of my entire life. As a child watching the battlefield pretend to explode with cannons and muskets firing blanks, men and horses charging, casualties falling, and chaos reigning, I had been overwhelmed, hiding behind my mother's hooped skirts in terror. But as the years passed, it became a big play, and I loved making up plays. Sometimes the ladies would let me help card the cotton and hold the spindle as the large wheels spun our cotton into thread. Sometimes I would take a turn plunging the dasher into heavy cream as they churned homemade butter, or help pour cornbread batter into the cast-iron, long-legged spider that straddled a campfire. The best part, though, was after the weekend was over. Ausley, our best friend Jackson and I would search for buried treasures left by the pirates of the Civil War.

There was no use disliking the thing. Putting it on was our duty as the descendants of the Weekes Family, the original owners of Red Oaks. We lived in the same house that witnessed the battle; our ancestors lived there, fought there and died there. A monument to the fallen stood about half a mile past the old kitchen in the edge of what is now woods. Mr. Calvin Reiter and about ten other volunteers with the 6th Regiment Alabama Cavalry, Delta Company worked year round making sure that the paths through the woods stayed hiker-friendly for any interested in strolling through history.

Resigning myself to the inevitable, I forced a smile. No sense making it harder for any of us by protesting. "Adair, what am I doing this week? Making baskets from straw I gather in my free time, or showing the wounded to the infirmary?" I shuddered, remembering two years prior when I'd had to pretend that a bunch of grown men had just had their legs or arms blown off. Seriously, grown men.

"Or can I just collect tickets for the BBQ?"

"I will find a place for you and your copious skill sets, Veelee," Adair said without looking up from her list. She held onto it like it was a map of the world, and she was the only sailor who could read it. "But I'm not sure just where those skill sets will best be utilized. Where, oh where, do you put someone with such a smart mouth? Maybe showing people to the port-a-potties? ' Cause you know they are full of the same stuff you are." Adair's laugh was contagious. I laughed with her as I tossed a piece of toast at her from across the table.

"I'm shocked, Adair. Potty-talk so early in the morning is not very ladylike." I tried to look genuinely disappointed.

She rolled her eyes and smiled, "I learned from the best,

little sister."

"If you want, you could start calling me your comedic mentor. Or just ' mentor' if that makes you feel better," I offered.

She bit her tongue to keep from laughing, "For the umpteenth time, you are *not* my mentor."

"If mentor is too telling, you could just start calling me Madam President or something," I said as I slid into a chair.

" Or something' is more like it," Adair straightened her face and set it to business. "Seriously, can you do the deliveries for Mother this week? You know that will take a lot of stress off of her. Ausley can go with you." She gave me a pleading look, which she knew would convince me. I could not stand turning down either of my sisters when she needed something. They had both mastered this look of complete innocence when they begged.

"Sure thing. This morning I woke up ready to do whatever you needed, because that makes my day worth living." I said, dripping with sarcasm as I peeled back the lid of my yogurt. Adair rolled her eyes and smiled smugly. The truth is, I welcomed this job because I knew it would keep me out of the tornado that was about to descend on the house once the preparations got into full swing.

Just then, Mother drifted into the room, her long silk robe flowing around her tiny feet and several pencils sticking out behind her ears. She had a way of floating in that made the entire room feel as though it had been waiting for her the entire time. She was enchanting; everyone wanted to be near her. Even though I favored her in many ways, she, like everyone else in the family, stood taller than my five-foot-two inches. Her short, angular mahogany hair framed her picturesque face, which was dominated by those silver-grey eyes. The contrast of her dark hair made her eyes even more striking. With colorful fabrics in one hand and some kind of flower template in the other, she sat down lightly in front of her coffee cup like a queen before her court.

"Good morning, ladies!" She almost sang. "Adair, how's the planning? Have you figured out what to do with Mrs. Hamstra? Please remember not to place her with any of the baked goods. Bless her heart, last year she forgot she was selling them and packed up half of the table and took home baskets of cakes and pies, all before lunch. Miss Cleo won't be too happy if most of her cakes go uneaten. She prides herself on her baking and comes back to the table to make sure her cakes have sold." Then, remembering something important, she slapped her delicate hand down on the table, and sighed. "Oh, and do try to touch base with Mrs. Hinsley to remind her to show her collection of Civil War photographs. She has the best collection in all the South. She has called here three times this week, but I have missed her every time. She has a new photo to show us. You know how excited she gets about these things," Mother drawled, peering over her cup.

With her free hand, she slid the Augmented Reality glass, or AR glass, over the surface of the kitchen table before her, bringing it to life. Her fingers danced across the screen as she typed in our encrypted password, allowing the daily news to stream in. The headlines ran across the screen, "Is War Inevitable?" War. That was a constant dialogue for the Friguscor. They did not trust one another, and it seemed, Americans trusted Russia and Iran even less.

Mother used the AR screen for her daily news, but as Simulacrum, we had to be very careful with technology. The Friguscor were tracked, watched 24 hours a day by the technology that they depended upon to do everyday activities. We did not want to be watched and we certainly could not afford to be tracked. So, we limited our use of the Friguscor's technology. As a result, our lives were simpler, slower in many ways. We lived as if we were fifty years behind the Friguscor, but I liked it this way. Life felt more deliberate, more meaningful.

"Yes, Mrs. Hinsley won't want to miss the 175th anniversary of the battle of Red Oaks." Mother said absentmindedly as she read over the headline, "Mystery Virus Has Arrived."

Trying to keep Mrs. Hinsley and her boxes upon boxes of antique photos away from the celebration would be like trying to keep the President out of the White House. She lived to share those photos and often spoke of the hours she spent organizing them and keeping them in pristine condition. The woman had made it her life's work traveling from town to town, rifling through antique shops for portraits: of families, soldiers, weddings, funerals, and anything else she could find that captured the Civil War era. Adair smiled patiently at Mother, her admiration obvious. Knowing Adair, she had already talked with Mrs. Hamstra and Mrs. Hinsley months ago and had sent reminder letters on the official Red Oaks stationery. Still, she humored Mother and nodded obediently. "Yes, Ma'am, I'm on it," she said.

Most of the visitors coming to Red Oaks would be Friguscor. Very few Simulacrum lived around us. This was our existence; we were foreigners in a foreign land. Most of them were vaguely aware something was different about us, but they could not identify it, so they accepted us as "normal." The only clue that seemed to tip them off was our slower pace of aging, well, that and our fragrance.

"Speaking of those old pictures, did you see the one of the family with the bug eyes last year?" I laughed.

Adair perked straight up from her papers already laughing, "I did! I was looking in the glass box with the magnifying glass in my hand when I scanned across and then BAM! That entire family looked like they could knock me out with their eyeballs. They were bulging out so far that I thought I had 3D glasses on for a minute. Talk about some thyroid problems!"

I tried to make my eyes as big as I could to demonstrate what the family looked like. Adair and I laughed exactly the same: loud and louder.

I weighed in, "I spent half the morning watching people get the shock of their lives while looking at the pictures." I stood up to make it more dramatic as I recreated the scene, "They would bend over the glass box, looking with the magnifying glass," I leaned over, pretending to hold the magnifying glass in my hand, "and I was like, wait for it, and then they would jump back with a shout," I jumped back with my hand over my mouth to demonstrate. "And that's when I knew they had seen the family of bug eyes! One lady jumped back just as Mr. Hinsley walked up with a piece of lemon meringue pie, and he literally got a pie in the face! You should have seen his face and the poor lady's that hit him!" Mother laughed, spraying drops of coffee all over the table. She grabbed a napkin to mop of the mess and looked at us sternly.

"Girls," she said, drawing it out so it sounded more like ' girrllsss' when she was getting on us, "one day someone may look at our family photos and make fun of you. They will say," Mother channeled her best Scarlet O'Hara, "look at those poowah, weeud-lookin' girls, bless thayuh hearts... with the most Bee-YOU-ti-ful muthuh I have evuh seen. Or is that fiiiinnne woman the beautiful sister, I just cannot tell which." She lifted her right eyebrow and added in her own voice, "Yes, that's what they might say. So, don't forget that even though time marches on, those people in the pictures were just as real as we are...they just wore different clothes." Mother smiled with satisfaction. She was just so witty. I like to think I did inherit that fine quality from her, too.

"Yep, that's exactly what they are going to say, I'm sure of it." I nodded my head dramatically, widening my eyes to emphasize my sarcasm.

Adair poured hot-chocolate mix into her coffee as she spoke. "Anyway, we have lots to do this week. Saturday will be here before we know it!" With that, she went back to her list.

"Mmm-hmmm," Mother slowly sipped her coffee with that faraway look that meant she was no longer really sitting at the kitchen table, but was already in her sewing room staring at her worktable full of little pieces of fabric. It was an amazing talent she had. The power to be in two places at one time. It was like her superpower.

"Hey, is Daddy going to be home tonight? Phineas needs help loading the picnic benches into the truck this afternoon," said Adair.

"He has a meeting with the CG at 1700, so he will be late," Mother explained. Meetings with the Commanding General were happening more and more frequently these days. Daddy was a Colonel—soon to be a General—in the Alabama National Guard. Since the Iranian-Israeli War, he had gone on active duty Guard and worked in Montgomery most days. He would come home from those meetings completely drained. I could tell that he would much rather be bush hogging the back forty acres or helping me perfect my aim at the shooting range than meeting with generals. To hide his age, he had held several jobs, but the one he loved the most was working on the grounds of Red Oaks. He had never complained a day in his life, but I could see it in the way he collapsed on the couch when he came home on those late nights. The work was a heavy load to carry.

Daddy was the kind of man who would be there before anyone else to turn the lights on in the building, and he would not leave until his last soldier had gone home. "Lead by example, and never ask others to do what you yourself are not willing to do," he'd say, and "integrity is doing the right thing even when others are not looking." Daddy was a man of wisdom, and people from all walks of life often sought his counsel.

Adair sighed heavily, "Okay, I'll tell Phineas to ask Mr. Reiter to help him out." Mother and I smiled at Adair. Phineas, or PH as we called him, was Adair's husband of six years. He was going to love the idea of gentle but older-than-dirt Mr. Reiter lifting benches into the truck with him. Mr. Reiter had volunteered over twenty years ago to head the group of local Civil War enthusiasts who helped maintain the battlegrounds at Red Oaks. He had never finished school, but he had worked hard as a carpenter to make a living for his family. Now his grown kids repaid him for his sacrifice by taking care of him in his retirement. Working at Red Oaks gave purpose to a man who was accustomed to hard work and long days. You could tell, though, by his hunched upper back and calloused, arthritic hands that both had taken a toll on his body. PH would never let Mr. Reiter risk injuring himself by lifting picnic benches, but Adair liked to have a plan for every turn of events.

"I'm sure Daddy can do it tomorrow night. Or we can get Jackson to lend PH a hand, he won't mind. He's good help. Daddy has been a little preoccupied these last couple of weeks. He's under a lot of stress. He needs more rest." Mother stood and kissed Adair's head as she went to refill her coffee cup again. Three cups were Mother's limit each morning. One to kick-start the day, two for good measure, and three just because she loved the taste so much.

The back door of the kitchen, which led out to the gardens, opened quickly.

"Good morning, ladies," Rosa Westbrooke walked in balancing a bushel of fresh-picked okra. She lived on the plantation adjacent to ours and was Mother's closest friend.

"Y'all had this much okra?" Mother asked, incredulous. Rosa laughed, a full laugh that warmed the room. She was only a little over five feet tall and was round where some women were angular. She looked soft, like a child could sleep on her shoulder and never need to move due to discomfort.

"Morning Mrs. Westbrooke," I said as I hugged her neck and kissed her cheek. She bear hugged me and left me feeling like the kitchen needed more air, but did not stop her conversation with Mother.

"We have okra to last for months and months. I just might

have to figure out a way to make clothes out of it," Rosa joked as she started to put the bounty in the sink, " Jackson picked another two buckets this morning, so I thought I would share." Jackson was Rosa's oldest son, and still my best friend.

"I was just about to sew, but I think I shall be putting up okra instead." Mother said as she reached for her blanching pots. "But, I think you owe me a hand for bestowing so much generosity on me." She held up two fistfuls of okra to Rosa.

Rosa knitted her eyebrows together, "Well, why do you think I brought them over so early for? I needed time to scratch your ears about a few things." With that, Rosa began to talk about the farm and plans she had for selling her needlework at the 175th Celebration.

Adair packed up her list and went to the living room to scoop up Mattie and her lovely doll, Evie. Mattie looked just like Adair, which secretly made me love her even more. Although I fought with my sisters, I loved them dearly. And it made me smile to see a little Adair in Mattie's face each day.

I waved as they headed out the door for a day full of exciting errands and list accomplishments. Mother and Rosa were eagerly chatting away as I slipped upstairs to shower and dress for school. I had missed my run, but I still had plenty of time to make it to my 10:00 a.m. class. As I started up the back stairs, Ausley blew past me, dressed and looking more than slightly frazzled. "Hey Veelee. I gotta run, I overslept this morning. I thought I set the alarm on my phone." At the mention of her phone she started digging frantically into her oversized blue bag.

"Lost your phone?" I smiled knowing that this was not the first time this morning, nor the last time today that she would lose the tiny runaway.

"Umm... I..." digging deeply into that Mary Poppins bag, she sounded muffled. "I... oh, oh! No, nope. Here it is!" She produced the phone in a victorious wave.

"Missed you at coffee this morning. Where are you going anyway?" I asked. Her hair was pulled into a low, side ponytail with stray pieces of her curly, honey-glazed mane escaping in wisps around her round face. She looked absolutely breathtaking... like a Hollywood star from the 20's. She yanked at her jean jacket and then tossed the heavy bag over her shoulder, "Oh, I have to work at the clinic this morning. They called last night. With the outbreak of this new flu thing they are really short-handed. It's crazy how fast this thing is spreading among them. They are just so defenseless. It seems to affect each one of them a little bit differently. I am trying to find a pattern in it, but so far it seems random. Well, I guess that is not exactly true. I have noticed that some get the disease and die within a day or two, while others seem to rally after a time of sickness and then some..." She adjusted her bag to even out the weight on her shoulders, while her eyes looked as though they were doing a mental inventory to make sure she didn't leave anything necessary behind. She glanced quickly at her watch, which she still wore on the wrong arm. "Some... but oh..oh I'm already late, and I'll be there most of the day, so I'll catch up with you tonight."

"Do you still go to school? Or is that way too overrated these days?" I asked, jokingly. Ausley was a senior in high school but had completed all of her required hours and was just biding her time until she could graduate. School was never difficult for any of us, but Daddy always taught us that it was important to apply ourselves anyway. So, with her free time, Ausley volunteered at the local Rural Health Clinic that treated low-income families in the area. She had always been tenderhearted and passionate about people, all people.

"I don't have school today... I have the same schedule every week, you know." She only attended school three days a week now. Curling her naturally deep-red lips into an wry smile, she turned and waved goodbye behind her as she bounded down the stairs and out the door.

I continued up the stairs. Although they had been renovated several times, the pipes still made a groaning sound in the mornings. I had come to acknowledge it as a kind of morning bell. Time to brush your teeth, *BAAAAA*, time for a shower, *BAAAAA...chug...chug....chug...* and finally warm water. Oh, the joys of living in an antique house. I stepped into the shower and lathered shampoo into my hair. As the old pipes banged a rhythm and the steaming water washed over my head and crashed to the floor, a fragment of memory hit me hard. It was from the dream I had had last night. But, what was it? *Bang, bang, bang,* the old pipes boomed as the rush of water splashed down my arms and legs, and then I heard the drums. Suddenly the debris from my dream last night surfaced in front of my eyes. And I remembered it all.

I am moving through the labyrinth of trees at Red Oaks, leaving the safety of the gardens and passing the monument at the edge of the far fields. Something is pulling me forward. It is the rhythm of distant, sonorous drums, which call to me like sirens in the night. Military drums? I am not sure. As I cross the arched, wooden footbridge Mr. Reiter built across the creek, I feel the reverberating pitch increase the intensity of my every heartbeat. There is an alarm, an echoing summons embedded in the unrelenting beat. My feet match the beat until I am running. I don't know why, but I'm sure I have to get there quickly. But where am I going? I am following the drums. The beat becomes more insistent, more demanding, more compelling as they come closer and closer. I have to get to them before they pass me by! Beginning to panic, I run so fast that the trees pull at my clothes and rip at my hair. I don't care; speed is more important than pain. I must reach the drums. They beckon me forward, pulling me on to an unknown destination. The rhythm awakens resonance deep within my bones, and my life-beat echoes in concert with it. Something inside me knows that this is a song sung to me before I was born. A song poured into my marrow and stretched into my ligaments. As I run with dogged determination, I become aware that I am not alone in this.

I turn to see Adair and Ausley running with me, match-

ing me stride for stride. We run together, each feeling the shared urgency. Suddenly, we stop as the full scene comes into view. We have reached the river that flows along the back of Red Oaks. Only this is not the peaceful, lazy river I know. This is a deep, menacing presence of dark blue, a swift and dangerous oceanfront with waves that roll and churn and crash against a rocky shore. Black storm clouds roll and boil overhead, mirroring the tumultuous river. Standing by the riverbank searching for a good entry point, I notice others pacing along the bank. They look completely lost, unsure of how they arrived at the river, or what they should do from here. Adair and Ausley see them, too, and rush to them, gathering them together into one group. They seem to rally, to strengthen, and to focus. As a group they find purpose of some sort. But, it is not my purpose.

Mud oozes between my toes, and the cold runs up my legs. My bloodied feet are raw, my limbs scratched and bruised from the journey here, but I don't care. The drums thrum louder and louder, closer and closer. I realize with a start that they are battle drums. BOOM, BOOM, BOOM, BOOM; it is deafening. My heart freezes as I see what is coming down the river. Thrashing, and churning the water, they are driving forward.

Giants! Giant warriors, the size of buildings, march down the middle of the river heeding the call of the drums. The drums are on the move, and the giants follow them. COME, COME, COME, COME, the drums drive onward. Girded *with helmets and breastplates of gleaming gold, the giants have greaves and shields of burnished silver and wield great swords of polished steel. The shields and swords bear odd symbols and engravings but I cannot read the words. Despite the overcast sky, their armor is so bright I use my hand to shield my eyes. One thing is clear: They follow the drums, these marching giants with purpose. The insistent cadence of the drums commands action, the steadfast rhythm demands response. I cannot stay safely on the side; I have to go with them. It is time to follow, time to fight.*

Before I can count the cost, I jump into the river. The giants' march churns the water and spins me under its current. Waves of frigid water rush down my throat, and my lungs begin to fill. I thrash frantically to stay afloat or to feel the bottom beneath my feet, but I can't. I kick and push to get out of the water, but I am no match for the massive swells. Panic chokes me; the churning water claims my screams. My lungs feel like they are exploding as the river drags me down, down with its icy fingers into the dark depths. I fight with my last burst of energy to break the surface, but my effort is futile. I am drowning. Ausley and Adair do not even know where I am. They will not know what happened to me.

Suddenly, flesh surrounds me. A great hand lifts me in its open palm from the water into the sky. I rise so high that I can see all the way across Red Oaks. The woods of Red Oaks are ablaze. I see a swarm through the smoke. Instinctively, I know. Friguscor. Red Oaks is overrun with Friguscor. Armies of depraved men are everywhere, pouring across the land like fire ants from an anthill that has been kicked. Iron axes strike the ancient wood, and the oaks come crashing down to wild screams of triumph. With their bloody hands they rip at the smaller trees and bushes, wrench landscape rocks from the ground and trample flowers in their manicured beds. A hapless doe is caught and hoisted high above their heads then ripped apart and savagely devoured in a mindless feeding frenzy. Their dead eyes are black, and their skin is the ashen pale of death. Flames feed the chaos, and murderous screams bellow from their throats. The deer does not satisfy them. They are hungry and searching for blood...the Eiani in our blood.

I fall back into the fleshy hand that holds me, reeling. The Esurio, the Hunger, has begun in the Friguscor again. They know about us, they are searching for us here at Red Oaks. At Red Oaks! Red Oaks is no longer safe! Each of these thoughts slams against me, blow by blow.

I am moving again, the giant hand slowly lowering me to the ground. I roll to my knees with my hands splayed out in front of me, looking up slowly to see what has saved me from the river. He bends low so that one of his eyes is equal to my face. A giant. A real giant. Silver hair falls in waves to his massive shoulders, and his inhuman cat-eye twitches and refocuses. For a moment, I am paralyzed by fear. Leaning uncomfortably close he studies my face before speaking. "Fear not, Child of the Blood," his bass voice booms. His breath rustles my hair as he speaks, and I tremble as the vocal waves go through me. Then, more gently he chides, "This is not your fight, Little One."

His words help me find my voice. "I can hear the drums! I want to fight, I must go with you! They are destroying Red Oaks, they are coming for us. Can't you see? They will devour us if we do not have help. Ausley and Adair! Mother and Daddy! Mattie! Jackson! They will kill them all! Let me come with you; let me fight while I still can. I want to die fighting, not caged like an animal. At least if I fight, I die with hope in me still. You must take me with you!" I scream back at him with a passion that rushes from the very depths of me.

"You will fight, but not now, not yet. Just because you hear the drums does not mean that this is your fight," he answers with a sad, knowing smile. "Very soon, Child of the Blood, your fight will come, but this is not your day. Answer the call of the drum only when it is your time. Be vigilant, practice discernment, and seek wisdom. Ready yourself. The days are near."

Shampoo dripped down into my eyes. *Oh that burned.* It burned much deeper than it should have; because I could feel it deep inside my chest. The days are near.

{ 3 }

Clear as Mud

The door to my worn, dependable white Honda Civic always stuck if you swung it out too far, which I always did. Still, it was much better than the even older car I drove in high school. The automatic window on the driver's side of that car would freeze when it was cracked open about an inch, so Daddy took the door panel off to work on it. I drove it like that for weeks. After he tinkered with it unsuccessfully, I helped him push the window up and duct taped the mechanism in place. We couldn't get the door panel back on, so he had "fixed" it by covering every square inch in silver duct-tape. Then, Daddy "fixed" her once again by spraying the rusted spots with Rust-Oleum, so she looked like a leper with the pox. I loved that car.

My parents did not believe that living at Red Oaks entitled me to drive a fancy car, wear designer jeans, or have a cell phone embedded in an electronic chip in my ear, like all of the other kids my age did. Cell phones were for drug dealers and gossips, Daddy jokingly said. I was neither, so Daddy declared that I did not need one until high school. However, we lived so far out in the country and the reception was so bad that it didn't really matter anyway. We joked that you could only get cell reception on the first Saturday after the first full moon of the Equinox, and then only if you held a coat hanger outstretched in your free hand while balancing your weight on the opposite foot.

Even if my car did look like a misfit compared to the others, I still loved that reliable Civic. It was a huge step-up. It had taken me four years working at the local vegetable market, Fresh Tomato, in order to afford her. She was mine, and I liked that her door stuck and groaned a little. It gave her character, and maybe it gave me some, too.

Putting all my weight into it, I slammed the cranky door closed and swung my red leather messenger over my shoulder. I loved that bag. It had my initials, VHG, embossed in the right corner in that overly fancy, scroll lettering. Mother gave it to me for my high-school graduation. The leather was soft, like it had been handled for years, and the red was rich and deep like the trees of Red Oaks in autumn. Even though it was three years old, the smell of tanned leather lingered, and I inhaled deeply every time I opened it.

Wallace State was a small school, so walking across the parking lot did not take long. Tall, mossy oaks that surrounded the buildings hung almost to the ground, and gave the school an old-world, romantic feel. The aged limestone buildings had recently been renovated. When I stepped through the doors, the pungent smell of new paint hit me like the perfume of an old southern woman. I loved that smell.

New paint reminded me of the smell of new books, and new books made me think of new beginnings.

I couldn't explain it, but something new hung just out of my reach. It waited on the other side of that closed door in my dream, but I couldn't name it yet. The man from the dream flashed through my mind, but angry, protesting voices from the parking lot interrupted my reverie. I watched as a small group of students marched in a circle with giant augmented screens, made to look like picket signs from forty years ago.

This was becoming an increasingly common fixture here on campus, students protesting some sort of perceived injustice. It wasn't too surprising; righteous indignation was practically the calling card of a college student. They were experts at single-mindedly championing any cause they saw as deserving, but having few practical ideas on how to really change things.

But they weren't all wrong–something *was* changing, all over the country. Daddy had discussed it in hushed tones with Mother in the library after dinner many nights, and I saw it more and more on the news channels. We mostly stayed on the outskirts of the Friguscor culture, but at school I got a firsthand look at what they believed, what they thought and what they questioned. It seemed like a rip had opened in society, just like a run starting in a pair of pantyhose. It had begun somewhere small, somewhere inconsequential, but it was spreading until it threatened to lay bare almost every part of their society. Sickness spread among the Friguscor, crowding the hospitals, jobs disappeared, shipped overseas, displacing local workers, fuel and food prices soared, and everyone seemed generally miserable. The rip was spreading.

"WAR....it's coming, man, it's coming!" a professor bellowed from the first classroom on the right. "We will not stand for this oppression anymore. We will not stand for this bigotry; they will force our hand and find justice at the end of it. The government has invented this disease and put it in the water systems. They are killing us on purpose! The time is coming. We will be forced to take back what we deserve from the government. They send our men and women to fight in wars that are centered on greed. But they lie to us. They tell us that it is for our safety, for our freedom. But we know the truth. We know that the wars are for greed, to fill the rich man's pockets, and the disease is a genetic weapon unleashed by the rich to kill off the poor. War is coming! Not the war they want, but the war we will give them!"

Mr. Steadman had started class with his typical rant against the anonymous "they" of government. I sat down and listened with mild curiosity. He often spent the first twenty minutes of class reliving his glory days, the Occupy Washington protest that led him to dance naked at rock concerts and march up and down the streets of the city, decrying the cause du jour. But now he was just another angry old man, determined that we young people should pick up the placards and press on with the passion that had fueled his youth.

I had heard variations of this speech a hundred times; I think he felt he needed to "convert" us in order to validate and redeem his own squandered idealism. He seemed mad at the world, but I don't think he was. Really he was angry that, at one time, he had fostered dreams for a greater purpose for himself than what he seemed to be living out at this small community college in Geneva, Alabama.

He didn't know it, but I was not a part of his wars, or his idealism, or even his culture. I usually skipped the first 20 minutes of his class, Evolutionary Psychology, and worked on my homework for Statistics or Child Development. My world was so far away from the Friguscor's, so distant, that it seemed impossible most of the time to connect with the alternate universe that existed outside of the Simulacrum. As the class ended, I sighed relief that I would not have to face Mr. Steadman's rants again until next week.

Emmalie, my only Friguscor friend, was already sitting in the window seat of my next class, hoping the warm sun would tint her pale skin with a bit of color. No chance. She was always the same shade, unless she happened to sunburn, when she looked more like a plastic mannequin splashed with a bit of red paint. She had the ashen, pallid complexion of the Friguscor and the slight odor of decay they all carried. Her skin was rough, dry, and flaked off in large patches and her dull brown hair was brittle from too much hairspray. But she was, in some way, my friend, so I still found her beautiful. Her dull red hair was dry and brittle from too much hairspray and curling irons, I assumed. She chatted with someone on her phone. I had grown accustomed to the Friguscor talking on invisible phones, but at first it had been alarming. They used an electronic chip, embedded behind their right ears. That chip corresponded to one on their right wrists, which produced a hologram on their palm when they needed to search the Internet or dial a number.

"Alright, talk to you later!" Emmalie said excitedly, then turned to me. "Hey, how's it going? Did you survive the parking mess out there? I know you have to drive that old car and park with the self-parks." She folded her legs up against the cold, silver bar of the desk, disregarding the fact that she was wearing a skirt that was shorter than her heels were long. Emmalie, like most of the other students, drove a new, auto-piloted car. The students liked to protest in the self-parking lot because it was closer to the road and allowed for more visibility. I watched as she inhaled my scent. Her pupils dilated slightly, and she swallowed hard

"You smell so good, Veralee....have I told you that?"

Only every single time I see you, I thought. "Mmm, nope, not recently, but thanks for the compliment. So what's going on out there?" I said, feigning ignorance while I slipped into the seat beside her. I saw the signs and heard them chanting, but I wanted to hear Emmalie's take.

"It's the rally; didn't you see all of the signs? They are going to march around campus today. How many people were out there when you drove up?" She jumped from her desk back to the large window, licking her dry, cracked lips. She was like one of those tiny bouncing balls that Mattie always wanted from the 25-cent machine at a restaurant.

"I'm not sure, maybe thirty people, which I figure is a lot, considering where we go to school and all."

Thirty unhappy people with signs and hostile voices, I sighed. Increasingly, the atmosphere seemed charged with anger lately. Don't get me wrong, I loved the college feel. I loved that there was always a ship to go down on, a fight worth fighting, a lost cause for every soap box, but at the same time I was tired of the constant bickering, lightly veiled as intelligent debate. I had noticed that the angrier people got, the less intelligent the debate became. Passion was one thing, but drawing lines in the sand where neutral ground had once existed could be deafening for those who chose to hear. How could one debate with ears that could not hear? Mother had always told me that we are made with two ears and one mouth for a reason. "You should listen twice as much as you speak." she would say.

"These people are seriously crazy. They talk about mythical creatures and cures for the Vampire disease." Emmalie sat down and pulled out a bag of Twizzlers to accompany her Starbucks. Breakfast of champions. I hate Twizzlers. It's like eating wax.

"I always want something sweet when you come around; it's like you bring out my sweet tooth or something," she said casually as she bit through the red wax. I cringed inwardly but smiled before looking down at the ground to avoid watching her tear through the licorice. *Yes, it's just like that actually,* I thought to myself as I tried not to breathe in the faint smell of feet in old leather sandals that permeated the room. The subtle odor was not uncomfortable anymore, just slightly unpleasant. I guessed it was kind of like growing up next to chicken houses. You got used to it, but the smell never really went away. But they smelled the honey-sweetness of life in our blood, and it roused a vague longing in them. They did not know what they smelled, but we did. Fortunately for us, the more they were around us, the more immune to our smell they became, and the less they seemed to be affected by it.

Then Emmalie's words dawned on me. She said,

"mythical creatures." The words rolled around in my mind, crashing into possibilities. What was she talking about? *Who* was talking about mythical creatures?

"Helloooooo, Veralee." She waved a long, floppy Twizzler in front of my face. I swatted it away and gave a weak a smile as she continued, "Well, everyone has some special brand of crazy they like to drink in the morning. Theirs happen to be warlocks and unicorns, I guess," she said.

My heart beat hard. I didn't know what she was talking about, but it didn't sound good "Emmalie, why did you call it the Vampire disease instead of the Mad-Dog disease?"

I had heard that name, but I wasn't really sure what it meant. The disease had first appeared about ten years ago in the Friguscor. I had learned a lot about it by watching a news special on it. The newscaster, Petra Asbry, was interviewing a research physician from Johns Hopkins Hospital in Baltimore. A Dr. Neufeld, or something like that.

The doctor had said, "The virus, TSE_3, starts with flu-like symptoms: headache, muscle-aches, low-grade fever, sore throat, and nasal and chest congestion." He went on to explain further, "The cough is high-pitched and brassy, and it sounds something like a small dog barking. Some people recover, so it is hard to know at first if the person has TSE_3 or another virus with similar symptoms."

The reporter had asked, "But the disease obviously causes some serious mental derangements as well. What about the paranoia and murder? Mothers have murdered their children, children their parents. There are many stories of mass murder. It is horrifying."

Dr. Neufeld replied, "Yes, if a person is truly infected with TSE3, or Mad-Dog disease, as you called it, the disease will enter a chronic state where it causes progressive degeneration of the brain. Those infected can become paranoid and aggressive, turning violent and even murderous at times."

Petra asked, "What is TSE3? How is it transmitted? "

Dr. Neufeld answered, "The good news is, we are learning more each day; so each new finding brings us that much closer to a cure—and believe me, we are working fervently for a cure. We do believe that the disease might be transmitted by a prion, like Mad-Cow disease. If you want to know the technical term, TSE is short for transmissible spongiform encephalopathy. That's a two-dollar word that means it is infectious, and it causes "holes" to develop in brain tissue as the brain degenerates. We believe it has jumped to man from another source, like Ebola was first transmitted to man from infected primates. It seems to attach to the host's DNA and alter the shape of essential proteins at the cellular level. Proteins are the building blocks of cellular structures and hormones, even DNA. So change the proteins and you potentially change everything about cell function, microscopically, and then macroscopically, everything about the person."

Asbry continued, "That sounds truly disturbing. So, then how do we protect ourselves and our loved ones from it?"

Dr. Neufeld replied," Unfortunately, the results of our research are not yet conclusive. It seems most likely, though, that TSE3 is transmitted through blood and body fluids. So, use universal precautions, and don't forget to use the UV light disinfectants in public places and at home whenever possible. We are working around the clock to find a cure or a vaccine, but until then, be aware of your surroundings and use common sense."

What I had gotten from that report was that even the researchers didn't seem to know much for sure. When we had first heard about the disease, they said it took years to progress to the stage where the infected were dangerous. But now it only seemed to take a couple of months or weeks. Maybe people called it Mad-Dog Disease because of the cough and the drooling, or maybe because people went as mad as rabid dogs in the end. But, apparently, they were calling it the Vampire Virus. That was even more ominous for us. Simulacrum did not catch the disease, but we did not want to get caught up in a group of angry Friguscor either.

"Come on, Veralee. Sometimes I think you live under a rock or came from another planet or something. " She was enjoying herself. She loved to deliver the news like a little boy throwing the paper at your front door in the morning.

"I guess they've found bite marks on the bodies of the people who have come into the hospital infected, so people are saying vampires are doing it." She giggled and rolled her eyes at the insane thought.

"Yeah, that's crazy. They really think it's vampires?" I wanted to know what she believed in order to gauge what others our age believed.

She shrugged and pushed her hair back over one

shoulder, "That's what they're saying, and it *is* weird. I mean, why would they have bite marks all over their bodies?"

"Well, don't they go crazy with the disease? Maybe they are biting themselves," I suggested, trying to inject some common sense into the topic.

Emmalie shook her head, "Well, they do go crazy, I mean they supposedly start drinking animal blood and stuff like that. So maybe they could be biting themselves. I mean, I had not really thought about that before. Who cares, really? I have more important news."

Before she had a chance to share it, I looked back out the window at the protestors. People marched on the sidewalks with signs demanding cures or vaccines, or condemning the government for not helping the sick. Emmalie's words stayed with me. Vampires. If they only knew that they themselves were the vampires. That inside each of them lay the *Esurio*, the hunger for our blood that would drive them insane before transforming them into blood-seeking monsters. I looked at Emmalie and shuddered. She too was one simple step away from becoming her worst nightmare. And mine. All it would take would be one drop of my blood. That is why the Simulacrum have the absolute law that cannot be broken. Under no circumstance do we ever reveal who we are, and even more importantly, we never ever share our blood with the Friguscor.

Mrs. Glenn slammed her screen down onto the desk, signaling the start of class, and I straightened in my seat. Grateful for the interruption, I turned and searched my red leather bag for my screen. Emmalie started taking notes on her AR screen, forgetting all about vampires, and bite-marks and the unexplainable disease.

I watched her for a moment out of the corner of my eye. Emmalie and I had known each other since I started attending public school in tenth grade. Up until that point I had attended school at Red Oaks with the rest of the local Simulacrum children. We were taught to read and speak Latin so that we could study the Histories that were kept on the top shelves of the library at Red Oaks. The Histories recorded the stories of our people from the beginning of time. I loved to open their giant leather bindings and see the colorful paintings inside. Reading those stories felt like glimpsing into another world that existed at the edge of my fingertips as I held the book.

Emmalie had opened my world up to the Friguscor more than anything had before. She was as foreign to me as someone from the other side of the world, yet she lived only five miles from me. Often I did not understand what motivated her, what caused her to react the way she did, or what she found interesting. She had lived her entire life in Samson, shuffling between her mom and dad. They had divorced when she was in middle school. It must have been a crushing blow to her, because brokenness had settled into her eyes like the remnants of a once-whole ship lying at the bottom of the sea. Some pain reshapes who we are, restructures how we see the world and leaves us trying to piece our fractured reality back together. That was Emmalie, always trying to patch the crumbled foundations of certainty that she had once known.

But as the years had passed, it seemed Emmalie had grown numb to the pain as she became more and more

the Oaks Remain

Friguscor. It was difficult to watch, and I had tried so many times to show her the Simulacrum way even though I knew I could not tell her. I even thought about breaking every rule and telling her what I am, but somehow I knew that Emmalie did not want to know. She saw that I did not deal with the same Friguscor problems. I did not need the lotions, did not endure the constant shedding of skin, did not require the sick days that they did.

Friguscor frequently visited salons to remove the excess dead skin that accumulated and created calluses on their skin. They spent incredible amounts of time and money trying to find the perfect lotion or ointment to keep their skin somewhat moist. They often developed deep sores and abscesses from scratching the almost constant itch.

It was not that way with Friguscor babies; most of the time, you couldn't tell them from Simulacrum. The process didn't usually start in earnest until around puberty. But lately it seemed to be starting even earlier, so more and more beautification products for children had begun appearing on the shelves of the stores in town.

Emmalie knew that I was warm to the touch, "a constant furnace," she would say, but she asked no questions and wanted no answers. At first I thought she was just simpleminded, but behind her giggly facade, I could see there was more. I guess in many ways she had already resigned herself to the broken world she lived in and feared a new, unknown way more than the familiar ruined one.

A couple of years ago she had asked me to make a pact with her. We had agreed that if we were not married by 21, we would go to Europe, see the world. We often joked about the trip, but I don't think either of us really ever considered going. We had never even been to each other's houses, so I think we knew Europe was only a pipe dream. Things seemed to be slowly changing between us; the years of friendship were stretching thinner. Maybe this was just the natural progression as people aged, matured, and changed, but it didn't seem like it. It seemed that the line being drawn between Simulacrum and Friguscor was seeping into our relationship more each day. Knowing Emmalie was changing me. I wanted her to know more than the death in her veins; I wanted her to know a life worth living, but she would have to change for that to happen. And that was impossible.

"By the way, I have a date on Friday. That's what I was going to tell you!" she whispered out of the corner of her mouth.

"With whom?" I asked without taking my eyes off the smart board at the front of the room. Emmalie always had a date on Friday night.

"Andrew Leute." She said his name slowly to make it feel more dramatic. It didn't work.

I hadn't even known that Emmalie was interested in him. Andrew did not grow up here; he was from a town closer to Montgomery. He had planned to play football at college, but then he got injured in one of his final high school games, landing him at community college like the rest of us. But he was very sure of himself and very proud to tell you that he was supposed to play for Alabama, that he was supposed to have had a full ride, that he was supposed to be in a big time fraternity;

the list of "supposed to's" went on and on. It seemed to me he was very arrogant, not leaving much room for concern about anyone else.

"Hmm," I pretended to be listening intently to Mrs. Glenn's explanation of the human larynx compared to the owl's larynx.

"Oh, Veralee, you can be such a prude. He's great! It's going to be a lot of fun!" Emmalie was obviously annoyed with me.

I had always wanted so much more for her, but I didn't know if that was even fair. I tried to be excited for her when she dated those worthless guys, but I just couldn't muster enthusiasm. In the last year she had dated one bottom feeder after another. They were always the same: wanting to have fun, to live in the moment with no regard for how it impacted the future. They were obnoxious boys who drove big trucks and tried to pass as men. I couldn't possibly find them attractive. They were Friguscor, and I could smell their skin decaying whenever they got close. Their odors were always something like overfilled, over-ripe dumpsters in July, mixed with soured, sweaty tee shirts. Plus, the current look for the Friguscor was not my style. Facial hair and any body hair was out, or so Emmalie had told me. No guy wanted facial hair or body hair, which I thought, would have made them look like men. The fresh and clean look of youth was in, Emmalie had said, so they paid for treatments to kill their hair follicles. Sensationally smooth, the billboards boasted. They wanted to preserve their baby faces, to look younger instead of mature. Their fascination with youth perplexed me. With each passing year, they were more willing to mutilate more of their body to capture their ever-fleeting youth. I guess this came with the knowledge of death. Death was inevitable for them. So they clung to a facade of vitality.

I looked sadly at Emmalie, knowing we would never progress past the shallow friendship and polite conversations we had in the hallways. Though my relationship with Emmalie was the closest I had ever come to having a friendship with the Friguscor, it still ended at the doors to the parking lot.

Class ended and Emmalie left a little too quickly. I sighed heavily watching her bounce down the hall.

"Hey there, Little Bird." His voice was light and deeply southern. It molded around his words like warm taffy. His crisp, blue shirt highlighted his milk chocolate skin and bright caramel-rich eyes.

"Um, hi, Jackson." Even though I had known Jackson all of my life, it always seemed excessive for him to call me by my family nickname. But he did it with such a warm smile that I always forgave him. We had grown up together, playing in the woods of Red Oaks. But lately, things had become more awkward between us, as things naturally do when romantic feelings arise between one half of a pair of childhood friends.

Leaning against the wall, he placed his body between the exit and me. He was taller than me, like everyone else on the planet, but I thought he always tried to seem even taller by spreading his shoulders out wide whenever we were close.

"You done for the day?" he asked.

"Nope, still have one more class," I said, wondering how long he would hold me hostage. Too bad we were too old to wrestle; I always beat him when we were little. I looked at his forearms. Didn't think I would win anymore.

He smiled his brilliant smile, which made me smile in return. How could it not? He was the happiest guy I knew. Happy Jackson. "I bet your house is getting pretty busy right about now with all there is to do for the 175th."

"You can't even imagine."

He straightened and looked very official, "I have my uniform ready, and I am willing to give the ultimate sacrifice for my country."

"The ultimate sacrifice, really? For a bunch of grown men who want desperately to dream of the day when the war will end with the South the victor?" I smiled with raised eyebrows, fully mocking him.

He leaned in a little too close, and I smelled his sweet breath on my face. "You know I am willing to sacrifice anything for what I love." He said, with eyes that danced and a mouth that trembled to be kissed. Jackson did not hide his feelings, and neither did I. The problem was Jackson knew what he wanted, but lately, I was having doubts. Everybody had always expected us to be together one day. What was wrong with me? I let him stay close to me and tested what it felt like to have him so near. I searched my heart for fireworks, for the longing and desire that I saw in his eyes to be mirrored in my own.

The man from my dreams reached out across my

memory and held out his hand, *"Jump...we will make it together,"* he whispered into my ear.

I jerked back from Jackson.

"Hey, hey don't be so skittish, Little Bird. I'm not going to bite. I meant what I said. I will give you time. Anyway," he said, changing the subject, "I love to see the old guys' faces when they see a black man in a Confederate Uniform. It really messes with their heads," he laughed loudly.

Jackson was fun. He had the kind of compassion for others that made you change the way you saw the world. Not to mention, he was beautiful. He was everything I should have wanted in a partner, in a match. I did love him, I always had. But something was missing...something that I could not fake or create. It would have been so easy to say yes to him, easy to live down the road from Red Oaks the rest of my life and raise the child that we could bear. And yet, something stopped me like a chair on the other side a door. I was pushing, trying to swing it wide open, but I could not get it to budge.

"No, no it's...it's not you, Jackson. Thank you for your thoughtfulness. I really am considering, and I really want to give you a true answer," I said honestly. He smiled and pushed a strand of my dark hair behind my ear. I blushed and looked down at my favorite knee-high riding boots.

"Don't worry, I'm a patient man. And I told you already; you are worth waiting for, Veralee. I'll wait as long as you need me to. I've loved you for years. What are a couple of days or weeks compared to that?" Jackson always said exactly what he meant.

"Well, let me take your arm and escort you to your next class. Shall we, my dear?" his smile was back, the one I loved to see. I tucked my hand into his arm, and I enjoyed the warmth of him against the cold, breezy hallway. Yes, life could be so simple with him. So easy. Why couldn't I just dive in the way he did? I imagined myself on the diving board, willing myself to jump.

"Here you are, safe and sound," he announced as we stood outside of my next classroom. "I'll come by later and see if I can help out at Red Oaks. Phineas will need a hand with Adair's list, I'm sure," he laughed.

"You really don't have to, but if you're volunteering, then I know Phineas will appreciate it. But I won't tell Adair that you're coming. She will surely have a list of chores waiting for you if I do." I started to turn into my class, "Oh, tell your mother we appreciate the okra she brought this morning." Jackson was an only child, like most Simulacrum. Our family was one of the only families I had ever met with three children. Actually, we were the only family I had ever known to have more than two children.

"You should come by, have dinner. They would love to see you." Jackson ate at our house a couple times a week, but for some reason over the past couple of months, I had been going to his home less and less. It felt too much like a promise of something I was not ready to give. People glanced at us as they filed into the classroom. Jackson nodded sheepishly at the stream of students and then looked back at me. "Okay, well. I better go. I don't want to be that creepy stalker guy who hangs on your every word...cause that would be creepy...and stalkerish," he said with a straight face and one raised eyebrow to enforce the creepiness.

"Very, very creepy," I said, smiling, and then turned to go into the classroom.

"Like a clown with little baby hands," he said wickedly as he caught my arm.

My eyes grew big instantly, "Hey, it's not the clowns that scare me. It's the thought of little baby hands running through my hair or stirring soup that gets me." I shuddered and added, "Since we saw that scary movie that I *told* you I didn't want to watch, I can't stop thinking about it."

Jackson rolled with laughter, "Of all the things for you, the fearless Veralee, to be afraid of, you pick little baby hands? I just don't get it."

"Well, at least I am not afraid of cats," I rebutted. Jackson turned serious with laughing eyes, "I am not afraid of them...it's just that they have no soul. A dog, that's a man's animal, but a cat, who needs that?" I shoved a firm shoulder into his side and laughed with him. He put an arm around me and took advantage of the moment. Tenderly, he lifted my face and kissed my forehead.

"See ya later, Little Bird. Watch out for the phantom baby hands running around out there." And then he was gone and I was left wondering. *What if? What if I choose Jackson?*

I drove home a bit slower than usual, which made me feel only a little guilty. Knowing that Adair would be at the house giving marching orders to anyone in her path made the rolling hills and dusty farms I passed on my way home seem even more compelling. Faded red barns, fields of cotton, peanut dust, and abandoned wooden houses painted the landscape while the drone of tractors and combines filled the air.

I thought briefly of Emmalie and her date with Andrew. I thought of Jackson. I imagined myself telling him yes. *Yes, I will bond myself with you for life. I will stand beneath the sacred oaks at Terebinths of Mamre and promise myself to you, Jackson. I will become one with you and walk the earth as yours.* This had been the unspoken plan between our families for years.

That would be the *easy* plan, the way it should be for my life. But I kept seeing *his* face. The man from my dream. My heart ached so gently I was not sure what was happening. Could I miss someone I had never even met? The feelings I remembered from the dream felt so strong that it seemed difficult to untangle myself from them, even when I was awake. *I don't know him. I don't even know his name.* But those words felt like a lie, even as I said them to myself.

Something caught my eye in the tree line as I turned down the well-worn, red dirt road. Whatever it was, it was running very quickly through the woods. I slowed the car and peered out my window. Nothing was there. I waited for several minutes. Then something flashed by my eyes. It was too quick for me to see it clearly. I left the car idling in the middle of the road as I got out for a closer look. I approached the edge of the woods and waited. I stood motionless; I could do this well. As a child I practiced how long I could stand without moving, without being noticed. But nothing happened. Assuming it had been a deer, I turned back to the car, then stopped. I stole a glance around.

The trees seemed different, redder even than this morning. I thought I heard a faint buzzing in the air but still, I saw nothing. The wind blew and brought with it a scent that I had never smelled before. Animals from the woods all have a distinctive odor, like the Friguscor have their smell and we have ours. But this one, I could not place. Maybe something like the rarefied air after a lightning strike. The trees seemed to be humming, and I felt the vibration on my arm. Something stirred in the forest; something was there. Or maybe it was just my imagination, what with the dream, Emmalie, and Jackson all on my mind as I drove, maybe I was a bit on edge. After waiting and listening to the wind blow through the trees for several minutes, I walked back to the car. I fastened my seatbelt and stepped on the gas, absently thinking about everything that had to be done for the 175th.

The house buzzed with activity when I arrived home. Mr. Westbrooke, Jackson's father, and Daddy were working in the front yard when I pulled up. I ducked into the house quickly, but Adair caught me before I could even reach the kitchen. She threw her arms around my neck. "Yay! You're home! I know you have been waiting all day to come home and help, little sister!" How was she simultaneously so annoying and so endearing? With a bang of the screen door, Adair was outside already.

"Okay, okay, just give me the run down on what I need to be doing." I called after her.

Jackson walked by carrying a basket of old ironworkings. "She's on a roll Veelee, you better get to work before she releases the hounds."

I looked at him curiously, "Do you think I could fit in that basket and hide for the rest of the evening?"

"Probably. You *are* the size of a small child, or a pygmy villager."

I laughed and looked up at him, "You only say that because you are like the Jolly Green Giant."

His smile widened flirtatiously, "I'm not green, small one; I'm a beautiful sun-kissed brown. So I would appreciate if you address me as Mr. Jolly Brown Giant, thank you very much."

Adair stuck her head back into the kitchen, "Veralee, come on."

"Hey, where's Ausley?" Jackson asked us both.

Adair looked at her watch and back at Jackson, "She's late, that's what she is. She spends too much time at that clinic." A twinge of nervousness fluttered in my stomach. She did spend a lot of time at that clinic, with the sick Friguscor, who had a disease that we did not yet fully understand.

Jackson gave Adair his signature peace-making smile, "Don't be hard on our Ausley; she's the only person I know who has a true heart of gold. Not to mention, she has the hair of little baby angel. Could be painted on a wall in Europe for all we know."

"He's right." I added. "Or instead of a wall in Europe, she could be on a wall at the post-office, for loving people to death, which is basically the same level of prestige in this country." Adair glared at the two of us and motioned out the door, "Veralee, follow me, and, Jackson, get that stuff out to the campground area before I am put on a wall for taking out two lazy teenagers."

"Lazy?" Jackson was already walking away with his basket, "Nah, she's not lazy, she's just always got her own agenda to follow." I smiled at Adair and shrugged my shoulders like I couldn't help who I was.

The rest of the day flew as we set up tables, dragged benches around the grassy areas, raised the tents and a hundred more things. Mother announced that she was too exhausted to cook, so we ordered pizza and sat around the fire pit enjoying the cooler autumn air that was moving in. Mother sat beside me on a log made chair.

"How's it going, Little Bird? Why so pensive?" she asked, and I entwined my arm with hers.

"I was just thinking about something that I saw, or thought I saw today." I explained the alleged deer that were running through the woods earlier today. But I did not mention that I could smell something different in the woods, something that I had never smelled before, because I could not explain what I did not know.

"But, something tells me that they were not deer at all. The trees seemed different, and the air was buzzing with motion. I can't explain it, but I think something is coming or has come to Red Oaks."

She looked at me without a trace of mockery in her

eyes, "Well, my eagle-eyed girl, I don't know what it was, but you seem to see when others do not. Let me know if it turns out to be anything I should know about. Your intuition is sharp, Veralee, and you have been given the gift of sight. Use it, my sweet Little Bird."

"Mmm, if it were only that easy," I said.

"It is that easy. That's what you've got to learn. You complicate things in your head, Veralee. It *is* just that easy. You'll figure it out. There is too much strength in you to be wasted," she said quietly.

"You have to say that; you're my mother," I joked.

"Of course." She said unapologetically. "That's my job." She patted my knee and stood to leave, "Now let me see what Ausley has been up to. She has to be exhausted. You know I need to check on all of my little chicks before I can sleep tonight." She walked toward the house briskly with purpose in her stride.

The fire jumped and danced hypnotically in the night air as I thought about my conversations with Emmalie and Jackson, the dreams that had been haunting me each night for the past several weeks, and the picture of the man who was permanently burned behind my eyes.

"Veralee, I've been waiting for you to talk to me," Daddy said, trying to sound official, but smiling too broadly for me to be convinced.

I looked up like a bubble had been popped in my face. "Talk to you? What about?" I said, confused.

"I spoke with young Mr. Westbrooke a couple of weeks ago," he said in his deep Alabama drawl.

"So you know," I said, resigned, "I mean, I knew you knew. He told me that he asked you first."

Jackson was wonderful, above reproach—there was no need to have the conversation. Daddy knew Jackson, had known him all of his life. He looked hard at me for a moment, and then he looked at me like he did when I was little and had scraped my knee. He would gather me in his arms and make the pain feel all better.

"I don't have an answer, Daddy," I said quietly. It was the truth.

He moved a log in the fire and spoke slowly, like smoke rising to the sky, "Then," he pressed his lips together, "that might be your answer, Veralee."

"Maybe," I said, but his words had the weight of truth in them already. Daddy was like that, he always saw through the problem straight to the answer at the end. "I just thought, well, I know it means a lot to y'all."

He nodded, "Yes. But apparently you don't fully understand me. I like the boy, I always have. He is from good people, and has a strong sense of character. But if he is not the one you wish to be bonded to for life, then I don't like him *for you*. You need to be sure of this, Veralee. It's hands-down one of the most important decisions you will ever make. It's not a decision to be made lightly or because of the desires of anyone except you and whoever the lucky guy ends up being."

"You won't be disappointed if I don't choose Jackson?" I asked with a slightly defiant raised eyebrow.

That caused him to laugh. "Since when did you become so concerned with disappointing other people?" he laughed again. "You, my strong-willed girl, have always decided what you would do based on your good sense and reason, not the opinions of men."

"Well, if you find him...whoever he is, let me know." I said wistfully, shrugging my shoulders against the night air.

Daddy winked at me, "You never know. He might be on his way here now, or he might take ten more years to get here, but I'll tell ya what, whoever he is, I hate him, just a little bit...for taking my girl away." I rolled my eyes and then smiled at him. A solid log rolled down in the fire and settled in the hot blue flame.

"Do you see that?" Daddy looked up and pointed to the sky above my head with a stick. "It's here! Amazing, isn't it?!" he exclaimed. I followed his finger. There it was. I had been so busy staring into the flames that I had not noticed the moon. A full moon as big as the sky, round and brilliant against the night. But, it was not the size that stole the breath from my lungs. It was the color. The moon was crimson red, as deep and rich as blood.

"It's called a blood moon. They are very rare," Daddy explained without looking away from the sky. We sat and watched the moon. Then without taking his eyes off of the moon he said, "Maybe you're right, Veelee. Maybe something is coming to Red Oaks. The Histories say that the blood moon announces change, like the leaves turning in the seasons. And this year, there will be four. Four blood moons." As a Guardian, Daddy watched for things like this, the changes in the moon, the seasons and the trees. It was his job, his calling to ensure the safety of the Gateway to the Terebinths of Mamre, which lay hidden deep within the forest of Red Oaks. Daddy sat on the Council of the Simulacrum as a Guardian of the Gate.

"Daddy, I have to ask you something. A couple of weeks ago, I woke up early and I heard you and Mom talking in your study. I should not have listened, but I did. But I have to know something. *Who* is looking for us?" I had not realized until this moment that this was one of the stones that had been weighing heavy on my chest, causing me to struggle to breathe for months. But now that it was out in the open, I felt the release of it as soon as the words passed through my lips.

Daddy watched me with eyes that looked at once fully alert and totally exhausted. He looked down at his hands, then back up at the moon. His face, always controlled, rarely betrayed his inner thoughts like mine did. What happened behind his eyes was a vault, only opened by choice... his choice. But tonight as the moon beamed down around us, he looked unmistakably sad.

"Veralee, I wish I could lie to you now." He rubbed his hands down the sides of his pants and sighed deeply, like it hurt. He began again, but softer, "I wish I could tell you that nothing would ever change here at Red Oaks, that the most important thing for you to worry about would be what classes you should take, or finding the boy you could love for life, like Jackson, or any of the other things that girls your age worry about. But you are no longer a child, though in my eyes you will always be my Little Bird."

He continued, "The blood moon signals change is coming. I hope it is change for the better, but truthfully, I'm concerned. I fear that for you and for your sisters, life will not be as easy as it has been for your mother and me."

He looked up at the moon and back again before he continued. "The safe-haven of Red Oaks might not be strong enough to stand against the tsunami of evil that is coming. I cannot tell you that I understand it all, because I do not. I am simply watching and waiting for what is coming, and trying to prepare the best I can for us, for our family." He stopped talking for a moment. Then he seemed to search for words like we had searched for sand dollars on the beach last summer.

"You have seen the news, and I'm sure you know about this disease. They are calling it Mad-Dog Disease." He spoke slowly as if his words were heavy weights he had to lift one at a time.

"Yes. At school they are even calling it the Vampire Virus now," I added, showing my understanding.

He did not look surprised, but nodded solemnly before he spoke, "That would be a more accurate name, I guess. Veralee, the disease...I'm afraid it's not new. Many in the Council do not agree with me, but I am worried that it is much more than another outbreak of disease among the Friguscor like the flu or chicken pox. Something does not seem right about it, and I cannot put my finger on it." He sat quietly as if working out a calculus problem on a whiteboard that I could not see. "Ahh, regardless, what I do know right now is that it is spreading much more quickly than even the news is reporting, and a virus that has the potential to become an epidemic gets great attention."

"I've seen it on the news. They are constantly talking about it. People are getting very scared, and it's heartbreaking to see them when they are sick." Heartbreaking did not quite describe my emotion when seeing the dead look on the people's faces and the anger in their eyes, but it was the best I could do. It was simultaneously heartbreaking and terrifying.

"More and more rallies are being held, and more and more people are getting sick. And they are getting sicker faster. Living in such close quarters in the EcoCities makes people more susceptible to this kind of epidemic. We are developing a plan for the state in case of a widespread epidemic. Meanwhile, Simulacrum and Friguscor doctors are trying to develop cures or vaccines. Rumors, whispers are growing louder that there is a group of people who are immune to the virus. Certain doctors are asking permission to look at a widespread population variance to see if they can find those who are naturally immune."

I heard the underlying problem in the words, "naturally immune." We Simulacrum were immune because our blood was different. We were not like the Friguscor, and we kept a healthy distance to ensure that they did not find out our secret.

"If they find our blood...if...if they take a sample from one of us..." The words tumbled slowly out of my mouth like I was lazy or tired, but they were just so colossal that I could barely think. The implications were devastating. Daddy turned to look at me, then spoke as if I were not sitting right beside him. He spoke as though he were a million miles away already.

"They are looking for us even though they do not know it is us they seek. It has always been this way; from the beginning it has never changed. They are drawn to us; the death in them aches for the life in us, and they cannot stay away for long. I fear it will begin again. They will start to hunt us though they do not know yet, it is us they want."

I saw Mother and Ausley laughing through the large kitchen windows, the light from inside pushing through the dark night. Quietly, I asked, "How close are they to finding us? How long do we have?"

He breathed in deeply and exhaled through his nose, "If they haven't already found us, it won't be long now. There is something more to this, something more than mere coincidence. It's like someone is helping them find us, like someone is almost deliberately leading them to us."

"But *who*? We are the only ones that know about us, and no Simulacrum would give our secrets up to the Friguscor," I said, confused and alarmed.

"No, no you wouldn't think so...but still...something is not right."

"Do they talk about us at your work?" I said feeling afraid of my own question.

Daddy pulled back and looked straight up into the bloody red globe, hanging low and full against the black sky, like an ominous womb about to give birth to something new. What could the omen of the blood in the moon mean? "No. Well, some do, maybe. But, to be honest, we are so busy at work. They have elevated our country to a high-alert status. We are saturated with information coming out of Russia and Iran right now. I'm afraid we could be fighting battles on two fronts very soon. And that is what bothers me most. When people get scared...when rumors of war couple with economic trouble and then something like this disease adds to the corporate stress...when things like these begin to circulate, it becomes a perfect recipe for scapegoats. People want something or someone to pin the blame on when things go wrong. If they are looking for us, we might just be the answer to their problems."

"Do you really think it could come to that? I mean, do you really think the Friguscor will go to war again?" I asked naively.

Daddy huffed sarcastically as he poked the fire, sending a great flame into the night, "They will always go to war again, Veralee. It's in their very nature to eat and devour one another. That is not the question. The question is when, and where."

We sat silently, lost in our thoughts, until the fire died down. Then Daddy tugged at my jacket, pulling me back to the present. "All right, Little Bird, don't you have to play deliveryman in the morning for Mother?" He was back to himself, and I welcomed the comfort of it.

"Deliverywoman, Daddy, and yes, Ausley and I will be heading out in the morning." I stood slowly and wiped my

the Oaks Remain

hands on my thighs. He pulled me close, "Stay away from those who are sick in the city. Be smart, Veralee. I have taught you how to be invisible among the Friguscor. Keep Ausley safe, and keep to our rules. These are not the days to rebel, Veralee." His fierceness frightened me, and he knew it did. The intensity in his eyes made me feel the weight of the warning in his voice. Slowly I nodded and he pulled me into a deep, warm hug.

"Alright, now go on into the house. Tell your mother I'll be along shortly."

"Night, Daddy." I kissed him on the head as I stood up, and turned towards the house. The light from the brooding blood moon fell red as a warning sign across my face as I walked through the night.

{ 4 }

Everything Changes

My car lurched and struggled to get out of the driveway under the weight of its load. Ausley and I had been tasked with delivering Civil War-era clothing to Mother's customers. We stacked the boxes so high that I couldn't see out the back window. Ausley downloaded the addresses from the cloud, and we headed off. From Red Oaks to Montgomery, our final destination was about ninety miles as the crow flies. We could have zipped there in about 30 minutes if we had used the new SIH, the solar information highway that stretched between Nashville and Destin, Florida. It passed just east of Samson, but most Simulacrum avoided the SIH because of the tracking system it used. My car was much too old to have the factory-installed information system that transmitted data about any vehicle that travelled the SIH, but Daddy wanted us to avoid it anyway, just to be safe. Instead we twisted around winding farm-to-market roads to reach the old asphalt highway, so the trip would take us about two hours or so with the stops. We were used to the old way, and besides, my car still burned natural gas, so it couldn't recharge on the highway like the newer solar cars could.

Ausley shrugged her shoes off and stuck her bare feet up on the dashboard while her hand hung outside the window, waving in rhythm to the rush of the breeze. I turned the radio up, and we sang in unison at the top of our lungs. She was a great companion on missions like this. She didn't mind silence, but she also enjoyed singing along to every song. Her long, curly blonde hair framed her round face with soft ringlets. Behind those gray-blue eyes was a bottomless well of generosity, compassion, and joy. As a child, she reminded me of a modern Shirley Temple, with her perfect curls and bouncing steps. And like Shirley, she was always ready to break out in a little song and dance.

When Ausley listened to you, she genuinely *listened*, and you knew she was really interested in you and what you had to say. Plus, she would laugh at any story I told her, which made her a great audience. These days she was looking much more womanly than that chubby little girl I fondly remembered. Though she was 18 and finishing her senior year of high school, she did it without any trace of the typical nostalgia you might expect. Ausley wanted to be a nurse, as soon as possible. She was ready to help, ready to change the world, and high school, she reasoned, was not helping her reach that goal.

"So, Jackson..." she said teasingly, trying unsuccessfully to hide her schoolgirl smile.

I looked at her and then back at the road, "Yep." I was not planning to drag this out today.

She pulled her feet down and leaned over toward me, "Come on, I know. I know that he asked you; I know he wants to bond himself to you." Ausley exaggerated every word and grew more excited with each passing second; by the end of the sentence, she was bouncing up and down in her seat.

I couldn't help but laugh. She pouted, "Veelee, it's not funny. He is asking for you! It's really romantic. Jackson is one of the best guys we know. You will not find a better match. I mean, he is downright beautiful with that caramel skin and golden-brown eyes, but he is more than that...he is funny, and kind, and he cares about everyone he has ever met. Not to mention that he will give you the shirt off of his back if you ask for it," she added quickly.

She was right. She was not exaggerating any of it. "I know," I said quieter, "I know you're right. He is an amazing person. But I'm not sure. I'm just not sure that I can bond myself to him for all of time. To be honest, the more I think about it, the more I'm becoming sure that I can't do that at all. I'm going to tell him tomorrow." Making the decision, saying it out loud dropped the weight of his question off my chest, and I felt instantly lighter. I was not his match, and he was not mine; somehow I just knew it. The more I thought about it, the surer I became that he was not even really in love with me, but more in love with the *idea* of me.

It had always been Jackson, Ausley, and me. Tres Amigos, the Three Musketeers. I *did* love him, but he was more like the brother I never had. I would never want to hurt him. In fact, I think I would fight any girl that tried to hurt him. But I just couldn't feel any fireworks when I thought about him and me together. It would not be fair to him to say yes. He deserved someone who could love him completely, and I knew that it was not me.

"Wow, I thought you would say yes," Ausley said, clearly surprised.

I turned to her and raised my eyebrows, "Why?"

She thought and then said, "I don't know...because he's Jackson. Because it's always been you and Jackson. Because he is amazing and because he asked. There are not a million Simulacrum guys out there, and even fewer lining up on the driveway, you know. You might just be missing out on the best one."

"That is not a reason to bond yourself to someone," I proclaimed.

"*What* is not a reason?" she asked.

"Limited options. Just because you don't know who is coming next or if there are no other options doesn't mean you should choose the first guy that comes around. It's not fair to him, either. He deserves more than me. He deserves more than I could give him." I looked at Ausley, with her heart of gold. "Actually he would be much happier with someone like you. You are a much better person than I am. You are like him in a lot of ways."

Ausley blushed a deep raspberry hue. "Veralee, he looks at me like I'm his little sister. Actually, when I think about it, he looks at me like *you* look at him. Besides, he did not ask me. He asked you." I saw it in her face: Ausley had more than a friendly admiration for Jackson. Underneath that curly hair she was harboring more. I did not press her further, out of respect, but I smiled inwardly thinking of the fine match they would make.

"Well, life does funny things. You never know where you might end up," I said just as the NavSat announced that we had "reached our destination, on the right." Ausley pulled her shoes back on. *Besides*, I thought, *I am waiting for someone else.* The man from my dream. *How could I explain that?*

We pulled up to the first house outside of Enterprise, and I jumped out to carry one of Mother's massive red boxes to the door. All of mother's gowns arrived in her signature red box. "A unique box for a unique dress," she would say with her tiny, black-framed glasses sitting at the end of her nose. Of course she did not need glasses, but they made her feel "more creative." They also helped her look less Simulacrum to the Friguscor world. We all used these subtle props to help us blend, to mesh with the others.

Ausley mashed the doorbell as the door swung open, "Good Morning, Mrs. Hinsley. We have your box from Mother." The round, short woman reminded me of a friendly pug. She smelled of dead roses that had sat much too long in fetid water and she had the dull, grey skin of the Friguscor.

Squinting, she toddled up, opened her little sausage fingers and took the box from me. Mrs. Hinsley had glaucoma and cataracts, as most Friguscor eventually do. She had had lens replacements in both eyes, and a new gene therapy, but it hadn't totally cleared her blurry vision. She looked up and smiled, but the effect was unnerving, because her face hardly moved. Layers of caked make-up marked the crevices in her face, and her eyebrows raised in permanent surprise or excitement, I'm not sure which. Obviously the result of one too many facelifts.

"Oh, I have waited for this! Tell your mother that I have been beside myself with worry. Why must she always push everything to the last minute? Why does she always make my heart so anxious? I did not know if I would have anything to wear to the big event at all! Then what would I have done?" Dragging her thick tongue across her lips she sniffed the air and then unconsciously licked her lips again several times.

I eyed Ausley, and she nodded. We were accustomed to this. Mrs. Hinsley didn't know it, but she detected the Eiani in our blood.

"Oh, I must get back to my coffee, mmm, yes. You girls came right in the middle of my breakfast. I can just taste those biscuits with homemade blackberry jam! I get it from Miss Cleo Whittaker; she makes the best! Blackberry jam... oh, it's just a little taste of paradise on my palate!"

I glanced at Ausley who was smiling broadly and nodding fervently like Mrs. Hinsley was telling her one of the secrets of life. A snicker escaped my mouth, and I tried to cover it with a cough. Ausley shot me a glance then looked away quickly to keep herself from laughing.

"Yes, we always get pear relish and pepper jelly from Miss Cleo, too," Ausley said. "Have you tried her 21-layer chocolate cake? The layers are thin as a dime, and the chocolate just melts in your mouth. Yum!"

"Did somebody say they had Miss Cleo's chocolate

cake? That stuff if so good, it'll make you wanna slap your Grandma! I'll take me some of that right now!" Mr. Hinsley boomed as he came to the door. He looked peaked, and somewhat winded, but much better than the last time I had seen him. Mrs. Hinsley loved to pore over fabrics and designs with mother when she came to Red Oaks to order her dress. Mr. Hinsley filled the time by telling his stories to Ausley and me. When I was younger, his tall tales and outrageous idioms fascinated me, but as I grew older, the repetitions became tiresome.

"Mr. Hinsley! What a thing to say. You wouldn't dare slap your Grandmother, bless her soul! Been gone on now for years, may she rest in peace," Mrs. Hinsley chided.

He chuckled, "Now, Nancy, you know I'm just kidding. It's just a saying. But, I do love Miss Cleo's cakes, that's the honest truth! Makes a man grin like a jackass eatin' briars just to think of it. Girls, how you doing? You come to bring your mother's dress to Mrs. Hinsley here? I do love to see what Miss Gail whips up for her! "Mr. Hinsley admired his wife and whistled, as if picturing her in one of Mother's gowns. "Mrs. Hinsley looks as purty as a newborn filly in a clover patch in everything your Mama makes, fine seamstress she is." Mrs. Hinsley beamed at what must have been a compliment.

"Thank you, Mr. Hinsley. I'll convey the compliment to Mother," Ausley smiled. "How are you feeling these days?"

Mr. Hinsley was undergoing treatment for advanced cancer. It didn't look good, but he was determined to "beat the cancer" which had spread from lungs to bone.

"I'm doing much better, I can breathe a lot better these days...not nearly the pressure in my chest. My leg doesn't hurt nearly as much either. Thank you for asking. Thanks to your uncle, I'm feeling much better these days."

"My uncle?" I asked, completely confused.

"Yeah, we played ball together years ago, we were real buddies. I guess he heard about my cancer, because I got a note from him saying he was coming to see me at the treatment center up in Birmingham. Hadn't seen him in ages. Lawd, he hadn't aged a day! He looks the exact same as when we was playing ball. We talked on and on about how he made that winning touchdown for Samson against Slocomb High, but he always forgets that it was *my* block that cleared the way." The nostalgia in his eyes matched the confusion in mine as he continued to gush. "We pulled some pranks together, too. He ever tell you about taping that catfish under Doc Steeley's desk? She thought it was something dead in the walls, or a chemistry experiment gone wrong! That thing stunk up that room for a week before she found it. It was awful! She never did find out it was us that did it!!" Mr. Hinsley started guffawing at the memory until his laugh devolved into spasms of coughing. It took a minute for him to stop. "Hey, don't make me laugh," he wheezed, "guess the lungs can't take that yet!"

"Are you talking about Uncle Austin?" I asked again, trying to make sense of his ramblings.

"One and the same, such a nice fella! Yeah, hadn't seen him in years, and then he just appeared out of nowhere. Looks exactly the same," he said, shaking his head back and

the Oaks Remain

forth. "He said he was going to help me, he did, gonna help an old buddy like myself." Then as if something caught his attention he jerked his head up, "Girls, you sure do smell nice. Like, like a candy cane that's been left out in the sun to bake." His nostrils flared, and he licked his lips feverishly. I saw hunger in his eyes as his fingers clawed into the side of his door. We stepped back instinctively, but thanked him out of habit.

I looked at Ausley again. We needed to go. Mr. Hinsley was not himself. Uncle Austin had not been to Alabama in more than five years, maybe more. Mr. Hinsley was old and sick. He must have seen someone else who looked like Uncle Austin.

Mrs. Hinsley felt our unease and shooed Mr. Hinsley, "Gibson Hinsley, you get yourself back to that oxygen concentrator! You know better than to work yourself up! Really, Gip, act your age!" But, though her tone was stern, her eyes radiated concern as they followed the gravely ill man down the hall. I wondered what she'd do when he was gone. The Hinsleys were nice folks, but something was obviously wrong.

"Well, we will see you out at Red Oaks for the reenactment, Mrs. Hinsley. We hope you enjoy your dress, I'm sure you'll look like a million dollars in it. You and Mr. Hinsley always make such a handsome couple!" Ausley smeared it on thick as blackberry jam as we backed away from the house.

Mrs. Hinsley toddled back through her screen door smacking her dry, cracked lips so loudly that we could hear it as we turned toward the car.

"Oh wait!" I almost forgot to snip the tag.

Mrs. Hinsley rolled around to see me, "Yes?"

"I just need to snip the lower half of the tag. It's the proof of delivery tag for Mother's records. She likes to keep accurate records."

Ausley smiled, "You mean Adair likes to keep accurate records." I pulled the silver Gingher scissors from my purse and took the bottom half of the golden tag before placing them back into their special carrying case. Mother was crazy about these scissors. Once I had used them to cut construction paper, and it was almost the end of me.

Mrs. Hinsley watched us as we climbed back into the car. I waved and drove away with a sense of grief and foreboding.

Ausley punched in the next address, and we started off. She turned the music down.

"What was that?" I asked once we were safely away.

"I don't know, but something is definitely wrong with Mr. Hinsley. There is no way he saw Uncle Austin. He's in California," Ausley answered.

"Yeah," I said slowly, "Maybe his medicines or the treatment messed with his brain somehow. Or maybe the cancer's gone to his brain. But he did look better than he did a few months ago." Still, something did not sit well. I remembered the conversation I had overheard a couple of months ago between Mother and Daddy. They had mentioned Uncle

Austin. I made a mental note to talk to Daddy when we got home.

On our way out of Enterprise, we pulled into the Big Little gas station. "Want something to eat?" Ausley asked as she jumped out of the car.

"Um, no. Well, maybe some boiled peanuts and a Coke." Grabbing the gas pump I started filling the tank with natural gas as Ausley bounced into the store. There was only one gas pump here; all the rest had been replaced with electric plug-ins. After a few minutes I heard the click of a full tank, but Ausley was still inside. $89.48 to fill up my thirteen-gallon tank. There seemed to be no end in sight for how high fuel costs would go this year.

Grabbing my purse I went to pay for the gas, which the store-clerk would inevitably find annoying. The Friguscor did not like operating with cash. But, the Simulacrum did not use traceable devices, such as the chips in their arms or the old credit card systems.

A dirty young man hovered by the door to the gas station, like a fly over your sweet tea. He approached me quickly, and I turned to face him head-on. I guess I could have walked on in and ignored him, but I found that facing men like these usually surprised them and quieted them quicker. He cocked his head slightly and squinted at me. I saw into his eyes. He had thin, grayish membranes that started at the corners of his eyes and grew to his pupils, partially obscuring his vision. It looked like tiny hands reached up from the periphery to play peek-a-boo with his sight. He unconsciously scratched at an eczematous patch on his pitted cheek, leaving jagged scrapes behind his dirty nails. He smiled at me. Gruesome desire dripped from his toothless mouth. No doubt he sought to charm me, but that was not quite the effect he had. Though he could not see well, he assumed I was beautiful, and he knew that I was pleasing to his sense of smell and would be warm to the touch. Obviously, he did not know why.

The Friguscor as babies, were as beautiful as they would ever be. It was impossible to tell the difference for the first few weeks of life. Time and age only worked against them, solidifying their tissue and spreading the cold decay throughout their body. Soon after puberty, widespread vitiligo slowly robbed their skin of color so that they eventually took on the signature ashen-white complexion, regardless of their ethnicity. Most could have played an extra on Michael Jackson's "Thriller" video, without any makeup.

"Hey Baby, What's yurrr name?" His slurred salutation jolted me back to the here and now. He swayed like a dead tree ready to tumble. I looked him dead in the eye, even though he was a head taller than me. I put my hand out to stop his forward approach. He stopped in his tracks and looked down at my hand. "You wanna get sumpin' to eat wit' me?"

"No, no thank you. I am just getting gas and getting on my way." Turning from him I grabbed the door handle and jerked it open. I did not enjoy being around the Friguscor, but I did not hate them or even dislike them. I truly felt sorry for them. They did not choose to be born who or how they were any more than I chose to be born Simulacrum.

The man slouched back down against the dirty concrete wall and sat in a drunken stupor. My heart ached for him; what a waste of life. The acrid smell of death stung my nose, much stronger than the usual decay of the Friguscor. I could smell it all over him. I knew he did not have much longer to live.

Inside by the hotdogs turning on spindles, Ausley stood talking to a young woman with a baby on her hip and two other children around her feet. I watched as the two older children drank the coffee creamers. They popped one open after another and drank the syrupy mixture down.

"You need to see a doctor. Not eating for more than 24 hours is not normal for a six-month-old. Is she drinking at all?" Ausley asked.

The young girl shifted the baby to her other hip so that Ausley could see the child more closely, "Nah, not really. I got ' er to take a little co-cola from a spoon, but she ain't taken no bottle or nothing like that."

Ausley touched the baby's small head, "She has a fever. Is there any way you can take her to the doctor?" The young mother rocked slightly to the left. Ausley and I grabbed her arm just before she tumbled over. I quickly pulled the baby from her arms while Ausley helped her to the floor. Ausley bent down to feel the woman's forehead.

"You have a fever as well, ma'am," Ausley said, touching the woman's clammy skin. The woman managed to answer, "Well, I can take the baby ' cause she's got Unicare, and she don't have no co-pay. But I can't go myself; I ain't been down to the county office to sign up. It's funny, ain't it?

They tell us we got the free health care, and then they put one sign-up office in the whole county." She half-laughed derisively, "Like I can get there with no car or nothing. I been out of work for a while now and Davion, he done run off, and I heered he's livin' off his mama again. He ain't workin' neither, and he don't help me none." I caught Ausley's eye and nodded in agreement with her. We could not leave this woman.

"What's your name?" I asked. She was frail and thin, with sores covering her face, like she had been drug addicted for quite some time. Her hair was thin and dirty like her clothes.

"Sandy," she replied weakly. This woman looked beaten, like life had pummeled her, and she was just waiting for the next cruel blow.

After paying for the gas, we crammed the red boxes into the back of the trunk to make room for the young, dirt-covered family. We bought what groceries we could for them at the gas station, stuffing the bags around the red boxes and headed toward the nearest doctor's office, just a few miles down the road. As we drove, Sandy told us that she had been working nights at the only bar in town; but she has been sick over the past month and hadn't been able to work at all. I looked in the rearview mirror at the three children. They all looked thin, frail, and sickly as well. We listened to Sandy's small, defeated voice while we drove, and my heart felt heavy with pain. The children looked as though they had never been bathed.

At the clinic, Ausley got the four of them seated in the waiting room while I walked up to the receptionist to get them registered. She sat behind a glass window chewing bubble gum and wearing a hot pink sweater and a phone headset. "Hello, Brunson's Medical Clinic," she chirped in an exaggerated southern drawl.

"Hi, um... I wanted to see about getting help for..." The gum chewer held up an index finger and then pointed to her headset. She continued to talk to the person on the other end of the headset. This was the problem with some of the AR screens. I could not see the person she was apparently speaking with, she could from her vantage point.

"Oh," I said. A running sign, in large black letters scrolled across the window.

FLU VISITS: $150

MUST PAY BEFORE BEING SEEN.

Reaching into my purse I pulled out cash and waited.

"Well, Hello! Are you for information on the new fertilization program? Do you have an appointment today?" Her smile was huge, and her lipstick the color of a ripe, red tomato, which matched the color of her hair. I breathed in the odd smell of her gum mixed with the slight odor of spoiled bacon.

"Um, no, no I don't. You see my friend Sandy over there is really sick, and so are her three kids. I was hoping you might be able to see them today." The red-headed gum chewer looked hesitantly at her computer screen while picking absentmindedly at a dry patch of dead skin on her forehead. "The children have Unicare, and I will pay for her visit today...up front," I said pointing to the sign.

"Oh honey, I'm sure you will. This must be your lucky day because we have two cancelations right after lunch... in about 45 minutes. We'll just put them all together in one room. Sound good, sugar?" *Smack, smack, smack* went her gum.

"Sounds great. Thank you," I put my hand out with the cash. Red-headed gum chewer briefly stopped chewing, "Um, no need for that honey, we'll just swipe your arm," she said as she motioned to the hand-held chip scanner. Most of the Friguscor used the electronic chip in their arm to pay via credit. The chips held more information than a traditional wallet did at one time. That was too much information for the Simulacrum. We stuck mainly to cash and protected our secrecy by keeping their identity chips out of our arms.

I was used to the Friguscor disliking cash. "I would like to pay in cash today, but thank you for the offer."

She stopped chewing and eyed me cautiously, but never let her smile fade, "Well, with the flu outbreak or the Mad-Dog Disease or whatever this is...we really don't like to use cash anymore...it spreads germs, ya know."

I didn't move, but continued to hold out the cash.

"Well, guess you gonna do what you gonna do, huh?" she took the cash in her fingertips, like it held a million flesh-eating viruses.

"Thank you," I said.

She smiled sweetly, "Well, bless your heart, I'm sure you don't know any better, but germs can be very dangerous, ya know. Maybe you can use those pretty little listening ears in science class this week. Education is a wonderful thing, isn't it, sugar?"

"Oh, it certainly is, ma'am. Just talkin' with you has been so very educational," I said, matching her southern drawl and her southern smile.

I stifled a laugh as I turned from the window. Southerners can insult you and call you stupid with a smile on their faces and a "bless your heart" on their tongues and leave you feeling warm and fuzzy. I'm not sure if the ability was hereditary or learned. Not that I would ever do such a thing.

Scanning the waiting room, I found Ausley and the little ones. Ausley wiped the baby's face with a wet paper towel, and Sandy gnawed at her fingernails while the two other children watched T.V. Their small noses were crusted over, and their greasy hair stuck flat on top of their heads. Their faded clothes hung either too loosely or pulled too tight against their thin frames. I thought of Adair and Ausley at this age, and I ached for these children, for the hard life they lived, and for the harder life they would most likely endure.

Ausley rocked the baby and sang to the middle child who had also climbed into her lap. Children had always loved Ausley; they reveled in her warmth. Bending down, I spoke to Sandy, "They are going to let you all see the doctor in about forty-five minutes or so."

"But, I can't pay to see no doctor!" she cried in a panic-stricken voice.

"No, Sandy, don't worry, it's already paid for. You

don't have to pay anything. Just see the doctor. If you need medicine they will send your prescriptions to the pharmacy in town. I will make sure those are paid for as well. Just get you and your babies better." I smiled at her, trying to cover the sadness in my eyes. Then, pulling cash out of my purse, I pressed her hand, "Here, in case you need to call a cab to get home."

Sandy looked down at her feet for a moment and then lifted her tear-stained eyes to me. "I see it in you..." she said. My breath caught in my throat. She looked too intently at me. "I see it in your face, the face of them that my Grandmaw used to tell me about."

I listened without moving. *She sees me, she sees.* I panicked. What should I tell her? She knows! "Sandy, I -"

Sandy interrupted quickly, "I know, I know, they all tell me I say the craziest things. I ain't very educated, but I can tell a good person when I see ' em. And my Grandmaw used to tell me about your kind when I was little. She said they's magical creatures that live here like regular folks. They kinda look like ever'body else, but they ain't the same, really. They's dif runt somehow. She said that they is kind, and that they did good things for us regular folks."

I smiled again, covering my shock, "Well, I don't know about all of that Sandy, but I'm really glad that I got to meet you."

"Veralee," Sandy said as she grabbed my hand, "Will it get any better?" She looked at her three little girls, and I followed her gaze.

No, I said to myself. *No, it will not get any better for your kind.* But I knew I could not leave this woman and her three little girls with such words. So I lied. "You will get medicine, and you'll feel better soon. You'll see." Then I stood and turned around before she could see the lie in my eyes or the tears on my cheeks.

Ausley and I waved goodbye as Sandy engaged her phone on her wrist and pulled a box of cigarettes from her purse. I knew that taking them to the doctor's office was not an answer for their problems, but merely a Band-Aid. Sadly, I pulled the red boxes out of the trunk and put them back on the seats, and then we were on the road again.

Ausley and I sat silently, both of us heavy with the sadness of this broken life. "Veralee, what were you going to tell her? Were you going to tell her about us?"

"No! No....I, I don't know. She knew about us in a way. She said her grandmother had told her stories about people like us. But she really didn't know anything because even as she told me the story I saw her doubting her own words."

Ausley gazed out her window and rested her forehead against the cool glass. "But do you ever think that telling them could help them? What if we told them, what if we did something for them...what if we tried to change them?" The words hung suspended in the car and travelled between us as if in slow motion. She was talking heresy, treason even. I knew that it was against every rule we had, but this was Ausley. I loved her for even thinking against the rules.

"They tried before. It didn't change anything. The Friguscor just wanted the Eiani in our blood, but not the change. You know the stories in the Histories. It drove them to madness and distorted their bodies and minds. We can't change them; it doesn't work that way."

"But what if we could?" she said, as if inching toward the edge of a cliff.

"Could what? Change them?" I added, heading toward the cliff with her.

I realized that I had been taught for so long to protect the Simulacrum secret that I had never really asked if the Friguscor could change. *Was it possible to change them? Could it be? How could it be done? Who had tried it?* No one in our lifetime, at least that we knew of. The thoughts drilled their way through my brain like carpenter bees boring into our cypress rose arbor. My thoughts buzzed, equal parts unease and fascination. A veritable hive of deliberation...and possibilities.

"I know what it says in the Histories," Ausley continued. "I have read about Rome and the madness that consumed the empire. But, I just look at them, and my heart almost bursts with their hopelessness and pain. It's so unfair. We have it all; they have so little. We were born who we are. We didn't do anything to deserve it, and they didn't do anything to deserve being born Friguscor. Why us and not them?" Ausley covered her face with both of her hands. Her golden ringlets fell over her fingers, and she slowly pulled her hands down her face, as if trying to wipe away the feelings of indignation. "I can't stop it; it flows over me and consumes me.

Those people out there are desperate and hurting. How can we look at that poor woman and those babies and just do nothing? There must be more we can do than pay a couple of bills. That's only a short-term solution." Tears pooled in her eyes, and she wiped at them with the edge of her sleeve.

"But what can we do? We are Simulacrum and they are Friguscor."

"Veralee, we know what happens to us. But if we *don't* do something, if we don't help, if we don't take a risk...what will happen to them?" A heavy silence filled the car. We both let it work its way between us, knowing that we were uttering dangerous words.

"But our blood isn't the answer, Ausley. It turns them into monsters," I said more to myself than to her.

"I'm not talking about the ones that turn into the monsters. I'm talking about the ones that can change. You *know* there are some stories in the Histories that indicate some can be changed. Some of them *can* be transformed," she said slowly, knowing the danger of her own words but gathering the courage to speak them anyway.

"The Boged," I whispered, and she nodded silently. Friguscor who could be changed into Simulacrum. Those Histories were obscure, and no one talked about them. "But we don't know which ones they are. There is no way of knowing who can change and who cannot," I said, feeling a prickle of hope run down my spine. *What if there was a way to identify them? What if we could find them? What if we could help Sandy and those three doomed little girls?*

"I know. I know there is not a way. I just wish there was. I just wish we could help them," Ausley conceded, her voice heavy with defeat.

I let the fresh air and the next song on the radio drown out my questions. Five more quick stops, and we were finally in Montgomery. We took Taylor Road to bypass the SIH and cut across to old Interstate 85. At the on-ramp, traffic crawled just trying to get onto the interstate, which itself looked like a parking lot. I decided to bypass the interstate and take the old Atlanta Highway toward Union Street. "Why is it so busy? It's not rush hour," I said more to myself than to Ausley.

"I dunno, but it sure is a deadlock. Going downtown will be nice. We can walk around and maybe eat by the capital building or down on the river." Ausley said, always with the glass half-full.

"How many more boxes do we have back there?" I asked. Leaning over the seat, Ausley counted boxes.

"One, two, three, four...no wait. Three of these boxes are going to the same place. So, we have two more stops." She plopped back down and adjusted her seat belt. We made better time going up Perry Street until we got close to downtown. Then we saw masses of people flooding the streets like the Alabama River in 2018. Swarms of people drifted toward the downtown area holding giant painted signs glued to wooden handles and mix of the more upscale AR screens.

"What is this?" I pulled over and threw the car into

park.

Ausley stared out the window, "I don't know. What are they protesting?" She squinted. "Their signs say:

STOP THE MADNESS,

FIND THE CURE."

Scanning the crowd I saw sign after sign.

WE NEED RESEARCH

NOT BROKEN PROMISES!

KEEP YOUR PROMISE FIND A CURE!

KEEP THE PROMISE NOW!

And then the odd:

ALIENS ARE AMONG US

INJECTING US WITH THE DISEASE

The epidemic. This was what Daddy had been talking about, and the kids at school. It was growing out of control, terrifying the people and leading them to desperate measures. Daddy's words echoed in my head, "They are looking for us now, maybe they haven't found us yet, but it won't be long now." I shivered as I watched scores of determined Friguscor marching down the street.

"Let's walk the box to the bookstore. It's only a couple of blocks from here," Ausley suggested excitedly.

"Um okay, but we need to stay away from the crowd." It was a bad idea. Daddy had warned me to stay away from the crowds, but sometimes I was just as nosy as Ausley was. So, I grabbed my purse, and Ausley grabbed the red box. *Stay invisible* I told myself.

"Where are we going?" I asked.

Watching the little dot on her phone, Ausley gestured past some scaffolding and said, "Looks like two blocks and then it should be on the right." Construction sites were common in Friguscor cities. Nearly every month it seemed, new technology had to be implemented to aid in the ease and comfort of the Friguscor daily life. I didn't know how they kept up with such novel contraptions, or why they would want to live life totally defined by computer chips, but they did. Life at Red Oaks was so much slower, so much simpler, and yet, it seemed so much richer. Here, it felt chaotic, like life was in fast-forward all of the time.

We walked against the buildings, trying to keep a wide berth between us and them. We avoided the solar walkways, which transformed the pressure of footsteps into power for street lights and public service announcement boards. The anger in the streets was palpable, and bitter resentment hung heavy in the air. We tried to keep our distance, but people were everywhere. Some sat along the road in wheelchairs, visibly sick. They looked like they should have been lying in hospital beds, not out on the streets. Men, women and children marched through the streets calling for justice, calling for a cure, calling for an answer. They pushed up against me, shoved and bumped me more times than I wanted to count.

It happened slowly at first, almost imperceptibly. The crowd started closing in on us. At first I thought more people were joining the march, but that was not the case. I watched as the Friguscor would pass us and then, as if a silent alarm were sounding, they would stop and sniff the air. They would then turn and look around, searching for something. My tsee-yen began to warn me of danger.

I grabbed Ausley's arm and pulled her hard, away from the crowd as quickly as I could. I regretted my stupid decision to walk on the streets immediately and even more so with Ausley by my side. Daddy had charged me with protecting her, and I had put her in harm's way. Zipping up my black jacket, I pulled the hood up over my head. Ausley did the same with hers.

"How far are we from the bookstore?" I asked anxiously. We should not have gotten out of the car. It was not safe here; things could easily get out of hand in a crowd like this.

"It's just right there. Page and Pallet, just ahead!" Ausley pointed with her phone.

"Yes, let's go!" I grabbed her arm and pulled her up the stairs more forcibly than I meant to. I pushed her into the door first, trying to protect her from whatever was out there.

The chime announced our entrance when we stepped inside, just like it should in an old bookstore. Immediately, the smell of new books calmed and enchanted me, books that graced the shelves like garlands on a Christmas tree. This was my idea of paradise, my happy place. A room filled with books, real books. Places like this were hard to come by. Books had not been printed on paper in over ten years, they were only allowed on screens. So bookstores were a thing from the past, kind of like our Simulacrum ways. Most considered books a waste of environmental resources. Save the trees, don't print books, they'd say. I breathed deeply the sweet and musty scent of the pages. I loved the past and all it had to offer.

Ausley walked to the counter with the red box, and I wandered to the back of the store, letting my fingers drag along the spines of the books. The noisy crowd outside felt chaotic, but here with the heavy black wooden door closed, it felt quiet and serene. The only sound was the low murmur of Ausley and the bookkeeper talking toward the front. I found my favorite section and fingered through the greats. I let my hand pass by each book, as if touching them would somehow let me get closer to them. *Jane Eyre, Anna Karenina, Pride and Prejudice, The Agony and the Ecstasy, East of Eden* and of course, *Gone with the Wind*. Some of my closest friends. I closed my eyes and enjoyed the moment.

"Lignum Vitae. Good afternoon, Miss Veralee." Agatha Dupree stood holding a pile of books at the end of the shelves. Agatha was tall, narrow, softly angular and very beautiful. She always wore long skirts that went to the ground and large, gemmed earrings, which looked more appropriate for a ball than a bookstore. She wore stacks of golden bangle bracelets on her bare arms, and her black braided hair was pulled into a sweet side bun with two chopsticks sticking out of the top. Loose tendrils fell over her cheeks and shoulders making her look like she belonged on the cover of a librarian magazine.

"Et Sanguis est essentia. Hello, Mrs. Dupree."

She set the books down and smiled at me. "Why are

you here today? You're quite a ways from Red Oaks."

"Delivering the red box. Mr. Dupree's uniform is ready." I glanced back at the books as if one had called my name.

"They are wonderful, aren't they? The books," she inhaled deeply, "I love the smell of them, don't you?" She never stopped watching my face while she spoke. She stepped closer to me, too close.

"Yes, they're my favorite." Awkwardly, we stood inches away from each other. The lack of personal space did not seem to bother Mrs. Dupree at all. Then in one graceful motion, she grabbed my right hand and twisted until our tseeyens were touching. I tried to step back from this personal embrace but she held my hand firmly with the strength of her centenarian years. I never knew how many years Agatha actually had, but I knew it was more than Daddy, for Daddy had said Agatha was old when he was young.

"Veralee" she whispered slowly, holding on to my name like it was a fond, but distant memory, "Something is coming for you. It moves soon. A river runs, though you do not understand its current. Do not be afraid to run hard after it. Remember, those who lose what they cannot keep will gain the world, and those who gain the world will lose in the end." She held my eyes with hers before she added, "And do not be afraid. Fear will make you unusable. Trust him when he comes, for he is already a part of you."

Then she leaned in even closer, cocked her head as if listening to something that no one else could hear, and put her delicate hand on my chest. She looked curiously into my eyes until revelation dawned in her own, "Your heart, it beats with a thrill."

    I stopped breathing for a moment, alarmed. But then, Agatha had always been a little odd. Just then the door chimed joyfully through the store. Agatha snapped back into her smiling demeanor and picked up her books.

    "Have an enjoyable drive back to Red Oaks and give Gail my love. She really is amazing, isn't she?" Then before I could answer or even find my voice, she floated around the corner.

    Ausley reappeared and asked, "Do you have the scissors?" I stood staring after Agatha, like I had seen a ghost.

    "Veralee, do you have the scissors in your purse?"

    Jerking up as if I had been underwater, I saw Ausley standing with her hands on her hips. "Yes, yes I have them, the scissors. I have them, I'm coming," swallowing hard, I followed after Ausley.

    Back on the street we decided to stop for lunch, but after finding three restaurants hopelessly overcrowded, we resigned to hunger and headed back to the car. The streets seemed to have closed their eyes and gone to sleep in the warm afternoon sun. The angry people had become hungry people—there were fewer of them on the streets now. Homemade posters sat propped outside restaurants, abandoned. We passed the oldest part of downtown, where crumbling walls stood covered in ivy, reminding of a Victorian past. Live oaks with Spanish moss draped over their branches and stretched over the stone wall to create a romantic canopy overhead. October daisies pushed their way through cracks in the wall, their lavender heads delicate against the deep crimson of the old brick. It was beautiful and whispered of Montgomery's Victorian past. Normally, I would have appreciated it, but it had been a long day, filled with unexpected oddities. I longed to see the red trees that always welcomed me home.

Behind us, a family walked, and we smiled as we heard a little boy's voice, exclaiming, "Look, I'm Superman! I'm flying!"

I glanced back. The fallen stones made perfect steps for the boy to scurry straight up to the top of the wall, which stood higher than a grown man could reach. I wondered what secret garden the wall must have guarded behind its back, so many years ago.

"Nathan, be careful up there. Better yet, come on and get down off that wall! You could fall and break your neck! That wall is old as shit," said a man in an obvious "Daddy" voice.

"I won't fall, I'm Superman. I can never fall. Superman can fly," the boy replied, confidently.

Without turning around, I heard the father reprimand the child again just as the little Superman ran right passed us with arms stretched out in flight, "Look, I'm flying! See, Daddy?" He made the whooshing sound of wind as he flew.

The wall did look unstable and dangerous, so I could understand the father's concern. The young boy hesitated, and then ran on ahead of his parents over and over like an imaginary bungee cord connected them. His parents passed us, hurrying to keep up with their carefree little boy. I saw the mother motioning to the boy for him to come down with exasperated hand motions. The Daddy called anxiously, "Nathan, that's enough! Stop right there, right now!"

The child tried to stop, and I looked up just as he lost his footing and fell from the top of the wall. The horrifying sight broke something in me, and I ran at full speed, pushing past his father as I tried to reach the boy before he hit the ground. Out of terrified confusion, his mother pulled hard at my shoulder, yanking me back. She desperately tried to reach him as well. Before any of us could catch him, the little boy cracked his head hard against the edge of the wall and landed with a horrifying thud onto the concrete. There he lay, deathly silent, his arms and legs splayed unnaturally across the concrete. The woman began screaming hysterically as she gathered the boy's bloody head onto her lap. Bending on his knees, the man tried to gather the blood in his hands that was seeping out of the back of his son's skull.

"My baby, my baby, somebody help my baby! Nathan, wake up! Wake up!" The mother screamed frantically over and over in desperate cries and guttural moans like I had never heard before. She started to hyperventilate. Ausley rushed to her side, trying to calm and comfort her. The man stared in shock and horror, still trying to collect the boy's lost blood in his hands like he might be able to put it back, to save it somehow. The boy lay motionless; he did not cry or twitch. His lips hung open and his eyes stared at nothing. I had never seen death before, never been so close to its sickening emptiness.

He was so small, so young, so beautiful, so precious, but one look at his face told me that the boy was slipping away; he was dying before my eyes.

I'm not sure what happened next. The horror of loss numbed my thoughts, and I felt my pulse throbbing into my fingertips. The street began to spin around me. I saw Ausley trying to help the mother, the father screaming at the dying child to wake-up, and the blood puddling onto the pavement...but everything else was spinning. The spinning became faster and faster while the screaming became louder and louder. Then, a still small sound pricked the air. It was the sound of my heart beating. A trilling so low, that I was not sure if I was hearing it or feeling it. I looked down at my shaking hands. "*The way is in your blood,*" echoed from my dream.

Before reason or rational thought could stop me, I reached into my purse and frantically pulled the Ginghers out of the case. The blade did not even sting as I slid it deeply across the vein in my wrist and let the blood of life, the Eiani, flow freely into the tiny, broken boy's gaping mouth. The blood dripped into his mouth and down his throat. The man stopped pooling the child's blood long enough to see what I was doing, but he was too late to stop me.

He jerked my shoulders backward screaming something that I could not hear. Ausley dove over to the ground where the man had tossed me, crouching protectively between the crying father and me.

"What are you doing? What are you doing? Who are you? Get away from my son!" The man was screaming with his hands on both sides of his head. Then the mother screamed again, and we heard the tiny sound rip through the air around us. The boy coughed, gurgled, and swallowed. His chest moved up and down, and he coughed over and over while gulping for air. The wound on his head stopped seeping immediately but still lay open. Ausley sprang into action. She checked the boy's head and then grabbed the man by the arm, "Call 911," she demanded. He nodded, confused and dazed. With tears streaming down his face, he struggled to press his ear and activate his phone. Ausley saw that he could not make the call and grabbed my phone off of the ground where it had landed beside me. She dialed the three numbers.

I saw the blue-grey color begin to recede, and the ashen white color slowly returning to the boy's cheeks. He started crying and reached for his mother.

"Veralee, look! He's, he's coming back!" Ausley whispered in awe.

The father turned with a mix of astonishment and disbelief in his wide eyes and looked directly at me.

"We need to go," I whispered back. We had stayed too long already. Quickly, I picked myself up and shot Ausley a worried look. Holding my wrist tightly we ran from the scene. Ausley got into the driver's seat, still shaking, and threw the car into drive. We did not look in the rearview mirror or turn around until we were out of the city. My mind raced.

What had I just done? Ausley kept looking at me out of the corner of her eye, but she was too stunned to say anything. Lost for words, I put my seat back and wrapped my wrist in a scarf I found on the floorboard. We healed quickly, much faster than the Friguscor, but still, it would take time for the skin to weave itself back together.

We rode in silence during the trip back to Red Oaks, trying to process what had just happened. Sweet Ausley looked so concerned, so afraid, the worry apparent as she stole furtive glances at me all the way home. Ausley stopped and ran the last boxes into the last house as I sat and stewed in this morass I had created.

What had happened to me? I had done the unthinkable, the unforgivable. I had broken our law today. I had gone against the Simulacrum way in a moment of complete panic. We were not to let anyone know about us. There were rules for a reason. We had to protect our people. I looked down at my trembling hands. What had I done? What would happen to me if they found out? Then a cold thought crept into my mind, and I stopped wondering about me. My body shook and a shiver ran down my spine.

What would happen to the boy?

{ 5 }

the Great Trees

Lying on a blanket under the trees in the cool October morning sun made yesterday's horror seem faded, like remnants of a half-forgotten nightmare. I always could push anything that bothered me to the back burner of my mind. I pretended that the problem at hand was as small as a mouse in our sprawling house. Of course it cowered, somewhere under the boards of the floor, making a nest and scavenging on crumbs, but it didn't affect the whole of the house. The difference this time, of course, was that this mouse could grow into an elephant.

    I inhaled a deep, calming breath and forced myself to concentrate on the warmth of the sun resting on my cheeks. Even with my eyes closed, I could still "see" the sunrays flickering between the leaves of the trees. It had a hypnotizing effect, and I relaxed deeper into the green grass. I held up my wrist...even the evidence of the deep laceration was gone, the edges fused together by the Eiani as I slept. Only a thin white line remained to testify against me.

Last night I had slept in the depths, that dreamless recess of the mind where consciousness does not exist or call you to action. I had not realized how much energy giving the blood had robbed from my body, until I fell deeper and deeper into the black ocean of sleep. Countless times I replayed the scene in my mind like an antique vinyl record skipping over and over again at the same point. Each time, I willed myself to make it to the boy before he fell, but each time he still lay silent and broken on the concrete. Each time the smell of rust and rot splattered into the air as his tainted blood seeped across the concrete. The mother's anguished screams, and the father's desperate questions wrapped the tragedy into a tightly coiled time warp. And orbiting the unending warp was the question I could not answer: *What had I done?* It probed with its piercing tentacles. The searing questions kept erupting: *What would the repercussions be? How would this affect Ausley? What would this mean for my family, for Mother, Daddy, Adair, Mattie, PH? What would happen if anyone found out? What had I done to the Simulacrum, to our way of life?*

And then the most probing question of all: *What had happened to the boy? What had I done to that boy?*

The Simulacrum way of life was *my* way of life ... or, was it? That radical thought invaded my consciousness. *Was this* my *way of life or* their *way of life?* I had always heard the stories about the essence that dwelt inside our blood, the Eiani. As I grew I saw for myself that we were different, marked by the One Tree, by our tseeyens, and by the Eiani. The Eiani was mystical, even to those of us who understood it best. It flowed as the life force within our veins, but in the veins of the Friguscor it turned to poison, a double-edged sword.

What happened to them was not a complete mystery. The horror stories were drilled into the Simulacrum as children. We heard over and over of the monsters, the bloodseekers, like other children heard about the boogeyman or vampires. But these monsters were different from fairytales; these monsters were real. And we could create them with only a drop of our blood. How it happened, exactly, was still somewhat of a mystery. Like a legend, all we knew came from stories of long ago, passed down by elder Simulacrum and recorded in the Histories. But what we did know haunted my childhood dreams. Bloodthirsty Friguscor, moving in packs, prowling like hungry wolves, hunted and pursued me night after night, until Mother would hear my cries and come to soothe the panic from my trembling body and mind. Peaceful sleep came wrapped in Mother's arms but the terrifying images never slept for long.

It was the vague whispers of the "others" that left me feeling that I had not been everything. The mysterious *Boged*, people who were Friguscor on the surface, but who carried a remnant, a lingering trace of Simulacrum lying dormant in their veins. The stories said there might be hope for them, that they could be changed. The minute memory of Eiani in them somehow created a pathway for living blood to pulse its way through the decaying veins and tissues and revive them. But, it wasn't an easy transition; they paid a price. I had never seen it, and no one spoke of it, because it was strictly forbidden to give Friguscor our blood.

We did not know who or what the Boged were. We

didn't know if they existed anymore, or if, like so much in our stories, if they had simply vanished from the race of men. Maybe they had never existed at all. Maybe they were just a myth, born out of the desperate hope to believe that the Friguscor could be changed. Still, something in me told me that they were real, that they were out there. Something in me yearned to believe that redemption was possible for Sandy, for Emmalie, for Mr. and Mrs. Hinsley and for Nathan. I couldn't decide why I was so desperate to believe. Was it a longing for our Histories to be true, not just ancient fairytales? Or was it something deeper? Was it some reality that lay at the bottom of that deep ocean of truth and fiction?

    I rolled over onto my stomach in the soft, smooth grass and propped myself up on one elbow. Longing for distraction, I flipped through a volume of the Histories I had "borrowed" from the top shelf in Daddy's library while he was away at work. I had loved these magical books as a child, with their intricate pictures colored with gold, red, green, and silver hues. The stories of the Simulacrum of old.

    "So, what's wrong, Veralee?" Jackson eased his way towards me from across the trees. He spoke softly, his smooth voice matching his smooth skin when I glanced up at him.

    "Nothing," I said sullenly. He leaned against an old oak tree and slid down the trunk to sit beside me. He pulled up a piece of onion grass and chewed on its end.

    "Nothing? Really? Now why would you be sitting out here with *that* book in your hands if nothing was wrong? I have seen you like this a million times. So what did you do *this* time? You seem a little old for ' time out," he laughed.

I scowled at him and sat up. He could be so annoying sometimes, especially those times that he seemed to be able to see right through me. The page blew slightly in the wind, and the picture of the One Tree stirred slightly on the page. The pictures were always moving in this book, which had always fascinated me. It was no normal book. Normal books never changed. They were flat, bound by the boundaries of ink and paper. But this book lived and breathed.

Jackson leaned over me and read, "*All things begin and end with The Trees.*" I felt him tremble as the words drifted off of his tongue. I traced the picture of the One Tree lightly with my fingertips.

"It's amazing, isn't it?" he said softly, like he didn't want to disturb the forest around us or the Tree on the page.

"Yes," I said, feeling the power of the Tree through the picture. I did not need the pictures to know these trees. I had seen them with my own eyes in the painting on my bedroom wall and, once, in my dreams.

"I've seen it before."

Jackson kept his eyes on the picture and ran a long finger across it. He did not look up, "In your dreams?" he asked. His fingers briefly touched mine.

"Yes...the One Tree...it's, it's," I struggled for words, but found none that felt adequate. "Really, Jackson, it's hard to describe. It's like trying to describe a color you have never seen. The Tree itself was colossal, overwhelming, even. And it was on fire, like an inferno, like some massive building totally engulfed by flames. Everything around it glowed a deep red.

It gave off so much heat that I had to shade my eyes and squint to even look at it. But with all those flames—that white-hot fire—it didn't consume the Tree. It burned and burned, the flames roared and billowed," I gestured with my hands to try to show him, "but the Tree didn't burn at all. It was like the fire, the flames were the very *essence* of the Tree. Somehow, the fire and the Tree were one. Does that make sense at all? "

    Jackson, suddenly serious, nodded, "Wow." He stared at the picture, attempting to grasp what I tried to convey, and then pointed to the picture again, "Did you see this? Did it grow like that?"

    "Pretty much. The trunk was actually comprised of three trunks that twisted around each other, but they were also interconnected so that they made one trunk, not three separate ones, like a banyan tree. And at the bottom," I pointed to the roots of the tree, "the Tree wasn't anchored to the ground, but it was like it was hovering over the earth. Its roots fanned out in all directions," I swept my outstretched arms in a circle around my body as far as I could reach, "and they were suspended in air, too. The roots seemed to be in some kind of order, but I could not figure out the pattern."

    I wrinkled my brow trying to solve that puzzle then shook my head. I still couldn't get it. So I went on, "Underneath the floating Tree there was a vast pool of water. Emerald green, like Ireland in liquid form. It was so clear, so pure. And, all of the colors from the fire danced across the surface of the water, like thousands of suns rising and setting at once. The water was alive with movement and color."

    I reached into my mind's eye for a closer look; "It was

..." I stopped. "I wish I could describe it better, Jackson. I wish you could see it."

As I watched the picture in the book, the waters began to ripple, and I heard a faint sound brush across the top of the water. The ripples rolled into waves, and the waves crashed up towards the roots of the One Tree. Then millions of voice broke through the air, swirling and surrounding the Tree with an antiphonal vortex of song. Rich harmonies and intricate rhythms blended into a symphonic chorale that made Palestrina's polyphony pale in comparison. It was like nothing I had ever heard before. It was as if it was the first song ever written, ever composed. I closed my eyes and sat mesmerized, letting the splendor of the music wash through me. It was a siren call, a love song, a cleansing infusion, a healing potion. This was more complex than Bach, more lush than Brahms, more passionate than Rachmaninoff, more everything. Was I remembering it now? Or was the book singing it to me here under the trees of Red Oaks? Regardless, I never wanted it to end.

Jackson shook me slightly, "Veralee? Veelee ... Little Bird!" I blinked hard and returned reluctantly to the moment, opening my eyes. Jackson's face was very close to mine, "Where did you go?"

I stammered, "I ... um, I was just remembering..."

He patted my head like I was a small puppy, "I could see that. One more minute, and I thought you were going to spin your head around and start speaking in a dark menacing voice, like, ' Jackson. I. Am. Your. Father.'" He was just so charming, like a five-year-old boy on a sugar trip.

"Did you hear that? Did you hear the song the Tree was singing?" I looked at him expectantly.

Jackson raised his eyebrows, "What? What song?"

I collected my emotions, "Nothing. I just thought... oh, never mind."

"Veralee, sometimes you talk about the weirdest things."

I sighed, "I know Jackson. I know."

"Come on, don't be so melodramatic. You know you are a little odd, right?" he said with an overly theatrical smile.

In the light between the trees I saw him then. Though we were such good friends, he had never really understood me.

Jackson put a warm hand on my back, "Er, okay, well, I'm going to the house to see what they have to eat. Hope your Mama has some fried okra and cornbread left. Ausley wants me to go with her today to the clinic or something. But if you want, I could just stay here with you. We could read big ole books about prophecy and dark days and mythological creatures. Then we could get all depressed together ... maybe cry a little and hug it out over some chocolate cake and dill pickles. That would probably lead to a romantic chick-flick and some cuddling or possibly spooning, which let me tell you, I was built to spoon!" He lifted up his shirt, showing off his rippling abs. He *was* built to spoon, but right now he was spooning it on a little too thick.

"Think I'll pass on the crying and hugging it out, and the chick-flick and the cake and pickles," I laughed in spite of myself and focused on the book, trying to keep my eyes off of his rippled stomach. He lowered his shirt and sighed.

Immediately I put my hand over his, "But I really do appreciate the gesture, I do. I just need some time alone today. Go, help Ausley. She says they are really short-handed at the clinic. More people are coming in with the virus every day." I patted him to console him. He raised an eyebrow at me and smiled. But, I knew he was disappointed.

"All right, Miss Ice Queen. Have it your way. But don't come crying to me when that book is too heavy for you to carry back inside all by your lonesome. I mean, seriously, you've got two twigs for arms."

As he walked back towards the house I flipped the pages forward, to the picture of the Tree of Shadows. The second tree in my dream, the second tree on my bedroom wall.

In my dream, the *Tree of Shadows* dominated a barren wasteland, which stretched as far as I could see in every direction. The sun burned hot and ruthless. Every now and then a dry, eroding wind blew through, kicking up dark clouds of thick dust. The Tree's gnarled roots grasped at the soil like arthritic knuckles before they dug into the earth. This time two trunks, not three, grew into one. The Tree's girth was massive, and it weighed so much that its roots delved into the core of creation itself.

Looking up, I saw that the Tree of Shadows spiraled into the sky, and I could not see the end of it. Its great limbs reached across rivers and oceans, and towered over the vastness of the land. Branches laden with two types of succulent fruit stretched to the four corners of the earth to offer food to the whole world. Twisted from two, bound as one, it stood tethering the world between its roots and shade.

Then I heard it. The Tree of Shadows seemed to breathe, emitting a continuous, humming sound, like it was calling to the earth. It never rested, never slept. Never silent, never still. Even when there was no wind, its boughs quivered and its leaves trembled.

In middle school, I had toured a power generating plant and stood near the lines that transmitted high-voltage electricity from its source. The lines vibrated, hummed, and swayed with the force that pulsed along them, and I felt the pull, a sort of tingling through my body being near to such a powerful surge of energy. This was something like that, but so much more.

Even in my dream I could feel that the Tree was not tame, not safe, though it was incredibly alluring. I could not look away; I could not understand it.

The Histories said that the Tree of Shadows was filled with the knowledge of good and evil. It separated and infused all at the same time. Good and evil. Could both truly exist on the same tree? Did both exist inside of me ... deep inside my blood?

My blood. The vinyl record skipped again in my mind, as I saw my deep red blood dripping from my wrist and into the limp boy's mouth. The boy and I were separated by so

the Oaks Remain

much, and yet in my moment of panic, I had felt like we were connected enough to share the blood. The thought of the boy pulled at my heart, and I felt a hopeless need to touch his face, to know that he was alive and thriving, to hold him and protect him. These thoughts confused me. I did not even know that boy, but something in me felt him out there. Somehow I *knew* he was alive, and I could feel his heartbeat just as sure as I could feel my own. He was *alive*, but was he well? Had he recovered? I couldn't just leave him there like that, so pale, so little, so helpless...so hopeless. I couldn't just ignore his mother's screams for help or his Daddy's desperate, but futile attempts to save him. I couldn't...could I?

No matter how I justified it, I knew that it was strictly forbidden to share our blood, for good reason. It was just too dangerous. My people had spent centuries erasing the memory of our blood from the minds of the Friguscor; we were frequently reminded that one mistake could undo the work of the generations. And yet, in a moment of terror, in a panic of compassion, I reacted without hesitation to heal, to help, to make right what was broken. *Why?* How could I overcome everything I had been taught in one unthinking moment? Why did my instincts betray me, and with me, the entire Simulacrum race? Closing the book and my eyes, I rolled onto my back to feel the cool morning air and the warm sunlight on my face.

I felt her before she spoke.

"I spoke with Ausley."

All of my life Adair's voice had been the same, solid, unwavering presence. She had been an adult since she turned five. Adair never understood the world of children; as a child I had realized she understood nothing of the trifling games of little girls. While I was writing stories about faraway lands, she was organizing her shoes in her closet and discussing her financial portfolio with Daddy. The world was black and white for Adair, without a hint of grey. Her view of the world always eluded me, as I'm sure mine did hers. What would it be like to always accept and never question the answers given? To feel freedom in the rules instead of a noose around your neck? To find comfort in the age-old formulas? I didn't know.

To me, the grey held mystery, adventure and possibility, but it simply blurred the lines for Adair. Her paint colors never blended, but stayed put in their separate splotches on each side of the paper plate. Mine seemed to find themselves swirled together before I could even decide what color they were in the first place.

Her shadow stood over me but did not completely block out the sun. Without opening my eyes I acerbically answered, "Of course you did." Ausley could not keep a secret, but it was not a betrayal. Secrets did not slip out of her mouth as one who had an excessive need to talk. No, she simply did not believe in holding back information that was marked, in her mind, as critical.

Even with my eyes closed, I could feel Adair's condemning frown, "Veralee, this is serious. Are you hurt?" she jerked my wrist up and gasped.

"Veralee! You really did it! Oh no! How could you? How stupid could you possibly be? Do you know what you've done?" she screamed, swaying slightly. I could feel tears forming in her eyes even as anger radiated from them.

I sprang up on my elbows a little too quickly and glared at her, "Do *you*?" I blurted back more forcefully than I had intended. I wanted her to answer me; I wanted her to explain it to me because I was completely confused, completely lost in uncharted territory.

Narrowing her eyes, she spoke through clenched teeth, "What are you going to do if someone finds out? You didn't just break a rule, Veralee, like driving over the speed limit or skipping class, this time. You've broken *our law*! This is not something small. You are always breaking rules; you think it's cute, like it's a game or something, to see just how much you can get away with. But this is *not* a game, Veralee. This affects us all...you have endangered us all!"

She was right; this was not a child's game that I had played. She didn't need to say it, but hearing it made it even worse. "I know. I know you're right, Adair. Is that what you want to hear?" I shot at her, glaring through the heat that was rising in my face.

Adair fired back, "You are such a child Veralee. This is not about being right. This is about our *lives*. But I am sure you never thought of that. I'm sure you just did whatever you wanted to do. I have a child, Veralee. I have a baby I have to protect! And one day, I will be the Guardian of the Gate. You don't have that sitting on your shoulders, no. You just act out of your rebellion." Adair was shaking with anger.

I launched my defense back at her, "Rebellion? You think I did this out of some need to rebel? Rebel against what,

Adair? Come down off your high horse for a minute and realize that I have this under control. No one knows anything about this except us! Stop blowing this out of proportion!"

Adair took two large steps towards me and pointed a condemning finger at me and raged, "Out of proportion? Out of proportion?! Do you have any idea what can happen if they find us? Did you *ever* listen to *anything* Mother taught us in school? Are you so naive? What you have done? You could get us in trouble with the Council. You could get Daddy in trouble. You could get us all killed!" Her tears burned hot with fury, "That law is the only protection we have, Veralee. It's the only way I can protect *Mattie* from the animals of this world!"

My heart dropped. She was right. She was always right. "I honestly don't know what I did. I don't know *why* I did it. I just...panicked. The little boy, he was Mattie's age. He was so small, his blood was everywhere, and I could see the life draining out of him. His mother was screaming, his Daddy was screaming, and he was so still, so helpless. Something snapped in me, and I couldn't watch him die. I couldn't just stand there and let him die. I gave him the blood before I even realized what I was doing." Tears burned on the edges of my eyelashes, and Adair's shoulders softened slightly. I saw some pieces of understanding in her eyes before she looked away, out over the fields.

Adair glared hard at me as she spoke, "Veralee. I can't imagine having to see that happen to a child. But the child was Friguscor. We are Simulacrum. It's the way things are. You cannot change everything you don't like. You must accept that the law was created to protect us," and she spoke in a softer, quieter tone as she glanced down at her perfect fingernails, "to protect Mattie."

    I saw the mother in her then. It had always been there, and I had resented it for years. Before it had just seemed bossy and controlling, but now...watching the tears stream down her face, it was different. Control was a balm for her fear, like rebellion was for mine. It kept the nightmares away.

    Then, in a moment of clarity, I said, "Adair, we are not going to tell anyone about this. The little boy's parents don't know who I am. They probably don't even understand what I did. I'm sure they rushed him to the hospital and spent the night with doctors and nurses patching him back together. I think he had a broken arm or leg, too. No one knows I had anything to do with this, that my blood had anything to do with it. It will blow over, but you cannot tell anyone. There is no way they can trace this back to me, and it will not help anyone to worry over something that cannot be changed. We *must* keep this between us."

    Adair bit her lower lip like she always did when she was thinking, weighing options. She dabbed her eyes and seemed to brush more than grass off her hands as she wiped them on her cornflower blue skirt. Her voice shook slightly as she spoke, "You are probably right. They would never be smart enough to connect what you did to the child's recovery anyhow. Their rational minds will explain this away for them. But what if the child turns? What if he is turning now? What will happen then?"

    She was working it all out in her head as she spoke to me, and I had no answers. She sat silently for a long while, calculating the odds, weighing the black against the white in her mind, "Okay, Veralee. Against my better judgment, we won't tell anyone." She rolled her eyes, and started again, "Why do you do these things? Why can't you just do what you are supposed to do?" Pointing at me, she said, "You have to start thinking before you just jump off a cliff. You are not a child anymore, and what you do has real implications, for all of us." She picked up my tattered copy of *Gone with the Wind* that lay beside the Histories. "You are not a character in a book." She shook the book a little, and I got the impression she was pretending the book was me. "You're too old to go around pretending that you're some heroine in a great story. This is not Tara, this is Red Oaks. Real life, Veralee, with real people, and what you've done could start a real war. Not between the North and the South, but between the Friguscor and the Simulacrum. You're nineteen years old; it's time to grow up."

She tossed the book back onto the blanket and stood above me again. She gave me an exasperated look and then, with great purpose, the only adult in the conversation started back toward the house.

"Come on, I can't talk to you about this right now...you won't listen to me anyway. In the end, you always do whatever you want to do." She knew me too well. "Besides, we only have two days until these fields will be red with *that* war. I have an entire list of things for you to do today. And you need to return that book to the library before Daddy catches you out here with it. Those are ancient books, Veralee. Put it back before you drop it in a mud puddle or something," she called back over her shoulder. Adair would use work to distract her mind. She would retreat to the safety of her lists.

"Of co–uhse, deuh sistuh!" I called back, using an exaggerated accent, trying to break the somber mood with a little humor. I swallowed the anxiety that made my hands shake and willed myself to believe what I had just said to Adair. I wanted it to be true. Maybe Adair didn't really believe it either. But what were our options?

Bending down I gathered the blanket, the Histories and my worn copy of *Gone with the Wind* and started back for the house. I guess if I were a character in that classic story, I *would* be Scarlett, because try as I might, I was no Melanie.

I loved Red Oaks like she loved Tara, and I planned to stay close to it and my family all my days. Scarlett had lost so much during the Civil War. The irony was not lost on me: North against South, a bloody feud causing horrendous death and destruction with nothing left unscathed or unchanged. Friguscor vs. Simulacrum had potential for the same. I shook my head. I did not want Scarlett's tragedy, or even her nineteen-inch waist, for that matter. She had caused a lot of her own misery through her impulsive actions and rebellious nature. I hoped that part was not like me. That would not be me. I looked up at the house and around me. *No, that would not be me.*

Turning under the red oaks, I took it all in: those trees, the rolling hills, the deep forest, the creek, the river, the landscaped grounds and gardens, and the house. I loved every inch of the 1240 acres that made up the property. If you arrived in autumn, the beauty of the red oaks would move you, but if you arrived in the summer, their magic would still dazzle you. Those oaks were an anomaly, a puzzle and a riddle. Their leaves were always red, no matter the season, no matter the weather. Some claimed that the soil content was different; others contended that the water had colored the trees somehow, or maybe that they were a special type of oak. Many specialists and certified arborists from Auburn, Mississippi State, Georgia, and the University of Alabama had studied the soil, water, and the trees, but nobody had come up with anything definite. The truth ran much deeper than the myriad theories.

We knew the truth about the Eiani within our blood. So it was here, in the midst of the unexplainable that we Harpers made our home, under the red wings of the mysterious trees. My family's roots ran as deep as the towering oaks that lined the drive up to the house. And it was safe, because Red Oaks was off the beaten path. Who would be looking for a gorgeous plantation just outside the little town of Samson, Alabama, population 2,000 (if you counted the cows and chickens)? The only outside people who came through Samson were looking for a meal or some fuel on the way to Panama City Beach, unless they came to visit family or for the re-enactment of the Battle of Red Oaks.

When Ernest Weekes, my great-great-grandfather, had come to this plot of land, he was looking for a place to call home. He had been discharged from the Army in Louisiana after the War of 1812 and was working his way back to Georgia. Needing some money when he reached this area, he worked helping a settler clear some land, part of which would become Red Oaks plantation. When he saw the trees, the red of their leaves, and felt the richness of the dirt between his fingers, he planted his feet and grew to love every inch of the land. He also fell for the owner's daughter, Barthenia Ausley

the Oaks Remain

McDuffie. Barthenia, affectionately known as Thenie, was seventeen when she married Ernest. She was half Creek Indian through her mother and half Scotch-Irish through her father.

Thenie's maternal family had held the land longer than anyone could even trace. The Simulacrum First Americans had long protected the Gateway on these hallowed grounds. By 1814 when Ernest came to Alabama Territory at the age of 19, hostilities between the Creeks and the white settlers were ramping up, with each side committing atrocities against the other. Simulacrum Creeks recognized they could soon be pushed off the land they loved. Knowing this, Chief Opothle of the Poarch Creek tribe passed the Guardianship to his daughter, who in turn, passed it to Thenie when she came of age. Thenie and Ernest had been married less than a year when her parents were ambushed and killed while trying to negotiate peace between a tribe of angry Creeks and a group of arrogant white settlers. Of course, both sides blamed the other for the murders. With her parents' deaths, Thenie had inherited the land and the Guardianship.

To increase their income, Ernest built a sawmill on the Pea River at the edge of the property and soon had a lively business selling lumber from trees that he harvested from what would become the cotton fields. Through the junction with the Choctahatchee River, his barges could reach up to Georgia and central Alabama and down the Gulf Coast to Florida, Mississippi, and Louisiana. His market was wide. The excellent quality of the red oak and yellow pine fueled the business, helping it grow rapidly, and soon everyone sought his product for plantation homes and floors. Weekes Lumber

Company made Ernest a wealthy man.

Ernest had a vision for Red Oaks. He wanted a safe haven for the Simulacrum, a place where any and all could come and live safely, protected from the outside world. He and Thenie lived for many years in the small house her parents had built until the Big House was finished. He ultimately turned the little house into the kitchen house. Years before he built the Big House, he planted the rows of red oaks to line the drive to the house that was yet to be. As if the land understood, the tree lines began to thicken all around the borders of Red Oaks protecting it from the outside world.

Eventually, Ernest built the stables and the work quarters and reclaimed several fields from the forest, who gave them up without protest. It took decades to make Red Oaks a fully functioning cotton plantation, but it was done through a partnership with the trees and the land that not even Ernest could explain. He poured his life into the work, and he and Thenie in some ways became as calloused as their hands. Living on the land, carving out a life from the dirt beneath them, and watching as the land took on a life of its own was not easy, but it was good.

Ernest could not farm a cotton plantation in 1843 with only the six hands in his household. So he, Thenie and their daughter Vera turned to the slave markets in Montgomery and Mobile for help.

Most Simulacrum avoided the southern states during this time because of the heavy hand that the Friguscor held there. The Friguscor ran the slave trade; they were indifferent to the unfathomable horrors they perpetrated. They only re-

the Oaks Remain

sponded to the sound of gold clinking into their wallets. So, the Friguscor prospered greatly during this time of immeasurable shame and sorrow for the nation, and particularly, the South. Ernest Weekes knew that Simulacrum came in every color, and many Simulacrum had lived and died as slaves throughout the ages of time. So when my great-great-grandfather was financially able, he made it his mission to buy Simulacrum slaves and let them live and work to earn their freedom on his plantation. There were few large plantations this far south in Alabama; most were just subsistence farmers, so he did not have to deal with other slave owners often. He was able to keep his mission quiet. He had seen the horrors of slavery, and he knew that he alone could not change the whole world. So he changed the world one slave at a time.

  Ernest worked hard himself, and he believed it preserved a man's dignity to allow him to work for what he got. So, when he bought slaves, he required them to work five years or until they worked off their purchase price, whichever came first. Then, Ernest gave them a sum of money equivalent to their purchase price, wrote out their emancipation papers, and they and their families were free to go. Some left, but it was perilous for freed slaves to travel, and most had nowhere else to go. They usually stayed. Ernest helped them build them small homes out of lumber from the mill, and he built a schoolhouse where everyone who desired to could learn to read and write. He took meticulous notes of marriages, births, and deaths, in addition to purchase price and freedom earned, so we had good records from the time. When the Civil War erupted red over the white cotton fields, Red Oaks housed more than 100 former slaves and about 50 who were working off their debt. During the war, most of the freed slaves stayed, protecting their families at Red Oaks. After the war, many stayed on again, because they were just as much a part of Red Oaks as the Weekes family. In fact, that is how Jackson's family ended up next door; Jackson's Great-Grandfather Abram was Vera's right-hand man, and she deeded him property in appreciation for his loyalty and hard work over the years.

As children, Ausley, Jackson, and I had spent hours playing in the old quarters tucked between the old kitchen house and the river along the edges of our property. For a long time Mother did not allow us to play so far from the house, but as we grew, she relented or maybe she just got distracted. Knowing Mother, she always knew just where we were. So when she would start up her sewing machine to create a new masterpiece quilt to auction off as a fundraiser for the Wiregrass Museum of Art or another hooped ball gown for the Civil War enthusiasts, we would escape down the rabbit's hole and end up on the other side of the world in our secret realm of children's play.

Ausley and I loved the shacks and turned them into the backdrop for characters and stories that I published in my mind. We knew we had found our own *Secret Garden*, our *Bridge to Terabithia*. The characters and lives we created for them were so real, so vivid for us that I can still recall them to this day. I knew their names, their pets' names, and what they liked to eat for dinner.

The best day of our little-girl lives was the day we discovered that the library in our house and the second slave shack, (where our own pretend character Rebecca Jane lived), were actually connected through an underground tunnel. Could there be anything more magical than a secret passage-

the Oaks Remain

way? I guess finding it wasn't really an accident, considering the countless hours we spent searching for secret passages that might whisk us away to Narnia in the blink of an eye. So, finding it might more accurately be described as a product of hard work and determination.

After the tin-foiled treasure maps and endless secret letters written to us by our "Great-grandmother Vera" had failed us again and again, we finally found something worth finding. I believe that mostly it was because we gave up following the maps and letters that were written with Adair's sparkling pink highlighter. I explained to Ausley that Great-grandmother Vera must have loved that sparkling pink highlighter, because she used it so much. (And Adair never could understand why her highlighters dried up so quickly.) Everyone probably used those during the Civil War, I'd say to Ausley, who bought it every time. Though she was only sixteen months younger than I, she trusted me completely. Wide-eyed, she would nod her curly blonde head up and down, practically bursting with pure excitement and devotion. Like I said, she was a great audience.

We discovered the tunnel on a hot and rainy morning in July during the wettest summer we ever had—I knew this because Rick Peterson, the weatherman on WGTV Channel 4 News said so. He looked so official that I knew it had to be true. Mother had whipped up a big breakfast of buttermilk cat-head biscuits, bacon, grits and eggs like she did most every morning and set off to her sewing room. That was her sacred hideaway where she could escape for hours on end. That room amazed us with all of its colors and fabric smells and little scissors and buttons.

Mother "discouraged" us from playing in the sewing room after the "Veralee Runway Extravaganza" disaster. It sounded like a good idea at the beginning, but featured a lot of crying in the end. Looking back on it, I could see that Mother was right: cutting Ausley's glorious golden curls had *not* been essential for the fabulous outfit I had created for her to wear. But, how was I supposed to know that until I tried?

Once we heard the presser foot hit the fabric, we knew we could expect long periods of unsupervised, unstructured, and unlimited play. I decided we would start our adventure in the library that morning. Ausley thought it was time to play dolls in our bedrooms, but I explained how important it was for her growing mind to go to school each and every day. Once she agreed to go to school like I said, we set off for the library where I kept all of my best teaching supplies and instructing sticks. I had been given a real teacher's pointer for my birthday and thought it so great that I found even more sticks around the yard to use, too. Who wanted to point with the same stick for every class? So I had a whole collection of pointers to instruct Ausley in important matters like knowing a capital A from a lower case a.

Ausley sat at her normal seat in the library even though it was raining, and she could not see our secret garden from the window today. She loved to sit where she could usually feel the sun on her round, chubby cheeks. Her cheeks turned bright pink when she laughed; she was always full of warm color. The argument began over who would write the schedule for the day. I, being the teacher, was the most obvious choice. The fact that I could write in cursive and not just scratch out letters like a caveman gave me a clear advantage as well. But that morning Ausley insisted and grabbed the dry-erase board from my hands.

"I'm gonna write down when we eat lunch," she held the board above her head.

"Only the teacher can decide when to eat lunch, Ausley! Give me that back before I move your star down, and I have to write a letter home to your mother. You got three just last week," I warned in my sternest teacher voice.

"NOOOOO, VEEEELEE," Ausley turned in one swift motion and started her chubby legs to running. She had not planned her escape route well, because she ended up slamming face first into a bookshelf. The board went sliding across the floor, and Ausley was left laid up like a crumpled rag-doll.

Not one waste an opportunity, I scrambled for the board like a rat let out of its cage, all nails and teeth. Ausley saw my move and used her position on the floor to block me and jockey herself toward the board. Victory was in sight just as I hit the board with my right foot and slammed into Ausley and floor all at once. Dazed, we glared at each other.

Then we froze and listened for a moment. Thankfully, the sewing machine was still going strong. Mother had not heard our scuffle over the dry-erase board. We surveyed the damage to the library. We were always fighting like cats, and Mother kept our fingernails short to keep the nail marks to a minimum. The rug was pushed all the way back to the great desk that sat in the middle of the library and a pile of books laid sprawled out across the room. We pushed each other back and forth as we set to picking up the books. I was picking up an old copy of *The Lord of the Rings* when I noticed the round ring of metal in one of the wooden floor panels. It was hidden down in the wood in some kind of pocket that had been dug out of the wood.

"Look at that thing!" Forgetting that I was not holding my pointer, I used the book to motion toward the metal ring.

"What thing?" Ausley crinkled her nose and cocked her head to the right side like she always did when confused.

I bent down and traced the ring with my finger. Magic was wound into this metal, I was sure of it. "It's some kind of metal thingy in the wood. Oh look, I think it lifts up. I think it's a handle, a funny handle in the floor!!"

"Wait, Let me pull on it! I love to pull on things, oh please, let me pull on it!" Ausley bobbed up and down.

"It's stuck, I can't get it," I pulled and pulled waiting for the magic to burst forth, but nothing happened. "Let's get Daddy's oil can from the workshop".

"We aren't supposed to go in there. It's a rule. He said it, I ' member and he said it with the really, real voice." Ausley, the ever-obedient one, warned.

"Well you have to get it ' cause I have to sit here and figure out how to get this thing to open. It's a treasure, a real treasure, Ausley, so hurry up!"

"Get what?" Jackson had arrived and stood in his denim overalls by the library door.

Ausley set her lips like the closed-mouth of a Ziploc bag, planted her feet and crossed her arms, "No, Veelee! Daddy said!" We ignored Jackson's entrance.

"Fine, then! Just stay here with Jackson and guard our treasure. I'll be right back." By the time I got the thing to open, it was almost lunch. It took a generous helping of oil, but with Jackson's help, we finally inched the metal ring up and off the wood. Then we could pull it and find the magic inside, simple. It *was* a door, a small door, but a door nonetheless. The metal ring was the way to open the door in the floor. The "floor door," as we called it.

I pried into the darkness with fluttering hands and squinted eyes. "It's a floor door that leads under the room. I'm gonna jump in, but I need a flashlight."

"It's dark down there...really dark," Jackson said as he leaned over into the black hole.

"Oh! Oh! I have one! My Barbie flashlight! I'll get it!" Ausley ran to find her treasured flashlight and returned quickly.

With flashlight in hand, I jumped in. Jackson hit the ground behind me with a thud. If I stood up I could still see into the library. The floor was made with the same stone pavers that decorated the paths through the back gardens. They were smallish, square and smooth, like old tiles. I could smell the earth, wet, musty, and old. Ducking my head down, I could walk forward and still use the light pouring in from the library to see that the pathway was, in fact, a passageway.

"It's a passageway! A real one! Oh, Ausley get down here, but leave the floor door open."

"Uh, is it safe? I don't wanna die. Mommy would be so mad with me if I die down there. I don't wanna get in trouble."

"Get down here, you big ole baby, or I'll leave you behind," I threatened with a bravado I didn't really feel. I said it just to make Ausley come, because I didn't want to leave her behind. Besides, three against the dark made for much better odds.

"It's okay, Ausley. I'll hold your hand if you're scared." Jackson was always so kind. He worked to help Ausley down into the hole, as I ran ahead.

"You can't go without me! I'm coming, just wait. Veelee! Veelee! VEEEELEE???" Ausley called after me.

Silence.

"Stop yelling! I just went a little farther. I'm back. Come on, I think it goes outside!"

All three of us followed the passage all the way to another little door at the end. We climbed an old wooden ladder and pushed and pushed on the door, until it finally flopped open. We came out on the floor of the second slave shack. What a discovery! A secret tunnel! I explained to Ausley and Jackson that this must have been how Rebecca Jane escaped with her prince to live in the castle so very long ago. Why else would they have needed a secret passage? Jackson did not agree with my story. He invented his own about a Civil War soldier escaping from the Union Army through the tunnel.

"Why would you think that some soldier was running from the Union Army?" I had asked with extreme annoyance and frustration. As usual, he seemed intent on ruining my pretend play with his stupid boy stories.

"Because I found this!" he said in a half-yell. He held up a small, oddly-shaped dagger. The dagger curved unexpectedly and had a bronze hilt and an iron blade. The hilt was inscribed with ancient symbols that I had never seen before. "And this," Jackson continued, "clearly belongs to a soldier."

"Did he save the beautiful princess that lived in the Big House?" Ausley asked Jackson dreamily. He patted her curly head, "Sure he did, Ausley."

Finding the tunnel was the most exciting thing that had ever happened to us, and we pinky-promised to never, ever tell anyone about it. No matter what, no matter who asked, we were to keep this an absolute secret.

So, naturally, Ausley told everyone about it at dinner that night. I didn't remember how Ausley told them or what she said, but I did remember Daddy's knowing smile. He was not a man that had much to say, only just enough. He was tolerant and open-minded, but never long-winded. When he laughed his boiling-water-on-the-stove laugh, his mouth could barely hold his teeth in from the pressure.

Daddy hit the table with his hand and let the laughter boil over, "What an exciting day! I remember when I discovered that little secret myself." Then he cut his eyes over at Mother, and I thought for just a moment the laughter was fake.

"But you didn't be little here! When did you 'escover it?" Ausley looked up at Daddy in wonder. Daddy smiled a true smile down at Ausley. She was so cute. Even I could see it, and it warmed me, even if she did break our promise. Ausley was my best friend, and right there I vowed she would always be.

"No, he was not little here," smiled Mother, "but I showed him when we became friends." I watched my mother carefully cut her meat. I saw her as something altogether holy, unnaturally kind and loving. She was set apart in my mind as one of the warmest women ever to walk the earth. Each night she would lean down and kiss me goodnight, and I would wish for time to stand still as she held me in a bottomless, comforting hug. I would kiss her cheek and see her small upper lip and her eyes that seemed they could be too easily hurt by the outside world. Ausley had those same eyes, which caused me to fight on the playgrounds. I was always championing a fight for sweet, kind, gentle Ausley. I could not stand to see her hurt, maybe because she seemed so much like Mother. They reminded me of birds who needed not to leave the nest. It was my personal mission to protect them both, even though I was always the runt of the family, standing a head shorter than Ausley most of the time. Maybe that's why they called me "Little Bird."

Daddy stretched his hand across the table to cover mother's small hand. "Yes, and that was a *very* exciting day." Daddy raised his eyebrows and grinned at mother, which made her blush just like Ausley.

I held onto that picture of us in my mind. I loved to remember them just like that. Happy, playful, and without the weight of the knowledge of how I might have put all of this—all of us—in danger. With one rash action I threatened my whole world, and theirs, too. Something like guilt tugged at my heart, and I bit down hard on my lip. *I cannot think about that now, if I do I will go crazy. I will think about that tomorrow*, I thought.

Still walking, I crossed the rows of tea olives, blue hydrangeas, and white geraniums that led the way up the back path to the kitchen. I breathed in their sweet fragrance greedily. We did not know how long the Simulacrum had made their lives here on this land, but this land had always called to me as a mother calls her child home after a long day of playing outside. I heard it when the trees blew in the wind and felt it when the sun smiled its warm greeting at the morning sky. This was where I belonged, and this was where I intended to stay.

Maybe it was the call of the ones who shared my blood and who had walked here before me. Maybe it was the work of their hands. Maybe it was the drops of sweat that had fallen on every inch of the dirt beneath my feet that testified to their dedication to the land and anchored me too. Their message drummed with every raindrop and blew through every breeze that brushed through the oaks, "Commit to this land." It called me to commit to this home and family and submit to the power it had in my life. It was here at Red Oaks that I belonged, and I knew like those who walked here before me, I must protect it as well.

Julia J. Gibbs

I stopped at the kitchen door and surveyed the land. Back then, as a little girl with big brown eyes my bold curiosity had led me down tunnels that always ended up back here, back at home. But now? Looking down, I felt surprised that my wrist looked exactly the same as it had yesterday, before my mistake. It felt like I should look different now. That I should be scarred somehow, or maybe marked as a traitor to my people. And now the innocent curiosity of a brown-eyed girl had gone, replaced by questions and decisions that might not lead me home at all. *What if I had to leave here, leave Red Oaks? If I'm not Veralee of Red Oaks, who am I?*

Swallowing hard I opened the kitchen door and set my shoulders towards what lay ahead.

{ 6 }

He Arrives

At 6:00 a.m. the bells announced it was time for the Confederacy to rise again, and then, by the end of the day, to fall back down into history. By 6:15 the Cavalry had arrived, and the Infantry soldiers stood in formation, marching up and down the dirt road in front of the house, practicing for the White Flag Ceremony. I lay for a minute longer, already missing my bed, and enjoyed what was sure to be the last moment of peace I would be able to steal all day.

Daddy poked his head in my bedroom, "You up, Veelee? Rise and shine. Got to get up and get the cotton." Before he started singing his favorite, terribly off-key song about picking cotton and a bird that gets its worm early in the morning, I sat up in bed and forced a smile.

"Of course! Going to jump in the shower, be down in just a minute." My fake enthusiasm amazed even myself.

"Atta girl," he said with a wink, flashing a smile that spanned his entire face. He closed the door, and I simultaneously threw myself backward into the welcoming pillows.

Ausley, already in costume, emerged through our shared bathroom and stopped short at the narrow doorway into my room. I threw my arm over my eyes, trying to ignore her presence.

"Veelee, help me through the door. I can't get through in this thing, and I need you to lace me up." I raised my arm and arched an eyebrow in her direction.

"Shouldn't have eaten so much last night," I said, flopping over again in my bed.

Right on cue, Ausley huffed, "Veelee, seriously, come on. Help me." I begrudgingly acquiesced and slunk from the bed to pull her through the doorway. Her hooped skirt popped out, taking its full shape, like a newly-freed prisoner. Fully formal and period correct, Ausley was wearing pantaloons and a corset underneath the giant frame of the metal hoop. "Are you even wearing the pantaloons?" I asked her.

"Of course, it's part of the costume," she said, then with a knowing look she added, "and you have to wear yours too. Mother made them for us and it's part of the romance of the whole experience," she said dramatically.

"I think it will be just as romantic if I skip the whole pantaloons part and enjoy the breeze under my skirt. Besides, it would ruin some of the ' romance' if I died of a heat stroke today."

"But Veelee, everyone will know you aren't in full costume! The soldiers expect us to be in full costume." Ausley was

the Oaks Remain

truly affronted, but not really surprised.

"Well, if the Confederate soldiers were planning on checking under my skirt to validate my loyalty to the cause of adding to the romance of the experience, then they are in for a battle of a different kind. I'll not be wearing pantaloons."

"Oh yes, you will!" Adair rushed into the room holding her hairpin box and dressed in an amazing robin's-egg blue taffeta gown. Her golden braids were tied with a peach ribbon just under the nape of her neck which, of course, matched the embroidered accents and ribbons on her dress perfectly.

"Will what?" asked Mattie as she bounced in and twirled in her peach dress with blue accents that made her golden hair shine like a crown on top of her head. She had robin's-egg blue ribbons braided through her hair. Mother and daughter wore coordinating blue and peach outfits. With perfect hair, naturally.

Adair started to set up her beauty shop in front of the large oval, stand-alone mirror in the corner of my room, which sat by the open French doors to the balcony. The breeze blew the curtains and filled the room with sounds of the Confederate Army preparing for battle. "Veelee, get in the shower. By the time I get Ausley's hair done and her dress tied, I will be ready for you. Ausley, take that hoop off so that you can sit down. Mattie, get my brushes, and the box of ribbon out of my bag ... please." The general had arrived, and marching orders had begun. Ausley quickly complied with a smile on her face and started to chatter about the day's events.

Mattie's tiny hand found mine, and she pulled me towards the balcony. I knew I really shouldn't walk out there in just my pajamas, but Mattie was eager to show me something.

The balcony wrapped around the entire second story of the house. My room faced the front of the house, so when I walked out the twenty-eight giant oak trees that lined the cobbled path to our front door greeted me. These trees were almost as old as the Constitution and probably wiser too. At least they had not been stripped apart and glued back together to fit the needs of the current day like the constitution had been. They bent toward the rising sun, like they were bowing to the King each morning. Their gnarled roots broke free from the earth and twisted upward, almost touching their low hanging branches in some places. The fields of green, which stretched beyond the red oaks as far as the eye could see, teemed with grey and blue uniforms.

Closer to our home in the middle of the circular driveway sat a huge copper pot, used at one time to stir sugar cane into molasses. Repurposed long ago, now it functioned as a fountain with clear water dancing from its center. Pink and purple asters, red and yellow chrysanthemums, sapphire blue salvia, and white daisies surrounded the copper pot, created an enchanted garden of color. It was so beautiful that I knew I'd never tire of looking at it.

"Focus, Veelee, I need you to get ready," Adair's bossy voice carried through the window. Was she my sister or my mother?

"All right, Mattie, I've got to get in the shower. The general is calling." She was standing on her tiptoes looking over the edge of the balcony rail. She looked like a ghost from the past, standing there in her period gown and gold buckle boots with ribbons in her hair.

"What general?" Her eyes filled with wonder, "is there

a general here?" I laughed and turned to go inside.

"Um, yeah, there is a general here. One day, you will know what I mean," I answered amused.

"Okay, I'm gonna watch all the peoples," she said excitedly.

"Pantaloons, Veelee," Ausley said, as I passed through the room. "It's the rule."

"Not gonna happen," I sang before shutting the door to the bathroom. No way was I wearing those things. They made me feel like a stuffed piglet.

"Wait...Veelee," Ausley called through the door. I cracked the door slightly.

"What? I need to shower."

"Can I borrow your pearls? The ones that belonged to Vera?" she pleaded.

"I was going to wear those," I said, "but you can wear the ones Mother gave me for my sixteenth birthday. They're in my jewelry box."

"You have so much junk in this box," Ausley said from the other side of the room as she rifled through the box, searching for the pearls. "Oh look! I haven't seen this thing in years. Did Jackson give this to you?"

Wrapped in a towel, I stuck my head out the door and asked, "Give me what?"

Ausley held out the ancient dagger we had found so long ago in the tunnel that ran between the library and the old slave quarters. "Yeah, I guess so. He gave that to me years ago."

Adair broke in, "Ausley, could you sit back down. I need to finish your hair so that I can do Veralee's." Ausley obediently returned to the chair, and I jumped into the shower.

A hectic hour later, my hair was done, my coffee poured, and I was dressed in my big hoop skirt, thanks to Adair's help with the laces and hooks. Mother made all of our Civil War re-enactment clothes, but she usually let us choose the material. I wanted a blue ball gown, with a wide neckline that rested just under my collarbone and sleeves that fell just below my shoulders. She had compromised with me by using the same pattern but not the same royal blue silk I had requested. "No one with a lick of sense would be running around the fields of Red Oaks in a silk ball gown all day in the Alabama heat, even if it is October" she had said. She was, of course, right. My dress was patterned royal blue voile over cotton batiste, and I had to admit it was a work of art. My dark hair played well against the rich blue, and I was proud to show it off to the crowds of people.

Walking out of the house, I spotted Ausley helping the "pioneers" set up their campsites at the edge of the battlefield. Mattie was with her, darting through the tents, coming dangerously close to knocking the poles out from under them. She looked like one of Mrs. Hinsley's photographs with her dress, period boots, and braids. Adair was a hair guru.

I smiled and waved, and Ausley gave me two thumbs up while motioning to my dress. I twirled the big hoop around and then returned the admiration for her dress. Mother had made her dress of green and white floral fabric that made her blonde curls shine even brighter than usual in the warm morning sun. She was a veritable blonde Scarlet O'Hara at the picnic at Twelve Oaks. Mother was a master with fabric and used it to help bring out the best in the people she clothed. Ausley yelled something from across the field. She cupped her hands over her mouth and motioned toward the sign-in tables.

Got it. Go see Adair for my marching orders. I bet she's already shot three people with her label gun. Watch out, she labels!

After lunch I was so tired of standing in my narrow, black lace-up boots that I had taken to hiding in the air-conditioned tents. I sat on one of the long wooden benches so I could watch the people view Mrs. Hinsley's famed portraits. I loved watching their reactions when they saw that bug-eyed family. I still chuckled out loud every time I thought of the lemon-pie incident.

I wondered who the people in all those pictures were. That was the kind of sad mystery of the photographs. At one time they had meant something to the families they captured, but now, no one among the living knew anything about them. Mothers holding babies, fathers standing proudly by their sons, sisters forever frozen in a warm embrace. They were real people, with dreams, fears, love and loss, but now, these many years later, they were just tinted shadows of people long gone and forgotten. The pictures were the only evidence that they had once lived. Such was the way of life for the Friguscor.

Soon, not long from now, no one would remember the little boy in the city either. The thought felt freeing, but painful at the same time, and I shifted my shoulders to relieve the hurt in my chest.

"Vera," a rough, smoky voice full of carcinogens and mothballs bellowed out to me.

I turned and realized the elderly man in a civilian costume meant me.

"Oh, I'm Veralee," I said, smiling kindly. He was not Simulacrum, but his foggy eyes could not tell him we were different.

"Good, good," he coughed into a handkerchief, "I thought that was you, Vera of the Red Oaks." He winked at me as he bowed at the waist as if to remind me that we are all in character here.

I was accustomed to this. They always wanted me to pretend to be Vera, my great-grandmother. They thought I looked just like her, or so my Grandmother had told me, because I had her coloring, but I have never agreed with that assessment. So while they pretended their legs had been blown off or that they still talked in a lovely Southern drawl, I pretended, for their amusement, to be Vera. A game to fill their time. It reminded me of when I was little, when I would sit by Daddy during long business meetings. He would give me his hand and hide one of his fingers bent down at the knuckle. I would pull that finger straight just as another one bent up. I got through many boring meetings by filling my time with games. Maybe this was what the Friguscor did to fill the boring parts of their lives.

"Yes sir, I'm Vera Weekes of Red Oaks. And who might you be, kind sir?"

"Beg your pardon, ma'am. I'm Mr. James Faust, from the Faust farm about thirty miles north as the crow flies. It's nice to make your acquaintance, little lady."

"Thank you, sir. It is nice to make your acquaintance as well," I held out my hand for him to take and give his little bow over it, which would have been the custom back then.

He pulled out a pipe and lit the end. Coughing, he inhaled deeply. Then as if remembering his manners, he attempted to dissipate the smoke by waving his hand back and forth, shooing the smoke away from my face.

Mr. Faust continued talking about his pretend farm and the re-enactment. The pretending was appealing, I gathered, because it helped him to forget his real problems. This man was obviously sick. I could smell death on him, most likely cancer. He smelled faintly of meat going bad, the kind you forgot at the back of the fridge and had to lift the lid and take several sniffs before you knew for sure. That was the typical odor of the Friguscor, but his was mixed with a bit of noxious sulphur, like untreated ground water at the beach. His skin, sallow and wan, was the color left when life begins to recede. His eyes were slightly yellowed around the edges, and were sad everywhere else. But more than physical illness, he seemed to suffer from a sickness of the soul, the kind that slowly kills the spirit when the heart has been irreparably shattered.

He talked of his "bride" who had travelled with him to these events for thirty years. They had made a lifestyle of following the re-enactments, and had had so many adventures together. They had always wanted children, but it had never happened. Finally, they had resolved that they had each other, and it was enough. She made his shirts and helped him pack his gunpowder. He built her cook fires and sang old songs on his beat-up guitar for her at night. Mostly they laughed and cried and played and relished life together. They had been best friends and lovers. Then one morning, they were talking over their coffee when she cried out once and fell silent forever. The pain in his voice as he described it was as raw as if he were still cradling her lifeless body. I listened to him as he poured out his life's story and tried to think of something to say, but found I could not. So moved by this man's tale of love and loss, I found myself caught up in his every word. Suddenly, I longed to be loved by someone as passionately as this man had loved his wife, to share a closeness, an intimacy of soul and spirit like the one he described. I felt my heart going out to him as he talked. I could see that his grief had robbed him of any zest for life. He was simply going through the motions until the disease in his lungs released him from his real suffering.

It was hard to watch the lives of the Friguscor sometimes. Their pain was so brutal that it bruised every part of them and bled into hopelessness. Though he left it unspoken, Mr. Faust seemed to feel the only cure for his sorrow was death, and the depth of his misery stirred a yearning in me. I wanted there to be a solution, a way to truly help him, but I knew that there was not—I could not. It just seemed so unfair, so calloused of us to watch them suffer so. Suddenly, I thought of the boy again, and I pushed those dangerous thoughts aside. It was just too risky, I knew that, but he kept creeping in.

Long ago, sympathetic Simulacrum had offered their blood to the Friguscor. They freely gave it as needed. But instead of the intended result, it created a frenzied madness among the Friguscor, like a narcotics addiction. The madness quickly led to murderous rage. Eventually, the Friguscor hunted and killed Simulacrum for their blood, with many Friguscor among the casualties as well. So my people went into hiding.

The Simulacrum banded together and elected a ruling Council to guide and protect us. To be Simulacrum was to follow the rules of the Council. Mostly, we protected our way of life and our people through secrecy, and we never, ever told others about our blood. With the Council's advice, we started something like an Orwellian campaign of doublespeak, weaving our existence into Friguscor fireside stories and folklore. Eventually we became a myth to them, and in that lie we found safety. Science also helped us hide. The Friguscor did not believe in what they could not explain. If they could not see it, measure it or test it in a lab, then it must not exist. Since they could not "see" us, they reasoned, we must not be real. And so we lived in the shadows of their imagination. It was best for everyone that way.

So now, if I had told this kind man my life's true story, that I was Simulacrum, he would laugh and move on, thinking that I was spinning yarns to pass the time. He might think I was simply being funny, or maybe he would think I was mad, but he would never believe the truth about me.

"Well, here now, I have taken up a good hour or so of your day, ma'am. Pardon me for delaying you so. I'll be moseyin' on along now." He held out his hand for me to take so that he could bid me a Southern good day.

With deep sincerity, I told him how sorry I was for his loss and how much I appreciated his sharing his story with me, and then I hugged him. When I touched him, I felt death's cool sickle on his skin. It would not be long now. My heart dropped for a second. I hugged him again for his story, for his willingness to tell me about his life. Stories made up our lives, but most of us only shared superficial things, the things that didn't really matter, or didn't come from the depth of us. But, every now and then when you least expected it, you got a gift. You got the story of a man who wrote with an honest pen, a story that moved you so greatly it reached the depths of your own soul.

"I'm going to have to go find myself something sweet to eat. I've just got a strong hankering for some honey and biscuits." He turned and walked away licking his lips. It was probably not wise of me to hug him.

Over the sizzle of Boston butts smoking on a bed of hickory wood and hot corn on the cob roasting on the open-fire grill, I heard Daddy talking to a group of men as I walked to the food tent. I stood against the lemonade table as I listened to his voice rise. He was the perfect picture of a soldier standing in his Confederate uniform. He was bronzed from the sun, a little round in the middle where he had once been lean, but still a sight in his Confederate grays. He was keeping his arms down, forcing his body to stay casual, but I could see from where I stood that his right hand was twitching, signaling his anger.

"Something is happening; something is not right. I think the government knows. I think they are hiding the cause or the cure. I think they've got the vaccine, or the cure, and they're giving it out to their people. Those people'll just let all the rest of us die, for all they care," one soldier blurted out.

"We have an elected official who believes he no longer answers to the people, and he was elected by only half the people of this country. This part of the country didn't vote for him, and those people in his party only look out for themselves, they don't care about any of us down here! You know, there's some out West talking about leaving the Union again. They are fed up with that bunch in Washington. I thought they was crazy at first, but now, I'm beginning to see the reason in it!" added another angry voice.

A third man weighed in, "If you ask me, our main problem is not the Mad-Dog or Vampire disease, our main problem is the people stealing jobs from us, and the big businesses cheating the workers out of fair earnings. Where I'm from, half the real Americans are out of a job! We need to stop those foreigners from coming here and taking over. Washington doesn't seem to be doing anything about that either! We just can't keep on going like this, something's gotta give!"

A wiry man who reminded me of rabid Italian Greyhound cried out, "It's aliens, that's what it is! They've been here before, and they're back! They're doing tests on us, messing with our DNA and stuff! They're taking people up in their spaceships and injecting them with this mad disease! I know you think it's crazy, but it's true! My wife's second cousin's husband was one of them. Just ask my wife; she can tell you all about it!"

Daddy's eyes cut quickly over to the man, and he tried to inject reason into the conversation. "Well, our country has seen hard times before. We're Americans, we are hard workers, and even as Southerners, we have that Yankee ingenuity on our side. We'll come out of this. What we do need to remember is that America is great because of our diverse backgrounds, but we are strong because of our unity. We don't need to be fracturing into segments against each other, blaming each other. Look around you! Have you forgotten? The very reason we are here today, wearing grays and blues is because we did that once before...and look at the devastation that caused us! We do not need to jump at crazy ideas like seceding from the Union or give in to fear. We *have* to work together if we are going to secure the continued success of this country."

The men studied Daddy carefully, and then slowly began to nod agreement. They weren't completely convinced, but it was hard to argue with his logic.

I had heard this kind of talk at school, with the angry students, but something about this seemed different. At school, they were just crazy kids who just wanted a focus for their righteous indignation, not men in uniforms. *Pretend uniforms*, I reminded myself. Still, a chill rolled down my spine as I recognized a portent for the future rushing in with their words. As I left the tent, Daddy caught my eye. He nodded in my direction, but did not smile. He knew that I had heard.

The October sun blazed high in the sky. Down here, there are four seasons: almost summer, summer, still summer, and New Year's. Despite my discomfort, I reminded myself that, had it been July, we would have just melted where we stood. Ladies everywhere tried to fan away the heat and humidity that seemed likely to smother the very life out of them. Looking around I did not see Adair, Ausley or Mother. They were all busy with the day's events. *Perfect.* An opportune time for me to escape.

I headed up the hill toward the quiet of the old slave quarters. While walking, the thought occurred to me that it had, in fact, been years since I had hidden away in Rebecca Jane's shack. I wondered if she was still with her prince. I never did write the rest of that story. It always ended at the "happily ever after." I smiled remembering the hidden pathway that lay underneath the old shack: the rabbit's hole, which had once fascinated me more than anything else. The way to the tiny wooden shack led me by the path to the pretend hospital where soldiers drank iced tea and rested in the air conditioning, discussing the ongoing battle. I decided I could muster the energy to smile at the men with imaginary injuries, so I started up the hill.

"Veralee! Veralee!" I heard my name on the wind before I saw him. Then from between the hedge burst Jackson. He looked glorious, if not a bit incongruous, in his Confederate uniform. So many years ago any girl would have counted herself the luckiest alive to have that soldier running toward her with such a wide grin on his face. But then again, 175 years ago it was unlikely that he would have worn that uniform at all. He reached me quickly, closing the gap between us in large strides. I felt sad, knowing that he could not close the emotional gap I felt.

He reached for my hand and spun me around lightly, "Now this is worth fighting for!" he said proudly. Jackson was over the top, but somehow it was endearing on him.

He flashed his beautiful smile and melted my objections away. "Oh, all the boys say that to any girl they see after they have been in the field with sweaty men for, what, four or five whole hours?" I said smartly.

Jackson shrugged, "Give me some credit; we got massacred at the 0900 battle. I lost a leg," he said, pointing down to his two legs. "So now I'm a pirate. Call me Old Peg-leg Jackson from now on," he said between fits of laughter. I shook my head, laughing with him.

"I will. I actually like that name better than just plain old Jackson, which is of course what I used to call you before you became a Civil War pirate."

He wiped the sweat, which was barely visible, from his brow. "It's been a great day out here, I really do love this place," he said absentmindedly as he glanced around. "I've always loved this place. Hey, Veelee, now that I am officially a pirate, maybe we can look for buried treasure again after the battle, just like when we were kids," he added. I felt his need to bridge the gap in our conversation. Like he was afraid of a silent moment.

"Peg-leg Jackson, if you remember, we often spent a good part of the day arguing over who could be the pirate captain while Ausley actually found all the cool treasure. So...Jackson," I said very slowly, with the southern drawl I usually used with the Friguscor.

"Veralee, don't answer me today, not here. Give me the day. I want to enjoy it, and I want us to talk alone." He said quickly but sincerely.

He knew. I looked at him and tried to smile, but his eyes looked defeated. I could not honor his request. He probably had figured out what I had, that we were not really meant for each other; that the bond it took for two to become matched for life just did not exist between us. I looked up at him once again. Yes, he knew. He knew as well as I did.

"Sure," I nodded. "It is a great day, and I'm glad you

are having such a good time."

His shoulders dropped an inch but his smile stayed solid. Ignoring his own request, he plunged ahead anyway.

"I would have loved you, Veralee," he said candidly. "You would never have wondered if you were loved. I would have given you everything I had. We could have lived here, made our life under these trees where we grew up playing and, eventually, watched our child grow up under them as well." His words floated away with the wind. I saw his dream of a life together for a fleeting moment as it passed by like a leaf drifting on the breeze.

We would have lived on Veritas Hills, Jackson's family farm that bordered Red Oaks. Jackson would have worked the land like his father and his grandfather before him. I would have walked barefoot in the summer through the creek beds and fished with my grandmother's cane pole at the big pond on the back of the property. We could have grown old together in a little house, raised our children on the land that we both loved and shared dinner with our families every weekend. I could have lain for hours on a handmade quilt under the Alabama sun and read my favorite books to him while he rubbed my shoulders. Later, a baby would sit there on that same quilt and learn to crawl, walk and then run under the maternal gaze of the vigilant oak trees.

The sun felt warm in that dream and his hands were kind, but even in the dream my heart was not in it. Yes, it would have been so easy to say yes, to take his offer, but it would not have been right. Even though it was the life I had daydreamed about and had been certain I wanted, I was sure that it was not the life I was meant to lead. Regardless of how hard I tried to fight it, something pulled me into an unknown world that did not offer the comfort of old quilts and sandy creek beds. Wasn't this my dream just a year ago? Wasn't this the life I had planned since we were children? When had the dreams of a child become the prison bars of a woman?

I fought the urge to look down at my hands or my feet; I owed it to him to look him in the eye. He was brave to say these things, and I did not want to dishonor him.

"I know, Jackson. And I have tried, really tried to make it true. I do love you, and I always will. But the truth is," I rubbed at my tseeyen as I spoke, "we are not bonded. We do not have what it takes to make the bond for all of time. You can feel it. You know it isn't there, Jackson, I know you do," I said softly, as if the words were walking on their tiptoes.

He dropped his head a little and then rubbed his hands together. "Yeah, I know. But sometimes, don't you just want something, even though you know it's not right? Something that would just be easy?" He breathed out the words that I understood all too well.

"Yes. I would be lying if I said I didn't understand that feeling," I responded gently.

We stood for a moment longer, letting the sound of the breeze and the noise of the people drown out our thoughts. After a while he said something about going to get a sandwich, and I found myself wistfully hoping that our friendship would keep.

"See ya around, Little Bird," he said with a raw edge in his voice.

"Soon, I hope, Peg-leg Jackson," I added. He turned

the Oaks Remain

and gave me a half-hearted smile. I watched him walk back down the hill, and then I turned and started back toward the slave quarters. The pain in his face left a hollow place in my chest that echoed with loneliness.

It was cool in the wooden shack, though the warm sun stole through the slits of the old wooden walls. So much of my childhood had been spent in this one-room, wooden-floored shack, mostly with Jackson and Ausley. *Boom!* I jumped and grabbed the door handle to steady myself against the shock of the cannons. *Boom! Boom!* I covered my ears and peered through the slats. I caught my breath and realized it must be time for the cavalry to be riding into the battle. *Boom! Boom! Boom!* I couldn't hear anything except for the ringing in my ears; the noise was strangely disorienting. *Boom!* Blessed silence fell, smelling of gunpowder, even up here on the hill. Then a voice broke the silence.

"Vera?"

I jumped back, nearly across the room and slammed into the wall as I screamed one quick, staccato sound. A man. A man with disheveled, jet-black hair sat on the floor of the shack. A shiver ran down my back.

"Oh my goodness, you scared me half to death! I didn't realize anyone was in here!" My nerves were rattled, and I instinctively reached for comfort, holding my hand over my tseeyen. I laughed nervously, my heart racing and my breath short and shallow, like I had just finished a marathon. I stood patting my chest a little too frantically, still staring at the man on the ground, whom I could barely see in the dim light.

"Vera?" He repeated.

"Lee," I stumbled over my own tongue. Something familiar was happening here. Something I could almost touch... I knew it so well. Something I had seen before?

He kept his eyes down, opening and closing them slowly several times. With his hands on his knees, he steadied himself like he had just come off of the teacups at Disneyworld for the third or fourth time. "Lee? What? Vera, where am I?" he shook his head briefly, and then opened his eyes wide and blinked like he was trying to stop the world from spinning.

"No. No, my name is not Vera, my name is Veralee." *And you're a strange guy in our slave shacks, and we are far from the main house, and maybe I should go. Yes, I know that is the right answer. I should go now, while he is still spinning from his teacup ride or whatever he has taken.*

I turned to slip out of the door that stood halfway ajar allowing the bright sun to pour onto the wooden floor. But something stopped me. Something I could not place danced on the edge of my mind. Something about his voice...

Keeping a safe hand on the door behind me, I inhaled deeply to calm myself. That's when I smelled him. Pine, musk and ... honey. Honey. The smell erupted into my mind like an alarm clock.

I spun around and looked curiously at the man on the ground. With slow, calculated movement he raised his head and looked up at me. He had sharp, angled cheekbones, which cast a shadow over his black-feathered lashes and eyes. But his eyes. Those brilliantly green eyes.

I gasped and searched his face for confirmation. I had

seen those eyes a hundred times before while I slept. I would have known them anywhere. I would have known *him* anywhere. It was the man from my dreams. *He* had arrived.

My chest tightened, and the world slowed around me. It was him. His eyes were as green as an emerald, as rich as the rolling pastures of Red Oaks, and they shone, even in the dim light. "It's you," I said like breathing a name out from the dark. *It's him.* My mind swirled, and I felt faint.

He was the one. The one who was running beside me, the one I had been waiting for. The one whom, for no rational reason, I was sure I would be willing to die for. My heart hammered and my fingertips thrummed with blood. This man in front of me, sitting on the old floor, so close I could touch him, he was the man in my dreams.

My hand closed over my gaping mouth, and I tried to remind myself that I must breathe to live. *It's him? He's real!* I knew he was; I knew he was! "What are you doing here? Who are you? It is you, isn't it? You are the one..." I could barely control the excitement that was washing through my body like the dam had been broken over me.

He dropped his head onto his hands and vigorously rubbed at his temples. "Shh, Vera, give me time to...stop...spinning."

"Lee, Veralee. And...how do you know my name?" I asked tentatively.

Sounding weak and scratchy, his voice escaped his lips with slow and precise effort, "Vera, how are you here? How did you come with me? Did you get too close? Where is Jeremiah? Did he follow us into the tunnel? Do you have the baby? Is Moses safe?"

It was him, I knew it was him, but I didn't know who he was or why I had dreamed of him. I didn't know why I felt like I could stay in that room forever if he would stay with me. Did he know me? Had he dreamed of me? My mind stopped suddenly as I registered what he had just said. Was he talking about the old tunnel to the library?

"How do you know about this tunnel? Were you in the house?" What was happening here? *Steady, Veralee, steady.* I was always putting the cart before the horse.

My questions seemed to alert him and his posture changed as his eyes wavered over me. With one quick and fluid motion he stood up, filling the room with his presence. His black, lacquered hair curled slightly around his ears and ruffled every which way, but it was thick and fell perfectly over his eyes. His deeply defined jaw reminded me of a Roman guard from my history books and was covered in a five o'clock shadow which made him look even more authentic.

Then I noticed his clothes. A Confederate uniform. Was he here with the re-enactors? Why had he come in here? I guessed people had been wandering over the grounds all day long. We had, on more than one occasion, found a traveling visitor in Confederate or Union uniform wandering through the old kitchen or the slave shacks. Because of the age and delicate condition of the buildings, visitors were supposed to wait for a guided tour, but there was a rebel in every group, it seemed.

"Oh, I didn't realize you were here with the re-enactors," my mind raced ahead of me like it had just gone to warp speed. He knew my name, but he didn't seem to know me. *Why should he?* I argued with myself silently. *He has never met me. Never seen me before. I have been dreaming about you ... no, I can't tell him that, because that is definitely not a normal way to start a conversation with a total stranger.* A million questions bubbled up inside my throat.

He stepped forward cautiously, and studied my face for a few seconds. I saw a light flicker in his eyes as recognition, or rather, lack of, dawned into his face. Calculating each step he slowly started toward me watching my face for signs of ... of what?

"You are not Vera," it was not a question. "Your clothes seem right, but, ah, you said your name is Veralee?" His eyes wild, he searched me for answers. Standing silently before me, he waited for me to speak.

"Yes, Veralee." My cheeks burned as he came closer, and my eyes darted toward his for longer than they should have. But I could not look away. The shock of really seeing him for the first time slowly dripped into me like a slow leak at our kitchen faucet.

Briskly, he brushed back the hair that had fallen into his eyes. Measuring each step on my reaction, he moved so close to me that I could feel the heat rolling from him and smell him more intensely. His scent was intoxicating and pleasantly familiar. His eyes were deep and rich, not dull and void of life; his olive-toned skin clean and smooth. His hands looked callused from hard work, but not cold and hard from the sting of death. I let myself look up into his eyes, which hovered above mine. I gazed into the face that I had dreamt about for months. *You are real...and you are here.* Leaning down, he placed a gentle hand on my shoulder and eased me closer to him as he spoke into my ear.

"Lignum Vitae," he breathed. I closed my eyes before I spoke, calming my voice and my breathing before it became hyperventilation.

Still, my voice, embarrassingly, betrayed me, "Et Sanguis est essentia," I whispered back in quivering staccatos.

We stood frozen for a moment, processing this new information. He was Simulacrum. These were our words. The words we learned as children, words that identified us, words we used to greet each other.

He spoke what we were both thinking, "You are Simulacrum." I nodded, reading his reaction. He seemed much taller now that he was standing next to my five-foot-two inches, than he had looked a second ago.

Gently, as if asking my permission with his eyes, he took my arm and entwined it in his, while keeping my steady gaze. The low, trill sound of my heart pounded in my ears as his tseeyen lay on top of mine, and I stopped breathing again. The bolt of electricity shot through me as our skin touched, and I felt a fire burn between us. Usually it felt warm and comforting to touch another's Simulacrum mark, but this was different, this was ... complete. Like the flow of energy did not stop on my skin but flowed between and through us and then back again. In him I could feel a place for me, and in me I felt a place already built for him. *What was this?*

Boom! I jerked and pulled my arm back involuntarily. Like a bird-dog on point, his entire body went rigid, and his head ripped toward the direction of the cannon. "The battle continues?" he said, his tone fierce with trepidation. "Get down, girl." He threw one hand out to my shoulder and pulled me to the ground with him. "How many are out there? Do you have a weapon? Give me what you have!" He stretched his open palm into my face so fiercely, that for a moment I sat flustered, straight on my rear in the dirt, watching the mad man hunt an invisible enemy.

"It's, um, it's not real. It's just the show; they have started the main push to end the battle. It will be over soon." I had seen animals ready themselves for a fight. The back tuft of their fur stood straight up, and their muscles went rigid with adrenaline. Likewise, the man in front of me was poised for an attack. His eyes narrowed and watched me but did not believe or comprehend what I was saying.

"What are you speaking of? I can smell the gunpowder from here. Do you want to die in this shack?" He began to stand, but I grabbed his sleeve to stop him.

"This is a show. This is not real. The cannons, they always rattle me even when I know the sound is coming, but they're not real. It's just a show you see?" The hair on his tuft came down slowly as he watched my face.

"Not real. We are not in the middle of the battle?" he asked for confirmation.

"Right," I whispered. He swallowed and took one more sweeping glance around the shack, looking for answers in the surroundings. He stood slowly and offered a warm hand to me. I took it, and he pulled me upright.

"My apologies" he said with a slight tilt of his rugged chin. Was it embarrassment in his eyes? I couldn't read him. His face was a trained blank slate. I was so good at reading something in everyone, but not in this man. It was as if a curtain had been pulled in front of his feelings. The shock of that made me step back, realizing how close we had just been. I smoothed my dress because I suddenly did not know how else to make use of my hands.

"How do you know when the battle will be over?"

"It's the end of the demonstration, the day is almost over, and everyone will be packing up to go home," I explained quickly, trying to calm him and myself at the same time.

I could see he was trying to understand what I had just said, so I continued, "They have been re-enacting the Battle of Red Oaks all day, and it's almost over now."

He narrowed his eyes again and frowned for a second. Then some sort of understanding inched its way over his face, but not certainty, there was still too much confusion for certainty. "*Re*-enacting the battle," he thought for a moment. "You are saying this is not a *real* battle. That the battle is over." He shifted his weight and forced himself to uncoil, "Vera...lee, um, if you would be so kind," he coughed and cleared his throat while rubbing his chin with his right hand, "would you be kind enough to please tell me the date of today?" He tried to appear calm, but I saw the panicked animal behind his eyes.

"The date?" *What?* "You're here for the 175th celebration right? So, it's October 13th." *The date? He wanted to know the date?*

"Um, yes?" Why did he answer with a question? He looked at me waiting for me to say more.

I obliged him and rambled on, "Right, the whole 175 years since the battle at Red Oaks. That's why you're in your uniform, and why we are all sporting such lovely outfits that are just too wonderful for words, and why we are pretending that air conditioning was not just as glorious an invention as the good ole butter churner, and why 1,000 of our best friends are climbing the hills of Red Oaks, to see if they can be lucky enough to find a stray bullet and, consequentially, why I am hiding up here to get a moment of silence and peace."

"It's been 175 years..." the words tumbled from him slowly and deliberately. "Yes, of course. And Vera*lee*, not Vera."

"Vera was my great-grandmother who lived here during the Civil War and everyone seems to enjoy calling me Vera, but my name is actually Veralee."

"Is," he said quietly as he looked around the shack with new interest.

"What?" I was confused.

"Vera is your grandmother?"

I stared at him completely confused. *Am I missing something?* I felt like he was having a one-sided conversation with himself.

"Um, excuse me, my apologies," he offered with his hand gesturing into what looked like some sort of bow. *Is this for real or is he just playing his part?*

His jaw tightened, and he seemed to be reading every piece of my body language. Slowly, he relaxed his stern stance and took on a much more informal posture, mirroring my own.

"So you are Veralee, and the Battle of Red Oaks was

175 years ago, and Vera was your great-great-grandmother."

"Great-grandmother, just one great," I smiled awkwardly. "She was my great-grandmother." I slid my tongue across my lips and said the word "grandmother" slowly, realizing that I might be over-emphasizing the "great." I was still trying to wrap my arms around all of this. "And you are Simulacrum, like me," I said getting back on track.

As if to reassure the slower side of my brain, he pulled up his shirtsleeve and turned his right wrist over exposing his mark once again, "Yes."

"Yes," I agreed much more awkwardly than I intended.

"Why didn't you tell us you were coming? We always have a place for travelers to stay in the south cottage. Are you here to speak with my family?" I inquired, trying to figure him out, trying to peer further into who he was.

He did not answer my questions. "This is still Red Oaks, and you are the Weekes family?" he asked. He knew us. A thrill ran through me. But he did not know *me*, not like I knew him. I reminded myself again that I did not, in fact, know this man. But I knew his face and his eyes, those green eyes, and his firm, strong hands.

"Um, no. Well, yes, this is still Red Oaks, and yes, my mother is a Weekes descendant. But we are now Harpers because my mother got married, so..." I swallowed down the anxiety and forced myself not to ramble. He was Simulacrum; I had seen and felt his mark. "Do you want me to take you to my father?" I didn't know why I asked that, but it seemed like the right thing to do. Usually when Simulacrum came to Red

Oaks they came to meet with Daddy. "He is the Guardian of the Gate here at Red Oaks," I added.

"Yes," he answered, before turning to look at the spot on the ground where he had been sitting. Bending down he felt around on the old dirt filled wood floors.

"Looking for something?" I asked. He stopped suddenly and stood up.

"No, I thought I might have lost my knife, but it appears that I lost it a long time ago." He said, with somewhat of a smile in his voice. He seemed to be laughing at a joke I didn't get.

"All right, so are you ready to go to my father now?"

"Yes ma'am, that might be very helpful. I thank you for your kindness, Veralee of Red Oaks." And the man from my dreams stepped to my side and offered his arm.

{ 7 }

Pictures from the Past

Outside, in the fresh air, I could think better. Lifting my dress above my black costume boots, I tried to avoid sliding down the hill on my well-dressed bottom. I wished I were wearing my own boots. These shoes gave no support, pinched my toes together, and were as slick as a greased pig.

"What's your name?" I asked him. "You know mine, but I didn't catch yours." His name. I had wondered about it so many times. Knowing his name would feel so permanent to me, like he was real, not just a character in my dreams.

"Please accept my apology, Miss ... Harper, did you say? I am afraid I have been rude." He stopped, extending his right hand toward me, "I am Atticus." He smiled slightly as I shook his hand, which seemed to confuse him. He looked around quickly and then back at me. It was like he was trying to figure out a great puzzle that I did not see.

Odd. A tremble ran down my spine. Was this real? He had just appeared in my life twenty minutes ago, yet I found myself hoping against hope that he would never leave. The emotion was too intense, but I didn't want it to stop, even though my rational side yelled at me to slow down and think. In his eyes I felt a pull; he was drawing me into him. I was the moth and he was the flame.

Everyday clothes mingled with period costumes all around us. Atticus looked in every direction, taking in everything but commenting on nothing. He tripped slightly as a woman in shorts and a tank top passed by. His eyes widened, and it took him a second to recover his balance, but still he said nothing. When a Union soldier walked by, Atticus reached for a sword that was clearly no longer there. The officer smiled and waved, leaving Atticus completely bewildered. He did not stop or slow his steps, but matched my pace as we walked through what was—to him—a totally perplexing crowd of people.

"Are you *okay*?" I asked.

That stopped him. He looked down at me like he had been dropped into the middle of foreign country with no map. He blinked several times and long, uncomfortable seconds passed before he spoke, "I am just fine, if that is what you are asking. I am not familiar with, ' okay,' or what did you say?" There was a bit of an unfamiliar accent there, something that I couldn't place. European? Not German, French, or Spanish. No, I couldn't put my finger on it, but English was definitely not his first language. But everyone knew "okay."

I pursed my lips, unsmiling, as I searched his face for

some clue to whatever was happening to him. *He was so odd, but still, I couldn't walk away from him.* I realized we were standing face to face again, with a crowd of people splitting around us. Stumps in the middle of the river of people.

Who was this man? What was wrong with him?

"If you're sure you're okay, I mean, fine, let's go. Follow me." Silently, he nodded and walked slowly beside me trying to shorten his long stride to match mine. I felt the confusion of his nearness in my head, like I had had too much wine, but without the fog of clumsiness. Something was happening now, something in my world had just shifted, changed...or maybe begun. I looked at Atticus and felt a sort of pain shoot across my chest. *I knew you would come*, I thought to myself as we walked into the battlefield.

Daddy stood at the far end of the battlefield by the cannons. He and another man were inspecting an old musket. Daddy had changed out of his uniform and was dressed in the civilian garb of the day, intended to look like Ernest Weekes, my great-great-grandfather and the original owner of Red Oaks. He wore a ruffled white shirt and tan vest. A beige cravat hung smartly around his neck, the gold chain of his pocket watch glimmering in the sun when he moved. Mother had given that watch to Daddy on their first anniversary. It was authentic, having belonged to Richard Ernest Weekes, and had the initials, REW, engraved on the back. Barthenia had given it to her husband on his 60th birthday. There was an old lithograph of them together from the day, and in it you could see the chain hanging from Ernest's vest pocket. Mother had used that image to craft Daddy's costume. To complete the ensemble, Mother had made him a deep burgundy long coat that was made to fit like his own skin. He looked so handsome.

Atticus muttered something under his breath, and I replied, "I told you already, this is the 175th celebration of the Battle of Red Oaks. They have just finished re-enacting the main battle. That's why everything looks so disheveled. Were you supposed to be with your regiment?" I asked.

He looked stunned, "My regiment...here? My regiment?!" He scanned the area frantically for a second, and then he shook his head like he had recalled some important information. "No, no, I do not believe so, Miss Harper."

"Call me Veralee, for goodness sake. You can drop the formality. The battle is over. Are you still dizzy? Do you have a headache or something? You sound a little frazzled. Are you sure everything is all right *Mr.* Atticus?" I probed again.

He scanned the horizon for a few seconds, and then looked down at me and smiled. "Yes, I think everything will be just fine, Miss Veralee. It always has a way of coming up right." His smile was brilliant for a moment. And for no reason at all, I believed him. "So, shall we go to your father, ma'am?" He gestured, indicating that I should lead the way. He looked like a picture from a book. With his black hair, curling slightly around his ears, his short black beard, and his green eyes that stood out like a beacon on his chiseled face. I must have stared at him too long, because he dropped his hand and smiled confidently at me. "Miss Veralee?" he said gently.

Ripped from my reverie, I answered, "Yes. Yes, of course."

Daddy finished up a conversation with a Confederate soldier who left as we approached. "Well hello there, Little Bird!" His excitement over the day's accomplishments was evident. "How have you been fairing on this fine day?" He tinkered with the musket and had still not looked up at me. Pulling the gun to his shoulder, he stepped forward. Facing the empty woods to his right, he fired a shoot. A small clicking sound followed, but no bang. "I cannot figure out what is wrong with this gun," he growled to himself as he looked the gun over again.

"I believe it is a jam in the feeding system," Atticus offered.

Daddy stopped and looked up then, suddenly aware that I was not alone. "The tape primer? No, I've checked it. Nothing's wrong with the primer."

Atticus reached a hand out, "May I?" he asked, cordially.

Daddy handed over the gun, "You can try, but I am not altogether sure that this thing hasn't gone Tango Uniform for good."

Atticus cocked the hammer back on the old gun, pulled out the primer tape and dried it off on his pant leg, then blew into the empty hole before replacing the tape. Cocking the hammer back, he raised the gun and pulled the trigger. *Boom.* The air smelled smartly of gun powder.

Daddy clapped his hands, "That is wonderful! How did you know what it needed?"

"That model always had a bad habit of sticking when the air was too wet. Terrible design, they got much better when they reverted back to the original percussion locks."

"You don't say? Well, I guess I will have to do a little more homework on this gun. I just got it today. It's in fine condition, isn't it?" Daddy offered me the gun.

I took it in both hands, "Yes, and Mother is going to be thrilled to see another gun in your armory," I said, sarcastically.

"She'll be so excited, she'll make it a nice dress to wear," Daddy joked.

I remembered my manners then. "Daddy, this is, um, Mr. Atticus." I said his name slowly, feeling it on my tongue. "I'm sorry, but you didn't give me your last name."

"I just go by Atticus now, Miss Veralee."

Daddy had clearly noticed that Atticus was not Friguscor and was visibly letting down the shield we all kept up when we were among them. He was more himself, more relaxed, more comfortable.

"I don't believe we have met, Mr. Atticus," Daddy extended his hand, "Come to partake in the celebration today?" He shook Atticus's hand vigorously and then checked his golden watch that hung on its chain.

"No, sir, I have not." Atticus scanned the surroundings and the amount of people walking by. "Lignum Vitae," he said in a low, almost whispering voice.

Daddy responded even lower, "Et Sanguis est essentia," and gave Atticus a long curious look that I could not read.

Atticus continued, "Is there a place we might converse in private?" Daddy noted the edge that had crept into Atticus's voice.

"Yes, but at the moment we have many *guests*, so maybe this evening would be a better time to discuss." Daddy waved at a man who was pretending to be hit in the upper leg as he limped by. We smiled as he waved back, then hobbled past us. Atticus just stared.

"This evening at the house would be best. Welcome to Red Oaks, my brother. You are safe here and welcome at our table tonight. But, now I must finish playing the host for a few more hours. I thank you for your help with the gun." Daddy turned to face me, "Veralee, can you show our guest around until then?" After greeting a few more passersby, Daddy turned and headed toward the big tent to find Mother. When he was about five feet away, he turned back to Atticus, "Where did you say you were from?" His face was warm, but I could see his eyes were hiding something.

I looked at Atticus too. "I did not, but I will tonight, at dinner. Thank you for the invitation, and I accept," he said with authority well past his apparent years.

"Are you hungry now? It will be a few hours until dinner. They've packed up a lot of the food, but I'm sure we can find a couple of plates still." At the mention of food my stomach lurched; I was starving and just now realized it.

"That would be extremely pleasant. Thank you so

much, but" he looked around, "will you be in need of an escort to join us?"

Was he for real? "Nope, I don't think so," I laughed. "We don't carry the re-enactment that far. I'll be *your* escort, how about that?"

"Why, yes, of course," He answered, a bit embarrassed. He held his arm out to me. It took me a moment to realize that he wanted me to take it. Trying for nonchalance, I offered him my hand, which he wrapped in the crook of his arm. He was warm against the cool autumn breeze that had started to blow. "You live here, Miss Veralee, at Red Oaks?"

"Yes, I have lived here all of my life with my two sisters, and Mother and Daddy."

"Two sisters?" he raised an eyebrow in surprise before continuing, "And the battle that you celebrated today? You celebrate because your people won this battle?" He was trying to sound casual but I could hear the urgent need for information in his voice.

"Um, well, yes and no. We remember it because it was a terrible war, and it is a piece of our history as Americans, but no, we did not win this battle or the war, for that matter. Red Oaks stood throughout the war, and still stands today, so it's an amazing piece of living history." That he did not know who won the battle *or* the war slammed against me like a door hitting a doorstop at full force. Maybe he *was* from Outer Mongolia or somewhere strange. Like Mars. Here he stood, in Alabama, the Heart of Dixis, and he didn't know the South had lost the Civil War?

"Living history," he replied thoughtfully. He considered this for a few seconds and then continued, "Did Vera...I mean, did your great-grandmother Vera, did she," he hesitated as though he wasn't sure he wanted to hear the answer. "Did Vera survive the war?"

"Yes, she did, in fact," I replied. "She was an extremely resourceful woman. Her father died during the war, but with the help of her mother and the slaves that lived here, they managed to hang onto Red Oaks through the war and even through Reconstruction, which was the hardest part, if you ask me. They ended up opening a school here at Red Oaks for the freed slaves and ran it out of the little white cabin down the road until the day she died."

Visible relief ran across his face. It was bizarre, because he looked like he actually knew the people I was talking about. It seemed like I had just told him a close friend had survived a war that occurred more than 175 years ago. "Good, good," he said heavy with relief, as he smiled and looked out over Red Oaks. "And her husband? Did he survive as well?" he asked more solemnly.

I looked at him, confused by his question. "Vera didn't have a husband during the war. She married years later, to a man who came to help with the school."

Atticus digested this for a moment. "Of course," he said with a sad smile.

When we entered the food tent, Atticus stopped short. I couldn't tell what caught him off-guard, but he seemed to be taking everything in at once. He looked at the picnic benches and tables, then at the tables laden with large tin trays of barbecue, corn and beans. He watched the people standing in line with plastic forks and Styrofoam plates, and then at the blue-grass band singing into their microphones, their speakers belting out "Dixieland Delight." Still on his arm, I pulled him closer, "It's all right. Come on, I'll show you around." He pulled even closer to me, like a disoriented child.

We stood in line for food, and I handed him utensils. Without being too obvious, he started to examine the plastic fork and plate. No one around us noticed a thing, but I watched his every move. It was fascinating, and I couldn't look away from his odd behavior. We got to the front of the line slowly. He examined almost everything we passed. I found us a seat by a fan that was, thankfully, turned off. Like it often does in October in Alabama, the midday heat had dissipated as the morning sun retreated into the afternoon winds.

"You want sweet tea or a Coke to drink?" I headed over to the drink table. He seemed to recognize tea but startled a bit over my mention of Coke.

"Ah...sweet tea would be refreshing. May I get you some refreshment as well?" he offered, with his best Civil War era manners.

"Ah, you just have a seat; I'll get it for us both. He obviously wasn't sure what to do about me going and him sitting, but he did as I suggested

"Here you go," I set the iced tea down in front of him. He stood as I approached the table, pulled out my chair, and then adjusted it back to the table for me. I felt like I was at a cotillion or something. With the big hoop skirt, it was helpful though. "Thank you," *Rhett*, I added in my mind.

He looked at his food and waited for me to take the first bite. "It's okay, you can eat now." He picked up his fork and put a little pressure on it, like he was trying to figure out what it was made of. He bent it a little too far, and it snapped, "Oh, Miss Harper, I mean, Miss Veralee, I am afraid I have broken one of your glass forks! I am so embarrassed! Please accept my deepest apology, and I will have to make this right, somehow."

"What? That's just a plastic fork, you ni-" I caught my tongue just before it said ' ninny' and made it say "know." "You throw them away after you use them once. You certainly don't have to ' make it right,'" I explained, chuckling.

"Plas...tic?" He asked. It came out like ' plaz...teek.'

"Yes, plas*tic*, see?" I waved my fork around in front of him. "It's just clear plastic instead of white or something. We've got hundreds of them." He tried to relax. "I'll just go back to the serving table and get you another one." He started to rise, "No." I said, "You just stay here and try to...to... never mind, stay here, I'll be right back."

Maybe he had suffered a head injury? That would explain it; people with brain injuries often had trouble remembering things they once knew. Something in me knew that wasn't right, though. I could smell his blood and it was pure, no scent of illness or injury. But I could not make what I was seeing and what I smelled add up. I got another fork.

"Where are you from, really?" I asked after I settled

down next to him, gaping at him like he was a monkey in the zoo. His head snapped up from the side of the table where he was pulling on the electrical cord that connected the fan to the wall. He sat straight up realizing what the tone in my voice meant. Once again, taking on a casual stance, he stopped fidgeting around and focused on the food in front of him.

"Oh, um, I am not from here," he answered. I waited, but he said nothing else.

I laughed loudly. "Yeah, I can see that, Mr. Atticus, you are inspecting things like you just got off the 4:00 shuttle from the moon," sometimes the sarcasm just came out, it was such a part of me that it was hard to control.

"From the moon? I assure you, ma'am, I have not come from the moon," he said matter-of-factly.

I sighed, "Yes, I *know* that much."

He purposely looked away from me and stared down at his food like his corn on the cob was the most interesting piece of food he'd ever seen. I leaned in closer to him so that no one could hear me, "Atticus, have you been to Red Oaks before?" He leaned in to me and considered my face. I enjoyed this closeness much more than I should have.

The current pulsing in my body felt so new sitting beside him. Never had anyone made me feel like this. Not even Jackson, sweet Jackson. Mother had mentioned the upcoming Council meeting about a thousand times, emphasizing that many new Simulacrum families would be coming and that, she said, "Held great possibilities for me." I was less than hopeful; something seemed to be broken in me in the romance department, or so I thought. Now, for the first time in my life, I was much more interested in a man than I should have been, and he was obviously... *crazy*. Leave it to me to find the crazy one. I could already hear the jokes from Ausley and Adair. Don't even mention what a field day PH would have with this one. Maybe I should wait until after Daddy met with him tonight before I introduced him to those three. Still, I had the urge to ask him if I could keep his crazy self, but thankfully I found enough dignity left within to refrain from embarrassing myself further.

"There you are, Veralee!" Ausley's high-pitched voice rose above all of the commotion in the food tent. We both jumped back from each other when the entire tent stopped and looked in the direction that Ausley was waving. Classic Ausley. *Awesome.* She bounced over like she was hopping across bubbles that were blown just for her and sat down quickly in the seat nearest to me. "I've been looking everywhere for you for, like, an hour." Her winded words came out in spurts of energy, "You have to come see what Mrs. Hinsley has found for us this year in the portraits! She wants to pack up everything and she's waiting, so we have to hurry!" She grabbed my hand and stood up.

"Um, Ausley, I'm eating."

She looked down at my plate, "No you're not. What else are you planning on eating, the plate? You have no food left." Then she noticed him. "Oh...." was her response. Clearly, he was breathtaking because Ausley stood awestruck in front of the table.

"Ausley, this is our new friend, Atticus. He's going to

be eating dinner with us tonight. Atticus, my little sister, Ausley."

Ausley smiled and looked like a golden angel, "Hello, Atticus, I'm Ausley."

He was already on his feet making his little bow, "It is a pleasure to make your acquaintance, Miss Ausley."

She giggled, then quickly composed herself. Her eyes cut over to me and then as if a light bulb had gone off, she began again, "Well, Atticus you'll just have to come along as well. Veralee, you have to see what Mrs. Hinsley has brought this year. You just have to!"

As we walked, Ausley excitedly explained why she was so insistent that we go see Mrs. Hinsley. During her searches for Civil War portraits, Mrs. Hinsley had struck gold in an antique shop in Wicksburg, a little town about 30 miles from Red Oaks. Mrs. Hinsley had not been positive until she compared the picture to the small portrait that hung in our sitting room, but once she saw the portrait of Vera, she knew she had found a treasure. "She found a picture of our Great-grandmother Vera! Our Vera!" Ausley clapped her hands.

I was skeptical, "But we've only seen the one photo!" Photographs were not as common during the Civil War as they were now. In fact, they were only taken for very special occasions. Now, we take pictures of everything, dirty dishes on a table to show we have eaten at a certain restaurant, babies with food all over their faces, light fixtures we have put in our houses, even pictures of our dogs dressed up in silly costumes. Maybe we had gotten a little excessive with our picture taking, but during the Civil War a picture cost money and was taken sparingly and only by those who could afford it. We had one photo of Vera, on the day she married. Besides that one, I didn't think any others existed.

Ausley jumped up a little, "I know... that's why it's so amazing. Who would have ever thought that another picture would be floating around the country? It's just crazy." Atticus walked close by my side, listening as we walked.

The disagreeable stench of rancid pork and cheap perfume was strong under the heavy canvas tent. "There you are, sweet girl," said Mrs. Hinsley, "I've been asking for you all day. I saw you earlier, and I tried to grab you then, but before I knew it, poof, you were gone again."

I smiled and walked over to where she stood holding the picture in question. "Oh, I'm sorry, I didn't know. It's been a..." I looked toward Atticus, who was now standing against the back of the tent across from me. Oddly I already missed his closeness. "It's been an interesting day." Mrs. Hinsley delicately placed the picture in my hand and turned on one of her crooked-neck reading lamps that she kept in order to see details in the old pictures more clearly. She did not know that, with my eyes, I did not need a lamp.

As we leaned in together, I heard her inhale deeply as she caught my scent, "Oh, you girls always smell so nice." She said, as she licked at her dry lips.

My mouth fell open as I focused on the picture. There were three people in it, and the woman in the center was most certainly Vera Lee Weekes. I recognized her thick, dark hair, the small eyes, and the shape of the face that looked so much like Mother's. In fact, she looked like she could be Mother's sister. A large black man stood to her left. I didn't have a clue who he was. Then, I heard my own sharp intake of breath when I turned my focus to the other man in the picture. It did not take me two seconds to recognize what I was looking at. The man did not have on a full Confederate uniform, just a Confederate coat layered over his clothes. It looked like he had on regular slacks, a checkered shirt of some kind, and black boots. He had a short beard and a shock of black hair that curled slightly behind his ears.

I looked up at Atticus, standing so still at the edge of the tent. I had not noticed that he was not wearing the entire uniform until now, until I saw the picture. He wore a Confederate coat layered on top of brown slacks, a light blue-checkered shirt and black boots. He had a short beard and thick black hair that curled slightly behind his ears. I looked at Atticus and back down at the picture, and up again at the man looking back at me from both the picture and the edge of the tent. My heart beat wildly as my brain tried to comprehend what I was seeing. Somehow, though I could not say how, I knew the answer to the question I had just asked Atticus.

Mrs. Hinsley said something to Ausley, and they talked about the picture and the declining health of Mr. Hinsley, but I did not listen. I stared at Atticus like he was the only person in the room. His eyes did not falter for one moment, and he returned my intense gaze like he was trying to tell me something. I looked down at the picture and back up to him several times until my head finally engaged with what was right before my eyes. Yes, of course. Atticus had been to

Red Oaks before

I mumbled something to Mrs. Hinsley about needing to keep the picture to show Daddy. "Of course, honey, this belongs to your family. I was going to give it to him myself, but the day has just plum gotten away from me." She squinted at her watch. "Oh, look at the time; I must start packing this stuff up. It will take me ages to get everything in the car."

The proximity of all of us standing together started to incite her craving; her pupils dilated, her nostrils flared, and her tongue jutted out and dragged across her dry, cracked lips, "And I do believe I'm half-starved for something sweet after working all day in this garb. Do you know if there is any of Miss Cleo's chocolate cake left? I wanted to get Mr. Hinsley a piece for sure. As I was telling Ausley, he was doing so much better, but now ... now something is terribly wrong again." Her face drew into a worried, confused frown. She leaned over and whispered, "I'm so worried about him. I'm afraid he's caught this terrible flu disease that's going around. You know the one, where they start biting at everything and acting like a wild dog? No, no, that can't be it. He's just not my Gibson right now. Maybe it's just the chemo, messing with his brain or something." She continued with feigned confidence, trying to convince herself. "He'll be all right, I know he will. He always bounces back. He's just at a low point. But, I do need to pack up and go check on him. I would love some helping hands from the sweet Harper girls."

"What? Oh, yes, help. Um, Ausley will get right on that." I rudely interrupted her speech. Ausley gave me an incredulous look, "I have to um, I have to..." Atticus was waiting for me. "I have to go." Without another word of explanation I took the picture and walked out of the tent. I did not look back to see the look of perplexed disdain Ausley was sure to be giving me.

He was oddly calm, not jumpy like he had seemed just an hour ago. Now, I was the jumpy one. Without having to discuss it we headed toward the slave quarters once again. The crowds were all making their way to their cars, and the cleanup teams were finishing up their job.

We passed PH, and he waved with a worn-out smile. He held his hands out to the sides in a triumphant, "we did it" gesture. I smiled, but did not stop to talk. Once we reached the slave quarters, we sat outside the old buildings on the soft green grass. I attempted to pull my knees up under my chin, but the amount of fabric around my waist made that impossible. So I sat with my legs bent to the side, resting my weight on my left arm. Atticus stood awkwardly for a long moment and then relented to sitting beside me in the grass.

"It's you," I swallowed down my own disbelief. "It's you in this picture, isn't it?" It was more of a statement and much less of a question. He sat and picked a few blades of grass and then threw them back onto the ground.

"Miss Veralee, I would rather speak with you about these things in the presence of your father." He was serious.

What year was it? In the presence of my father? "Look, something very odd is happening here, and I'm not sure what is going on but somehow you are in this picture. I can't figure out if the picture is a fake or if somebody's playing a joke, or if something even more...more...I mean, it's been 175 years since the Battle of Red Oaks, so that picture must be close to that old. That's a lot more than the 110 years we can stay here, and besides you are obviously not anywhere *near* that age, but there you are in that picture, or somebody that looks just like you! I don't like being kept in the dark. I might be crazy for saying this but something tells me that picture is *not* a fake. I don't know what that means exactly, but...," there, I had nothing left to say. That was the entirety of the rant going on in my head.

Atticus looked at me with an odd sort of pity, "I know this is hard, it never really gets any easier, but I will not lie to you, Miss Veralee. I have not lied to you thus far, and I will not begin to lie to you. May I see the photograph? I believe I know the one, but I would like to see it all the same."

A thought hit me. "You haven't seen it?"

"No," he replied.

"Then why do you think you know what picture I am talking about?"

He looked almost annoyed, "Miss Veralee, I believe I know what photograph you are referring to, because clearly from your reaction in the tent I am in it, and because I have only been in one photograph in all of my life that I know about, and that photograph was taken on the morning before the Union Army marched onto Red Oaks. I was standing with Mrs. Vera and Abram. A man traveling to take photos of the battle had come that morning and asked for a photograph of Mrs. Vera. She refused unless Abram and I would stand with her." Atticus slowly trailed off once he saw the shock in my eyes. His tseeyen started to hum loudly. We sat listening to the sounds of the cleanup crews loading benches, tables and tents onto flatbed trucks.

When I was a child, the Histories taught me mystical stories of the Simulacrum. I would lie awake at night trying to imagine what it would be like if the drawings in the great leather-bound book came to life. Although I knew they were not fairytales, they still seemed so removed from my reality that I lumped them into the same category. Maybe it was a simple way for me to understand them, or maybe it was my inability to truly believe in what I had never seen. When I was young it was much easier to believe in such things, to close my eyes and imagine a world in which the rules of reality did not define our every decision. But with time and age those things seemed less and less likely to be true. I started seeing them more for what I believed they were stories to help us understand the unexplainable. Somewhere along the way I had lost the ability to believe that they were real, tangible truths. Sometimes I was not much different than the Friguscor, with whom I walk every day. They could see me, yet they still do not believe that I exist.

I opened my eyes wider and looked at this man called Atticus. Some of the Council members were very old, much older than this. But they looked like older adults, not like twenty-somethings. *Could this be? Could he be a drawing from the leather-bound book that had actually come to life? Impossible. And yet...* "Atticus, I don't know how to ask you this, so I am just going to ask you." He turned and looked at me like the question would free him.

"Hey there, you two!" Daddy called from the bottom

of the hill and waved us to him. Atticus stood up and held his hand out for me. I looked up at him and saw the unbelievable before me.

"Coming!" I called back to Daddy as a gust of wind tore down through the valley and ripped my hair from its bun. Dark clouds swept closer, and the trees swayed, announcing the coming rain.

Atticus looked up, "It looks like a storm is coming." Just as he said it, small drops hit my nose and eyelashes. I gave him a knowing look as the heavens opened, and the rain started to pour down. "No, I think it's already here."

{ 8 }

Called out of the Dark

We stood in the foyer dripping water all over the marble floor. Daddy shook off his coat and laughed at the mess. "Thank goodness that storm held off until the re-enactment was over," he stretched his arms out like an eagle spreading its wet wings. "It is *over* Harper family! We did it!" He let his boiling-water laugh spill out over everyone.

Mother came running in, already wearing a pair of jeans, with warm towels in hand, "Yes, it was a resounding success! Everyone worked so hard. And look at you, dripping all over my—" she stopped short when she saw Atticus. "Oh, hello. I didn't realize we had a guest!"

Daddy chimed in, "Gail, I'm sorry, it was so hectic this afternoon we didn't get a chance to introduce you. This is Atticus, and he is staying for dinner tonight. Atticus, this is my wife, Gail."

"Lignum Vitae. I am pleased to make your acquaintance, Mrs. Harper, and I appreciate your kind hospitality for dinner. I hope it will not be too much of an inconvenience," Atticus did his little bow for Mother.

As a military wife of many years, Mother was used to extras and unexpected guests for dinner. Daddy was always bringing soldiers who needed a warm meal and a little touch of home to Red Oaks, not to mention business associates. Ausley had the same big heart, so we often had acquaintances from her school over, or anyone Ausley thought needed a friend. Mother was a perfect hostess and welcomed them all, so she wasn't surprised that Daddy had brought in another stray.

"Et Sanguis est essentia. Hello, Mr. Atticus, welcome to Red Oaks." She nodded politely to acknowledge his bow. "It's no bother at all, there's always room for another pair of boots under our table." She looked over the towels in her hands, to ensure she had enough for all of us. "Well, here, you three," she handed out towels. "Don't just stand there dripping all over my clean floor. Take a towel and get upstairs and change into some dry clothes."

I could hear Adair and Ausley helping to get dinner ready in the kitchen.

"I'm afraid Atticus does not have any other clothes. Do you think PH could lend him something to wear?" I asked.

Mother and Daddy looked curiously at Atticus, but held their questions for the sake of hospitality. "Oh. Why, I'm sure we can come up with something," Mother said, though she was clearly confused as to why one would show up at someone's house in costume, completely unannounced, without a change of clothes or an extra pair of shoes.

When Daddy saw Mother taking charge, he went upstairs to dry off and change. "See you in a minute, Atticus," he called from halfway up the stairs.

Mother called into the kitchen, "Adair, come here a sec, please." As Adair entered the foyer, Mother continued, "This is Mr. Atticus; he is staying for dinner, but I think the rain took us all by surprise. Think you can find him a change of clothes, and maybe some dry shoes?"

Adair ran upstairs to grab some of PH's things out of the bedroom they kept at the Big House.

"Mother, can you help me?" I pulled up my hem to show her a glimpse of my hoop. I couldn't get out of that steel trap by myself.

"Sure thing Veelee, step into the kitchen." She motioned towards the kitchen, "Mr. Atticus just stay put for a moment. Adair will be down soon." Handing him a towel, she ushered me away. I forced myself not to stare at him as I left the room, but I had the sinking feeling he just might disappear while I was gone.

"Who is that man Veralee?" Mother asked in a casual tone as she worked quickly to free me from the hoop.

"I don't really know." I said trying to cover the blush that was coming into my cheeks. Mother spun around me and offered me her hand as she helped me out of the metal hoop.

But she stopped when she saw my face. She smiled broadly. "Well, well, Veelee. Getting out of that hoop should not have made you blush so," she stifled a laugh, "but maybe it is the mention of our guest that causes your cheeks to ripen?"

I walked out of the kitchen as I said, "I don't know what you're talking about."

Atticus stood, still waiting on Adair. Hiding the blush on my cheeks, I sat on the bottom step and pulled off my shoes and drenched knee-high stockings and dried my feet on the towel Mother had given me. Atticus watched me, wide-eyed for a second, then turned away slightly before he, in turn, pulled his boots off as well. That's when I noticed that he was filthy. The rain must have brought out the dirt in his clothes because he looked like he had just rolled in a puddle of mud.

"Here ya go," Adair held out a stack of clothes to Atticus.

"Thank you, ma'am, I am much obliged," he said as he bowed slightly, making his wet hair slip over his eyes. Adair shot a look in my direction and smiled curiously back at the beautiful man in our foyer.

"Dinner will be ready in about thirty minutes." She said and then turned back to the kitchen singing, "look away, look away, look away, Dixie Land."

Atticus looked down at the clothes and then up at me with eyes full of questions. "I'll show you where you can get cleaned up. You'll probably want to shower before dinner." *Cause you need to*, I thought.

He followed me up the stairs looking around the house as we went. Once upstairs, I led him down the servant's hallway to the back guest bedroom. I noticed that he did not seem lost, but more at home than I would have expected. I opened the door and walked through the bedroom into the bathroom. "Towels are in here," I said reaching in and grabbing a towel and washcloth. "If you need a toothbrush, we keep extras in here. There's a comb, disposable razor, stuff like that if you need it. Can you think of anything else you need?" I opened up the drawer that housed every extra toothbrush the Harper family had ever received at the dentist office, plus toiletries of all sorts. I pulled back the shower curtain and pointed to the rack, "You are welcome to use any of the shampoo/soap stuff you need." Atticus stared at the bathroom with zero recognition in his eyes. Try as I may, I did not understand his confusion. He looked completely lost again. I started towards the door, but couldn't stop myself from wondering what he was thinking. "Um, Atticus, is everything all right? Do you need anything else?"

"No, thank you, I am..." he started. Then I remembered the trick to hot water in this bathroom.

"Oh, I forgot, the pipes are old in the house, even though they have been worked on about 8 million times," I reached in and turned the water on in the shower, "You need to put the knob about here for the hot water to start, and you will hear that groaning sound, but just give it a second and then....see? Hot water." Atticus stood with his mouth slightly open, staring at the shower. An eerie feeling crept up my legs. He didn't seem to know what to do in the bathroom; it was as if he had never seen indoor plumbing. "When you are done showering you just pull this handle down, and it will turn the water off," I added, at the risk of sounding like a moron.

Then, on a hunch, I walked to the little door that housed the toilet. "Um, if you need to...um...use the restroom, it's in here." I pointed to the toilet, and Atticus came quickly to peek inside the small room. His face reddened a bit, but he quickly nodded. "You push the handle down when you are finished," I flushed the toilet quickly. He did not laugh at me or make fun of how I was behaving. In fact, he seemed to be listening intently to everything I said, like a two-year-old learning how to maneuver themselves in a bathroom for the first time. "Do you have any questions?" I asked genuinely. Atticus considered me carefully for a long moment as if he were looking for something in my eyes.

Then, as if he had found it, he asked, "What is...toothbrush, Miss Veralee?"

That was not what I was expecting at all. "Well, we use them to brush our teeth like this..." I picked up a toothbrush and demonstrated putting on the toothpaste and brushing my teeth. He watched everything I did with silent appreciation. Suddenly, I became aware that I was still dripping water all over the floor and a cold chill ran down my spine. "Um, okay. I'm going to get cleaned up for dinner. Just come downstairs when you're done." I closed the door and went to my room trying not to think about what he might look like with his shirt off. *What was happening here?* I thought about the photograph with Vera. *Who was this guy and more importantly where was he from...I didn't think Kansas was the answer.*

When I got out of the shower, I could already smell the tantalizing aroma of Mother's wonderful roast and potatoes. Every year we celebrated the ending of the battle re-enactment by sitting around the table together and stuffing ourselves on Mother's roast, Cream 8 white peas, fried okra, and hot cornbread. I loved the roast slathered with Miss Cleo's hot pepper jelly. It was the perfect combination of sweet and hot with the tender, mouthwatering meat. We washed it all down with plenty of sweet tea, of course. Then we feasted on the leftover desserts until we nearly popped. Yum! The South might have lost the Civil War, but no doubt we would win the food war any day. It was a perfect southern ending to a long, long day.

I reached in the drawer for my comfy old flannel jammies, but then the thought of Atticus turned me toward the jeans drawer. I picked out my very cute but casual jeans with my deep navy-blue oversized sweater and brushed out my long, wet hair. It would just have to be wet; I wanted to get downstairs as quickly as I could. I grabbed the picture that Mrs. Hinsley gave me, and I quickly stuck it in the pages of my old journal. I fought the temptation to look at it, knowing it would throw me into confusion again. I knew answers were forthcoming, and it would be better to discuss it all with Daddy there.

I decided to take the servant stairs, which conveniently passed right by the guest bedroom. The door was slightly ajar, and I could hear him rummaging around in the room still. I walked heavily to signal that I was in the hallway. When I was halfway to the stairs he stuck his head out of the door.

"Miss Veralee?" His rugged face flushed a bit again as

he peeked around the door.

"Hey! Did the clothes fit?" I asked, enjoying the feeling of being next to him again. He stood awkwardly in a pair of PH's old khakis and a deep blue tee-shirt that claimed he had run in the Samson Fall Festival 10K last spring. His hair was still a little wet, but he had combed it down and back. I sucked in a gulp of air. He was absolutely perfect, like a storybook hero. His face was not soft, nor was it immediately inviting. His eyes were too intense to be inviting, and yet, I found them striking. He looked like he had seen many hard days, like his hands were ready for battle at a moment's notice, and his jaw was much too strong to be considered gentle. I thought about the models that smiled from the magazine covers of men's magazines in the checkout line. The difference between Atticus and those magazine models was that he made them look like boys, like gentle boys who needed their hair products and tanning beds. But Atticus... Atticus looked like a warrior; there was a bridled danger in him.

"Miss Veralee, I," he paused and then forced himself to continue, "I hate to be such a bother to you, but I may not be able to come down to dinner. Will you make my apologies to your kind Mother and Father?"

I was completely confused. "Why not? Are you sick? Dizzy again?"

"No, no, ma'am, it is nothing like that. I am well, thank you. Your sister was very kind to allow me to borrow her husband's clothes. However, I cannot... um....I do not think this is proper to say to you..."

I interrupted, "Atticus, if you're not sick, there must be something wrong with the clothes. Just tell me the holdup. I can probably help."

"Holdup?" He didn't get that word, obviously, but then he gave up and resignedly opened the door wider. "I cannot seem to hold my trousers up," he was holding them up as we spoke, "perhaps, could I trouble you for...a piece of rope or something? I am sure I can make do." He looked absolutely mortified to be discussing his belt problem with me, and his eyes darted around instead of looking at me. I giggled, but covered it with a cough.

"Wait one second."

I laid the journal on the side table in the hall so I wouldn't forget it. It didn't take but a second for me to locate a belt in the midst of PH's closet. Two years ago, Adair and Phineas had moved into the Big House while they renovated the north cottage, but they had never completely moved back out. They still kept half of their things here and half of their things in the cottage. That way they didn't have to run home every time they decided to stay the night after dinner. Mattie would beg to spend every night here, so most weekends they stayed in the blue room upstairs.

"Here's a belt. You thread it through the loops on the waistband of the pants," I said as I offered the solution to his baggy pants problem. I waited in the hall as he stepped back into the bathroom and came out standing much straighter than before.

"Thank you, Miss Veralee." He smiled and tried to

look comfortable in his new clothes, "The warm shower, that was…" I could tell he was searching for a word, "very nice. And the—" then he stopped and looked at me, concerned, "Miss Veralee, you are wearing men's pants?" He said it with such alarm that I looked down, expecting to find that I had forgotten to put on my jean.

"Oh, sort of. These are jeans. Women wear pants now." We both noticed that I said, "now." I was being pulled into his world where I seemed to be explaining very common things.

"'Who is this Gene? Why do you women wear his pants?" He seemed concerned and disappointed somehow.

"No, no! Not *Gene*, as in a man's name. *Jean*, as in short for blue jeans," I explained, trying not to laugh.

"They are blue," he said, studying my pant leg, "but they are not short."

"No," I laughed a little. "The type of pants you are wearing are called khaki pants for the beige color. We normally just say, ' khakis.' The pants I'm wearing are called blue jeans, or just ' jeans.'"

"Yes, yes I see," he gulped and swallowed hard and then looked away rubbing his hands together. "They are very nice, these just jeans for ladies." For a moment he looked like a twelve-year-old boy who had just seen a picture of the female form in an anatomy book. I loved it. I tried to hide my smile as I recovered the journal from the side table.

"Thanks. Well, let's go down for dinner," I invited. He

crossed the gap between us and held his arm out in a friendly gesture. I gladly placed my arm in his, and we headed to the kitchen.

Downstairs, the kitchen swirled with activity like glass flying in a hurricane, which was normal during dinnertime. Ausley set silverware on the table, Mother poured peas into a dish, Mattie handed ice cubes to Adair, one at a time, for her to put into glasses, PH shoved stolen pieces of roast into his mouth just as fast as Daddy could slice it, and everyone talked at once. I loved the comfort of this familiar chaos. "Grab the cornbread and bring it to the table, Veralee," Mother commanded with the authority of the Kitchen General. I placed the journal at my normal seat and quickly complied.

Once we were seated, Daddy made the formal introduction of Atticus, which was awkwardly short since we knew very little about our dinner guest, and what I *did* know was too odd to share. Atticus did not talk much during dinner, but ate like a starved man. He watched the entire room with observant eyes, taking everything in, and making note of every new thing. Trying to keep things more normal, I talked throughout dinner, all the while watching Atticus. Toward the end of dinner the telephone rang. I saw Atticus flip his dinner knife in his hand in one fluid motion, ready to attack.

"Don't touch it, we will not answer it. Let the machine get it until we have finished," Mother directed. Atticus relaxed slowly when the room went back to eating and talking. He glanced at me quickly and saw that I had been watching him. He looked apologetic, and then drank down the rest of his tea. I looked over in time to see Daddy's eyebrows go up curiously. He had seen it too.

"Atticus, why don't you tell us where you are from and how you have come to Red Oaks today?" Daddy said, using his glass of tea as a pointer. The entire table went silent out of respect to our guest, and because of our insatiable curiosity. Adair, who had been upstairs putting Mattie to bed, slipped quickly back into the room. "What did I miss?" she said, a little out of breath.

Phineas gestured toward Atticus, "Atticus here was just about to tell us about himself."

Atticus looked around the table. "Yes, where did you and Edwin meet?" Mother asked.

Daddy answered first, "Well, Veralee brought him to meet me this afternoon. So, Veelee, why don't you tell us?"

I looked at Atticus, and he nodded his head slightly. "I met Atticus today, well I guess I should say I found Atticus today," I said to the table.

Ausley chimed in, "You found him? Like a lost child? What do you mean, you found him?"

Atticus hastened to speak, his odd bit of an accent more apparent, "Miss Veralee found me in your slave quarters today. I am afraid I gave her quite a fright, and for that, I am very sorry. I ask your forgiveness, Miss Veralee." I nodded slightly in response, and he continued. Atticus put his right arm on the table and then lifted it up slightly showing his tsee-yen, "I should begin by telling you, as you already know, that I am Simulacrum." We acknowledged the mark. "I will tell you who I am, because I have arrived unexpectedly at your doorstep, but if I may, I would like to ask for your discretion from others until the time is right. When the time comes, all things will be revealed. But until then I hope to stay here with your family, if you will agree? I do not want to burden you, and I will work for my food and bed. Have I come to a year with a Council Meeting?" Atticus looked toward Daddy.

"Yes, we have a Council Meeting next week." Daddy answered, unsure what to make of Atticus' request or his question.

Atticus cleared his throat and pushed on, "The Council, it is still made of leaders for the Simulacrum tribes? Am I correct?"

PH responded, "Yes, of course."

Atticus continued, "And the Council meets every seven years, I am assuming?"

"Yes, every seven years. The other Council members from North America will start to arrive early next week." Adair added.

We all wondered why he was asking such odd questions. PH expressed what everyone was thinking, "Yes, you are correct, but why are you asking these questions? If you are Simulacrum you must know the traditions of the Council; as far as I know, those have never changed."

Atticus nodded, "I would not be surprised if many of those Council members are the same as they were when I was here before."

Ausley cut in, "When you were here before? At Red

Oaks? You have been to Red Oaks before?"

I could feel the answer, but I wanted to hear it from his lips. Somehow the answer would stop the jumble that was occurring in my head and give clarity to the chaos. I looked at him from across the table with the question hanging in my mouth. He could see it.

"Yes, Miss Ausley, I have been to Red Oaks before, but it was long ago, very long ago in fact."

Mother cut her eyes at Daddy, feeling the odd tension that began swarming in the room. Then she asked it. "How long ago were you here, Atticus? I have never met you before, I am sure of it, and I have lived here my entire life." She was using her business voice, which immediately reminded me how fierce she could be when necessary. I loved that about her. She was the most inviting, warm, caring creature I had ever known, and yet she was fierce when it came to protecting us, like most creatures that are truly wild at heart.

"I was last here, in this very dining room during the Civil War. I sat here at this table with Vera Weekes and told her who I was, just as I sit here this evening telling you now."

The hammer dropped in the room, and I heard it crash with the collective gasp from everyone in the room. Relief flooded me. Instinctively I knew this was true, and hearing it out loud calmed me. No one in the room spoke for what seemed like ages, the fullness of these words passed between unmoving lips and wide, stunned eyes.

"I know this is true." I heard myself speak before I had planned to do it, and I turned to face Mother, "I have dreamt of him; I have heard him in my dreams."

The grandfather clock chimed in the hallway, breaking through the stillness and announcing that time was still a reality, was still moving.

Ausley spoke first, "I'm sorry, I'm completely confused," she twirled her hair and then, as if someone had slapped her hand, she suddenly stopped. "You are saying that you knew our great-grandmother, Vera? That you were actually here during the Civil War?"

PH tuned in quickly, "Atticus, are you Chaim Arukim? Is that what you are telling us? Just come out and say it, goodness, it's not that common, but it's not that rare, either." PH seemed annoyed with the intensity of the room. Adair placed a calming hand on his leg; PH was normally very steady, but when pushed, he could become very agitated.

"Chaim Arukim? Oh, you mean those who outlive us all? Like Issachar who is like, thousands of years old?" Ausley asked.

Adair looked at her with annoyance, "Ausley," she said her name like a reproach, "Issachar is not thousands of years old. It is his gift to live a long life, just like most of the Council members."

Something told us all (except Ausley), that he was not Chaim Arukim; that it was not that simple. Mother sat silently, quietly communicating with Daddy, who sat across from her at the head of the table. Atticus sat still and silent as stone, not defending, not reiterating, but waiting. It was odd to me how concealed he kept his emotions. Slowly, I opened the journal I had brought to the table and pulled out the photo from Mrs. Hinsley. Atticus saw it, but again, said nothing.

Ausley leaned over and saw it as well, "That's the picture that Mrs. Hinsley gave us today." She turned to Mother, "It's really amazing; she actually found a picture of—" Ausley stopped talking mid-sentence as she observed the picture more closely. I passed the photo down to Mother. She held it in her delicate hands and then walked around the table and handed it to Daddy before taking her seat. Daddy looked at the photo for a long time, then back at Atticus.

Mother finally spoke, "I saw the picture early this morning. When you came in tonight I knew you looked familiar and I thought of the photo, but I did not understand what I was seeing..." Her voice trailed off. The clock ticked forward, but the air stood still around us.

Ausley spoke hastily again, "So you are a long-lifer...like you live for a long, long time? Right?"

Irritated by her persistence, I snapped, "No, I don't think it's that. I think it's more, Ausley. Try to keep up."

"Then what is it?" PH chimed in with his lawyer voice.

Atticus leaned forward slightly in his chair. In his face I saw a level of control that could only come through much experience with chaos. "I am older than the ones who are gifted with long lives. I am from much further back in time than just the Civil War. Instead of measuring my years in hundreds, as many of you do, and most of the Council does, I measure my years in thousands."

Daddy leaned back from his chair and then moved forward again, like he was looking at a puzzle and trying to make the pieces fit together, then he asked, "Veralee, you have heard of him in your dreams?" I nodded in confirmation. He continued, "I have learned not to doubt the gifts that my wife and daughters possess, but I have also learned through the years that hearing is a difficult gift to navigate. You can see one thing and hear it, but it is not completely clear until it has come to pass....Veralee, has this thing come to pass?" He was asking me if my dream was complete with Atticus' arrival. I thought of the drums, of the giants, and the river, of Ausley and Adair on the riverbanks and the voice that spoke to me.

"No, it has not come to pass entirely, but I believe..." I weighed my words carefully, "I believe that it is just beginning."

Adair looked at me from across the table. She did not hear in her dreams, and it had always been a struggle for her to completely understand what she did not possess herself. Yet, she did trust me and so she was careful to listen and believe.

Mother looked intently at Atticus, and then parted her lips and she inhaled deeply. "Thousands. You are thousands of years old? Why would you live for that long? Why would you not go on to the Terebinths of Mamre? What purpose would you serve to the Simulacrum?" She leaned forward stretching her mind to ask, "Atticus, are you..." She breathed heavily, "It can't be. Atticus, are you....Ayindalet?"

Could words choke you? The word that had been stuck in my head fell into my throat and seemed to choke the air from my body. Atticus looked at Mother like he carried—

and concealed–a world of answers. "Yes," was his only reply.

Daddy looked as if the room was spinning for a moment, and then he put his hands flat on the table to steady himself. "You can't be...you can't be." He repeated. But the truth was so rich, so palpable, and lying so heavily in the air that his denial held no weight.

Adair looked like she was dusting off an old book and trying to remember pieces of a story, "You are the Ayindalet, the Watcher for the Door?"

Ausley broke in, "I remember the name, but please remind me exactly what we are talking about. It feels like a name from long ago, but I just can't..."

I cut in, "Ayindalet, are the ones who watch for The Door. Remember, Ausley, when Mother would read to us from the Histories. The ones who.... do not stop living until the Door is opened."

"Time will not define them as men. They walk through the ages until the ages are no more," Mother quoted from the Histories.

"I thought Ayindalet only appeared when something big was happening. I mean, no one has ever really seen one, so..." Ausley asked what I had not been able to put into words, "So, what does this mean?"

Everyone looked at Atticus, and he looked right at me. "You dreamt that I was coming? You saw me?" I nodded, and I could see that he was struggling to wrap his mind around that. Maybe it was the intensity of the moment, or the stress of the day but I had to stifle a laugh. I had surprised *him*, an Ayindalet. Finally he nodded; that seemed to help explain my reaction to him.

He looked at Ausley then, "I cannot answer all of your questions, Miss Ausley." He continued, "There are things that I do not know about my life myself...things that my eyes cannot truly see until they come to pass, just like Miss Veralee's dreaming. I am pulled through the river of time for a purpose each time. It is not an accident, nor on a whim that I wade down, but I do not know for what purpose until it has come. With each move, I must participate in the events of the time while I wait. I have been waiting for so long, and I will continue to wait until the Door appears. I am Ayindalet, and I am to watch for the Door." He looked around the table at all of us; we were frozen in place, grappling with his words.

Only Ausley spoke freely, "When you say the Door, are you talking about the Gate to the Terebinths of Mamre?"

"No." it was Mother who answered, "He is not a Guardian of the Gate, Ausley. He is not looking for the Gate; he is looking for the actual Door. The Door that will allow all Simulacrum to leave this world once and for all and enter Elysium for eternity."

"Oh," Ausley made a small sound as her eyes widened to take it all in.

"You are also a sign that the age of the Simulacrum is coming to an end. Is that not so?" Daddy asked. Atticus did not blink, "Yes, one of them. But I am just one, and as you know just one bird in the sky will not show you where a carcass lies. It takes several birds to circle the sky before you know the exact location."

No one asked for dessert. We had too much to digest already.

Everyone was exhausted after dinner from the long day and the added weight of Atticus' revelation. After putting the kitchen back in order, we took turns fading away into our rooms for the night. I walked Atticus back up the servants' stairs, and we drifted toward my room where he stood by the door, not crossing the threshold of the room. "Veralee," he said quietly, matching the tone of the sleepy house, "you have the gift of seeing through your dreams?"

I bit down on my bottom lip and considered my words, "Yes." He leaned against the doorframe.

"Tonight, at dinner, you said that you had dreamt of me...that you knew I was coming. Is that true?" He said with an eager desire in his voice. I looked at his green eyes and felt my heart race inside of my chest. How could I tell him? He would think I was crazy. Then again, he *was* a time-traveling Ayindalet.

"Yes. I have been waiting for you, I guess you could say. I have dreamt of you for months now, but I never knew your name. Just your face." I let the last words drain out like the last drops of a fine wine. He watched me, unmoving. His eyes burned with life and hunger, and I felt the ardent vibration of my tseeyen. It was almost as if he was under my skin, setting it ablaze. Time slowed for moment around us, like a glass dome had been placed over us. Like we could live our lives inside of a winter wonderland snow globe for all of time as we stood, entranced in each other's eyes.

"Well," he said breaking the glass around us, "I'm glad that I know your name." He smiled and shook his hair away from his face. Then with great consideration he lowered his voice to a whisper, "And, even though I am not sure that I should, I like hearing you say my name."

He leaned in, closer to me, "A very long time ago, when I was a little boy, I got lost in the cellars underneath our home. My light had burned out, and I sat terrified in the cold dark tunnel. I must have fallen asleep, because I remember waking to the sound of my mother calling my name. And then I saw the light she was carrying down the stairs to find me. When you say my name, it feels like that again. Like I am being called out of the dark." I stood helpless in front of him. He seemed suddenly self-aware and straightened, "I am sorry, Miss Veralee. I have forgotten the hour...and myself, it seems. Goodnight." And then he turned about face and marched down the hallway to his room.

That night I lay in bed exhausted, but awake with wonder. The rest of the house seemed to be doing the same, for I could feel the dampened, muffled voices humming through the walls. I knew what he was, but the aching feeling in me reminded me that I did not know *who* he was, not really. I got up and wrapped one of my favorite cardigans around me and slipped my feet into warm socks. The hallway was empty as I made my way down to Daddy's office. The light from the desk warmed the room, making it feel like a safe haven in the middle of the dusty books and ancient words. I climbed the rolling ladder and reached for the Histories. Sitting in Daddy's wooden chair and inhaling his woodsy scent, I paged through the books until I found the section on the Ayindalet. These words had been written so long ago, but the colorful pictures seemed to be as fresh as the day they were put to paper. I traced the picture of the Ayindalet with my finger and began to read. Some of the Histories were written in the ancient language, but this one was penned in Latin. Though Simulacrum children were taught to read Latin from an early age, my grasp on the ancient language was a little more than rusty.

"At the foundation of the Earth, the Door was begotten. It was called out with the sea and the sky, but left uncut until the appointed time. Once cut, the Door will stand until the time for it to open." I skipped forward, "They will be men who walk with men, and yet time will not define them as men. They walk throughout the ages until the ages are no more. Watchers, placed to see, placed to wait until the Door is opened." *That's it?* I thumbed down, but I could find nothing else. *Well, that was helpful*, I grumbled. I closed the book silently and placed it back on the shelf. Somehow I found my bed and slept fitfully, dreaming of doors that were still closed.

In the morning I awoke and rushed down the stairs, only to find that Atticus had already left. Daddy had taken him to the south cottage to get settled in, and then to town to find clothes and other provisions. Coffee sat still and the house lay quiet until Mattie awoke and filled it with her three-year-old giggles. Everyone tried to wade through the words that had been spoken the night before.

I did not see Atticus at all that Sunday, Monday, or even Tuesday. He was busy catching up on the current century with Daddy and PH. But that did not stop him from occupying my every thought, even in my dreams.

{ 9 }

the Phone Call

Later that week, after school on Wednesday, I pulled up to Red Oaks and parked in my usual spot. A heavy mist hung over the grass and trees, making it feel as though morning had just broken, even though it was already 4:30 in the afternoon. It had stopped raining, mostly, though a cool drizzle still fell softly from the silent clouds. My hands felt damp, and stickiness seemed to descend over me the moment I stepped out of the car. Alabama humidity, even in October, was like living in a public pool all of the time; it was full of everyone's sweat. Everyone else must have been out; my car sat alone.

Before I even shut off the engine, I knew where I was going. I left my bag in the car and walked out of the garage that was built beside the house in the late 1950s and could be, in many ways, credited with my existence. Daddy's father had been a contract builder and great restorer of old things. He built homes and some businesses, but he had a special market on period building and restoring. He knew period-appropriate style, and he employed a group of skilled craftsmen who still carved beautiful banisters, painted ballroom ceilings and specialized in built-in wood bookcases for libraries. He could restore what was falling to pieces and have it looking like the day the paint first dried. I found it strange how some men could do things like that; they could pour so much care and attention into a skill, a job, or a project that they had nothing left for anything else, for *anyone* else. I think my grandfather must have been that kind of man. He worked his whole life to restore what was broken, but could never make his marriage to my grandmother completely whole.

As soon as he was old enough to wield a hammer, Daddy started traveling with his father to jobs, on weekends and summer vacations. He grew to love the dedication and loyalty it took to call out new life in the old houses they worked on. And maybe that's when he grew to love the old man that had been such a shadow over him otherwise. So when Mother's family decided it was time to build a garage at Red Oaks, they called Mr. Harper, who in turn brought his well-trained son.

Daddy said he still remembered the day he drove the old road from Samson to Red Oaks. It was late autumn, and the trees were ablaze with flaming fingers of sunlight and crimson. It was something you couldn't forget even if you wanted to, it was that alive. He met Mother that autumn while working on the add-on garage and fell in love with her and Red Oaks all in the same season.

Now those same oaks were painted deepest autumn red. Once again I felt the depth of my lineage here. It pulled at me often, reminding me that I belonged here. I remembered Mother pointing to the trees through my bedroom window as a child, "Look, Veralee, these are the trees of your lineage. The roots run deep, and they run through you just as much as they run through me. Do not ever doubt that, but most of all do not ever forget that this land is as much a part of you as you are a part of it." I breathed in the cool, wet air and let the smell of the woods remind me again. As always, she had been right.

The well-worn path from the Big House to the south cottage took about ten minutes to walk. Nietzsche said that all great thoughts came from walking, but I found more questions than anything else. About a million of them stacked themselves up in untidy rows inside my head. Atticus had told us he was Aiyendalet. But why was he here now? How long would he stay? How old was he? Where was he from? How did he move through time? But most importantly, I wanted to know something that I was sure he could not answer, "Why are you in my dreams, Atticus?" I mumbled out loud. *What did it all mean? Why do you make me feel this way?*

By the time I reached the door, my wet hair hung lifeless down my back, like a beaver pelt slung over a trader's shoulder. I shrugged. There was nothing to be done about it now. I knocked on the door with freezing hands, *rap, rap*....the door swung open before I could knock a third time.

"Miss Veralee, you are wet," Atticus stood in the doorway wearing dark blue jeans and a heather-grey, long-sleeved shirt that fit snugly around his chest. I breathed in a small, sharp breath, which filled my lungs with more cool air. He was just so handsome. "You must be freezing. If it is allowed, please come inside," he said, ushering me in with a warm hand on the small of my back.

"I forgot to grab my coat out of my car," I said, trying to explain why I looked the way I did, like a drowned rat or a run-over possum. *Why had I walked here in the rain?*

"I saw you come through the woods," he said, then put his hands into the pockets of his jeans. He looked nervously around the kitchen, like he was embarrassed about something unseen.

"I was cleaning the dishes," he started to explain, "and I saw you come from," he nodded toward the woods, "and I felt...I believed something was wrong. I apologize, Miss Veralee." He pushed his black hair from his eyes and looked at me expectantly.

The tension in the room felt stronger than the other night at dinner, if that was even possible. If someone struck two rocks together, it felt the whole room might ignite.

I sat on one of the yellow wooden chairs, trying to act casual. "I heard you talking to Daddy last night about working around the farm here. He told me that you wanted to work on fixing up the old kitchen?"

He relaxed a little with the mention of work. "Oh, yes. Yes, I like to make myself useful." He smiled lightly. "I do not live on the kindness of others without earning my food and bed in whatever way I can," he added, his tone serious.

"You don't have to earn your keep here; you are Simulacrum and this is Red Oaks. It is meant to be a respite, a place for all to come and rest when they need it," I explained, hoping to make him feel more comfortable.

"Yes, I know and I appreciate the generosity of your family very much. But it is my way. I do not like to live on the backs of others, even though I am forced to do so at times. So when I can help, when I can earn what I am given, I want to." He then added, "I am grateful for your help and the help your family gives me. I just like to earn what I take as mine." Then, he looked much older than the years that showed on his face. He looked like a man who had seen too much, maybe he looked like a man who had done too much. I struggled to connect my thoughts again.

"So, you're a carpenter?" I asked, desperate to unlock as many of his mysteries as I could.

"Oh, no. I would not say I am a carpenter. I have learned a few skills along the way, and I like busy hands. Working with my hands, it helps time to pass." His tone was almost wistful. I found myself wondering what it would be like to talk to him for hours, to listen to his thoughts and—more than anything—to touch his olive skin. "Your father needs me to begin with the slave quarters and work down the row. It will make me feel as though I am accomplishing something, to see something finished, that is." He spoke freely, and I sat watching his gestures and expressions as he described the work he had done that day. I smiled when he showed me the direction of the saw or the position of a hammer, as if his empty hands held real tools. I talked with my hands, too.

He was so animated that I found myself lost in his world of woodworking. "The original wood can be saved sometimes, but not always. You have to—" He stopped abruptly and smiled crookedly.

"I am very sorry, Miss Veralee. I am afraid I am talking you into a slumber."

I answered truthfully, "No, don't be sorry at all. I'm interested." He eyed me, testing my words, and then laughed as he shrugged his shoulders. How could I tell him that it was *him* that I found so interesting? He could be telling me about the internal workings of a car and I would find it interesting. *Or maybe the internal workings of a horse-drawn buggy.* I laughed.

"Have I amused you, Miss Veralee?"

"No," I said straightening my face, "I was just thinking about how different things must be for you. I mean, how different everything must seem here as opposed to your own time." I gestured to the appliances around the kitchen, "It's just that things were so different when you were hanging out during the Civil War."

"Hanging? What is this you mean, hanging? No, I did not hang in the Civil War," he was confused. I kept forgetting he did not understand my slang.

"Sorry, it's just an expression. It means you were there, you stayed in that era for a while," I explained.

"Oh yes, the Civil War times were much different from this time, but I was not from that time either, Miss Veralee."

"Then when, when were you born? And seriously, it's just, Veralee." I corrected.

He smiled slightly and held my eye for a moment too long before speaking, "I am not really sure, but I am from a little farther back than the Civil War." He hesitated a second, and then, "Sum Romanus," He said, matter-of-factly.

"You are *Roman*?" I asked, incredulous. "As in, ancient Rome, the Appian Way, chariots and gladiators in the Coliseum, *et tu Brute... that* kind of Roman? Not Spanish or French or Romanian or something like that?" No wonder I couldn't put my finger on the accent; not even Italians sounded Roman anymore.

I paused unintentionally, feeling frozen by his words. I swallowed hard, trying to rid myself of the disbelief that made my mouth go dry as cotton. He watched me carefully from across the room, evaluating my level of emotion. "I am not sure I am understanding all of that, but yes, I am *that* kind of Roman, as you say."

"So you're telling me you are over 2,000 years old?! Impressive." I ran my hand over the brick fireplace by the table, attempting to look calmer than I felt. The cabin looked spotlessly clean; there was fruit in a basket on the counter and bags from Wal-Mart put neatly by the fridge. Mother must have taken him shopping to fill the cupboards. The thought of Atticus in a Super Wal-Mart seemed laughable—if not impossible.

I looked at this man in front of me. He was tall and lean, and his thick, slightly curly black hair framed his face and hung almost to his collar. Not one thing seemed out of place on him, his clothes were as straight as his back, and he always looked as though he was calmly calculating the hour of the day in his head. But even with his new clothes, *he* seemed out of place here. Something about him—maybe it was his mannerisms, or the fact that he never seemed at ease or fully relaxed—he did not fit this time. It was as if an antique had come to life. A gorgeous, priceless antique.

He did not sit at the table with me, but instead leaned stiffly against the sink. Pulling a rag from his back pocket he wiped at his hands as he spoke, "Um, no. I do think so."

"You don't know how old you are? I thought you were thousands of years old, even though you look like you're maybe twenty." I could not hide the bewildered look that stretched across my face.

He looked straight at me, and then bent his head down with a shaggy grin that I loved instantly. A few rebel hairs slightly covered his eyes, but still he smiled with amusement. His smile was not broad like Jackson's, but more controlled, more stoic. Like he had seen things that had tempered his smile, or maybe he had known long periods of time where he had never smiled and then come to know happiness again. His smile seemed like something to be earned. I was addicted to it already.

"I am not 2,000 years old. I have not lived for 2,000 years. I have moved through the River so often that I would not put me having more than twenty-five or twenty-six years." He shuffled his boots back and forth on the ground, "I am not positive, because it is very hard for me to keep up with time that is related to me personally and time that is related to the environment where I watch. I was eighteen when I began, but I have not changed so greatly..." He looked out the window over my head, as if searching the sky for something that would tie him to the here and now.

With the mention of the River, I felt myself being pulled back under its rough waters. In reality I knew I sat at the little table in the south cottage, but just as strongly, I felt the choking water from the dream pouring into my lungs. Then, suddenly the giant lifted me and set me back on dry land. I blinked and gasped. The bleached scent of the kitchen brought me back instantly. I blinked several times, clearing the water from my eyes. It had not happened—I was still in the little cottage—but it felt so real. Atticus tracked me like I was a wild deer on the run. He did not speak, but I could feel that he was reading me like an open book.

I leaned forward, "What is the River?" I spit it out like I was emptying water from my mouth.

"The River," he began cautiously, "is what we use for the analogy of time. It is a current flowing with streams and creeks that are like arms or tentacles that stretch to every person. When I move, or go down river, the determined current pulls me forward. I do not have control over when or where I stop."

"Are we all being pulled down river?" I asked. He calculated his answer in his head like he was deciding how much to tell.

"Yes, but not like me. There are few people like me."

"So you are 'people?' I mean, I don't want to be rude, but I have to ask: are you human?" It was an embarrassing question to say out loud. Right up there with, do you have a cape or can you turn invisible or do you control the weather? Not things I normally asked people I had just met.

He did not laugh but said very seriously, "Yes, of course. I am not much different from you at all; I have just been called to a different....purpose. I am watching for a door–for *The* Door. And I think because of my previous profession, I happen to also be called each time to fight. But watching for The Door, it is what I have been called to live for. It is why I am still here, why I keep going, regardless of rules and regulations of time."

Not much different from me? I eyed him questioningly.

"To fight? What are you fighting? There is nothing here to fight." I winced as I asked it, knowing I would not like the answer. My mouth felt dry and my stomach was nervous. Immediately, I felt the weight of what had been pressing me, chasing me in my dreams, barreling toward me while I ran settling back down on my shoulders.

He stepped closer, placed both hands on the table, and leaned forward a little bit. "Veralee, how old are you?"

"Nineteen."

"And you are not bonded to another?" He inquired. *Was that a question or a judgment in his voice?*

"Nope, not married. Most women do not get bonded when they are 12 years old anymore. We can also vote and go to school. They let us out of the kitchen a long time ago. " I said hotly, regretting my tone immediately.

He laughed with his entire body, and his shoulders relaxed.

"From what I have observed, I am guessing that happened many years ago." He shifted his weight, but still stood by the table. Then, for a moment, the loudest thing in the room was our silence, but it was, surprisingly, extremely comfortable. I looked down at my hands that still rested on the table, but even then I could feel his strong, expectant gaze hovering over me. He did not look away, but watched me as if he could see a secret in me that was about to break open.

So many questions filled my head, but I did not know if I was ready for so many answers. He knew this about me already, I could see it by the way he carefully measured each answer before he poured it to me. He gauged the effect of his words on me like he had seen the truth drive others crazy. I knew the question I most wanted answered. I stood, and then sat on the table where I felt more on his level.

"Why are you here, now, in this time of the River?" It was the loaded question, the big one. No going back.

Then he spoke and with each word he seemed to come closer to where I sat.

"I am watching for The Door to open. But I also come for war. I move down river when wars are starting. I have told you this already. I am a warrior, and in the end when the door opens and then closes again, I will account for the actions of men."

He was so close that it was hard for me to concentrate. What was he saying? What did it mean? All thoughts drained from my mind. Slowly, as if a swarm of bees was coming from far away, a humming sound began to build in the space between us. I did not have to touch my arm to know where the sounds were coming from, but still, I did it out of habit. Weighing my actions, I gradually reached down and took his right hand. Unspoken words and thoughts filled the small kitchen as I wrapped my wrist around his. With shaking hands, I placed my mark on top of his.

Instantly, the connection pulled me to him. He seemed to flow into me, completing the missing parts of me like a puzzle finally connecting to form the big picture. I watched as his lips parted slightly and he closed his remarkable eyes. The essence of the energy flowing between us was tangible in the room, and we stood in the middle of it as if a lightning storm was raging all around us. Then, as quickly as it had begun, it ended. I opened my eyes and swallowed hard, feeling out of breath. He was standing two steps back now, holding his arm with his left hand.

He turned abruptly and clutched the coffee pot for stability before holding it up to me. "Do you know how to make this...uh...work? Would you show me?" He gestured towards the coffee maker. "Your mother, she was kind enough to show me several things this morning, and some I have figured out through trial and error, but this thing I do not understand."

My brain felt like scrambled eggs, and it took me a moment to reconnect the synapses.

"Um...coffee. Yes...Did Mother bring you coffee today?" I asked, trying to orient myself back to Earth again.

He watched me while he spoke, "Oh, your mother brought me what she called a welcome basket. It was filled with the most confusing, but wonderful things, I cannot believe all of the *things* you have here. You push that little lever over there on the wall—¡atro! There is light. There is power in the wall that creates light without fire? What did she call it?"

"Electricity," I answered.

"Yes, electricity. You will have to tell me more about electricity." His accent thickened slightly as his excitement grew. "Your Father tried to explain everything that occurred in the last years to me last night. I cannot believe how much has happened in so few years. He told me about this net of some type. You cannot see it. It is a spider web full of information." He did not look exasperated, but on the contrary, he looked exhilarated by all of the possibilities before him.

"Yes, that spider web of information is amazing." I laughed, and he pursed his lips into a smug smile.

"I must have said something wrong." his smile was still on his face as he shook his head, laughing at himself.

"No, nothing wrong, it just makes me appreciate those creature-comforts we kind of take for granted. I can show you more about the *int*ernet and the computer."

"Phineas said he would begin my education." Then he quickly sat down across from me and added, "But I would enjoy it if you would show me what I need to know." *Ask and you shall receive*, I thought.

Outside, the rain had stopped. I made the coffee and

was surprised to find cream in the fridge. It had Mother's signature all over it. She always made sure our guests wanted for nothing. She would never bring coffee and not cream.

My phone rang, disrupting my reverie and I jumped, banging my knee on the table leg. My ringtone sounded foreign in this little cabin with Atticus. He watched me with wide eyes. Quickly I reached into my pocket and held the phone up. "Cell phone," I said, shaking it in his direction. It was the same number that had already called me twice that morning while I was in class. I frowned and decided to take it. "Give me just a sec," I said as I headed toward the door for better reception. Atticus started to stand when I did and then sat abruptly looking confused again. It must be so hard to be in such a foreign time.

"Hello?" I answered, stepping outside.

An unfamiliar voice replied, "Um, hello? Is this the girl on the street? I mean, um...this is Nathan's Daddy. The little boy who...who fell off of the wall. Um, is this the girl who...who saved him?"

My eyes flew up to the sky. His words ricocheted through my body, hitting every major organ. I felt the earth tilt slightly and vertigo set in. My heart pounded and my mouth went dry. *Should I hang up?* Silence. "I think that you might, um, I mean, I um..." I froze, not knowing what to say. I could hear the man breathing on the other end of the line.

"Please don't hang up!" He sounded desperate. "You see, my wife and I need to talk to you. No one believes us; the doctors don't have any answers. We need your help. You're the only one we could think to call." He stopped, waiting for me to answer.

"How...how did you get this number?" I blurted out, too harshly.

"Oh, well...um. I'm not proud of this, but I work at the police station in Montgomery and, well, when no one could help us, when no one could give us any answers about what is happening to Nathan, I remembered that you were the one that called 911 that day. So I checked the phone records at work and found your number. I know that I shouldn't have, I know that it's against the rules, but...I just didn't know what else to do." Against the rules. He had no idea how against the rules this was. What I had done was against every rule; every law actually.

"I'm sorry, I can't help you. If the doctors can't help, then there is no way I can—"

"Listen, I saw what you did." His voice had a hard edge, "I know that you did something to save my boy's life. He almost died, but he didn't. And then...then I thought he was going to die again. He was screaming and looked terrible. The doctors, they said it was just a slight head injury, they didn't understand why he was getting so sick. They didn't believe us when we told them about all the blood he lost. That he was not breathing, and then that you did something that made him come back. They said he must have just passed out, and then came back around. They said we just thought it was worse than it really was, but, but we *know* what we saw. You saved his life, you brought him back. You let him drink your blood and somehow that saved his life."

I could have hung up, but he would call again; I could hear it in his voice. Panic started to set in. He had my number; did he know where I lived? I could hear the desperation, the fear in the man's voice. And desperation made the Friguscor dangerous. He needed help, and I could tell that he would go to all lengths to find it. "Look, I still don't know how I can help. What's wrong with your son, with Nathan now?" I asked quietly.

It had been a couple of days, a week, 10 days maybe, since the accident. The days were running together. So much was happening now. Atticus, the boy, the dreams, everything was coming so quickly now. Like a snowball cascading into an avalanche and all plunging at breakneck speed toward me.

"Well, he was good the first couple of days. I mean better than good. He, he was great. He was our Nathan, except he didn't seem to get tired; he was a bundle of moving energy and seemed to be recovering with an amazing speed. But then, in the past few days, he's changed. He's not normal. He even looks different. He's started acting very odd, not like our little Nathan at all. I can't put my finger on it, but something is wrong with him. I'm, we're afraid it's....well, all I know is that something bad is happening."

I listened to the fear behind his words. "Sir, what do you need from me? Why are you calling me? Like I said, I'm not a doctor, I don't know what—"

The man barked back, "We need help, and you're the only person I could think of asking. I don't know what you did or how you did it, but you did something! Something happened, and you saved our son, or ...maybe you did something else to him. Will you come see him? Will you at least try? No one will help us; no one will help *him*. We are all alone here." The man began sobbing and giant, uncontrollable bursts of pain rolled through the phone. *All alone.* Those words rocked me.

I thought of Mother holding my hand and telling me that Simulacrum were never alone. Now, I heard in his tears the true depth of being all alone with no one to help. "Yes, I'll come. Give me a couple of days to figure it out—"

"Nathan may not have a couple of days," he interjected. We need you now—*he* needs you now."

I put the phone down slowly and stood in the yard of the small cottage as the sun began to dissolve into blurred streaks of red, pink and orange. What had I done? I thought it would all just go away...I thought...I was so naive. How was I going to fix this without anyone finding out? Adair would completely lose it if she found out. What would Mother and Daddy say?

"What is wrong, Veralee?" His voice broke through my frantic thoughts. Turning back to the porch I saw Atticus standing on the steps like a Marine braced to meet an enemy threat.

My face betrayed me, as always, but still I tried, "Um...oh just something from...no, nothing really...nothing I can't handle." I tried to cover my panic and rising alarm.

"Veralee, something is wrong. I could feel it from inside the house. Your tseeyen is vibrating so loudly that I can hear it over here; you are upset, maybe even scared. So I will ask you again, Veralee. What is wrong?"

What was he saying? How could he hear my mark without touching me? The wind blew as I stood contemplating what I should tell him. But his face, full of protective concern, made my decision easier. I didn't want to do this alone, and I wanted to be with him even more. The scene from my dream ran through my mind of holding his hand and running together. "I need to go and see about a sick boy." There, that was true.

Atticus watched me from the porch; he studied the forced relaxation in my stance and gave a tense smile.

"A boy," he repeated. I nodded, but offered no further explanation, "Who is sick," he jutted his chin out searching for more information. I gave him none. After a long moment he threw up his hands, "All right, Veralee, I guess I will get my coat." Then he added, "Will we have to ride in your carriage without horses?"

The question was so unexpected that I laughed out loud. "Yes, we will have to ride in my *car*."

"Fine, but do not drive your horses too fast. I like fast horses very much, but this is not a living creature who understands commands. I was in your father's car, and it was very..." He searched for a word again, "very...unsettling." He stomped into the cottage, and I smiled as I realized I was falling for a granddad.

{ 10 }

Wade in the Water

Atticus sat with his right arm braced against the door and his left wrapped tightly around the middle armrest of the seat, as if he were personally responsible for holding the car together. I couldn't imagine going from riding a horse to riding in a car overnight. I tried to keep the car as steady as I could as we hugged the curves that wrapped around the countryside.

"Atticus, relax," I said. You aren't going to fall out of the car; you have your seatbelt on. Besides I'm not *that* bad of a driver." I reached for the radio and then thought better of it. Maybe I shouldn't overwhelm every sense at once.

Without taking his eyes off the road he spoke, "Veralee, I do not wish to insult you, but I fear that you are similar to your namesake at reining in a horse. Vera was not the best at controlling a horse, and you may not be the best at controlling this horse either." He was not joking. He was stiff as a board and his every muscle was tight as a cat ready to spring, or maybe like a Roman soldier ready to attack.

"Excuse me? I'm a great driver." I smiled because I knew that I was, in fact, not a great driver at all, but a girl can try.

Atticus replied. "Why do you say ' excuse me' when you cannot leave the car? Will you be getting out?" Atticus watched the road and tried to look at me at the same time for an answer.

"Um, no, Atticus. It's a saying, it doesn't mean, ' excuse me, I am about to leave', it's just a saying." He was waiting for more, so I continued, "Like it means ' what are you talking about' more than it means ' pardon me." He thought for a moment.

"I see." Talk about a generation gap.

"Did you know my Great...did you know Vera well?" I asked, remembering the portrait of her in her wedding dress. Dark brown hair piled high on her head and a round face, just like Ausley's.

Atticus smiled deeply, "Yes, Vera was a wonderful friend to know." He relaxed a little in his seat, "Your sister Ausley favors her greatly, that is, if Ausley's features were dark like yours. Vera had your coloring and your eyes, but Ausley's face and maybe even her temperament, which got her into hard places more often than not. That's why I thought you were Vera the other day, with your dark hair, and profile...but then when I really looked at your face...I saw that it was not her." He was right, Ausley looked just like a blond version of

Vera, but I had her eyes.

I rolled the window down slowly so that the cool air could reach my face. Atticus watched with astonishment as the window descended into the door, and then looked for his own button to try. He inspected the button and then beamed with accomplishment when his window started to roll slowly down as well. I gave him the look you gave a child when he rides his bike the first time, and he looked at me with smug satisfaction. "You're learning," I shrugged. "That's great!"

Sitting back and releasing the arm rest for the first time, he looked more relaxed than I had ever seen him. "Veralee, I've been learning for longer than you have been alive, but thank you for the little-boy encouragement." I heard the smile in his voice.

"Atticus, can I ask you something?"

"Yes, ma'am." I loved his little archaic habits. They made him even more charming.

"When you first arrived, when I first saw you in the slave quarters, when you thought I was Vera, you asked me about someone named Jeremiah and a baby. What were you talking about?"

"So you remember that. Well, I guess an explanation would be in order," he searched the countryside for a starting point. "The night I was pulled down the River, this last time, was in the middle of the battle at Red Oaks. I had arrived on the shore of the morning of the first of January, eight months before the battle. By that time Jeremiah was gone and Ernest, Vera's father, was dead. A deserter who was passing through the plantation had killed him. Jeremiah, Vera's husband, had been drafted into the Confederacy. Vera was bonded to him the year the war began, but she had not seen or heard from him since the month before."

"Vera wasn't married during the Civil War." I said. "I told you, she wasn't married until after the war ended."

Atticus raised his eyebrows and said, "Well, she was married when I was there. To a man named Jeremiah. If she had not been married, she would have been a scandal. I met Jeremiah only briefly, the night the battle began, when he came back to Red Oaks."

"I have never heard of a Jeremiah." I said, confounded. "We know so much about her, so much has been passed down that I thought we knew the major facts and events of her life." Before I finished my thought I saw the error of my thinking. A major event in her life was sitting right beside me, and a couple of days ago I had no idea that Atticus had even existed. He followed my train of thought without needing my words to lead him.

"Well, the pages of history do not record every paragraph of life, just the ones they are lucky enough to catch in their net. Most fish slip right through a net and are never seen again." Atticus said.

"Wait," I said quickly, "why would she have been a scandal? Why did you say that?"

Atticus looked at me with raised eyebrows, "Because she was with child."

I looked at him and then back at the road. Pregnant? Did I just totally miss my history dates? Could she have been pregnant with my grandmother then? No, that could not be right. *If* Vera were pregnant during the civil war, then she must have lost the baby, because my grandmother had no siblings. That stung, even though I did not know Vera. The thought of losing a child made my chest ache. Swallowing hard, I pushed the thought out of my mind, "So when you arrived, this Jeremiah was gone and Vera's father was dead?" I asked, refocusing myself.

"The women, Thenie and Vera, were running the plantation with the help of the freed-slaves. Holden, the overseer, had disappeared months before I arrived, so Abram was in charge. Abram was a giant of a man, towering over most of the other men on the plantation, which gave him an honest advantage to take charge over things. He had a voice that could reach from one end of the fields to the other, deep and rich was his song that he sang. I can still hear it:

> *Wade in the water,*
>
> *Wade out in the water, children*
>
> *Wade in the water,*
>
> *The Man's gonna trouble the water.*
>
> *Now if you get there before I do*
>
> *(I know) The Man's gonna trouble the water.*
>
> *Tell all my friends Ima comin', too*
>
> *(I know) The Man's gonna trouble the wa-*

ter."

Atticus had a deep, unforgettable voice that soaked into my bones and made itself at home in my memory. He sat silently for a moment then continued.

"I would sit out on the back porch and listen to Abram sing as his people came in from the fields. That song got me every time. The words were so real for me. I had been wading in the water for so long by that point that I had forgotten what it was like to stay in one place. And the part that says, "If you get there before I do...tell all my friends I'm coming too" just haunted me. I would rock in that old white rocking chair and listen to those words and allow myself to wonder about reaching the end of the River. Wonder what it would be like at the end. And then I would wonder about how long the River is, how far it reaches and how much further I could travel. Sometimes," he sighed, "sometimes when I would see them come in from the fields, singing about the River, it would seem so very lonely, the vast River that I traveled day after day, night after night, year after year."

I stayed on the back roads, which took longer, but it gave us more time to be near each other. Besides, the on-ramp to the super-highway was still under construction in town. As I drove I felt the vibration of his tseeyen and instinctively, before I could stop myself, I reached for his hand and found that it was already lying open in anticipation of mine. We drove like that for a while, sitting quietly and listening to the warm completeness of the current between our marks.

Then the humming vibration settled and Atticus started his story again, "I arrived in the woods the first time early in the morning. I was disoriented and lay for some time in the sun trying to figure out where and when I was. It didn't take long for hunger to motivate me toward the smell of the kitchen. I approached cautiously, which probably made me look more criminal than I was. Addie and Phoebe saw me first and screamed for help, which brought big Abram out immediately and several of his men as well." Atticus smiled and laughed softly, "They did not like me at all, at first. Abram wanted me gone immediately, but thankfully Miss Vera was in the kitchen that morning and poked her head out the door to see what was occuring.

' Abram, wait one moment. He looks half-starved, and he doesn't even have a gun on him. He's not in uniform,' Vera had said.

' Missum, you ain't gunna let no trash run up in here, cause you got sum bleetin heart dat gunna get you kilt,' Abram had warned her. Vera had stood up as tall as she could, which just put her in the middle of Abram's large chest and then placed her hands on both hips.

' Abram, I'm telling you he's not to be harmed, and he's to have some breakfast with me so I can figure out who he is. Look at his skin; he has the Eiani in his blood. He is no danger to us. You can join us in the Big House if it makes you feel better.' She turned and gathered her skirts as she headed back into the kitchen.

' I ain't eatin' wit' you at dat table, Missus. It ain't proper.' Abram announced before he started pushing me toward the Big House."

Atticus continued, "I always try to gather as much information as possible when I arrive at a new place in time. Usually I look for differences in whatever everyone around me is wearing, then I listen to their speech and try to match their speech patterns as much as possible and even their body language. It doesn't always work, but for a short period of time it serves to get me around until I can figure out where I am. I had arrived into the Civil War from what they called the Revolution. I was not wearing a uniform, but was dressed as a common farmer from North Carolina. My clothes looked dated, but I was not as far out of my league as I was arriving during your time. So when I sat down at the table Vera didn't notice how out of time I looked, but it didn't take long for her to notice how out of date my knowledge was. I knew nothing of the ongoing Civil War, but talked once or twice about the war with England. She figured out quickly that something was wrong with me. But, she was Simulacrum so I showed her my mark and told her and her mother about the River. They listened and believed me. They gave me a place to live at Red Oaks, and I found that I was a welcomed asset to the plantation. I worked side by side with the other Simulacrum, who were freed slaves. Some of the freed slaves stayed and made their homes at Red Oaks, while others followed the Drinking Gourd north."

He adjusted his posture and began to speak as if he was trying to work out a puzzle for himself, "But the most curious thing about the plantation was the amount of Boged living there. I'm not sure, but I believe Jeremiah had something to do with that."

The Boged. "Wait. I have never heard about the

Boged at Red Oaks. What do you mean that the Boged lived at Red Oaks? I'm completely confused," I said with bewildered excitement. I thought I knew most of the history surrounding Red Oaks, but I had never heard about the Boged. "I thought the slaves they bought were all Simulacrum."

Atticus shook his head, which made his thick hair shine in the setting sun, "Well, many were Boged. So they were changed at some point."

"Changed?" I said, like the word held the key to a hidden treasure, "What do you mean changed?" I wanted to hear him say it. I wanted to hear him confirm the excitement and fear in my head.

"To have that many of the Boged living together, it would follow that someone was changing them, or at least someone was purposefully finding them and bringing them to Red Oaks. I have never known the Boged to live together like they were at Red Oaks" Atticus explained.

"Wait a minute. Are you trying to tell me that Vera gave her blood to people? That can't be...that's against the rule. She couldn't have!" My heart was pounding again, and I knew he could hear the vibration starting to hum on my arm. He looked completely confused.

"Veralee, I am not telling you that it was Vera. But you know that the Simulacrum can be created. You do know that...correct?" He looked astonished, like someone had told him they didn't believe in air.

"What do you mean? How are Simulacrum created?

We are born Simulacrum. I mean, yes, I know that there are some who can come over, and they call them Boged, but... but that is a rare and mysterious thing. We don't understand it, and it hasn't happened in so many years, we don't even know if it is really true anymore." I was speaking too fast, too forced and I knew it.

"Veralee, it doesn't just happen, it happens when a Simulacrum of pure blood, with the ability to change the Friguscor, gives some of their blood to a Boged."

"But how do you know that? I've read it in the Histories, but Vera couldn't have done it! This can't be true. There is no way to know who would change and who would die, or worse who would become ill and turn into a blood seeker!" I was at a loss for words as I tried to make this fit into everything I had ever known to be true. It felt like an asteroid colliding with the brick wall of certainties that I had always been taught; there was only a crater left at the point of impact.

"I know this, because I was Boged, and now I am Simulacrum." Atticus gave me space for the words to slam into the brick wall and then gave me a look of reassurance as the bricks fell down around me.

"You are... were... Boged?" I said it slowly, like I was speaking a foreign language for the first time. "But... but we don't change them. I know they say that the Boged exist. But we don't know where, or how, or who." I felt slow on the uptake, trying to make this add up and fall in line with what I thought I already knew. This was what I had been waiting to hear. What I had wished to hear but didn't ever really expect. *The possibility to help them, to change them might actually exist.* I looked at Atticus, a real, live Boged sitting here beside me...and yet his tseeyen proved that he was Simulacrum. "You..." I stumbled, "You are Boged? Truly?"

The whiny voice of the NavSat gave us the warning that our destination was on the right. I gradually pulled the car to a stop and looked at the small yellow house with the porch swing and asparagus ferns standing by the front door. "We're here," I half whispered. Atticus took the lead and opened his door. He came around and offered his hand to me as I got out of the car. I felt a little dazed. *Boged? Could this be true?* With my hand in his he led me to the front door. I marveled at him for a moment. He did not know where we were going or why, and yet he led the way because I had asked him to come.

The door opened before Atticus could knock. There in the dusky twilight stood the little boy, Nathan. Immediately I could smell fresh clover honey radiating from his skin. Color washed his cheeks, and his hair shone like fresh-washed flax. He stood up perfectly straight, not bent in the way of the Friguscor. I grabbed the door to stop myself from toppling over. His eyes. They were still blue, but they now looked like a neon sign announcing his change. This child was not Friguscor. He smiled at me with knowing eyes that were alive and crisp with clarity. Atticus reached for me and tucked his arm around my waist, supporting my weakening knees. Staring at the child, all I could hear was the sound of my heart, pounding wildly in my chest.

"You've come." A voice heavy with relief called from the dimly-lit room. Nathan's father walked to the door and placed his hand on the boy's shoulder. Instantly, I saw him lick his dry, cracked lips with his thick, swollen tongue. "Come in. Please, come in." Atticus and I followed him into a family room that was littered with family photos on a wall that changed its display like someone was changing the channel on an old TV set. Each photo reflected the tortuous joy that the Friguscor experienced. Joy for life, interlaced with confusion on how to fully embrace it.

"I didn't know if you would really come. I'm glad you did, don't get me wrong, I just didn't know if you were really real. I kept telling myself that you might be just a part of my imagination or something. But here you are; you're here now." The man slouched into his couch, pulling the boy to sit beside him. The boy sat, fully at rest with perfect posture. The room smelled of rancid meat. It was not as intense as the few other Friguscor homes I had been in, and I knew immediately that was because of Nathan, the boy. He smelled fresh, like the atmosphere just after a cleansing rain, the faint odor of sweet clover drifting from him.

I stared at the boy, my mind still grappling with the bricks that had once composed my wall of certainties until, just moments ago, when Atticus reduced them to rubble. I did not want to believe what was sitting right in front of me, but how could I deny this proof? The father began again, "I'm sorry I keep saying this, but I just can't believe you are real. I mean, I can't make sense of it all, you know?" The man held his hands palms up in a gesture of pure surrender.

"Yes, I know exactly what you mean," I croaked.

"Linda Faye, she's here! Come on out here," the man got up from the couch, using his wrist to switch the TV onto mute. "Excuse me just a minute; let me tell Linda Faye you're here." Then he left the small room that was made even smaller by the massive AR screen hung across one of the walls. The boy jumped down from the couch and made a beeline for Atticus and me. Atticus sat beside me with his hands tensed upon his knees. It was not a casual stance, more like a soldier at the ready.

Nathan put his hand on my cheek and brought his face very close to mine. "I'm Nathan," he said in a very tiny voice.

"I'm Veralee," I breathed.

"Hi, Miss Vewalee, I'm six years old." His smile was infectious, and it spread quickly over my face and then to Atticus's face.

"Well, Nathan, It's nice to meet you. I'm so glad you are feeling so much better."

That made him think, "I hurt my head really bad and then there was the fire that burned me," he said as if remembering a bad dream.

"No, you didn't get burned, you fell, remember? You fell off the brick wall you were climbing on, and it hurt your head," I corrected tenderly.

"No, no Miss Vewalee. The fire burned me, it hurt so bad, I was crying and crying and I couldn't even breathe. It sat on my chest and burned in my arms, and it burned in my legs, and it burned until all of the bad stuff in my body burned all up. Then I woke up, and I was like this." He held his hands out and flipped them from one side to the other over and over again so that I could see every part of them. I looked at Atticus and saw that he was starting to understand what had been done. His eyes did not miss anything, and he scanned the boy, reading into every hidden message.

"Here we are," said the father as he entered the room followed by a woman. I recognized her immediately from the day Nathan had taken the fall. Her square shoulders sat heavily on her bony legs, and her chubby face looked exhausted and ravaged by age. She wore an old pair of cut-off jeans and a Hard Rock Cafe t-shirt that looked like it had been at the opening of the very first restaurant. Her smile was worn and tired. Nathan immediately crawled into her lap and began petting her cracked pale hands.

Then Atticus knew. He looked at me and said a thousand words with his eyes. Both parents were Friguscor, but the boy was Simulacrum. We had come for a sick boy and found a boy suddenly alive. A jolt of fear went down my spine. He knew that I had done something terrible, something completely against the rules. I swallowed hard and spoke to the father.

"Nathan looks just fine to me. You said on the phone that he was sick, but…?"

"Fine? Shit, lady, he's not fine at all. Something is strange with the boy and everyone can see it, but we don't know what it is. We keep taking him back to the doctors, and they say there is nothing wrong with him. They won't even run any tests on him. They just look at him and say he looks healthy. Healthy? He looks weird, like a damn glow worm if you ask me, and he smells like a sickening sweet donut or something. I just don't know what to do. How do I get him back to normal?" He directed his question solely at me.

"I'm not sick, Papa, I'm better and I'm still me!" The little boy proudly turned and motioned to his mother. I watched as Nathan cuddled into his mother's arms. Then, as if pulled by the same string, they looked up at me together. The father looked sick with fear. But underneath the fear, I saw a storm of anger brewing in him. I had no idea what to tell these people. I didn't even fully understand what was happening myself. How was this boy Friguscor just days ago and now Simulacrum? Was the boy completely changed, or was it just my blood lingering on in his veins? I didn't know. But Atticus's words echoed in my head, "*I know this because I was Boged, and now I am Simulacrum.*"

"All I know," the father started, "is that you gave my boy your blood when he was dying, or maybe he was already dead, or maybe he was just knocked out like the doctor said. I'm not sure how it happened, but I can see that it did happen and now something is wrong, something is different about Nathan. Hell, it's like he's a new kid. He's still Nathan, but he's so different." The man put his face into his hands as he struggled to communicate what he couldn't comprehend. Pity and guilt ran through my body as I watched this man struggle for understanding on the worn-out blue couch. The clock on the wall chimed, but time felt stale. I made sure that I did not affirm the fact that I had given the child my blood.

"It does not look like Nathan is in any danger right now. I see the changes that you are talking about, and I understand that this is very confusing."

The man became enraged, "Confusing? Shit, this is my child. It's not confusing, it's terrifying, lady. What did you do to him? You did something and now he looks like... that." The man pointed at the boy.

Nathan sank back into his mother's arms. "Please, he can hear you." She said as she hugged Nathan to her chest. She looked scared as well, and I had not noticed until now how protective she was of the boy. But I could *feel* how afraid the boy was. I didn't know how, but I felt him inside of my veins.

The father stood suddenly. Atticus sprang into action and stood before me with an icy military composure. "Sit down. Veralee is trying to help you. We came to help you, not to harm you. Sit down and we can continue to talk. If not, we will be on our way."

The man snarled his lip at Atticus and then reluctantly obeyed by slamming his body back into the couch. He immediately began to wring his hands, and tears slipped down his cheeks. Atticus sat rigidly beside me with an ironclad resolve. I looked at Atticus, who kept his eyes focused on the man on the couch, watching his every move. I looked at Nathan and his mother and then back at the man on the couch. The tension was so palpable I found it hard to breathe.

"Give me a couple of days, and I will come back to check on Nathan. He is not in danger, and he will not get sick again," I said.

"Your son will continue to look as he does now." Atticus stated, "I understand that he looks and acts differently than he did before his fall but give him some time. He is just recovering from a severe head injury and that will take time."

The father looked unconvinced. Then he looked up sharply at me, "Who are you anyways?" he sneered.

I looked directly at the man and found a degree of self-control I didn't know I possessed, "I am Veralee, who saved your son's life, and that is all you need to know for now."

{ 11 }

the Wakeful One

I am planting in the fields of Red Oaks with Atticus. We are tired from working all day, and my back hurts from the constant motion of chopping the hoe into the stiff ground. But I am beside him, so I smile. Suddenly, Atticus trips, landing hard on his knees in the dirt. The earth rumbles then convulses beneath my feet as the ground abruptly heaves new life from its womb. A tree slices the surface and shoots upward into the heavens. Limbs unfold in every direction in one swift motion and then crawl across the sky as far as the eye can see. A bird's eye view shows me that the limbs have covered most of the earth.

The lush tree supplies a bounty of wondrous fruit. Sun streams through her verdant canopy, gilding the earth with brimming warmth and halcyon light. Animals stretch their necks skyward to forage among the branches and drink the gentle rain that cascades from the leaves. A utopia of sustenance, comfort, and shade extend from her trunk. Atticus *reaches up and picks a red, rich apple. It glimmers as he rolls it from hand to hand. I reach up and take a golden, yellow pear. Sweetness fills my mouth with the first bite. The juice runs down my neck, wetting my shirt. There is so much fruit that we would never be hungry, never be without.*

Contentment washes over me and stirs my heart. Laughing, I feel the cool breeze blowing my hair back, and the birds sing in chorus to the tree. I reach out and touch the trunk of the tree with both hands. But instead of the bliss I expect, I feel something unfamiliar moving within the tree. From deep within her epicenter, I feel quaking vibrations rise steadily toward the top. Turning frantically, I find Atticus's knowing eyes. He is not surprised; he knows what is coming.

The ground quivers again, and the animals feel the shifting under their hooves. Bum, bum, bum — a deep bellowing cracks the balanced tranquility. Heavy drums pound, and my heart begins to pulse in rhythm against my chest. The growing beat frightens me even as it beckons. The bass is driven by calling and the beat by purpose. It is the current of time pulling its clock-hands toward alignment, toward the ending point. Bum, bum, bum, it rolls on. Then a sudden silence engulfs us like the pregnant pause of warriors in that instant before their general signals them to take the battlefield. Every space of eternity that was just glutted with the thrums of the unrelenting timpani is just as quickly wrapped in a chrysalis of silence that hangs suspended in time. The silence is complete. The tree limbs lay still; the leaves hang motionless; the birds sit in silence. My hands make no sound when I wipe them on my jeans, and Atticus is completely still. The silence overwhelms me; it is like being lost inside a cave so dark you cannot see your hand in front of you. I snap my fingers. Silence.

A small rip opens in the scenery and then spreads like a run in a silk canvas. Brilliant light bursts from the seam, illuminating the form of a man stepping through it like a rock star taking the stage. He is radiant beyond the capability of human DNA, and he shines with a radiance and purity that emanates from within. He is as masculine as a warrior but as tender and fierce as a mother.

Like a woman in labor, the earth groans under his steps. He stands and gazes across the expanse of the tree. Surveying the animals, he gives a look of pity and acknowledges what he sees with a slight nod. He closes his eyes, taking in the warmth of the sun for a moment with a slip of a smile on his lips. Then, in a motion so quick that I am not certain how it happened, he claps his hands together once with the force of a million cymbals. The sound is terrible and majestic. It rings as far as the tree stretches, and the animals scream and howl. The tree shivers violently, its fruit dropping from its limbs. The tree is left naked, as if ashamed. An immense moon, full and luminous, rises and slowly devours the sun. But as the clarion sound of the man's clap reverberates into the heights, the moon begins to change. Its white light begins to bleed, and the sanguine rays drip through the holes in the tree. The color is as deep and thick as that which pulses through a man's veins. A blood moon. Signal of beginnings, seal of completion.

The man speaks with eyes wide open. Immediately I recognize that he is the Wakeful One.

"Cut it down," he whispers, but the sound thunders

across the land. "Take it down to the stump and bind it with bands of bronze." He turns his fearsome gaze directly upon me, and I am stricken like a mountain ogre petrified by the first ray of morning light. "You who have ears to hear, hear," he gently imparts, and the sound of cracking branches hits my ears like blunt trauma. "The Age of the Simulacrum is accomplished."

The tree comes down fast, and I am beneath her; I am under her colossal arms. How can I escape the weight of her fall? How will I survive? I stay frozen in place, paralyzed with fear, as the mighty tree sways. Atticus grabs me and we run. He pulls me, drags me forward. Then I see it: a great tree in the distance, three times the size of the one crashing down around me. Its bark shimmers, and a thin divide of sunlight slides down its trunk, creating a door. Desperate hope fills me, and I begin to run with every muscle, sinew, and bone in my body. We must reach the Door.

My muscles ached from outpoured adrenaline, my feet bruised from running, even before I took my first steps this morning. The scene from last night's dream played over and again in my head as I ran along the well-worn paths of Red Oaks. The sun peeped her red-gold bedhead over the horizon. The trees glowed a vibrant crimson in her welcoming embrace. Running helped me clear my head, so on this Saturday morning, I ran before anyone else stirred in the house. I didn't know what the dream meant. Who was the man who ordered the tree cut down? What did the tree symbolize? Was it us?

Over the past two days I had missed more classes than I had attended. I wanted to be with Atticus as much as possible. Next to him, school did not seem to matter anymore.

But my dreams did.

Increasingly, my dreams seemed to have the same recurring theme, though they were never the same. Trees, rivers, and doors, or rather, *the door*. It was obviously the same plot, the same message enacted by different players in different dramas. Yet, there was always danger–life-threatening, terrifying danger–and I was always running. What door was I meant to find? I thought of the tree coming down around me. What was about to happen to me? What was coming? It was the same question I had been asking for months now without an answer. But I had also been asking who the man in my dreams was, and Atticus had arrived. Remembering the heart-stopping terror, I decided I could wait for more answers to come when they were ready.

Breathless from my run, I slipped in the kitchen door and up the servants' steps before anyone saw me. After stripping off my sweaty clothes, I jumped into the shower and let the warm water do its work on my sore muscles.

"Hey...you almost done, Veralee? I need to get in the shower." Ausley stood in front of the mirror of our shared bathroom. She opened the cabinet and set a clean towel on the hook beside the door for me.

"Yep. Why are you up so early? Where are you going?" I asked, tucking the towel around my body.

"The clinic," she said, rubbing her eyes. "I feel like I

spend all of my waking hours there."

"You do," I replied. "I haven't seen you all week."

"I know. It's just that this virus is getting so out of control, Veelee. There are so many people catching it. Did you know that the government is thinking of putting sanctions on air-travel? It's not just here; it's in Africa, England, China, and parts of France."

"Are you sure you're safe working at the clinic, Ausley? Have you talked to Daddy about what's going on?" I asked, remembering my talk with Daddy by the fire last week.

She bit her lip and grabbed a hairbrush. "Does it matter?" she said softly.

"Does it matter?" I asked, bluntly. "Yes, it matters. Ausley, I know you care about people, but you have to protect yourself. Don't make stupid mistakes because of your bleeding heart." Heat rose through my neck like it always did when Ausley spoke so carelessly. She did not seem to have a self-preserving bone in her body, and it drove me crazy.

"Don't worry about it, Veralee. I'm fine. Seriously. I would stop if I thought it was dangerous." She was lying.

"Bull. You know something is wrong at the clinic, but you are still going there." I put my hands on my hips, "Ausley, you can't sacrifice yourself; it won't help anyone."

She put the brush down and turned towards me with tears in her tired eyes. "But you did." Her words hurt, but, she was right. Who was I to tell her to stop helping others? Who was I to give this speech? " I promise if it gets dangerous for me, I will come home. Seriously, I will not put our family in danger." She hugged me and I felt the damp towel press against my skin. Her words echoed in my mind: "But you did." What had I done?

"Ausley, what I did..." I let my voice fall silent. "Ausley, please don't make the same mistakes I have. You have no idea how much trouble I have created."

She pulled away, "But it was worth it, Veralee. You saved that boy's life." She seemed younger and older at the same time. So naive about what my actions truly meant, and yet so wise in terms of valuing life.

"Ausley, please just listen to me. Protect yourself. Don't get into trouble like I have." I turned and left the bathroom.

After dressing with shaking hands, I left my room.

"Veelee, you wake?" Mattie held her spaghetti-thin arms up to me as I emerged from my room, dressed and ready for the day. I scooped her up without breaking my trot down the stairs. As soon as my foot hit the cold marble floor, I heard their voices in the study. With Mattie on my hip, I waltzed into the study and plopped down onto the brown leather sofa. It sat under the large windows that gazed out over the trees.

Daddy's study looked and smelled just like him. Years and years of cigar ash and pipe smoke had penetrated the walls and the dark wood floors, creating a lingering tobacco odor. Even though Daddy did not smoke a pipe anymore, he occasionally lit a cigar and sat for hours reading books in his study. The smell reminded me of him and of home. All of the wood in the room, crafted in deep browns and reds, was as old as the house. The cumulative effect created an old-world charm to the room that one could not buy. Game that had been hunted generations before still hung on the walls. The same golden letter opener that Vera's mother had hidden at the beginning of the Civil War sat on the desk, fresh from a day's worth of work.

All conversation stopped as we girls entered the man cave. In the winged chair sat Phineas, while Daddy sat in the heavy wooden chair by the desk. "Good morning, Veralee," Atticus said from across the room. My name fit perfectly on his lips. Immediately I started raking over what I had just seen not five minutes ago in my bathroom mirror. I wore a tight pair of old blue jeans with holes in the knees and an old 10k race t-shirt. Adair would have looked amazing the moment she woke up. I was positive she brushed her hair and teeth even in her sleep, because she would roll over and look like the cover of some romance novel. Quickly I tried to wrap my long brown hair to one side of my face and position Mattie so that he could not see how shabbily I was dressed.

"Oh, hi, Atticus," I said trying to sound casual.

His emerald green eyes were sharp, and he smiled like he was covering up a laugh. He brought his hand up to his mouth feigning a cough, but I was positive he was laughing. Then I thought of the tree and of us together in my dream last night. Why was Atticus here so early? It's 6:00 in the morning, and the whole house is awake and having meetings? I clearly did not get the memo. Atticus was still watching me with amusement. My face flushed scarlet, and I was sure he could tell it was because of him.

"Good *morning*, Veelee," Daddy laughed, watching me fidget. He *would* think this was funny. I gave him a cut-it-out-now look with my eyes that told him to lay off. He nodded his head and redirected his efforts back to the conversation at hand. Daddy cleared his throat, "Veralee, its good you are here. We are discussing the plans for the Council Meeting." This was a surprise.

"When is everyone coming?" I asked.

"Two days," PH answered from the chair that he was almost too big to sit in. Two days. I had been so distracted with Nathan and Atticus that I had completely forgotten that the Council members were coming.

Daddy put down a large book, "We are going to be using all of the cottages, so your Mother is going to get the maid service to come today. She might need help making sure all of the cottages are opened up."

"Sure thing," I said.

Daddy continued, "We have been talking, and we all think it is best if Atticus lays low until the Council Meeting."

My eyes shot over to where Atticus sat in the window seat. "Yes, I think it would be best if everyone does not know about me at this time. I prefer to stay away from Council meetings whenever possible. So if I attend, I will stay out of way. I have found that my role does not intersect well with the role of the Council. My presence there seems to...complicate things. It is best if they do not know that I am here at all," Atticus said plainly.

The thought confounded me, "If you attend? Everyone who is of age *must* attend the meetings at the Terebinths of Mamre."

"I am not everyone," he said without apology. Something about him was so self-assured, so confident in who he was and who he was not, that in that moment I knew I could love him.

I wanted to be near him, to wrap my arm around his and to feel the warmth of the humming closeness. His eyes were full of an intensity that matched my own. I forced myself to breathe in a slow rhythm so that I would not betray myself to the entire room. He glanced up at me and smiled quickly as he looked down at his hands, and then at the books on the shelves. I was easier to read than they were.

Adair walked in holding a cup of coffee and offered it to PH as she sat on the arm of his chair. He slid his loving bear paw around her waist and kissed her cheek in thanks. Adair looked so small compared to PH, even though she was tall; PH was a bear of a man. Mattie saw her mother and jumped from my arms to crawl into her Papa's lap. They looked like a fashion ad, sitting there together, or maybe the three little bears from Goldilocks. I smiled at Adair when her eyes touched mine. She smiled back, completely satisfied in the moment.

Ausley and Mother also joined the crowd in the study. Ausley plopped down by the ancient bookcase, which held books older than the house. I loved those books and the way they encased snippets of lives that had long passed out of this world and into the next. Their voices still spoke through those pages, and not one bit of the magic was lost on me. Mother walked in and sat beside me in her white silk robe that made her look like a goddess recently freed from a Grecian sculptor's hand. Daddy smiled when she entered, like he did every time she came into a room. It was like the celebrity guest of the party had arrived, and he could not keep his eyes off of her. She smiled warmly and winked back at him over her steaming cup of coffee.

"Now that Mother has arrived, we can begin to discuss the serious matters of life." Daddy was enjoying himself this morning.

"Oh, hush, Edwin, you have been talking in here all morning," smiled Mother.

Daddy piled it on. "Ahh, but I saved the most important things for your arrival...besides with you looking as good as you do in that robe, I'm thinking we could just have a more private conversation," he winked and showed a toothy smile.

"I think that could be arranged," she said as if we were not all in the room.

I had to stop this gross display of affection between them. I mean, I loved that they still loved each other, but I was still their daughter. Sometimes they were really cute, but today was serious business.

"Really? Are going to do this now? Really?" I looked back and forth between them.

"I guess we digress, my love," Daddy leaned back in his chair while giving mother an over-the-top look. "The Council members will begin to arrive in two days' time, and this is a very special Council meeting for the Harper family. All of my girls will walk with us to the meeting this year. I have waited to do this, to walk side by side with each of you, as a completed family."

Daddy stopped and smiled at all of us for a moment. Daddy didn't show a lot of emotion, but I could tell he really was excited about this. I, too, had looked forward to this meeting for years; all my life really, to the time when I would wear the beautiful cloak of the Simulacrum for the first time and walk the secret path to the Terebinths of Mamre and join the Council as an adult.

"I cannot wait to see the Alabaster City and the Sacred Oaks!" Ausley cried, like the lid had just burst off of her excitement container. The Alabaster City was the mystical place where all of our family who no longer lived in this world now resided. I briefly thought of Vera. How odd it would be to be so close to her, and yet not be able to speak to her. Simulacrum were not allowed to enter the Alabaster City until we had reached 110 years.

Adair sat up and uncharacteristically squealed, "And you will finally get to taste the fruit from the trees! It is the best thing you will ever taste." She immediately worked to control her excitement and patted her dress down onto her thighs, hiding the blush that had entered her cheeks.

"Girls, calm down. We are all excited, but do you have to do the squealing thing?" Daddy put his hands to his ears and feigned pain. Mother suddenly looked uncomfortable and jumped up saying, "Oh, let me check the biscuits." Then she was out the door. Daddy turned and began talking to Adair about watching the Guardians and what she should learn while at the Council meetings. Adair would one day take Daddy's place as the Red Oaks Guardian, so she had the responsibility of learning her role.

I listened to the chatter but felt uneasy. Something was odd in Mother's response, or maybe I was just a bit jumpy because of what I had done. I had dreamt of going to the Terebinths of Mamre all of my life...but now with Nathan I felt uneasy. If they only knew what I had done, I would not be welcomed anymore. The thought of that made me nauseous. What would the Council members do if they discovered what I had done? I didn't know, and my excitement was descending into a growing sense of dread.

Mother returned and reclaimed her seat.

Ausley looked up with bright eyes. "When will Uncle Austin arrive?" She looked expectantly at Daddy while she twirled her blond curls around her forefinger. I saw Daddy's eyes cut over quickly to Mother. She looked equally concerned for a split second before they both covered their anxiety with smiles.

Adair piped up, "Is he coming? We haven't heard anything from him."

Ausley spoke with a mouth-full of jelly beans, "He said he was."

Mother looked disgusted for a moment, "Ausley, for

goodness' sake, remember your manners. Don't speak with your mouth full of candy...and isn't it a little early for sweets? We haven't even had breakfast yet."

Daddy laughed at Mother's constant need to raise a lady, and leaned across to eat a handful of Ausley's jellybeans. "Oh, he is always one of the last ones to arrive. I wouldn't expect him until Friday."

Adair went to work, "We need to open the other cottages today for the maid service and arrange who will be staying in the Big House." Daddy swiveled a bit in his chair kicking Ausley's elbow that was supporting her head out from under her. Ausley glared at him and then started to laugh in unison with him. It was going to be a good day, regardless of everything happening beneath the surface.

Everyone started individual conversations, but I noticed Mother give Daddy a strong look. Daddy cleared his throat again and said, "Everybody, listen up just a minute. I need you to know something about this Council meeting. You know how much I've looked forward to it. Veralee, you are now nineteen and Ausley you are eighteen, so you will both attend as full-fledged members for the first time. Your voices will be heard, and your votes will count, if needed. Your mother and I are thrilled, and we couldn't be prouder of the women you have both become." Mother smiled broadly and nodded her agreement.

Daddy held his hands and continued, "But, I need to talk to all of you. We are family, and as a family, we need to deal with the fact that there are changes in the air, and there are things happening that are...unsettling, to say the least. At work I am seeing more and more traffic cross my desk about this so-called Mad-Dog disease. It seems to be occurring more and more frequently, and the unfortunate ones who get it seem to be getting sicker faster. You know Simulacrum doctors and researchers are pouring a lot of money, time, and energy searching for a treatment or a cure, but so far nothing seems to be working. Now, there are very disturbing rumors among the Friguscor that some people are either immune or that they possess the cure in their blood."

The room went silent, and his words stole my breath. Adair shot a hard glance at me, and Ausley looked at me with pity in her eyes like she could cry at any second. I looked away, willing her to hold it together. Mother watched us closely, "And Ausley, we would like to speak with you privately about your involvement at the clinic."

Ausley narrowed her innocent eyes, "What? Why? I can't stop working at the clinic, I won't stop working there." She said, with surprising defiance.

Mother looked at her with understanding, "We will discuss it after this meeting is done, Ausley."

"Ausley, you can't put yourself in danger for the Friguscor. You put us *all* in danger if they find out what you are, or if the disease makes them crazy and they hurt you," Adair said, in a mothering tone.

"You haven't seen them. You can't know how much they need me. They are helpless victims of this disease. I can't walk away from them when they are so short-handed. They need me." She was on the verge of tears.

Mother looked at her with a stern but loving sigh, "Ausley, we will talk to you after this meeting."

Daddy leaned down and rested a steady hand on Ausley's knee before he continued, "You know that we cannot hide forever. We do not know what tomorrow will bring, but we are never alone, do not forget that for one moment. We will not fear tomorrow, because we know that in us flows the essence of life. But the Council has very important decisions to make this time that will affect what life for this family–and every other Simulacrum families–will look like from here on out. I cannot tell you why this is happening, though I wish I could, but I can tell you that something is coming. As the Guardian of the Gate at Red Oaks, I am bound by oath to this land, as is your mother. We must do whatever it takes to secure the Gate. Whatever it takes...we must protect this land and its secret. It is our responsibility to the Simulacrum; it is our duty as Guardians."

He turned and looked out the window at the great oaks that lined the road that led to our home. I looked at him, "I feel it as well, something is barreling toward us, but we won't know what it is until it is here," I said.

"It's like we can see the foliage bending under its weight from afar, but it hasn't revealed its true nature yet," added Mother. The grandfather clock in the hallway struck 7:00 and rang loudly through the house. Dong, dong, dong, dong, dong, dong, dong. Time was ticking, and it would not let us forget.

The room grew thick with anxious thought and then Mattie spoke, "I'm hungry! Mimi, can we have grits and eggs?" The moment passed and bacon and eggs, as it has it's way of doing, began to occupy everyone's thoughts.

Mother hopped up and took Mattie's hand, "Yes we can, my little princess. You come stir the grits while I make the gravy." Mother and Mattie went out together, singing, "Someone's in the kitchen with Dinah."

"Hello!" A cheerful voice called from the down the hall. I froze at the sound and looked over at Atticus.

"Hello! Y'all here?" Jackson's voice carried down the hall from the back door of the kitchen. Ausley jumped up and leaned out the library door.

"We're in the library, Jackson," she said, smiling and quickly brushing her hair with her fingers.

Jackson broke into the library with a robust, "Good morning Harper Family!" Then, noticing the somber mood, he adjusted. "Am I interrupting something?"

Daddy gave Jackson a warm, genuine smile, "No, not at all. We were just finishing up. Great to see you on this fine morning. What can we do for you? Did you come to eat Gail's famous cathead biscuits? If you did, you came at the right time, she's about to fix some gravy."

At the mention of biscuits and gravy, Jackson became even more animated, if that was even possible. "Sausage gravy or sawmill gravy?" he said eagerly.

"Sawmill gravy," Daddy said, a little disappointed. He liked Mother's signature milk gravy, but he loved her sausage gravy.

"Well, beggars can't be choosers! I'll take a plate of whatever you're offering." He turned and smiled right at me.

Adair cleared her throat, "Jackson, have you come to help me today? I left a message with your mama last night."

"Yep, she said y'all would need help getting ready for the Council's arrival. So...here I am. A strong back and a weak mind to the rescue," he echoed the teasing request Adair had spoken to his Mom.

I laughed at his playfulness, "That's how Adair prefers her minions and her men, which are pretty much the same thing for her."

Jackson turned intimately serious. "And how about you Veralee, how do you prefer your men?" It was not a mean comment, but a true question that he had clearly been rolling around in his head. The moment became a bit uncomfortable for the room full of people. Adair and PH slipped out of the room with Daddy and Ausley on their heels like a NASCAR race to the kitchen.

I looked sadly at Jackson, wishing I could have given him the answer he had wanted. His resolve softened and he sighed, "Well, time to let go of those dreams and build some new ones. But it's hard to let go of something that I have wanted for so long. It was always you, Little Bird." His voice dropped, and I saw that his heart had been wounded. If only I could erase that pain. I hated that he was hurting because of me.

"Jackson, I—"

He held up his gentle giant hand, "No, I'm sorry Veralee. I should not have brought it back up. I promise I will behave from now on." Then he flashed his million-dollar smile.

"No, you don't have to apologize. It's just that—"

"Don't look so down-trodden," he interjected, bumping my shoulder. "You look kinda terrible, you know."

"Um...thanks?" I rolled my eyes at him.

"I'm serious. What has happened between now and the last time I saw you that has you looking so...I don't know, like you have become some warrior with a mission...except your mission was a small kitten that died last night and now all of your dreams of building a new city populated by tiny kittens is gone because that was the last one in the world."

Well, I saw a boy die, and then gave him my blood, which is, of course, against every law we have and on top of that, that boy could possibly be turning Simulacrum now, but I'm not sure and then there is this guy, who is from the past and I barely know him, but something in me wants to love him for the rest of my life, or maybe just rip his shirt off...I'm not really sure which one, and the Council Meeting is coming and I'm scared that they just might behead me while I'm there. But, other than that, I'm fine. That's what I wanted to say, but I didn't say anything.

While I tried to think of a coherent reply, something shifted by the window. Atticus. He was still sitting in the windowsill. He had heard the whole conversation. My heart beat faster, and I felt the heat of embarrassment spread up to my cheeks. Jackson noticed him as well. "Um, Jackson, this is our guest and friend, Atticus." I tried to cover my discomfort.

Atticus rose slowly from his seated position. Jackson held out his hand, "Nice to meet you." His words were nice enough, but a little short for his usual demeanor. The awkwardness in the room was as thick as smoke from a fire started with damp wood and doused with kerosene.

Atticus nodded his head and took Jackson's hand. "It is a pleasure to meet any friend of Veralee's."

Jackson, the nicest guy in the world, everyone's best friend, the resident court jester, ruffled up like a prize rooster ready to defend his henhouse. "Yes, I am her oldest friend. We've known each other all our lives, grown up together. And when did you arrive at Red Oaks? I've never seen you before," Jackson parried, with a definite edge in his voice.

"I am quite sure I have never seen you either. You are young, and I do not remember meeting you before," Atticus had a look that claimed territory, but still kept his unnerving calmness.

I cut in between the two men who stood on either side of me like I was the prized sandwich meat. I hated sandwich meat, it was not natural; it was cut in weird shapes and grossed me out. So did being put in awkward situation like this. "Atticus arrived the day of the 175th celebration. He has been staying here at Red Oaks. And yes, Jackson and I grew up together. He lives a couple of miles away on his family farm. Now everyone is acquainted, and we can get some breakfast."

"Which farm?" asked Atticus with a quick change of tone and genuine curiosity.

"Veritas Hills," Jackson responded tersely.

Atticus's eyes relaxed a little, "I remember it well. But are not those lands still a part of Red Oaks?" he asked.

Jackson was clearly surprised by the change in the atmosphere, "Well, they were a long time ago. But Vera gave the land to one of her slaves who raised a baby she rescued during the Civil War."

Atticus smiled like he had just found an answer to a different question. "Moses," he said.

Jackson looked impressed, "Yes, and Abram who raised him. How did you know that?"

Atticus looked warmly at Jackson, "So you are the descendant of Moses?"

"Yes, a direct descendant," he said. Atticus stuck his hand out again, "It is truly my pleasure to meet you Jackson, descendant of Moses. I am so glad that you are here today."

Jackson looked at me with raised eyebrows like I had brought a lunatic into the house. I smiled quickly, like this was completely normal. But the truth was I was a little bit more than confused. Then I remembered. Atticus had said that when he came down the River of time, Vera had been coming through the tunnel behind him with a baby. I guessed that baby was Moses.

"Well, I'm going to get some breakfast before it gets cold." Jackson gave me another 'he's crazy' look and left the room dazed.

I turned to Atticus. "Moses? The baby who was coming through the tunnel with you and Vera?"

Atticus looked truly happy. "Yes. At least he made it. He and Vera made it out, I assume. I had feared, that with my disappearance, they would all be in trouble, but here is Jackson. Those two made it out alive."

"Atticus, why did she have a baby with her, and why were y'all going through the tunnel?"

Atticus rubbed his hands together and pushed his black hair from his eyes, "Moses was Vera's hand-maid's baby. She was killed searching for Abram during the battle. Vera had a mother's heart already and took the baby from Abram, promising to protect him. So when the Yankees overran the house, I rushed to get Vera and the babies to safety. Jeremiah was behind all of us. We were taking them through the tunnel when the River pulled me down, and I arrived here with you." He sighed, "I am glad to know that at least Vera and Moses made it out alive."

I followed his thought, "Jeremiah? But Jeremiah...we have never heard of him. He must not have made it."

"No, I think not." Atticus said sadly.

I leaned against Daddy's desk. Then, I remembered my anger, and burst out, "Hey, you could have said something you know."

Atticus looked amused at my outburst. "While Jackson was lamenting his love for you? It would have ruined the moment."

I glared at him, "It was rude. It embarrassed him. And there was no moment to ruin."

Atticus folded his arms, "I was at the back of the room, and to leave would have interrupted your conversation. Besides, I was in the room first; he was the one who came in and started talking without knowing his surroundings."

He was being childish. "Atticus, seriously, it's just Jackson. We grew up together. We ate sand together as babies."

Atticus stood in front of me, "You said you had not bonded yourself to another."

My old nemesis, my temper, raised its head. "And I haven't. If you had not been listening in to a private conversation, you would not be assuming I had. You know what they say about people who assume things?"

Atticus looked annoyed "No Veralee, I do not know what they say about people who assume. I just came from the 19th century, remember?"

"Well, they say that it makes an as...." his eyes were so green and clear. He looked beautiful, even when he was angry. "They say that...well, it's just not nice to listen in on private conversations."

Atticus dropped his arms, "You are right, I apologize. I had no right to listen to your conversation. In fact, I have no right to you at all."

"No, no that's not what I meant. I *want* you to have a right to me, I mean, I...not that you have to *want* that right, but I'm just saying that there might have been something between Jackson and me, but there is nothing there now. Everyone always assumed it would be Jackson and me, but we had already decided that we were not meant to be before you arrived. And now you're here, and I have dreamt for so long that you were coming. So, I guess what I'm saying is that..."

Atticus moved closer and placed his hands on the desk on either side of me. He came so close to me that there was no longer room for my temper. "He called you Little Bird. I am not good at what you call ' feelings,' but I know I did not like to hear him call you that. It was too...familiar for my taste." His words climbed into my heart and his expression stoked the hope inside. He raised his hand to my face and let a finger trace my jaw line. I watched his face intently, not wanting to miss the radiance of his eyes by closing mine. But instinct set in and my eyes closed as I tilted my mouth up to his. The buzzing sound of our tseeyens was so loud that I thought anyone in the house could hear it.

But then...nothing happened.

I opened my eyes. Atticus stood three steps back from me. I sat dumbfounded and embarrassed on the wooden desk.

Atticus shook his head, "My apologies, Miss Veralee. I am so sorry. I should not have imposed myself on you. "

"What? You didn't impose yourself on me. And why are we back to the Miss thing?" I said, at once annoyed and embarrassed by my reaction and his inaction. Atticus looked down sorrowfully at the Persian rug beneath his feet.

Then he pulled a veil over his face and his affect went flat. No emotion was left in his eyes, he was simply a blank slate as he said, "I apologize, Veralee. I have forgotten myself. I am an Ayindalet, after all. My life is not my own."

With that he turned and walked away from me.

{ 12 }

Waking Giants

"**V**ERALEE! How far are you going?" Mother leaned out the back door, yelling at the top of her lungs, her yellow, polka-dotted dress blowing gently in the cool October afternoon breeze. I loved October at Red Oaks. It rarely rained, and hot, sultry September had finally melted into cool mornings and low humidity, a rarity in south Alabama. The afternoons were warm enough for t-shirts, but the evenings brisk enough for s'mores by a bonfire. It was perfect weather for running.

"Five or seven miles," I called over my shoulder. I held my phone above my head and waved it in her direction as a preemptive strike for her next question. My shoes hit the dirt as I entered the well-worn path that my feet could travel in their sleep. I loved to run the same paths over and over through the Red Oaks. Some runners might find this a monotonous cauldron of motion, but I found only comfort in the familiarity. It was one of the few things Adair and I could agree on.

The trees blurred into an abstract painting of red, green and grey, as my legs mechanically pushed forward. When I entered the forest, I was free. The world became smaller and yet completely available at the same time, as I moved through the silent orchestra created by the heavily-blanketed trees. I heard only the pounding of my shoes hitting the earth and the sigh of the fresh, clean air as it moved quickly through my lungs and out through the trees. I was alone in what felt like a sacred place.

The dense canopy pushed back the sun, so the light progressively dimmed and the air cooled, as I traveled deeper and deeper into the trees. The path curved around the creek that flowed softly over sand and rock, the peaceful calm serenaded by the melody of the trickling water. Bending from the waist, the trees reached to embrace each other with old, heavy arms high above the path, some covered in thick Spanish moss that hung down like holiday lights. Alice's rabbit hole seemed open before me and, like she had, I followed it down, down, down as if I were late for a very important date.

The sounds of the outside world vanished. Here on this hallowed ground, I could forget that it even existed. Here in the midst of nature's poetry, I could believe that another world was possible. Golden leaves from the river birches floated down like snow and carpeted the path creating a yellow brick road before me. And so I followed.

At Red Oaks, at home under the trees that raised me, I felt whole. With so much changing around me, with Atticus and Nathan, and whatever was coming next, I relished the familiarity and comfort that was Red Oaks. She was like an old, worn security blanket that I had carried since infancy, the kind a child lovingly cradles when content, the irreplaceable kind that tears away a real piece of heart if lost. I was reminded of Dorothy, who had left home and had followed the yellow brick road. My favorite part had always been what she said when she returned to her own bed: "If I ever go looking for my heart's desire again, I won't look any further than my own back yard. Because if it isn't there, then I never really lost it to begin with."

I had started running with Daddy when I was a little girl. He was always up with the sun, standing on the porch in his running shoes. Maybe it was his time at West Point that had engraved the running habit into him, or maybe it was because the run washed the stress of yesterday's worries away. I would crack the door open and see him stretching his arms over his head. He would turn and send me back to bed with a hug and a smile. But I never stopped cracking that door open.

After some years passed, and I had grown a little taller, he stopped sending me back to bed. "Where are your shoes, Little Bird? Expecting to fly? Gotta have shoes if you're gonna keep up with me." I would race up the stairs and grab my shoes just in time to join him before he left the porch. We had spent hours on these trails, talking and not talking. He would talk to me about school, about our love for history, and about his life growing up. I would tell him about Ausley and Adair, and how I wanted to be a teacher when I grew up, and all of the great dramas that affected a middle school girl. He would sing the cadence songs from his Army years that framed his life as much as the degrees and accomplishments that hung over his desk in the study. I would call them after him, and he would end up running small circles around me when I thought I had gone my last step and wanted to quit. "One mile, Feels good, Two Miles, No sweat..." He would make it up as he went. I never quit either, but tried my best to go that "two miles, no sweat..." with him. When I just could not make it any farther, he would lift me onto his back and carry me the rest of the way home.

When I shared a problem or situation with him, he knew just how to cut to the marrow, laying out a clear, logical path for me to follow. Daddy was always a straight shooter and I believed he could solve any problem. But, when the hours at work added up to more hours than there are in the day, he had stopped running with me. I missed his warm laughter and his constant teasing. I was too big to ride on his back when I got tired now, but still, I missed him when I ran.

I had always run to relax, to feel the earth beneath my feet and to blend myself into the beauty of Red Oaks, but lately I had the sinking feeling that I was running *from* something. The dread was like a faucet left on in a plugged sink, filling, ready to overflow. It had started slowly over the past year, the feeling that I had to run to get away from something, never knowing what that something was. Hitting the trail only escalated the feeling of flight, the need to get away from something barreling toward me faster than I could run. I did not know what was coming, but I felt its presence gaining with every passing day.

Clinging to the right side of a curve I tripped and my feet left the ground before I could register what was happening. I landed on a sharp, jagged root and rolled hard down an embankment, hitting my head on an exposed rock. Dazed and with my head ringing from the impact, I lay looking up into the trees. I sat in the dirt slowly blinking my eyes until the black spots in my vision cleared. That's when I felt wrenching stabs of pain coming from my knee and leg. Cautiously, I brought my knee up to my chest and investigated the damage. My leg throbbed and my sock was already red with blood from the open gash below my knee. A wave of nausea rolled over me when I saw the broken stick protruding from my calf. I reached for my phone, but my armband was gone, and my phone along with it. I looked all around me, but my phone must have been flung further away. It was almost impossible to find those old-fashioned phones for sale these days. I would have to find it, wherever it had landed.

The smell of iron and sweet, wild clover honey poured down my leg and onto the ground. This bleeding wound would not heal as quickly as my wrist had. It would take a day or two to completely close back up. The sickening thought of what would come next choked me. I was going to have to pull the stick out of my calf.

Then a muted thundering echoed through the woods. I froze. The hair on my neck stood up, and my tseeyen went wild with vibration on my arm. Holding my leg and my breath at the same time, I kept completely still in the deep of the woods, biting my tongue to quiet the pain. Steadily I slowed my breathing as I searched the trees for any sign of life. Silence. The wind. A bird called to the sun, which seemed far away, above the heavy canopy of trees. Nothing moved; nothing broke the silence. Unable to bear it any longer, I let out the stifled cries. My broken voice echoed, the loudest thing in these woods. Looking down I decided it was time to start working my way back to the house. I abandoned the idea of pulling the branch out of my leg. How far had I gone? How far from the house had I traveled?

I spied a piece of fallen branch nearby that looked like it might work as a makeshift crutch. I inched toward it and wrestled it upright. With both hands anchored on the branch, I pushed up on my good leg, letting my bad leg hang freely in the air while my left supported the weight of two. I closed my eyes as the pain and nausea engulfed me in the effort.

When I opened them, a man stood in front of me like a magician appearing from thin air. I fell backwards from shock and fear, but as I tumbled, another caught me from behind and righted me. Two of them? Who? The man who faced me was taller than any I had ever seen, over seven feet if an inch, and his hands were the size of basketballs. He could have crushed me with one little finger.

Thick, silver hair began in a defined widow's peak on his forehead and ended like cleanly wrapped dreadlocks hanging past the middle of his back. It was coarse, and so long, I wondered if he had ever cut it. But what could cut such hair? It resembled braided rope more than anything else. His clothes were not clothes at all, but more like a warrior's uniform from some science-fiction adventure novel. The material looked like a rustic metal but moved with the softness of suede. It was patterned after...leaves? Like a thousand leaves laid one on top of the other, creating a feathered pattern all the way down his chest. A thick, wide belt crisscrossed from a bronzed buckle on his waist. A long scabbard hung from the belt and I could only see the pommel of the sword, which looked of ivory and mother of pearl, and the end of the sword which stopped just above his feet. I had never seen a weapon of that size, and I stared at it nervously. For that matter, I had never seen anything like this giant of a creature in all my life.

"Who…ahh…whaa- " unintelligible sounds slipped from my gaping mouth.

"Do not be afraid, Daughter of the Blood. We have come to help. We…Are…Archaon." Their voices all spoke at once, a sound more similar to singing than speaking that echoed as if inside a cave. It was an odd, foreign sound not made by human voices.

They stepped back, giving me space, being careful not to hover because of their intimidating size, but staying alert, lest I started to sway again. Large, but lean and muscular, they looked like warriors from frescoes that were now chipped and dull on ancient walls. It was hard to keep my balance, even with the support of the branch I was grasping, and I kept touching my wounded leg down to keep from falling. Ten of these strange creatures stood in a semi-circle within the trees. They stood silent, reading the emotions of my face or maybe reading my mind…I was not sure which.

As the silence continued, my body began to relax involuntarily. I felt a calm wash over me as their eyes search mine as if they were broadcasting unseen, unspoken reassurances through their steady gaze. An unworldly aroma, something like the rarefied air after a nearby lightning strike, floated among them. The wind stilled, and the trees stood erect, holding their branches at attention. Everything was still. The distinctive scent in the air triggered my memory.

Then, as if I were watching a movie, I saw myself step out of my car on the drive to the house and enter the forest. They were showing me a scene from my memory like someone would show a movie on a wall. I saw myself, a week ago, as I looked into the trees, searching for whatever had left the unique odor. Then the image was gone. I looked at the creature who cocked his head like a Bengal tiger, and he nodded. It was them. They had been the ones in the woods. I *had* sensed something.

Their words registered slowly, "The Archaon?" I whispered, as the dust blew off my memory. The pictures in the Histories, the gilded metal armor, the leather bindings that snaked up their arms, the belts tied with chords of golden thread and filled with knives and spears that gleamed without the sun. "The Archaon." I whispered again. The one who spoke to me stepped forward as if he had been called by name. His face. I knew his face. He was the giant in my dream. The one who pulled me from the river and set me on solid ground. My mouth opened, but no words escaped. He inclined his head knowingly, and I knew without being told, that he was answering the question spoken only in my mind.

Archaon, the Guardians of the Light, Watchers of Men, warriors and helpers. Ten minutes ago they were just pictures in an ancient book; they had not been seen in centuries, and then only by a handful of people, never as a group. The only time I had ever read about such creatures was in those few stories where Simulacrum claimed to have seen one. But no one knew if they still existed, if they were still....real. Now I stood in the midst of ten of them.

I stammered what seemed like nonsense, "You are the

Archaon....I have seen you in pictures, or in the Histories, but I didn't know...I mean, I didn't think you... I don't mean to be rude...but...you're real! I mean, you *are* real, aren't you?" I reached up to touch the goose egg on the back of my head, "How hard *did* I hit my head?" I looked from one creature to the next. They waited patiently. I reached out to touch the one speaking to me to reassure myself, but thought better of it and dropped my hand. My nattering should have embarrassed me, but I was too uncertain of reality to be concerned with southern manners.

"Do not fear us. We have heard the Red Oaks moan from afar, even the ground weeps for what is to be. Many times have we walked beneath the shade of these trees, and many times have we drunk deeply of their waters. We have seen you, Veralee Harper of the Crimson Terebinths, transformed from what was to what is; we have seen you, blood Daughter, as you have grown beneath their wings. Eiani runs in your veins, much richer than in the birth blood. And we see that what is to be will be for you as well." He paused and tilted his head like a lion reading its prey, "I am Achiel, servant of Paraclete the True, Liege of the Archaon." At the mention of Paraclete, all of the Archaon bowed their heads slightly and placed their right fists over their heart in salute.

Achiel continued, "You are hurt. Your blood spills, and the ground calls out." He did not move when he spoke, but stayed oddly still. His body language was as foreign as his dress and voice. "Yes, we would like to heal you, Daughter of the Blood. If you are willing to be healed."

Achiel moved slowly with exaggerated care onto one knee in front of me. I got the impression that he did not want to scare me with quick movement, as if I were a wounded rabbit. He flipped his hand over and grasped at an invisible nothingness. A slow, sudden pulse stirred in the air. A thrumming that I could not place. It was not musical, not like the sound of the heart beating in my chest, or the tapping of a foot...and yet it had a pattern. The huge creatures stood with mouths open, and eyes shut around me. The rhythm came from their breath, the breath of life. It filled the forest. The intake...yahhhh and the exhale...waaayy, over and over. Unsure of what was happening I looked down to see Achiel's hand still open, waiting on something unseen. Then there was light. Light, brilliant and pulsating, filled the palm of his hand and radiated into the air around us. Yahhhh...intake of breath....wayyyyyy...exhale of breath. Yahhh...wayyy...yahhhh wayyyy.

"Daughter of the Blood, are you willing to be healed?" Their voices, in one single sound of unity spoke rhythmically into the air. Yahhhhh...intake of breath...wayyyy...exhale.

I searched the creature's face for some piece of reality to hang onto. But I found inhuman eyes, having neither a begging nor a demand in them. They were like the remnants of a firework after detonation. Deep royal blue in the center, bursting with rays of rich purples and yellows toward the periphery, all ringed in silver-gray. Star sapphire, they looked like my grandmother's star sapphire ring my Mother wore on her right hand. Those unfathomable eyes were offering me a choice and waited for my decision. Yahhhh...intake of breath....wayyyyyy, exhale for life.

"I am... willing," I whispered. The words felt like an answer to a much bigger question. *I am willing*, I thought. *I am willing.* It rang through me like the old Liberty Bell.

Then I felt the excruciating pain of the branch as the Archaon removed it from my leg. I clenched my teeth but could not stop the sob from escaping my mouth. Still kneeling, Achiel steadied me with one hand on my hip. Then, where the pain had been, warmth flowed over my body like the sun had found me standing in the shade. It all moved so slowly that I thought time itself had stopped. As his hand covered my wound, warm fire engulfed the pain. A small flame began on the edge of the wound where the stick had protruded, and then spread like butter on toast across my calf and up and down my leg. The flame turned to a raging fire, which did not scorch, but instead spread glowing warmth to every fiber in my leg. Rather than devastate, this pain made me feel alive. I wanted it to last forever.

Suddenly, I was no longer in Red Oaks. Everything around me had changed. The sound of rushing wind completely surrounded me. I turned, expecting to see the trees of Red Oaks again, but they were gone. A vast ocean of wheat fields covered the land. The sky shone such a contrasting blue that I could not help but think of Van Gough's paint brush. I reached my hand out and felt the golden crunch of the wheat. If fell apart quickly in my hand. Wheat ready for harvest. *Where am I?*

"Have you not seen this place before?" Achiel inquired. I spun on my heels and found him standing behind me. His armor was no longer the rustic brown it had been just ten seconds ago; it now shimmered a brilliant gold.

I stammered, "No... I don't think so."

Achiel pointed behind me as he spoke, "Have your eyes never seen before?" I followed his outstretched arm and turned to look. A long, rectangular pool of vibrant emerald water hovered over the earth, and above it floated a flaming tree. It was the One Tree! The Tree from my dreams! The raging flames burned through the sky causing the clouds to take on hues of pink and purple and orange and blue. The colors rippled across the waters, mirroring the painted sky.

There was a detail I did not remember seeing in my dreams. Down the center of the trunk of the One Tree, where the three trunks twisted into one, a river of blood flowed. The river passed from the Tree into the roots, then into the mighty emerald waters below. Like oil, the blood did not mix with the water, but settled to the bottom of the sea, infiltrating earth and clay, fueling creation and calling forth life. Clouds billowed out along the roots systems.

"It is here, from this river, that the Simulacrum were born. The essence of the blood called you into being long ago," Achiel explained into my ear.

The words fell out of my mouth, "The Eiani."

Achiel nodded.

"The Eiani is the life in the blood, and it is very strong within you—much richer and stronger than you know." He fixed those wild, knowing eyes on me and studied me for a second, as if deciding something. "You are a descendant of the first Primogenes, or the First-borns, as your kind calls them," Achiel said.

"The Primogenes, who first drank from the One

Tree," I answered slowly, with dawning understanding.

"Not the first to drink, but the first *Friguscor* to drink of the One Tree," he corrected. "Before then, all of mankind drank freely from the One Tree. That was before the world of men changed."

The Primogenes were just a drawing in the Histories to me. The drawing did not show their faces, only twelve, grey-colored backs.

"Because of The Dulling," I said flatly. Originally, mankind was created to live forever, but everything changed with the first bite of fruit from the Tree of Shadows. With that bite, that one deadly bite, death entered the veins of man, and the story of life was forever altered.

"After the Dulling, when the Original men ate from the Tree of Shadows, the Shadow Age began. It was an age when time was not measured, when purpose was erased from mankind, and the seasons stopped moving forward. Heat, disease, and death burned through the lands. The Original men disappeared, for the Friguscor covered the earth. They destroyed the earth, each other, and all of mankind with them." Achiel spoke like he was reading from the Histories himself. His tone was like someone who had witnessed the events personally. His words were so compelling that they painted a live picture as he spoke.

"Then, in the midst of ruin, Friguscor were called. While they lay in darkness and desolation, the One Tree sang the ancient song, calling them to return. It bid them come and drink from the river of blood that would restore health and wholeness and life. Twelve responded, and across the barren lands, they drove their horses into the ground and pounded their fists in determination until the dry cracked ground turned into white, loose sand. Some grew weak and wanted to leave, to go back, when fear of the unknown and the harshness of the journey began to choke the resolve from them. Through the encouragement of the others, all persevered through long nights and unending days. Desperation spurred them forward until the white sand turned to rich earth underneath their feet, and still they rode on. When they found the place that sat on high and hovered above all things, they called to the One Tree. For four hundred years the twelve called to the Tree. They beat their fists and cried out for an answer. But there was only silence. Until the sky of brass fractured, and finally...the One Tree spoke. They sank to their knees and drank of the blood that transforms. The Eiani healed the cold deadness that had settled in their hearts, and then engraved each one with a tseeyen."

With my eyes still closed I whispered, "And then... we–they...were born."

We stood watching the great One Tree for a long time before I asked, "But, how did the First-borns find the One Tree? I mean...I know that they were called...but how did they know the way?"

Achiel inclined his head toward me and formed his lips into what could have been a slight smile, "They were called by the One Tree and directed by us...through their dreams."

"*You* showed them? You brought them? But I

thought you did not walk with men," I asked, astonished at this revelation.

"You think that, because that is all you have ever known. But we have a memory like the trees. We still remember the age when we watched over mankind and walked among them. To lead them to the One Tree was our last gesture of mercy before we left the world of men."

"But you are here now," I looked at him then, fully.

"Where is here, Daughter of the Blood?" he asked, quizzically

I opened my mouth to respond, but then the world around me tilted, and I was back in the woods of Red Oaks. Achiel stood just as he was before, bent down, with the strange light hovering in his hand. The warmth of the light still pulsed through my body. But then, as if retreating from battle, the warmth slowly pulled back to the wound on my leg. The flame burst into a flurry of soft floating lights, and I watched snowflakes of photons float down and around me. Whatever "it" was, "it" was over.

What had just happened? I trembled as the energy of the light left. But.... *something* stayed. I could feel it still, somewhere deep within me. The light. I smiled as my mind probed the light that was left inside of me.

The man-creature stood silently, and turned his head slightly to the side. A conversation of secret, silent words seemed to be transpiring around me, but I could not hear a thing. My fingers and toes tingled while I watched these creatures converse in silence. I wondered how they heard each other without using any spoken words. They did not shift their weight or look away from me. All ten stood perfectly still watching my face like it was a jack-in-a-box about to open.

"Thank you," I stammered in a voice that sounded to my own ears, surprisingly musical. "But where... where did we go?"

Their unusual scent, of a world long lost or maybe just far, far away, filled my lungs.

He did not answer my question, but instead said, "Tell the Simulacrum that we have arrived. We come in the authority of Paraclete himself, we come to walk once more beside you, to stand with you against the coming night. In the last light of the blood moon, we will come; let us meet together, as in the days of old. The Terebinths of Mamre will witness as they have since the beginning of days."

What is to be will be for you as well, Achiel's words ricocheted through me like a drum being pounded repeatedly. I felt as though I was standing at the end of a long hall that echoed and bounced his words back and to over and over.

"I will tell them." Then I added quickly, "But why now? Why are you here now?"

Achiel looked sharply at me and then as if he decided to grant me this request, he said, "The Age of Slumber is completed. We walk among you as foretold: the Age of Simulacrum is accomplished, the Age of Friguscor is become."

"The Age of Friguscor?" I echoed his words, "What do you mean that the Age of Simulacrum is accomplished? Do you mean ended, as in, over?"

"To everything a season, a time, is appointed. Do not fear, Daughter of the Blood. Do not fear simply because you do not yet know what is to be, but draw on the Eiani. Therein lies your strength. As the Eiani flows through you, your blood triumphs over what was, what is, or what is to come. It is more potent than your beginning or end, for it holds the power of all your people, those of all the Ages. Even now, you feel it in your being. Even now you know we speak Truth, for we speak the words of Paraclete, and there is no lie in Him." Achiel gave me a look charged with fortitude and resolve, and as I received his steady gaze, I felt courage and hope rise to counter the dread.

I did feel the strength in my blood. It was as if it were not mine, though still a part of who I was. Almost like a shield or a sword that could be wielded by my hand, but a tool that I had not yet mastered. The blood in me felt foreign and yet mine at the same time. The blood that pulsed through my veins was a weapon, a comfort, a shield, a sword, a book of knowledge, and a council of wisdom. All compiled from years of life I had never known, from days of living I had never seen, and toils of existence that I had never borne...and yet it was in me.

"I am willing." *I am sure of it.* I was willing to do my part, to go wherever I was called, to walk the unknown path.

Achiel faced me fully then, and allowed the weight of my words to fill the moment and to resonate through the silence. He offered me his hand, where my phone sat small and out of place in his palm. I took it, "Oh...Thank you." I said, or at least I thought I said it. Then, he nodded slightly, as if in some sort of salute to me and to my words.

And they were gone. I was alone. I looked around me, spinning on my heels. The empty space where their massive frames had just stood seemed barer than before. *Were they still here?* I detected no scent. The wind blew, and the trees moved methodically in the breeze while the squirrels scurried and the birds called. No, they were gone. The world, which had seemed frozen only moments ago, was once again in motion.

Quickly, I ran my hand down to where my black running pants flayed open. The skin not only showed no evidence of the gash, but it looked warm, golden and fresh. I turned toward the house, and then stole another glance at the trees. Change was coming, but it was hard to tell from what direction when you were standing in the midst of it. The Archaon were coming to the Simulacrum and Atticus, whoever he was, sat in the tiny south cottage of Red Oaks even now. The little boy, Nathan, had changed and a piece of me had changed with him.

Stories, read to me as a child, were coming to life, and rules had been broken. It was just like the painting on my bedroom wall. The Age of Simulacrum might be coming to an end....the Age of the Friguscor was rising? Had I always known this was coming? Is this what had haunted my dreams my entire life? I did not even feel the effort of running as my body pushed forward. I could hear the drums beating. It was time.

the Oaks Remain

I ran until I reached the clearing that wrapped itself around to the south cottage. With eyes bent on the cottage I ran straight to the door and pounded on the old wood. It rattled under my hand but nothing came of it. Where could Atticus be? *Working.* I spun and dashed toward the old kitchen. He had volunteered to work on restoring the old wood in the ancient kitchen. Daddy had agreed happily, and Atticus had relished the idea of working with his hands again.

I reached the old kitchen in what had to be a new world record, but it was eerily empty as well. The slave quarters sat still, undisturbed. Atticus was not there.

Breathing heavily, I raced through the gardens back to the Big House. I wondered briefly if Atticus had gone walking in the woods when I heard his voice at the back door. Then I saw him. He wore a pair of PH's blue jeans and a v-neck t-shirt and stood leaning against the edge of the back door with arms folded, talking to Daddy. Daddy was still in uniform, having just arrived home from work. Atticus saw me first and jerked his head up, like a string had pulled his attention toward me. Daddy craned out the door and waved.

"Hey there, Little Bird, been out running?" Daddy smiled and started toward me. Atticus could see I was struggling. I bent over, swallowing air down in large gulps, and put my hands on my knees to catch my breath.

I put my hands out in protest, "I'm...fine...I just need...a minute. I was running...in the woods, and I saw...something," more heavy breathing and gulping escaped my mouth.

Atticus perked up like a hunting dog that had caught the scent. "Veralee, where have you been? What did you see? That scent, I smell.... *who* did you meet?"

Daddy looked down at me confused. "What's going on?" he asked.

Finally I could talk in more than brief snatches. "I saw something in the woods; I mean I met a man in the woods. Only, he wasn't a man at all. He said he, well they, there were about ten of them....he said they were the....Daddy, I saw the Archaon!" The word fell like a metal ball on a tile floor, and crashed into us all.

"The Archaon?" Daddy swiftly broke in. "What are you talking about, Veralee? The Archaon? Why would you use that word?" Daddy's smile had left his face, and he focused intently on me. The wind blew hard across the fields, thrusting Daddy's cap to the ground as he spoke the name into the air. Instinctively, I looked toward the trees, half expecting to see Achiel, but nothing was there.

"I have never ever, seen anyone who looked like them...or sounded like them for that matter. When they spoke, it was like they all spoke at once, but only one actually moved his mouth. It was amazing. It was musical with the oddest cadence. It was not like speaking at all, actually." I spoke faster as I relayed the story.

"Their leader, his name was Achiel. He said he had come to walk with us again, to meet with the Simulacrum. He, or they, asked that we meet them in the last light of the next blood moon at the Terebinths of Mamre."

Daddy searched my face as if I held more answers than I did. As if an ancient voice were awakening inside him, he looked like he was trying to remember the Archaon through cobwebs and dust balls. I saw as remembrance entered his eyes, and maybe, just maybe, I saw understanding. He half-whispered, "Long will be the way that fate will lead them. When the days are dark and the nights are darker still. When the giants awake to walk as one, and the door will open wide, the Age of Blood will end, and the Age of Death will arise."

"He said that the Age of the Simulacrum was coming to an end, and the Age of the Friguscor was rising... yes, I'm sure that's what he meant," I said, as the wind whipped around me and sent fresh chills up my spine.

Atticus was quiet and appeared calm. Although he seemed composed, the vibration from his tseeyen told me otherwise. He stayed in that alert position, listening to every word. He did not speak or fidget, but stood as a statue, or maybe as a solider waiting for orders. Daddy looked at me for a long time, and then at Atticus.

"Did you know that this was going to happen? Did you know that the time had come for the Archaon to return? Is this why you are here?" He directed his question solely at Atticus.

Atticus did not speak immediately, but held his mouth in a thin line, contemplating and deliberating. He nodded slightly. "The blood moons have begun. It is what called me here, I believe. Another one comes soon; I can feel it approaching. I did not know that the time had come for the

Simulacrum to meet with the Archaon. I did not know they would come now, but now that they have, I understand more and more at what point I have landed in the River. If the Archaon have awakened, then the birds are circling, and dark days are near."

Atticus's eyes flickered to me and then back to Daddy. "So the words have come to life. The pages are being born," Daddy spoke more to the wind than to us.

"The Council meets in three-days' time. That is the morning before the blood moon rises. I will need to let them know that the Archaon have come and," Daddy looked at Atticus, "I will need you to let the Council know that you have arrived as well. They will have questions, of course."

Atticus inclined his head, "Yes, this is certain."

"Veralee, you know the Histories. The Archaon do not walk with men; they have not walked with men since the very beginning. If they are coming now, then we must be ready." Daddy added.

"Ready for what?" I asked the pregnant question

"I'm not certain. It can't be time for the dark days, it just doesn't seem real." Daddy looked as if he were in the middle of a bad dream and needed to be pinched back to Red Oaks. "But...the Archaon...here...I don't know, Veralee. I just don't know. Regardless," his face looked decided, "we will be ready for whatever is coming." He patted me on the back and then turned toward the house, "Give me some time; I need to read, to see what the Histories say, and I need to talk with Issachar. The Council will begin to arrive in the morning. We will have a plan, don't worry about that." Then he looked out across the oaks while holding the door open, "Do the trees look redder than they did this morning? I think they do ...I must go and speak with Gail."

He shut the screen door and disappeared into the house. I turned to Atticus, still spilling over with excitement, "The Archaon. I remember them from the pictures in the books when I was little. They are not Simulacrum and not Friguscor–they are not human–are they?" I tried to calm myself down, but it felt impossible against the rising mix of excitement and anxiety building inside of me. Atticus moved close enough for me to touch him. He touched my wrist tenderly. Then he tilted his head slightly and peered into my eyes, "Veralee, where were you hurt? Did the Archaon heal you?"

How did he know that? "Yes, on my leg." I pointed to the area on my leg where no less than an hour ago a bleeding gash had been. "I fell, and it was gross; my leg was hurt pretty badly because a branch went through the muscle. Not like a small little twig, it was a big stick. I was dreading having to make it back to the house because I knew it would not heal instantly, not being that deep into the skin. Then suddenly they were just there. I didn't see them come, they were just there. Achiel, he is the one who started talking to me, he asked to heal my leg. He had light in his hand–light! Then I felt that light throughout my entire body... it was...it was like nothing I have ever experienced before."

"I know well what it feels like, and it never leaves you. Once you have been healed by the Archaon, that light stays in you, a part of you, it changes you ever so slightly," Atticus said.

"Yes, but how did you know I had been hurt?" I wondered.

He looked at me, and I saw the wisdom of ages in his eyes. "I can smell it, Veralee. You have the scent of the Archaon on you. I have to tell you that others will know that you have been with the Archaon as well. I have been healed by them so I could feel the light, and almost smell the light on you. If you think about it you can feel and smell it on me now." He stopped talking so that I could try. Yes, I detected that faint scent of rarefied air, like ozone after a lightning strike. Then a familiarity rose between us, once I realized it was there, and I could tell exactly what he was talking about. The warmth in him flamed the warmth in me.

"Yes, yes I can feel it, and I can smell that scent, the scent of them on your skin, ever so faintly." I adopted my best British accent, "Heady like the scent of oak forest in deepest summer, with a slight hint of polished steel and composted earth." A tiny laugh escaped my throat, and then I felt awkward.

"Veralee, this is not a joke. I warn you, others will be able to tell as well, and it might not always be a good thing, a pleasantry for you."

His face hid pain behind it, and worry. He raised his hand to my shoulders, and I could feel his protective need to cover me from an invisible danger. What was he afraid of that I could not see? What does he know that he would not tell me? He squeezed my shoulders once and then forced his hand down by his side in a tight fist.

He broke the spell as he turned to walk toward the swing that looked out over the clearing.

"So, what do you know about the Archaon, about Achiel?" I asked as I followed him to the swing.

"Well, I thought Achiel had decided to sleep until the world had ended, but I guess he is awake now," Atticus laughed and smiled like he was a thousand years away.

"Sleep until the world ends? What does that mean? How long have they been sleeping? Did you know them before? How old *are* they?" I asked.

Like a rubber band he snapped back from his memories quickly and smiled shyly. "No, Achiel has been around for longer than anyone I have ever met. Much longer than I. He is First among the Archaon, first created by Paraclete. Paraclete is their sovereign leader, and if they are coming, then I am certain they come at the bidding of Paraclete and bring his message."

"Yes, he said something about a Paraclete. He said he spoke the words of this Paraclete. What or who is Paraclete?" I asked.

"The leader of the Archaon, he is a part of the Ancient One."

"Okay, that is clear as mud," I answered.

Atticus sat with me as the sun started to slowly descend from the azure October sky. "Sometimes I wonder, Veralee. You said you love the Histories; did you pay attention when you were learning them?"

"The parts I liked," I answered truthfully. "Okay, sometimes I got bored, so I kind of zoned out and started making up my own stories when I should have been paying attention to what Mother was teaching us. But we acted out some great plays that I wrote...Adair was too cool to actually act in our plays, so she did the commercial breaks."

Atticus looked at me with bunched brows and a crooked frown. "What are you talking about, Veralee? Plays? Do you mean theatrical dramas? You wrote dramas during your lessons?" He shook his head in disbelief, "My tutor would never have allowed such frivolity. He would have rapped my hand with his teaching stick, and then make me recite what he had just said until I could do it without mistake."

"Well, Mother didn't use a rapping stick; she used the power of the pen. I had to write an extra report on the subject matter and present it to the ' class' whenever she realized what I was doing," I confessed, "OKAY, so maybe I've written lots of extra reports. I do know about the Archaon, but I am foggy about some of the details—a lot of the details. Will you tell me what you know, please?" I must have looked like I was begging because he said,

"Hmm, I like the way your face looks when you ask so...nicely."

"I'm serious, tell me what you know," I said with an edge.

"There you are. That seems more like you," he said with a laugh, "You are so full of life."

"Have you known many women?" I asked impulsively, ignoring his backhanded compliment, in hopes of digging out more information about him. He smiled with half of his mouth and then rubbed his fist over his lips. He was still laughing inside, I could tell.

"Women?"

I shifted my weight slightly and then pressed on, maybe a little too forward, "Yes."

A smile seemed to be trapped inside of his mouth, literally bursting to get free, because his face looked absolutely frozen with amusement at my question. I didn't know why this was so funny to him.

"Yes, it is a hazard of my long life. To know many women, that is. You see, they are just as common as men happen to be, and so I have met many of them." He was playing with me. I felt like he had just moved his knight towards my queen. I pursed my lips.

"That is *not* what I was asking, and you know it!" I blurted out. Since he refused to take the bait, I would not give him any further satisfaction of hearing me ask about that again. So, I went back to the real subject, "But it doesn't matter. Didn't the Archaon live among us at one time?"

Atticus watched my face for a moment, and then began to retell the stories of old for me.

"The Archaon lived among men, long before my time or before the time of the Friguscor. But the world changed. Men found the Tree of Shadows and, fascinated by its apparent power, lusted to take knowledge for themselves. So they ate the fruit. Thus began the coldness."

"And then the first blood of man was spilled into the earth," I added, to show that I was not a complete idiot on the subject. Atticus nodded, "Yes, that is correct. The Archaon watched with alarm and dismay as this coldness in the heart of man, the Friguscor, spread. The Archaon began to withdraw, as man became more and more unsafe, more and more sick and unstable. They wanted nothing to do with the disease that brought the coldness. They did not want their race to be infected with the poison, and so many decided to leave this world. They simply walked away, leaving this earth to the fate of man."

"They walked away, all of them?" I asked.

"No," he answered, "some left, some...chose a different path entirely, and some stayed. Those who chose to stay watched and observed man's descent into utter depravity. They decided that it was too hard to watch, too grotesque, and so the great and mighty beings just closed their eyes on the world, deciding to sleep until the end arrived. As old as they were, they simply slipped beneath the trees and lived off their root systems like great bears hibernating through the winters."

"Achiel said something about drinking of the roots of the oaks," I remembered.

"Yes, but Paraclete had not given them the order to sleep; it was not their purpose. So he awakened them to help the Friguscor once more. It was the Archaon who led the first twelve to the One Tree during those days of old. At night, the Archaon would infuse the dreams of the twelve with the path to the tree, and by day, the Archaon would watch and guard the pilgrims' progress, silently and unseen. The Archaon hid their presence from the twelve because they had vowed never to walk with man anymore; yet, they stayed true to their given purpose, leading the men to the blood that heals.

I knew about the Archaon from the Histories. I had seen the pictures and read these words a million times, but they felt real for the first time. I looked at Atticus and marveled at how different the world looked today than it had yesterday.

"Atticus, you said they are much older than you are, and you are not from the time when the Archaon walked with men."

"This is truth," Atticus confirmed.

"Tell me about where you came from. About your home. Where did you grow up?" I wanted to know everything behind his stoic face. I had this feeling he only showed me what he wanted me to see. I wanted to see behind that facade. I wanted to see him.

He looked at his feet and swayed back and forth with the motion of the swing.

"Sum Romanus, a Roman citizen in fact, or I was at one time. I am from the time when Rome was supreme power of the world, and there was no country called America, or electric coffee pots."

I laughed freely and smiled, enjoying the relief for a moment. He smiled back, and I felt his warmth spread up my arm. I did not need a mirror to know that my face was betraying me by turning red. And I didn't care.

He turned to me and caught me off guard. He watched the color spread across my cheeks and then, as if stealing something sacred, he looked at me completely and unashamed. *Who are you Atticus?* I did not speak the words, but I was certain he still heard them.

As the past had pierced the present, he seemed to pierce and draw me into his world. I had often laughed that I, as Simulacrum, was a living fairytale to the world of the Friguscor. But here he was, a living fairytale from the book of Simulacrum. The irony was rich. The pages of history that fascinated me were now here, one in my own backyard, on our little swing, a man from our history with flesh on his bones and blood flowing through his veins. With eyes so clear and green, and hands warm to touch, but calloused from battle, he sat beside me. From far ends of time we have come to this one place together. The past had come rushing onto my doorstep, and its name was Atticus.

He did not look away from me but seemed to be answering my unspoken questions with his eyes. "I am Ayindalet,' he seemed to say without speaking. "I am one of those who watch and wait for the doors to open."

The Archaon had come, the Ayindalet sat beside me, and the trees did seem to be redder. He waited for me to put the pieces in the right spots, for the picture in the puzzle to become clear, but I did not have all of the pieces. I could not see it all, though I tried. But I did see him. I did see Atticus.

Something in me begged for his touch, for his strong hands to grasp mine. The same thing that flowed in my veins poured into his and back into mine. Is that what called me to him? Did that push me toward him, despite the fear of tripping and falling all the way into the unknown? Atticus stretched out his hand and tucked my hair behind my ear. My eyes closed as his warmth touched me. The humming vibration from our tseeyens began to burn into the air. I reached up and pulled his face to mine. With our foreheads touching and his arm wrapped around me, we sat and breathed in the scent of each other.

"Veralee, what are you doing to me? I have never met anyone...any woman who..." His words stopped, unsure of the next step on the rocky path in front of us.

"Atticus," the words escaped out of me, "I feel you even when you aren't next to me, I cannot stop what is happening to me, and I don't want to." Atticus closed his eyes and touched my cheek.

"Veralee, I...I do not know if this is the right thing for you or for me. You are filling my mind day and night. But, I do not know when I will..."

I stopped him before he could stop us. "Atticus, I don't care. All I know is that this is stronger than a feeling. It's as if you were meant to come to me before our days even began." I felt desperation in my chest that words could not explain. He pulled back, and I saw sorrow in his face. The lonely sorrow of a man who had spent centuries walking alone.

He pulled his hand back slowly, jammed it into his pocket and looked out to the clearing like the wind or the sun held an answer to his hidden request. I did not move, but sat still, listening to the silence between us that was heavy with words unspoken. He pushed his feet into the dirt, sending the swing a little higher. Time to change the subject.

"Rome," I let the word roll around in my dry mouth, "What did you do in Rome, Atticus? How did you become Ayindalet? Were you born Ayindalet even though you were Boged?"

His hand touched mine, and I felt relief as our marks touched and hummed in unison. He raised his eyebrows a little, and he seemed to be digging into memories like you would dig a quilt out of my Grandmother's hope chest. Then I saw him decide to open up, to speak and to be heard cross his face. Would he let me know who he was?

"Atticus, I want to know you; I want to know all of you." I spoke this revelation under my breath so that only I could hear its truth.

Seeing the expectation in my eyes, he allowed me a little further into his world. "No, I was not born Ayindalet, just like I was not born Simulacrum."

Mother stuck her head out of the kitchen door and called across the garden to us, "Y'all planning on sitting out there through dinner?" We pulled apart quickly.

"Nope, coming right in." I said, my face turning crimson. Atticus laughed and stood up. He offered me his hand. I knew what I wanted, so I took it.

He pulled me up and close to his chest. Then, softly, he lifted my face. My heart beat so wildly I was sure Mother could hear it in the house.

Leaning in close he whispered, "Earlier...you asked, and I wanted to give you an answer. I have been across the seas, through villages and cities across time, and never, ever have I known a woman like you."

I watched his face. He meant it. It was not a fanciful line like Jackson always delivered. Atticus did not know how to be anything but authentic.

"I like this Atticus," I gestured to his heart.

"Oh, do you know another one?" he said with a wry look in his eyes.

"No, I mean I like it when you are like this. When you let your guard down. When you let me really see you. I like when you are not just Atticus, the Ayindalet. It's nice to see you, just Atticus, with no strings of responsibility attached."

Atticus reluctantly pulled away from me, "If only it were that easy, Veralee. I would gladly be the kind of Atticus you would want...if only willing it would make it so." With that, he led me into the house.

{ 13 }

Midnight in Montgomery

My eyes flew open. It was the middle of the night, and the sound jarred me from a deep sleep. I jumped up, toppling out of bed as I attempted to reach the ringing miscreant. A tangle of sheets lay wrapped around my legs as I sat on the floor, heaving from the shock. *Ring, ring, ring.* Disoriented, I grabbed the phone without checking the number.

"Hello?" a small voice said.

"Um, what? Who is this?" I struggled to overcome the fog of sleep.

"Is it you? The girl? The girl who saved me? Vewalee?" said the tiny voice.

It was Nathan! I immediately snapped out of my

grogginess, "Nathan, is that you? Are you all right? What's going on?" Panic rolled over my body at the sound of his voice. Then I *felt* his fear from deep within me.

"It *is* you," said the slight voice, "we need help. You said you would come back," his voice cracked, "but you didn't. Daddy is being mean. He's not being my daddy anymore, he's...." the little voice started to cry, "He's mean, and he's hurting Mommy, and I'm scared."

The dark felt even more disorienting, even heavier as I tried to understand the hoarse voice on the phone. "Nathan, what do you mean? Where is your Daddy now? Where are you?"

"Please come, please. I'm scared. Mommy put me in my room and told Daddy to stay away from me. Then she was screaming."

A million scenarios ran through my mind at once. *Do I call the police?* These people were Friguscor. They were not *my* people, so should I call the police? My heart beat wildly and drummed into my fingertips; my tseeyen burned with adrenaline.

But, Nathan...I had seen the change in him myself. He was no longer Friguscor. I could not involve the police now; it was too late for that. I thought of him there, alone and scared, and I knew what I had to do. "I'm coming, Nathan. Hold tight, I'll be there as fast as I can."

Swiftly, I threw on the pair of jeans that was laying on the desk chair and my warmest hoodie. With my boots and purse in hand, I tiptoed down the hall. In order to avoid the front door, I crept down the servant's hallway and out the back door.

The air outside hung deathly still and humid. I sat on the stoop and pulled on a boot but stopped short when I reached for the second one. My tseeyen vibrated. I looked up, expectantly, toward the ominous tree line. Without seeing him, I knew he was there. A humming sound met me from the blackness. "You're here." I whispered into the night. He stepped out from the tree line at the edge of dark.

"Atticus," I breathed out. He acknowledged me with a nod, but there was no smile on his lips. Faster than I thought possible, he closed the gap between us. We stood silently, listening to the sound of the electricity in our marks. It was like hearing a telephone line pop in the heat of summer.

His voice was hushed and stern as he spoke, "What is wrong, Veralee? I was sleeping when I felt your tseeyen... what has happened to you?"

I couldn't pretend that I understood what was happening between us, but I knew what he was talking about. We could feel each other even when we were apart. It started the very first time we touched our marks together, the day he arrived from the Civil War. It was faint then, vague and cloudy. But with each day it grew stronger, more pronounced, more intense.

"Atticus, it's Nathan... he's in trouble. Something is wrong. He called my phone and said that he had tried to help his father. Now his daddy is trying to hurt his mother and possibly him as well. I don't know what is going on, but I have to go to him."

He whispered frantically, "Veralee, do not be rash; you do not know what has occurred."

"Atticus, this is all my fault. I can't leave that boy alone and terrified with no one to help him, regardless of what has occurred." I straightened my back and my mind at once. "I will not leave him alone when I am the one who did this to him. Besides, if I don't go, then who will?"

He made a sort of groan and then turned quickly back toward the tree line. *He's leaving. Fine... I can do this by myself.* My temper began to rise.

I turned toward my car and started, heatedly, across the yard. Before I took five steps, he was behind me again. Wordlessly, he followed me to the car. Relief flooded me, but I did not turn around to show him my appreciation because time was ticking for Nathan.

"So you decided to come after all?" I said quietly.

"I decided that when I left the comfort of my bed *and* my good sense to follow a girl into the unknown in the middle of the night," he said, matter-of-factly and without a trace of humor in his voice. I eyed him sideways, just in time to see the hint of a resignation twitch across his stoic face.

We pushed my car down the drive in neutral, taking care not to wake the sleeping house. The guardian oaks that lined the road to the Big House seemed to watch us with knowing eyes as we passed. With the tap of the key we were off, reeling toward the complete unknown that waited for us in Montgomery. As I drove, Atticus asked me to repeat every part of the conversation with Nathan. He pored over the details to make sure he understood what was happening as much as he could.

"What do you think the boy meant when he said that he had tried to help his father?"

"Atticus I have no idea; he's a little boy. That could mean anything." We paused at a red light, and then pushed on toward whatever was waiting for us.

"Yes, it could mean anything, but what if it means he has tried to *change* his father?" Atticus mused.

No. That would not be possible. He is only six years old. How could he do that? I could not say those words out loud, but Atticus read my face.

"Veralee, he *is* a small boy, but he is now a Simulacrum boy, who sees clearly. He no longer has the clouded vision of the Friguscor. From what you have told me, he understands that you saved his life and changed him by giving him your blood. He can also see that his family is different from him. So do you not think that a small boy would want to give that to his family?"

The clock ticked as I turned right. This possibility had never entered my mind. Surely, Atticus was giving Nathan too much credit. There is no way he would have figured that out. I chewed on my lower lip as I thought. Atticus watched me, and then looked out to the road.

"Veralee, have you ever seen a Friguscor who has tasted the Eiani?" his voice was so flat and void of emotion that I looked at him to make sure it was him who was speaking.

"No," I breathed into the night.

"I hope that you never do," he said icily. Was he angry or was that something else in his voice? He clenched his hands several times, showing the rippling muscles that wrapped around his strong arms.

"Atticus, when have you seen them?"

He didn't look at me, but watched the night pass by out the window. He was quiet, and I thought he would not speak again, but when he did speak, he seemed like he had aged a hundred years in just a few seconds.

"I have seen them more times than I would like to count. First, in Rome. That was a madness that still haunts my dreams." He thought for a minute. "Maybe I have seen too many things during this life, too many hard things."

He looked down at his hands. I wanted to touch them, to feel their calloused palms. What had it been like for this man who had walked most of his life alone? No family, no one to sit with at dinner, or to hold while swinging on the back porch, and no one to share his secrets. No one to write to or call when he was lost in a different country or a different time, no one to care for, no one to love him.

I reached over and put my hand in his. He closed his hands around mine, and his touch was enough to settle my nerves. I wanted to tell him that he would not be alone anymore, that he was safe with me, that he could stay here, with me, but the truth was that I couldn't promise any of that. He was Ayindalet. The reality of that made my lower lip shake. He had just arrived here in this time, in this place; he had just walked into my life. And he had no control over how long he would stay; soon he could leave me.

"We're here," I said, pulling down the lonely road to the house. Toys lay strewn across the jungle of a yard. It looked disheveled, unkempt. Had it been in such disarray the last time I was here? Maybe I had been too excited to notice that day? Something was definitely wrong. The anxiety in my racing heart was quickly replaced with the fear of what waited inside the foreboding house. Inside, a single light cast an eerie halo across the cluttered yard like a solar monument in a dark graveyard. "Here we go," I said to Atticus as we started toward the door.

Rap, rap, rap. I half expected the door to swing open like a jack-in-a-box, but it didn't. Nothing happened. Atticus knocked this time, louder and harder, but no one came to the door. I looked at Atticus for direction. He cased the house with his eyes. I waited, but when nothing happened, I tried the door.

"I have not driven to Montgomery in the middle of the night to stand on the doorstep of a house like a little girl with my knees knocking," I said, more to myself than to Atticus. With one twist, the door swung open. Atticus looked at me with a raised eyebrow, but did not reprimand me. Taking it as permission to proceed, I stepped inside, ignoring the warning from my tseeyen.

The house lay quiet and still, like everyone was sleeping. The only sign of life was the solitary lamp that shone feebly on a table in front of the picture window. Atticus was so close behind me that I could feel his warmth through my shirt.

"Hello, gurrrl," sneered a murky voice from the shadows behind me.

I pivoted, feeling unnerved, as I did when we would swim in Clyde Jones' wash hole as a child. The waters of the river were dark and swirling, and I never knew what lay beneath; cottonmouth moccasins were always a possibility.

There, in his worn, green recliner, sat Nathan's father. As my eyes acclimated to the dim light, I surveyed the man who sat within earshot of the door, but had not answered when we knocked. He sat as though the chair were charged with electricity; he could barely keep his body still. I noticed that he gripped the armrest so tightly that the material slowly ripped under his fingers. His eyes were red with hemorrhages, his filthy hair matted, and his skin had a morbid, grey pallor. Despite the chill of night, beads of sweat dripped down his nose and neck, but he did not bother to wipe them away. Something was very, very wrong.

"Where's Nathan, and where is his mother?" I demanded.

He cackled a sick, disgusting sound, full of mucus. "They are here, you filthy trash. I haven't finished them off...yet." It was clearly a threat. He spit a wad of bloody mucus onto the carpet.

I instinctively backed up a step from his venomous spray, hoping to find the strength of Atticus's arms, but to my surprise, he was not there. I did not want to alert the man to my panic, so I stood tall and looked him square in the face as he spewed his malicious tirade.

"You thought I wouldn't figure it out. You thought you were so very clever," he cackled again, then spit directly onto the carpet and slammed his fist into the chair. "You had me at first, you did. But it didn't take long for me to see what you had done to my boy. You *changed* him; he is no longer my boy, but some kind of freak you created. Then I knew *you* had to be some kind of mutant freak," he snorted and stopped briefly to wipe his nose on his sleeve.

He narrowed his eyes at me and cocked his head slightly, "Yeah, freak. That's what you are. Maybe you're not even human. Maybe you're some kind of freakin' alien or something. And you changed my boy into one. Both of you. Her, too. All of you...mutants!"

He wound himself tighter and tighter around his anger. "Now his skin is like yours. Freak's clothing, I call it. And then there's the smell; I couldn't sleep from the smell of that kid. It stunk up the whole house, every bit of it, every day. The sickening, sweet smell...it filled my every thought, too. It was all I could think about the moment I came into the house each night after work. The *smell* of him."

His mouth glistened with drool, and he glared at me as if he could kill me with his madness alone. Blood shone on his teeth and lips. I stood my ground, trying to listen for anyone else in the house as he spoke. I heard a low whimpering sound, and I knew it must be Nathan. I could feel him in the house. He was here, and he was alive. The man lit a cigarette and sucked on it deeply, licking his cracked, bloody lips. My stomach churned.

"Where is Nathan?" I asked again, looking the man in his terrifying eyes. *And where is Atticus?*

"Shut up! I'll tell you what I want you to know when I want you to know it. You're just like my little wifey was, always trying to change the subject, always got something to say," he whined. "That little freak did something to my wife, and then she got really sick. Just like Nathan. I thought she was going to die. I didn't know what was happening to her. But then, about three days later, she got up out of bed, and she looked just like my boy, like a circus freak herself. And the smell, the smell was always there. It's like she *wanted* me to taste it. Like she was tempting me with her smell. So I did. I thought I was going crazy at first. The thought of drinking her blood, of tasting it, made me feel sick at first, but the more I smelled her, the more I thought about it. Well, the better it sounded, ya know?" He smiled briefly at the memory, "That blood was like the best drug I've ever had–and I tried plenty of them in my earlier days."

I interrupted his mad rant, "You drank your wife's blood?" I felt sick.

"Don't look at me like *I* am the freak here; *you* are the one who did this!" He pointed his finger and shouted, "Don't you forget that! *You* did this to us. And yes, I drank her blood, been drinking it for days. She wouldn't have kept letting me if she didn't want me to. But then tonight, I..." He faltered for a second and his lips quivered as a tear fell down his cheek. With trembling hands he touched his face, and then looked at the tear on his finger as if it belonged to someone else. He shook his head and his eyes went black with rage, "Well, she'll recover. That whore always does."

He swayed in his chair, as sweat ran down his face. He coughed, making a high-pitched whooping sound, and then spit a wad of phlegm onto the carpet. Wiping his face, he rested his head on his hands.

"Are you okay? You look sick," I said, more calmly than I felt.

The man jerked his head up and glowered at me, "I've got some virus or something. It's been making me feel sick as a dog. I've been using Tylenol and that stuff for flu, but nothing is helping... and I'm always so thirsty." He sounded almost sane for a moment, like we were chatting at the pharmacy about the common cold.

I felt pity for him, like I would a rabid dog with a broken leg. Even though I might feel bad for the unfortunate animal, I would not get close enough to touch it. The man started licking his lips vigorously and watching me like a lion watches his prey. He started rubbing the arms of the chair repeatedly, and he positioned himself like he was ready to jump at any moment.

"I'm not going to stay long, I just wanted to check on Nathan, so if you will let me see him, then I—"

The man jerked up from his chair, snarling, "I've been waiting for you, girl. I knew if I let that little mutant call, then you'd come running. My wife, she was sweet, but *you*..." He swallowed hard and let his mouth hang open, "Your scent has haunted me since the day you came here. Over the past couple of days, I couldn't get it out of my head," He started moving slowly toward me.

"Oh, I'm going to enjoy *you*, my little freak. I'm going to drain you dry. You're so...pretty," he laughed darkly as the tip of his tongue darted out and around his lips, "maybe I will enjoy the rest of you after. Or maybe I can enjoy everything at the same time. You'd like that, wouldn't you?" His chest started to heave, and he unbuckled his belt.

"Don't you touch me!" I growled with broken glass in my voice. I took a step backward, mentally gauging the distance to the door. "Don't. Touch. Me."

He smiled with a sinister twist to his bloody mouth, "Good, good. I knew you'd have fight in ya. I like that." He crouched like a tiger and let out an inhuman growl as he lunged toward me.

He was faster than I had anticipated. I stumbled backwards and fell into a bookshelf filled with faded family photos. His full body slammed against me, and we fell down onto the brown, ash-filled carpet. His rough tongue licked up the side of my face, while his hand dug hard into my scalp, pulling my head back and exposing my neck. He pushed his mouth onto mine and dug his sandpaper tongue inside. My teeth felt like they would break under the force.

Instinctively, I threw my hands up to cover my face and kicked with all my might, but before my foot could make contact, he was gone. Just as fast as he had hit me, his weight was lifted from my body. His body flew across the room, landing hard against his chair, and then slid down to the floor. With a broken jerk and a ragged swift motion, he was up, much faster than I had ever seen a Friguscor move. He looked mad, like a starving rat trying to fight its way out of a bag. That's when I saw Atticus. He did not say a word, but stood in a fighting stance, ready to take on the deranged man.

Nathan's father growled, bile draining from the sides of his mouth. "You piece of shit...I'm gonna kill you," he barked in a low, malicious voice.

"Do not touch her," Atticus said with murder in his voice. He passed a long dagger between his hands. The animal-like man put his head down and emitted a deep, ugly laugh. Slowly, he raised his eyes to meet Atticus. He cracked his neck to each side and smiled, revealing a black film that covered his gums.

"Oh, that's where you're wrong boy; I'm gonna touch her in ways you can't even dream of, and that whore will enjoy it." He launched himself across the room with one goal: to kill me. In mid-air the man stopped suddenly. His eyes rolled back into his head. He fell forward onto his knees and the front of his shirt pooled with blood. Atticus lurched forward and used his foot to slam the blade deeper into the man's back. In one seamless motion, Atticus had plunged the knife through the man's back before he could touch me. The man did not fight back, or even move again. Instantly, he landed in a heap.

*What just happened...he couldn't be...*I couldn't think.

Atticus stood over the man and pulled the long dagger quickly from the body, wiped the blood on the man's shirt, and re-sheathed the dagger into a crisscrossed leather holster that lay hidden beneath his flannel shirt.

My stomach lurched, and I felt like I would be sick. I sat on the brown carpet and covered my mouth with both hands trying to muffle the sound of my screams that rose in waves with the nausea.

"He's....what did you do? Where...that knife? What...what have you done?"

Atticus kicked at the man's lifeless body and then turned to me, his hands dripping with fresh blood. "Veralee, listen now. That man would have killed you." He didn't come close to me but gave me space. "Veralee, I do not want you to be afraid. But you have to get up. You have to focus on the mission. Get the boy, Veralee. Be afraid later, but do not allow it to immobilize you now."

I couldn't move. I sat wide-eyed, trembling on the floor. What had just happened? Just a few hours ago I was in my bed at Red Oaks. I was safe at home....and now...I felt hysteria rising again. Then I heard a distant voice, the voice of Agatha Dupree in the bookstore from what felt like a lifetime ago; *Do not be afraid; fear will cause you to be unmalleable and unusable. Trust him when he comes, for he is already a part of you."*

"Get the boy, Veralee," Atticus said loudly, like a commander to a soldier, "Go. Now. You will find him in the back bedroom. Get the boy and bring him here, but *do not* go into the other room. Do now what I tell you. Now!" Atticus spoke directly into my face. *Trust him when he comes, for he is already a part of you.* His hands were red with blood, but he was the man from my dreams. The man who protected me from the darkness of my dreams. I was meant to trust him. I would trust him. Still shaking, I stood like a toddler just learning to walk and forced myself down the hallway.

The door to the back bedroom stood ajar, but the light was off. I saw Nathan lying face down at the end of the bed with both hands tied to the bedpost. He cried softly. Seeing him like that pulled my fraying edges together. He was scared and hurt. I pulled at the bandanas wrapped around his wrists. The smell of urine permeated the room, and I noticed that Nathan's fingernails were filthy. He began to sob when he saw me. His little frame fit perfectly in my arms as I lifted him from his soiled sheets. I wanted to sit and rock and cry with him, but we had to move, or I would never get up again. *I will do this; I will not fall apart now.*

"Vewalee, you came....my daddy, he hurt my mommy. Where's my mommy?" The boy looked as terrified as I felt. My fingers trembled.

"It's okay, Nathan, you're safe. I'm here. I'm here."

Was any of that true? I took the boy and pressed his newly marked arm onto my tseeyen. His was a simple design that resembled a circular clock of some kind. He relaxed instantly and stopped whimpering as the peace of the Simulacrum flowed into him. With Nathan wrapped in my arms, I pushed myself back down the hallway. Atticus stood in the living room, keeping a noticeable distance between us. Space for my fear to work itself out.

"We have to leave now. Get to your car. Put the boy in the back seat," he commanded.

"What? We can't leave. Where's his mother?" I protested.

The look from Atticus sunk any hope of finding her alive. I forced myself to swallow the groaning scream that was racing up my throat. *No, no, no, it can't be.* This can't be happening. I held on tight to the quivering boy and started toward the car. Then something stopped me. I turned halfway so that the boy faced the car and I faced Atticus. I was about to get in the car with someone I hardly knew, who had just killed a man.

"What are we going to do, Atticus?" I said frantically, "We can't call the police. These people are Friguscor...Friguscor, Atticus. And they are dead. Two people are dead!" I was losing any semblance of self-control. "Do you know what this could do to us? Atticus...this could expose us all. My family...what have I done?" I started to sob and hyperventilate, and Nathan in response began to cry harder.

Then a cold realization spread over me, numbing my thoughts: "He is chipped, Atticus. In his arm, he has a chip and they will be able to see my cell phone number in it. The police will know he called my phone. Oh, Atticus, they will know! They will know!"

"Where is this chip that they can follow?" Atticus said, confused.

"In their arms, Atticus, they have computer chips in their right arms," I said, frantically.

Atticus raised a hand to comfort me, but instinctively I flinched away from him. He did not try to touch me again.

"Veralee," his voice was low and extremely even, "Veralee, you have to control your breathing. Focus on the boy in your arms. He is a child, and he needs you to be an adult right now. Look at his face. The boy needs you, Veralee. Focus on the boy until you can control yourself."

I wanted to scream at him. How...what had just happened? I wanted to put Nathan down and run hard from the dirty house of horrors and never, ever look back. I looked down into the terrified little face, and I knew that I could not run away. I knew that I could not leave the small boy who was whimpering in my arms. And I knew, on some level, that even though I was terrified myself, I could not leave Atticus either.

I looked straight at him and found some grit within. "Are you... *safe*, Atticus? Am *I* safe with you?" My teeth chattered, and my hands shook around Nathan. My knees felt like they might give way at any moment.

The man in front of me had executed a man just like an actor in a Delta Force movie. My throat went dry, and I had no plan for what to do next. But I had to know, I had to ask him. Atticus gave me a steady look, which held no trace of a lie.

"Safe?" He looked at me long and hard like he was exposing his soul to mine,

"I am for *you*, Veralee. I am always safe.... for you. You have no reason to fear me, ever. But I will do whatever it takes to keep *you* safe, no matter the price. For the cost of safety is paid in blood."

I nodded, not fully knowing what his words meant, but feeling somewhat better. That was what I needed, something in me knew this, but I needed to hear it from his lips. My teeth chattered like I was lost in a snowstorm. My head told me that I should run from him, that he was a trained killer who had shown up only days ago, but I also knew that he was Simulacrum, and even now I could feel his tseeyen singing into my body. This was all that held me together, the thin hope of him. Besides, it was too late to run from him. I had known for months that something was coming, and I had raced through the trees of Red Oaks trying to outrun it. I thought of the dreams that had plagued my nights. Running in the dark from the unknown fear that chased me. Now I was here, standing at the beginning, and there was nowhere left to run.

Nathan slumped into the back seat as I buckled his seatbelt. My car door screeched loudly in the still night air as I climbed into the driver's seat. Atticus snatched opened the passenger door, and I jumped like a gun had gone off. He carefully slid into the seat. "We need to leave now. Do you think you can drive the car?" Atticus spoke like a counselor to an agitated mental patient who held a thin line on reality.

The sound of the engine starting seemed loud enough to wake the entire city. I reached for the steering wheel, but ended up grabbing the door handle instead. Holding my hair in one hand, I vomited all over the curb. When I shut the door, I jumped again, as Nathan cried out for his mother. My hands shook almost uncontrollably. Atticus's hands stayed calm. Without saying a word, he moved to the backseat and held the boy in his arms. Then he gave the order, "Drive, Veralee. We must leave *now*."

Focusing on the road as best as I could, I drove slowly, making sure I obeyed every traffic law. All of the training Daddy had drilled into my brain growing up started to kick-in. If you ever find yourself in trouble, stay off of the smart-highways, keep to the rural roads where they cannot track you, he had said. I was in more trouble now than I had ever been in. Fighting down the panic, I focused on the road. Incoherent words escaped my mouth before I could process them, "I thought... I thought... I wasn't—"

Atticus, a steady voice in the dark, spoke from the back seat, "What Veralee? You didn't think that this would happen?"

My lips trembled, "No. Yes. No. I thought that I would have been..." the memory of the man overtaking me so quickly chilled my words. Daddy had trained me to protect myself; he had trained me for this. "I thought," a rush of words, raw energy, verbal fear flowed out of me; "I thought I would be stronger. I thought I could fight back if someone ever tried to hurt me... I couldn't. I was too weak... I was weak."

"There is no way to know how anyone will react in battle....until the first blow is struck. Grown men become boys and boys become men. You stood your ground, Veralee, and you're alive. You're alive. That is all that matters when blood is spilled."

When blood is spilled.

Nathan fell asleep in an exhausted heap in the backseat with Atticus. We rode silently as I cried. Atticus sat so quietly that I had to keep checking the rearview mirror to make sure he had not disappeared. Two hours later we pulled up to the south cottage at Red Oaks. And somehow, just being home made the events of the night feel farther away as morning was breaking open across the tree line.

We sat motionless in the car. Every scene from the night colored my vision. The dirty house, the dingy light, the monster of a man, and Atticus...Atticus had killed that man. My legs had stopped shaking, but my hands still trembled. I caught Atticus's eye in the mirror. He watched me closely.

"Who *are* you?" I said between clenched teeth. Atticus did not reply. "I just saw you..." I gathered my voice and nerves together, "I saw you...you *killed* a man tonight, Atticus...like it was nothing. Like it was *easy!*" I stopped, forcing myself to calm down.

"I could not let him hurt you, Veralee. You know he was going to kill you–and the boy," Atticus said, without a quiver of doubt in his voice. "Then, he would have tried to kill me as well."

He could not let him hurt me. Atticus was right. That man would have killed me. I had seen it in his eyes when he attacked, the look of a wild animal ready to kill his prey. A shudder ran down my spine as I saw a new side. Atticus had *saved* me. He had risked his life to save mine and Nathan's.

Atticus continued, "I saw the man when we entered

the house, and I knew then what he was. I have seen the Friguscor who have turned after tasting the Eiani in our blood. They become monsters, and there is only one way to deal with a monster like that."

"When have you seen it before? When you were in Rome? Who *are* you?! You owe me the whole story; I need to know who you are." My voice was still stern, but softened with each word.

He turned toward me, "You want to know everything? I have been trying to tell you."

I stopped him. "You have been telling me bits and pieces as you gauge how much I can handle, like I am a small child, incapable of comprehending. I'm *done* with that; I'm *done* with not knowing. After what I just saw...after..." I stumbled over my words, "I want to know the whole thing. Who are you? Where did you come from? What *are* you, Atticus?"

He looked away into the night and said, "Sum Romanus. I am Roman."

"You already told me that!" I screamed, hitting the steering wheel with both hands.

He shot me a look like I was testing the last of his patience, and started again, "You must be quiet and allow me to tell you."

I was exhausted, completely undone, and I was talking without any filter. He was right. "Tell me your story, tell me the whole story, Atticus; have you killed someone before?"

He looked at me sadly. "Many times," he replied.

Silence spoke for us both.

"Where do you want me to start, Veralee?" His voice was so calm, so quiet that it felt like balm to my broken heart. I wiped at the tears that spilled down my face.

"Just start at the beginning, isn't that where all stories begin?"

{ 14 }

Home Sweet Rome

"I was a Roman soldier serving on assignment when my life changed, or should I say, moved forward. Time can be so confusing when there is no ending.

My father, Titus Lucius Amemilius, was a career Roman soldier. The Empire granted him land outside of Rome, as a reward for his loyal service. I lived with my mother and two younger sisters on this country estate, a large grain farm, outside Rome. My father was often away, fighting the Gauls in Germania, but even when he was not at war, he tended to stay at the dwelling he kept in Rome. My mother and I managed the estate in his absence, and business was good. Augustus had begun paying people with grain, and Rome needed more grain as the population grew.

We kept over 100 slaves between the two houses, and we stayed mostly in the country. Mother was not exactly a wise woman, but she was constant and kind. She loved us, but she had not seemed to have grown past the age of a child herself. Her name was Nereida, after the sea nymphs who lived under Neptune's protection. Like her namesake, she seemed to need protection and never came up from her world long enough to be considered a real part of the world of men. I was her first born, a capable boy, and by the age of five I would hold her hand and lead her to the market. She never could grasp the concept of money, so Pallos, the head house-slave and my tutor, taught me to count denarii so that I could keep Mother from being swindled.

High born and beautiful, my mother had attracted many suitors. Being born to a noble family had saved her from a much harder life, and her parents knew a good marriage could insulate her from life's cruelties. So, her parents had kept her childlike behavior hidden from my father until after their marriage. Later, my father hid her as well. Though I think he cared for her, he was too Roman to be proud of her.

I rarely saw my father during my childhood, but when I did, he was often drunk and angry. A lifetime of warfare had hardened a brutal shell over the once youthful man. He may have been a brilliant commander and successful soldier, but he never mastered the roles of husband and father. When I had fourteen years, he retired from the Army, having finished ten campaigns with the infantry. Lacking a clear enemy to fight, he focused on the details that came with running a prosperous farm as if he were still subduing an unruly people. He never focused on me for too long, except to correct me with his whipping tongue and heavy hand. Consequently, I spent most of that year in the city with Pallos while my father lived in the country with Mother and my sisters. My sisters, Varinia and Julia, were too young for me to be bothered with; I do not remember much about them anymore.

We were Friguscor, but now I assume we were descendants of Boged. A trace of the blood still lingered in our veins, which must have accounted for my father's great military career and my ability to learn quickly. I had waited for years to join the Army like my father, so the day I reached my fifteenth year, my father arranged for me to join the Legion. Every boy who joined the Army dreamt of the glory and riches that it would bring, but I wanted more. More than anything, I wanted to prove to my father that I could be a better soldier than he was. During those days, Augustus decided when and where the Roman Army would go to war, and then the gates of the temple of Janus would be flung open and remain open until Rome was at peace again. The gates were almost always open.

The Roman Army existed to keep the Pax Romana, the peace of Rome. Rome made it her mission to bring "peace," but I soon realized that she really just laid waste to lands and subjugated people and called it "peace." Still, we were the most powerful empire in the world, and very few conquered peoples raised their heads to oppose us. So, as long as Rome ruled with an iron hand, there was peace of a sort.

A couple of weeks after I reached my fifteenth year, the red flag of war had been hoisted above Rome. I stood with a group of Roman men and swore the oath, the sacramentum. The sacramentum sealed us as Roman soldiers; it was this oath that bound us to Rome and clinked the iron around our wrists. I quickly learned that it had the power to control a man and to move us to actions we never thought possible. When you serve with men in those close quarters, with your hands and your life, it changes who you have been into what you are becoming.

We left our white tunics on the steps and picked up the blood red tunic of the legionnaire. I had no idea how symbolic that red tunic was. I could not have known what Rome was capable of through the hands of ordinary men. Never had I thought about the realities of war beyond the dreams of glory I had as a boy. I faced a hard awakening, like a storm crashing over the sea.

Once I took the oath, I had a few days to go home and prepare to leave. Before we left for training, most wanted another night with their wives or children, but I was ready to go. I despised the days at home, and I watched for the sun to set each day, anxious to leave that part of my life behind me.

My mother cried when I told her it was time for me to go, but quickly forgot her grief when I gave her a shiny new coral necklace. When I placed it in her hands, she smiled and clapped her hands like the child that she was. I only vaguely remember her face now; I just remember her black hair and the smell of jasmine that always hung like a halo around her head. I bent to kiss her coarse hair and to feel the warmth of her cheek one more time, feeling sorry that I would not be there to walk her to the market, which she so loved. But I knew I did not have any need to stay.

With my father home I no longer had a place in that house. He made it clear it was time for me to prove myself to him and to Rome. My father spoke to me the night before and told me to make Rome proud, to remember my oath and to come home stronger than I left. If I were not to return, it would be even better, because that would mean I had died for Rome. Standing in his study, dressed in the white tunic of a Roman citizen, he railed against the barbarians that threatened the civil life of Rome.

' If it comes to it, die well, Atticus. Do not humiliate my name by begging or pleading, so that I can be proud of you.' That was the last thing the man named Titus ever said to me. He did not show up the morning I left. I guess I did not expect him to. Why would a stranger come to see me off?

Pallos stood where my father should have, in the atrium of the house, and held his old, thin arms out to me. A slave had become, over the years, the most loving person in my life. It pained me to leave him. It was uncommon for a master to embrace a slave, but Pallos was no longer a slave to me. Throwing my arms around him, I embraced Pallos, and he placed his old lips to my ear.

' Atticus, remember the blood that runs in your veins; it alone will guide you forward.' His words confused me. He had never spoken to me of my Roman blood, and I knew he had never valued it. He was a highly educated Greek before he was captured as a slave, so he had no love for Rome. I realized later that he was Simulacrum, and he was not speaking of my Roman blood that day, but of the traces of Simulacrum blood that still lay dormant in my veins.

As I walked out the door, my mother grabbed my hand, still wearing the coral necklace I had given her. She looked at me and, for a moment, I gazed into the eyes of an intelligent adult instead of the woman-child I had known all my life. Her hand opened and inside I saw a small clay statue of Vesta, to whom my mother prayed daily.

She hoarsely whispered to me, ' Remember us, Atticus. I am afraid you will not return to us, my sweet boy. That you will somehow be swept away by the sea-nymphs into their watery down-under.' She blinked slowly but held my gaze. Then she spoke in a commanding voice, one I had never heard before, ' Serve the oath faithfully, and do not draw back, even when you are weary or unsure. You must run with the horsemen and soar with the eagles until you reach the end, my sweet Atticus. The end will come when the River spits you out.' Her odd words left me frozen in place, but just as quickly as it had come, her lucid moment vanished. "Atticus, do bring me another beautiful necklace when you come next. I love them so.' She stood on her tiptoes, touched my hair and kissed my face. Then she turned and walked away into her gardens where she could play for hours. It was the last time I ever saw her, the last time I ever saw any of them.

I lived in a garrison north of Rome for several months learning hand-to-hand combat and other skills. I do not miss the days of marching 20 and 24 mille. That would be like 19 to 22 of your miles, carrying a fifty-pound pack on my back, but I do miss the men with whom I served. I made a good friend in Decimus. He was older than I, but he had been raised in a manner not much different than my own. We trained side by side and shared a tent at night. He was not only a good companion, but he was better than I was at most everything we did. Decimus could run faster, hit harder, block stronger and kill quicker than most men. His father, a soldier as well, had spent years training his son and had created a machine. My inability to match his strength and resolve triggered a need in me, so I stuck by him, willing myself to find it within me to be the soldier that Decimus was. I think in some ways he also reminded me of Pallos, the only thing I missed of home. He spent hours with me every night, hitting his sword against mine, teaching me and creating the machine within me. It was a gradual process, because I was not built for war then. My arms were weak and my legs would buckle with exhaustion, but Decimus would not stop. Then one day, I matched his arm and his speed.

We moved up quickly in training and made a name for ourselves among the soldiers when we marched north to fight. Battle soon became a drug that I craved more with each passing day. We fought the barbarians in the North, who had refused to accept the rule of Rome. The mixture of excitement and terror made it irresistible to a young boy raised in the Roman way. Not only was war better than I thought it would be, so was I, with the help of Decimus. We never fought alone, but developed a sixth-sense of each other and worked in concert through enemy lines like a two-headed wolf. The other soldiers called us the ' Hellhounds of Hades.'

But even in my accomplishments, I quickly found that there was no place for me to stand where my father's shadow did not eclipse the sun. Everywhere I went I heard stories of my father, and all that I did was attributed to being his son. This began to eat me alive with bitterness, so I set my resolve against going anywhere that Titus had been in battle. After months of training and then the campaigns in the north, I made a decision. I did not want to see Germania, or the edges of the earth in Asia, for my father had spoken often of these places. I wanted to go as far from him as possible. So when I discovered that my unit was headed to Britannia, another place my father had been, I had to act quickly. With Decimus by my side, I went before our commander and requested a transfer. Looking back, it never occurred to me to go without Decimus; he had become closer than a brother. He had saved my life more times than I could count, and I in turn had covered his.

The commander, Flagus, was not an unreasonable man and was greatly pleased with Decimus and me. Our success under his command had brought him much-needed good attention, and he was being transferred to where he had lived as a child before coming to Rome. He was my way out. So, just days before we were to leave, Decimus and I learned that we would be accompanying Flagus to Syria to join up with the Legion there.

About twenty-five of us started east by boat. I was never a sailor, so the first days on the ship were rough. I spent days and nights on the deck, breathing in the salt air and avoiding the masses below. Then, in the middle of our wretched journey, a storm nearly claimed all of us for Neptune. It blew us off course, and we had to stop in Alexandria for repairs and supplies.

Afterwards, we boarded a ship to Jerusalem. From there we planned to cut across to Mesopotamia. One night as the ship floated through unusually calm waters, I awakened. I felt something near where we slept. I stared into the darkness, but saw nothing. The only light came from the stars, and the darkness seemed to roll in like a carpet over my eyes. Then something moved, and I sat straight up and grabbed my sword. A slow, grating sound drew closer to where Decimus lay across from me. Then she was there, right beside me. A beautiful young girl with hair as black as the night that surrounded us. I could just make out the form of her lips and the arch of her cheekbones, but something was terribly wrong with this girl.

I heard her lick her lips several times, and then her rasping, desperate voice spoke, ' I could smell him all the way from down under. I have smelled him for weeks, but I could not find him. Until now.' She started to put her hands on Decimus and greedily sucked in the air around him.

' Woman, go back to your place, you are not needed here.' Thinking she had come to sell herself in the night, I dismissed her quickly. She was only a young girl, not much younger than I was. She flipped her head toward me and let out a low growl, and then bared her teeth at me. I could see the whites of her teeth even in the darkness. I froze, uncomprehending the animal that stood before me. I had never seen a woman, even of low-breeding, or a barbarian, resemble a wild animal before. In the split second that I stood frozen, she dipped her head too quickly for me to stop her and sunk her teeth into the flesh of Decimus' thigh. When I heard his roar of pain, I sprang to action and came down hard across the girl's back with my sword. She screamed, her face covered in blood, her voice an inhuman growl through bloody teeth as she felt the blade and stood to meet the challenge. I jumped over Decimus and drove the blade through her chest, through her heart. Decimus clenched his teeth and held his bleeding thigh.

' Atticus, did you kill her?''

'Yes, here wrap your leg with this,' I ripped off some of my blanket and handed it to him.

'Good,' said Decimus. I sat down, quickly out of breath from the moment's adrenaline rush. My bloody sword rested between my legs. The bite must have been deep because it bled like a fatal wound. It had to hurt badly, but Decimus never even moaned. He worked quickly to wrap his leg, but the blood soaked his blanket by now.

I had smelled a lot of blood over the years, even blood from Decimus. Most blood had a rusty, metallic odor mixed with the faint scent of sulphur. But Decimus' blood was different, and that night... I smelled it completely. The scent still had a metallic quality, but overall it was pleasant and slightly sweet, like the honey the slaves took from hives on our farm. Something was different that night on the boat. For a moment that scent of honeyed blood drifted down into my taste buds. My mouth began to water, and my lips quivered with thirst. My throat felt parched. Something in me snapped, and a ravenous hunger rose in me. I wanted to taste the blood on the blanket.

Decimus watched me carefully and must have seen the danger in my face, for just as I reached for the blanket, he threw it over the side of the ship. We stared at each other, motionless, as the ocean lapped gently against the side of the boat.

'Atticus, you need to get rid of the girl,' he said gravely. With the scent of his blood gone the fog receded, and I became myself again. With little effort I picked the lifeless body up and tossed it into the darkness.

'What was that thing?' said Felix, who slept beside Decimus. Neither Decimus nor I answered. Felix started to laugh hard, though he tried to cover the sound, 'Decimus, you fool, I told you not to let the turpis lupae please you. She was trying to earn her money off of you and ended up almost un-manning you with her teeth.' His laughter seemed out of place.

'Go to sleep, you idiot,' said Decimus, repositioning his hurt leg.

I sat with my back against the side of the boat, wondering what had just happened. I had heard that you could go mad on long voyages. Were the gods playing games with me? I crossed my arms over my chest and closed my eyes tightly. I had wanted to taste Decimus' blood. *Blood.* I was no animal, like the filthy woman I had just killed. The hunger had passed, but something in me had changed, had shifted somehow, and I felt its caged power lying silently inside of me. I began licking my lips. The scent still lingered somewhere in my memory, and I sought to enjoy it again as I drifted back to sleep that night.

I awoke to Decimus standing over me with a huge piece of bread. He tossed it at me. 'Wake up, we are getting off of this horrible sea monster today.' The sun already shone brightly in the sky. I pulled myself back into a sitting position against the deck while Decimus plopped down loudly beside me. He always made sure I had enough to eat, and I always made sure that he was up and in formation on time.

Was it a dream? I wondered. I saw no bandage on his leg and no blood on his thigh. I pulled my sword from under my blanket and saw the dried blood caked across its blade.

'Listen up,' said Flagus. The long trip had not been kind to him, and he looked older than when our journey had begun. We still had a long way to go. 'Because of the terrible weather Neptune bestowed on us, we are heading into a wretched city. I have documents to deliver here, so we will stay a few days while I make arrangements for us to head north. Don't get into any trouble and keep your heads down, the bottom feeders are talking about some kind of rebellion in the city.' He spit onto the deck and walked toward the edge of the boat to relieve himself.

'Where exactly are we landing?' asked Felix. We all looked to Flagus, curious.

'Joppa, then onto Jerusalem, the filthy city,' he said, with obvious contempt in his voice. Flagus had served once before, in Judea. Though the land was beautiful near the Mare Nostrum, the Judeans had a reputation for being stubborn and difficult, and most Romans dreaded an assignment there.

When we landed at the port of Joppa, no one came to tie us off. The captain was furious as his crew worked to secure the ship. As we unloaded, we noticed an eerie silence that sat over the city. We tried to recall if it was Caesar's birthday, or another one of his festivities. We wondered, where were all of the people? It was mid-morning and people should have been busy working the boats. Our horses barely had their land legs when we drove them hard towards Jerusalem.

Late that afternoon we arrived in Jerusalem, so our commander decided we would go directly to the prefect, Pon-

the Oaks Remain

tius Pilate. Flagus carried letters from Sejanus, who, at that time was essentially ruling in Rome while Tiberius retired to a life of leisure on Capri. Jerusalem was as desolate as Joppa. We passed through the gate and into the city without seeing a single person. The gust of wind blew up suddenly, and we drew our swords, fearing a bad omen. We started walking slower, more cautiously, our swords at the ready around every empty corner. Houses stood left opened, vegetables sat free for the taking at the markets, and animals roamed freely. I stopped at a stand and stuffed my face with dates. We were half-starved from being on the ship for so long, and the food sat baking in the sun. An old man walked into the street where we were stood.

' Sir, is it a celebration day? Where has everyone gathered?' Flagus asked. The man did not answer. ' Answer me, you filth. Where has everyone gone?' He rolled his eyes as he motioned for Felix and Decimus to take the man down. They started toward him when I noticed that something was wrong with the man. All of a sudden, his body twisted, and he put his nose up, sniffing the air like my hunting dogs did when they picked up the scent of their prey. The filthy man emitted the same low growl that rose into a primal scream, as the girl the night before. The sound was piercing, and I fought the urge to cover my ears while he screamed. His mouth was black, and his eyes were red. He set his shoulders and ran straight toward Decimus. Felix stepped in quickly and cut the man down with one blow.

' What is happening here?' asked Felix. Suddenly, the silence erupted into violent sound, as though the earth were birthing dragons. Screams of terror, high-pitched yelling, deep growls, howling, and strident voices mixed with the pounding of feet, the unmistakable cracking of bones, and the thudding of falling bodies. These were the sounds of war. We raced toward the unknown with swords drawn and hands braced for battle.

We crashed into the multitude before the smell hit our noses and throats. The foul odors of rotting garbage, sweat and feces were overwhelming. People were everywhere, bloodied and growling. In the midst of the city where people usually gathered for announcements or festivals, people paced like beasts waiting to eat. Blood dripped from their mouths and was smeared across their faces, down their bodies, and into their hair. Dazed children screamed and walked aimlessly. Some of the frenzied were completely naked, while others wore only shreds of fabric. Bodies of men, women, children, and even babies lay mutilated and trampled into the dirt.

I noticed a man sitting on a naked carcass, as if he were waiting for something.

' What in the name of Pluto and Hades has happened here?' I demanded of him. The skinny, middle-aged, man had yellow, leathery skin that was stretched much too tightly around his protruding bones. He licked his white, flaking lips and let his tongue hang out too far. His eyes darted back and forth from me to the door, revealing an unsettling wildness in him.

' We are waiting for more. They will only give us a certain amount a day, and so we are waiting for the doors to open,' he said, crazed.

' Waiting for more what?' I said without dropping my

sword.

The man looked at my sword and nonchalantly said, ' For more of them. They will only give us so many a day, and there are many of us here; we are starving.' My face must have shown my question, for the man continued. ' For more of *them*, the ones that taste of honey. We are waiting to eat, and if you want any I recommend getting closer to the doors. When they throw them out it starts a frenzy, and they will suck those bodies dry before most of us can get anything at all.' He stopped and looked at me then. ' You are a Roman, have you brought us something to eat?'

I stepped back extending my sword, 'No, I am a soldier; I am not here to bring you food.'

Flagus spoke, looking for clarification, ' You people are waiting for the doors to open so that—'

Just then the palace doors opened. Armed soldiers led a group of fifteen or twenty people into the square like cattle to the slaughterhouse. The masses began to yelp loudly, like hyenas circling a herd of antelope. Some in the crowd held boards with exposed nails, some brandished stones, and others bared long, jagged nails. A few, who looked as if they had once been soldiers, carried old weapons, short swords and an occasional bow. We drew our swords to keep the crowd at bay, turned quickly, and retreated toward the iron gates.

Then it began.

The hordes descended upon the men, women and children who stood helplessly in the middle of the square. As they attacked, it became obvious that their objective was blood. The unarmed overwhelmed their victims, so that five or ten fell on a hapless person and began biting him all over and drinking the blood. Those with weapons drew blood as quickly as they could and then gorged on the flow. Some of the stronger ones literally tore the victims to pieces and ran off with limbs or torsos, like mad dog with pieces of meat. They dropped to all fours like rabid animals, sank their teeth into the flesh and drank. Any blood that fell to the ground was instantly attacked. Bones broke and flesh tore. Even in the most brutal battle, I had never seen anything so sickening…or terrifying. I tore my eyes away from the scene and turned to our commander.

    ' Sir, we have to get out of here, we must leave the city. This is a …sickness, some kind of disease that is spreading.'

    His tired eyes were alive with fear. ' I have to get the letters to Pilate. Those are my orders,' he said. Roman to the end.

    Felix broke in, "What is that smell? It smells wonderful! Like fresh honeycombs."

    'The smell of human feces? That smells wonderful to you?' Decimus asked incredulously.

    Decimus turned to Flagus, ' If we stay here, we will be killed." Decimus remained in battle-ready position, ' If you do not give us the order, you sentence us to death.' He was out of line to speak to the commander in that tone, and the others froze as I positioned myself between Decimus and the commander. But, a fight between Flagus and Decimus was the least of our concerns, for a small number of the animal-people had begun darting back and forth around Decimus.

The commander ignored Decimus's insubordination, since he had also noticed the danger rising around us. 'Take half the men, Atticus, and get them outside the city. If we can find horses, we will have a better chance to get back to our ship. I will take the other half and deliver the letters, and then meet you outside the eastern city gate.' He pointed, 'It's in that direction. Get to the wall and follow it to the gate. We might be unnoticed by traveling in smaller groups. Felix, you are with me.'

Ten of us made our way through the maze of streets as fast as we could travel. The fear that rose in our throats was choked out each time we encountered another twisted woman or man, and we were forced into action. They flew at us quickly, but were no match for our steel. Our ignorance of the city complicated our mission, so we headed in the direction the commander had indicated. Once we found the wall, we desperately began to follow it, hoping to find a gate of freedom from this hellish nightmare. The winding streets made it difficult to stay in a fighting formation, and we were forced to spread ourselves thin. A group of men followed us like dogs nipping at our heels. We would take one out, but two more would take his place. They came faster than we could fight, and we were quickly fighting for our lives in the street. They came at our swords with their hands and teeth, but their numbers eventually overwhelmed us. When one of us would fall they would set their teeth on him, only to release him quickly, then speed their attack toward us, as if they wanted something other than the body they already had.

As we fought our way against a wall, Decimus yelled, 'Atticus, the gate has been left open.' I saw that our escape laid less than 100 paces away.

'Decimus, we move on tres: unus, duo...tres! '" I yelled and charged forward with Decimus. The remaining men fought us in a circular position. We moved together until one of the monsters broke through and raked Decimus' right arm open with a board fixed with nails. A jagged nail hung from his arm as blood poured from his body. That tantalizing smell of honey wafted between us, and then it was as if a volcano exploded in the middle of the street. The inhuman screams from the monsters exploded through my head like a battering ram. The screeching came moments before the frenzied madness tore from their throats and limbs. We stood only 50 paces from the gate, but I saw that some of the monsters had reached the gate tower and were closing the massive doors. Those on the street lunged at Decimus. We created a barrier with our bodies and our swords, but they would not be stopped. Like starving lions surrounding a mortally-injured buck, they launched themselves repeatedly at us, and at Decimus. One after another broke through to tear at Decimus with whatever weapons they could find, before we dispatched them into the bowels of Hades. Others dropped and licked at the blood-stained sand where Decimus had passed. Bruised and bleeding, Decimus limped toward the gate, fighting hard the whole way. The mighty doors were closing. Time was running out.

Then, just as the heavy doors swung closed, we slipped through the gate and landed hard on the dirt outside the city. The four other survivors got to their feet and ran as fast as they could. I kneeled before Decimus, who was gravely wounded. They had been tearing at him the entire time, ripping and clawing into his head, arms, legs, and body. He bled profusely. His face had begun to swell, and blood dripped into his eyes. The wind swirled around us, and I smelled the sweet honey of his blood.

"Atticus," he swallowed hard, "I need you to do something for me." The doors to the gate bulged, and I jumped back with surprise. They were coming, they were opening the gate.

"I'll carry you, Decimus." I looked frantically for a place to hide, but there was nowhere to go. I knew I would have to carry him, but we would not make it.

"No. Atticus, I was to bring you this far and I have. Go across the valley and up that hill until you reach the top of the mountain. Run as hard and fast as you can; do not stop until you see the words that form a man. The words, that's how I found him. They swirled around and around until they took a human form and then—"

The door began to move. "No, I will not leave you here, Decimus." I stared down at the only friend I had ever had, a man who had saved my life, taught me to fight and wanted nothing from me except for me to be his friend. The memories burned my eyes, and I wiped away the weakness that was closing in around my heart. "I can carry you," I said defeated. I knew even as I said it that I was lying.

"You are hurt, Atticus. Look at your leg. You never even noticed you have an arrow sticking out of your thigh."

Decimus tried to laugh but started to wheeze heavily. "Atticus, remember: find the man of words. Now, come close to me and say goodbye, my friend, so that I can give you a piece of life." I leaned down on one knee and kissed his forehead. Then he grabbed me with all of his might and buried my face into his wounded shoulder as hard as he could. His blood gushed into my mouth before I could pull back. As soon as the blood touched my lips the animal in me took over, and I grabbed his arm and drank deeply of the honey in his veins. He did not fight or struggle, but lay still as I drained life from his body.

    Decimus rallied as he heard the doors giving against the push from the other side. He ordered weakly,"Go NOW, Atticus, my....brother. Remember the man...of...words... Find...him."

    Then the doors gaped open, and the monsters began clawing their way out. I jerked my head up like a dog and growled. Even a dog knows that he cannot beat wolves, and so I left him there, lying in the dirt alone, to be eaten by the monsters.

I ran until I could go no farther, until the burning broke my gait, and I slammed into the red earth. There, in the heat of the sun, I writhed in pain and tore at the earth as the blood slowly burned away the death within my body. The sun baked me from outside while the blood scourged me within. The depth of misery was immeasurable, the pain unspeakable, the agony unrelenting, and I lay helpless as a newborn in its birth blood. I thought I was dying.

    But it was just the opposite. The Eiani cleansed, refreshed, and rejuvenated me. In order to heal, it first had to burn away the dead, consume the decay, and then force new life where death had once resided. I jerked from side to side as the blood made its way through my body like acid, burning away the decay inside me. The stench was overwhelming, and even in my semi-conscious state, I was overcome by waves of nausea as the odor of scalded flesh seeped from my body. No wild animal came to claim me, and no one passed by as I screamed for death to come. There is no healing without the pain, no change without the suffering, none that would last for eternity, at least. The flames slowly subsided and the burning became manageable. The fire lingered for months inside me as the blood continued to heal what had been destroyed, but it became a pain that I learned to welcome, because it meant that I was, for the first time in my life, fully alive.

When my eyes finally opened, I did not know where I was or what day it was. I lay still, trying to remember. I sat up and looked for Decimus. Where was he? Then, I remembered, and the pain felt like a new blade going through my chest. I cried like a child bereft of its mother. But then, I noticed my hands. Slowly, I examined them...they were my hands, but they were not my hands! These hands were full with color, they were warm and felt soft instead of dry and cracked. I stood up. Amazing, what energy I felt! Then I stumbled backward as I realized how much I could see! The world seemed like a new place as the sounds of every animal and tree reached my ears and the colors of creation blinded my eyes. I thought, *had I never heard before? Had I never seen before this moment?* Then as if he were standing beside me, I heard Decimus' words, "Run, until you get to the top of the mountain, where you will find the words that form a man."

Filthy from the dirt on the outside, but seared with new life on the inside, I broke into a run and found that I had the speed of eagles. I laughed out loud. "So this is how you did it, my old friend," I screamed into the sky, wanting Decimus to hear me as the earth flew beneath my feet.

The mountain seemed to mock me as I ran, because it grew taller with every step I took. The wind ripped at my body, and I had nothing to block its powerful gusts from my bones. The temperature dropped as I struggled upward, but the warmth in my body rose with the effort of my exertion in defiance of the cold. I was determined to gain ground and conquer this obstacle; I would not let it stop me now. Then, as I saw the pinnacle within reach, I ran between two strangely paired trees. As I passed between them, the skyline ripped open like a frayed seam. I fell through the hole in the air, but instead of falling to my death, I found myself instantly in another place. One moment I was running up a mountain in Judea, and the next, I felt soft grass beneath me and giant trees surrounding me. I stopped, inhaled the scent of fresh wood, and tried to steady myself. I remember thinking that I must be going mad. This was not Jerusalem or Judea! So I stretched my arm toward the obvious mirage, and to my surprise, my hand touched real bark on one of the massive trees. They were more than real–they were alive–and I could feel an energy and dynamism within their bark that I could neither understand nor define.

I did not know where I was or how I got there. The sound of shuffling feet interrupted my confusion. I looked up to see many men and women walking serenely, but determinedly, through the trees, all heading in the same direction.

Instinctively, I slipped behind a trunk for protection and peered around it cautiously. The people continued; they did not even seem to notice me. Even those within arms' length flowed past me like water spilling down a stream.

Was this the way? I knew it must be. I joined the procession, and we walked silently through the deep woods together. The trees were larger than anything I had ever seen before. The white trunks seemed to glimmer, lighting the forest with a soft glow like a full summer moon. Yellow, green and red leaves floated down from the sky like autumn snowflakes. Then we came to the largest tree. A tunnel was cut in the middle of its massive trunk, large enough for fifty men to march through at a time. As I entered I heard cracking and groaning, like the knees of an elderly giant as he stood to stretch. I was amazed to realize that the tree was still growing. The roof and sides of the passage displayed such intricate and beautiful motifs that I knew a human hand could not have crafted them. It was not carved, nor painted nor burned. It was if the artist has breathed onto the wood, warming and liquefying it so that he could press and shape, swirl and brush it, like oil on canvas. I stopped to run my fingers across the side of one wall, and it was burnished more smoothly than the finest silk robe of a daughter of Caesar.

The size of the tree astounded me, and I shivered in awe of it. The pathway was larger than any room I had ever seen. Only in nature had I seen such vastness, in the plains that stretched over the edge of the earth, the mountains that punctured the canopy of the skies, or the seas that swallowed up the horizon. *Where was I*, I wondered.

As I came to the end of the path within the tree, I

heard water before I saw it. A solid, roaring flume of water cascaded over the exit of the tunnel, like a waterfall over the mouth of a mountain cave. The men and women did not pause, but walked straight into the torrent and disappeared from my sight. *Into what* I wondered. I had been at the top of a mountain before I found myself in this forest. Would I step off the side of a mountain, into a free fall, into nothingness? Did the cataract feed a deep pool, or a treacherous river? I could not see to the other side, and there was no way to know. Clenching my teeth to brace myself, I pushed into the silvery-blue deluge. Unlike most of my men, I knew how to swim, so that did not make me fear. But not knowing what lay on the other side did turn my stomach upside down as I felt the water hit my face.

I thought again of Decimus. I would not dishonor his memory by giving up, I would see this to the end, and so I stepped forward. But the ground did not give way under my feet, and I had no need of my swimming skills. As I walked through this water, I felt it wash the filth of my years at battle, the scars of my childhood, the horror of the death of Decimus and my men; all of it, all that was dirty, it washed away from me. Cleanliness was not a high priority for a soldier. So the feeling of being clean, the smoothness of my new skin, and the warmth in my hands were invigorating. I felt as polished as a newly smelted sword that had never pierced armor, one without chink or flaw. I felt new, my calloused hands were smoother. I looked at my arms and felt my face; the deep scars from Germania and Jerusalem were still there, but now they were lighter, gentler somehow. It was like I was someone or something that I had never in my dreams thought of being. I asked myself again, *what is this place? How can these things be?*

    Then I remembered the blood, the blood that Decimus carried in his body and shared with me. These changes were not possible; this was not something I had done for myself. It was not my hands that had caused such change, but the blood that had worked upon my broken body. I pondered, *what tonic was this blood? What wondrous properties must it hold?*

    I had heard stories of Hebe's Fons Juventute, the water of youth, which gave you skin better than a newborn babe, warmer than the sun, and stronger than that of a bull. Hebe was the daughter of Zeus and the Goddess of youth. When she bathed in a pool she left some of her very essence behind. If you were fortunate enough to come upon these waters, and submerged yourself in them, you would be invigorated and rejuvenated, made new, like I was. But those were stories, told by old priestesses who preyed upon the masses. "Stories from crazy women who tricked you out of your coins," I muttered to myself. And yet, I looked back at the water, which poured down the back of the tree obscuring the path, and wondered, *was it the water?* On each side of the waterfall, two massive stone warriors stood guard. Slowly the last of the people emerged through the water and walked quickly forward. *Could this be it?* I turned my hands over and back again, like an answer would somehow appear. Then I looked around. I wore a white tunic, not the red cloak of a Roman soldier. Was I with the gods now? I laughed at myself and thought Decimus would have laughed if he could see me.

    "Atticus, you have arrived," a deep, musical voice floated through the trees and found me in the moving crowd. I searched for the source, and then I saw him, standing across the crystal pond under the cover of the heavy trees. At first I thought he was a large carving of Apollo, he was so perfect in shape and build. But this was no stone statue that stood before me. He was the most alive, the most vibrant being I had ever seen. "We have been waiting for you, Atticus," the words echoed into my mind.

"You know my name? How...who are you?" I stuttered.

"I am Achiel of the Archaon," the being said, without blinking, without moving and without words. "Atticus, we are glad to see that you have made the long journey. After traveling for so many months, your feet must be weary." Achiel somehow poured the words into my mind. I wondered, *how am I hearing him?* He was not speaking out loud. But, somehow, it seemed right, here in this strange place. The old language rolled easily off of my tongue, and I marveled at it as I spoke.

"Months? It has only been a few days." But was that right? No, days did not seem to summarize the time that had passed. Time was different here, like it was made of something flexible instead of iron.

"We will see to it that your needs are met soon, but first, you have been Called. Will you come?" Achiel spoke with me for hours then, or maybe just minutes or maybe days as we walked deeper into the Sacred Woods. He told me about the One Tree, the Tree of Shadows and the twelve Primogenes. Suddenly, so much of my world made sense. The wars I had seen, the desperate lives of the Friguscor, and the ever-present hunger that was so deeply a part of me that I had never known life without it. But now, more than being clean, more than the healing effect of the blood, was the absence of the hunger. It was an odd thing, to suddenly be separated from something so formative to my existence, and yet until now I did not even realize it had existed in me.

My thoughts brought me to the edge of a river. Not until my feet hit the ice-cold water did I realize my surroundings and that I was now alone. Achiel was gone.

Standing on a cliff, I watched the mighty river as it flowed through a deeply carved riverbed. The water moved like none I had ever seen. It was as if this river was not water at all. Instead, this river was smooth and metallic, like lava, and it moved more like liquid silver or melted rock.

Suddenly, the small rocks around my feet began to quiver. A thick mist came plunging down the riverbed like a stampede of horses, and the ground shook under its weight. As it advanced, fierce lightning flashed from its center, and thunderous booming shook the rocks on the cliff where I stood and threatened to topple me. I sunk down onto one knee to keep my balance as the rolling storm surrounded me, filling every space. The river was hidden, though I could still make out the rushing sound of movement.

"Atticus," out from the fog came my name. "Atticus," a still, small voice called to me, but from where...I did not know. Maybe it was from the storm, but still, I saw nothing. The fog was too thick. "Atticus," the voice called a third time. A pale light lingered at first in the distance, but grew stronger, penetrating the fog, advancing toward me. Despite my training, I was almost overcome by fear, but I forced it down and steeled myself to meet this unknown.

Trembling, I answered, "I am Atticus. What do you want of me?"

Then in the edges of the fog I saw a form. A silhouette of a man, but not a man at all. I tried to focus my eyes on the form, but it never solidified, never stopped moving. It was always in motion, as if a tangible body could not contain this being.

"Fear not, Atticus. The things that were, the things that are, all you have known is passed away. You are now Simulacrum. Grafted back to the image through the blood of the Eiani. You are made new. Now, you are Called. Now, you are Chosen."

I felt his words sear my heart and mind like a permanent mark of identification. I could feel the force of the storm in them. They were like a warhorse with a bridle, tremendous power completely controlled by the rider. *Simulacrum?* Who was this being? As I strained to see, the words from the man floated in the air and were more physical than he was. It was the words that concealed him from the eye. He was surrounded by them, swirling, turning, and coiling around him. *It was him! The Man of Words! The man Decimus had told me to find!*

The Man of Words continued, "Just like this River, the world you know has a beginning and a completion. You will travel this River to its completion...and to the completion of the world as well."

the Oaks Remain

Somehow I found my voice, which sounded impotent against his, "The River? You want me to travel down this River? And at the end of it, I will find the end of the world?"

"You, Atticus, are Called. You are a Chosen One. You will travel down the River, moving with it through what is, watching and listening until the full completion of time comes. As you travel, watch for the Door, the way to what will be. You will point them to The Door. You must watch and at the time of completion, you must lead them to the Door. Will you go?"

The words birthed something in me, forming a life of their own. They soothed my panic, and the soldier in me began to listen as one receiving orders for a mission. I longed to hear his voice again. But, the voice grew fainter, the man made of words was leaving. But the words he spoke were not leaving with him. The words became seeds that burrowed into the fertile brown soil. They sprouted small leaves and grew at an impossible pace, before my eyes, they became small trees. The small trees bolted into oaks. Jumping back, I just missed a mighty oak shooting up from the ground, unfolding its branches, and narrowly missing my head. All of the oaks in this forest had come from this man. It was his words that brought forth life.

I wondered, *what was this man who was not a man at all? How could a man be made of words? How could his words have such power?* I could not really see him through the fog. Panic rose again, and I called out, "I will lead them? I ...I cannot do this thing." I managed to stutter, "I have only just changed. I do not know the Door. I do not know the way! I do not know the ways of the Simulacrum! I do not know anything! How can you ask me to show anyone the way when I do not know the way myself?"

The kind, but firm voice pierced the fog, "You are Ayindalet, a Chosen One. Watch for the Door, and lead them through it. They will depend on you. Do not fear. Be strong and take courage. You will be given that which you need. Will you go?" As he asked a second time, I felt the words "strong" and "courage" sprout in my chest. Within me a tree of purpose, planted by his words took root, and I knew then that I would not be moved.

Simulacrum, I was *Simulacrum*. Yes, it made sense. Pallos must have been, too. That was why he had been so kind to me and why I had felt so loved when I was with him. Decimus had given his life to bring me here. He had sacrificed himself. I knew the Man of Words was asking if I would do for others what Decimus and Pallos had done for me. Could I lead others? I was a soldier, and soldiers take orders. *But he had given me a choice.*

The voice came again. "This journey, this path down the River, it will cost you much, Atticus. The life of the Ayindalet is one of sacrifice. I warn you, because you did not hate bloodshed, blood and bloodshed shall pursue you even through the path I have prepared for you. You will show them the way to the Door. Soon, the Door will appear, and you will know. You will carry the key within you. By your blood, the way will open, bringing them to the One Door." A third time he asked, "Will you go?"

"I am a soldier; I know well the cost of such missions," I said boldly.

"Yes, but do you know the cost of a life fully sacrificed?" The nebulous form leaned closer through the fog, and I saw the man within him. I could not bear to look directly at him. I was afraid, for in him was something dangerous, something unpredictable and unknown. Life and death were in his words, in his being. I knew a mere breath would consume me like a lightning bolt from the angriest sky. It was confusing, and yet, it was right somehow.

I lowered my eyes quickly as he answered, "No, you do not know fully, Atticus, but you will. Do not fear what is coming, you have been created for this life."

In that moment I fell to my knees, "I give you my sword, and I swear to you that I will give you my life as well."

"Receive that which you need," he breathed out, and I felt an eddy of wind wrap me before it rushed inside my lungs. He touched me, and the brilliant light pierced the very core of me as he locked the key inside my blood.

"Watch for the Door, Atticus, and lead them to its gates," he instructed me one last time.

"But...how do I know what it looks like? I don't even know what the One Door will look like...how will I find it?" My words echoed across the River, for the storm was receding, and I was alone among the new grove of trees. Trees grown from words of life.

My mother's strange parting words came to my mind, "*Serve the oath faithfully and do not draw back, even when you are weary or unsure. You must run with the horsemen and soar with the eagles until you reach the end, my sweet Atticus.*

The end will come when the River spits you out."

And then I leaped off the cliff, and into time."

{ 15 }

the Council Arrives

From the edge of the ballroom at Red Oaks, the light of a thousand candles shimmers on the Venetian chandeliers suspended around the room. I hold a fan fashioned of overlapping silver and gold feathers. I open it and watch the feathers spread, like a bird taking flight. The room smells of sweet pastries and cakes. Crystal balls tied with purple ribbons hang from a giant canopy of branches at the center of the ceiling. Black metal crows fashioned from clock parts circle underneath the skylight with slow, mechanical movements. One lands on my arm. I watch its eye tick open and close and then fly away.

My intricately detailed dress hangs heavy. Its elaborate design of golden tree roots twist across my bosom and wind around my naval. The back of my dress is dangerously low, much lower than Mother would typically allow. I step slowly towards women in exquisite gowns. They all wear hats, some with feathers and clock-pieces folded between free-flowing fabric, some with veils, and others with iron from old bird cages on them. I have no hat, just a dress of gold. Layers of golden chiffon and silk bustle under my lower back, creating a waterfall of illumination as I move under the candlelight.

Glasses clink, and the dulcimer strains of violins weave through the rhythm of conversation. Gowns of every color and suits of black and white swirl together on the dance floor. I watch, mesmerized, as women bend and float across the floor to the demand of meter and fortes.

The dance stops. The people split down the middle, and I see Mother standing at the front of the ballroom. Her royal blue gown fits like a second-skin. The high neckline accentuates her long, slender neck. She looks regal with her corset tied stiffly around her middle and her tall hat draping sequined netting over her eyes.

I want to touch her, to feel the material of her bustled gown. I reach for her, but my hand collides with something hard. Cautiously, I glide my hand out in front of me. A clear, glistening wall stands before me — like a giant pane of glass — blocking my way. I walk quickly, all the way to the edge of the room, but find no passage. My heart begins to beat faster. The glass separates me from the rest of the room. Suddenly, the edge of the ballroom where I have been standing feels small and tight.

I bang on the wall. Mother would get me out of this. But the violins crescendo and the cello strums harder. "Mother!" The music drowns my screams. I bang again and again on my glass prison. "Mother, I can't get out!" She turns without noticing me. She laughs and drinks champagne. I slide down the glass wall as the panic sets in. Why can't she hear me? Why am I separated from her? Tears roll down my face and soak my dress. I open my blurred eyes and see the stains on the once golden gown.

My gown was gold. Now, it is a dull brown; the brown of old tree roots. I hear it before I see it. The dress cracks and stiffens. Long roots grow from the material and reach for the ground. No one hears my screams. I struggle to stand, but the gown is growing and grasping the ground too tightly. I am forced to my knees again. I grab at anything, but nothing but the slick glass wall surrounds me. The roots turn and suddenly stop. They have anchored in the ground beneath me, and hold me fast in their wooden grasp. I cannot move. I am a prisoner now.

"Mother," I cry, in desperation and grief, but she is gone. They are all gone. The ballroom is gone. I am alone, surrounded by the unyielding roots in the ghostly light of the moon.

"Help me!" I scream into the night air. "Someone, anyone! Help me!" I begin to cry as the roots tighten around my legs and climb up my torso. I gasp as the roots choke my chest and dig into the skin on my neck. Panic rises in my throat. I am going to die.

Suddenly Nathan stands before me.

"Nathan, go and get help! Hurry! I try to swallow, but I gag and cough instead. "Please, Nathan, I'm going to die..."

Nathan walks past me. He stops and turns slightly in my direction, "You cannot change the roots of a tree, Veralee, so why do you fight what is so deeply rooted in you?"

I spent most of the night in the front seat of my car, listening to the story of Atticus's life. Just over an hour ago, I had collapsed onto my pillow, but now the sun demanded the start of the day. I needed more sleep. Daddy stuck his head into my room, "The Council arrives today. We have to get up and at it." He closed the door with a thud.

My eyes felt heavy. The dream from last night had robbed me of the little sleep I might have had. Little Nathan's voice echoed in my head, *"Why do you fight what is so deeply rooted in you?"*

I ached all over. I was not sure if my body really hurt, or if it was the mental exhaustion that plagued my bones. Moving slowly, I stood and stretched my back. The trees on my wall caught my eye. Something in the mural looked different. I rubbed at my eyes and tried to focus. The roots of the trees seemed more pronounced than they were yesterday, and the trees seemed to be closer this morning, like they had advanced in the night. What seemed so distant yesterday seemed close enough to touch today. Reaching up, I touched the painted trees. If everything changed in my world, I found great peace in knowing at least the oaks would remain.

Suddenly, I thought of Nathan and hoped he was still sleeping at the cottage with Atticus. *Would Atticus know what to feed a six year old?* He was a soldier, but he must have been around children at some point in his life. I chewed on my fingernails while I stood in front of the bathroom mirror, not seeing my reflection, but only the thoughts flashing before my eyes. I would be expected at coffee this morning. My body protested, but I showered and dressed quickly. I checked the mirror once more. I looked bad. The scene from last night played before me. Atticus had killed a man. Nathan was here at Red Oaks. I had lost control of the situation. I knew what I had to do. I couldn't keep this secret anymore; I had to tell Daddy. As I walked slowly to the kitchen, I tried to convince myself that everything would feel better with a warm cup of coffee in my hand.

"Have you even been to school this week, kiddo?" said PH as he walked a bag of trash out the back door of the kitchen. I made a face at his back. School was the least of my problems right now. "I'm going to go...besides fall break is coming up...and then I can just hang out here all day long and watch you do all the work."

"We will have company in a little over an hour, Veralee," Mother reminded me while hugging my neck.

"Mmmm, it feels so good to be near you." I grasped her tightly and buried my head into her shoulder for a moment, feeling the comfort of her embrace. After last night's events, I rocked on an ocean of disbelief and shock. Holding Mother made the wind stop blowing long enough for me to find some calm. I was home with the people that I loved, and they would help me. We would find a way to make this right. Simulacrum were never alone, *I* was not alone. That age-old truth pounded through the fear and confusion that sat like rocks on my chest. Mother tried to pull away but I clung to her. When I released her, she pulled my face up with her hand on my chin and looked into my eyes.

"What is it, Veelee?" she asked, searching for a trace of what plagued me.

I said nothing, sure that I would cry if I started talking. I hated to cry in front of others, but Mother had a way of pulling the tears out of me. Shaking my head, I moved toward the coffee. She stood quietly for a moment, watching me with hawk eyes, as the kitchen filled with Ausley, Adair, PH and Mattie. The morning chatter began, but Mother continued to watch me from across the room. She sighed and gave me a smile that did not disguise her searching eyes.

I poured my coffee without speaking, testing my self-control. Slowly the emotions receded to a manageable state.

"All right, it's another big day. Do we know when they will begin to arrive?" PH said as he shoved an entire piece of buttered toast into his mouth in one disgusting bite.

My face screwed in disgust.

"What?" he said in exaggerated response so that pieces of bread spit out of his mouth.

Adair looked at me and at PH and then said, "Gross, Phineas. Seriously, try to eat like a human being, and not like a wild animal."

He laughed and coughed so loudly that I spilled some of my coffee onto my sleeve. "This is why you three needed a brother growing up. You are so, so....girly about everything. I'm a hungry man, and I eat like a hungry man, he said, as he shoved the second of many piled-up pieces of bread into his mouth without chewing. PH was obviously enjoying himself, aggravating us on purpose... just like brothers sometimes did.

"You eat like a pig," Ausley said, equally disgusted.

PH turned to her and opened his full mouth wide, "See food..." he said.

"Oh, you are a pig! Gross!" Ausley complained and slapped his arm playfully.

"Papa's a funny piggy," said Mattie as she clapped her hands wildly. Adair took a wet dishcloth and rubbed it all over PH's face to clean it. We all dissolved into a fit of laughter. It felt good to laugh with them.

"They should be here in an hour or so," Adair said, as she gave Mattie a high-five for her one-liner.

"Who?" said the pig with the bread.

"The Council, that's what you asked about, isn't it? Come on now, keep up, pig-man," answered Ausley.

There were twelve Council members, one representative from each faction within the Simulacrum. Four of those Council members, plus their family members, and many other Simulacrum would be arriving over the next two days. The rest of the Council and the Simulacrum would meet us in the Terebinths of Mamre. I was so excited to say "us". Council meetings, which occurred once every seven years, were open to all Simulacrum who were sixteen and older. Ausley was 18, and I was 19, so we would be attending for the first time. Adair had been sixteen at the last meeting; this would be her second time to attend.

Mother and Daddy had always updated us girls on decisions the Council made, but I had always longed to attend. I wanted to see and hear everything for myself. Even though I understood the rule of minimum age to attend a Council meeting, what happened in the Terebinths of Mamre seemed like a mystery that had been kept from me for far too long.

We had been told the Terebinths of Mamre was the most beautiful land ever created. It was a place that was not visited by anyone in this world, except for once every seven years. Yet, it was the destination for Simulacrum when our years were completed in this world. There, they lived in the great Alabaster City until *the Door* opened.

Though I knew every path, every crevice of the land at Red Oaks, I did not know the way to the Terebinths of Mamre, which lay somewhere deep within the forest. I had always been fascinated with finding the location of the Gateway, even as a child. Still to this day, when I was out running through the trees of Red Oaks I found myself wondering, was this it...or was this it, with each place I passed. That secret was for Council members alone.

The Histories said that an original Terebinth grew in twelve locations around this world. Though they each had separate and distinct forms, they all originated from one root system, interconnecting them below the earth. The roots of the Mamre Oaks were the first to develop from the roots of the One Tree and the Tree of Shadows.

The Histories also said that the Terebinths of Mamre were born in the first days of time in order to bring about the end of time. No one seemed to know exactly what those words meant, but they stuck to my mouth like peanut butter every time I read them. They sounded like ancient words that had been sewn into my bones. I knew they held an answer, but I just didn't know the question.

While the family laughed in the kitchen I slipped down the hallway with my warm coffee cup in hand. I tiptoed by the study. *Maybe he's not there.*

"Veralee, is that you?" Daddy called from his study. A bouquet of antique guns lay across his desk. He seemed to be getting ready for target practice. Maybe this was not the time to talk to him.

"Yep, it's me," I said, cautiously edging my way into the library. I knew I should tell him, but I was afraid. I had broken so many rules; I had made the biggest mistake of my life. Keeping secrets had not helped me at all so far. *What if I had asked for help after the incident in Montgomery the first time?*

I gathered my courage and spoke up, "Daddy I...I need to talk to you." My voice sounded smaller than I meant it to, so I made myself stand up a little taller.

His eyes were captive to the Berretta M9 pistol in front of him as he stood gathering ammunition into his dark olive shooting jacket. "Well, perfect timing. I was hoping you would take a walk with me and give your trigger finger some exercise before everyone arrives." I had grown up shooting with Daddy.

Living in the country brought lethal dangers of rattlesnakes, feral boars, and water moccasins. Old Mr. Davis had been found dead in his soybean field a few years ago, gored and trampled by what must have been a huge wild boar hog. Daddy made sure we knew how to use a gun safely. We often had barbeque made from the wild hogs that had been destroying his cotton and peanuts or roast venison when he needed to cull the deer herd so that the fawns wouldn't starve. I had bagged several deer and wild turkeys, but I couldn't say I loved hunting. I loved shooting at the small clay targets that burst across the sky, though, and I was pretty good at it.

Adair and Ausley had learned the bare minimum of gun safety as children, but neither one of them had ever really enjoyed marksmanship. Once, when Ausley was around ten years old, I stood by her side as Daddy instructed us on the kill shot.

"In a boar, try to hit just below the shoulder. That way you will fell him, and can get another shot if you need to," Daddy advised. "And if you are ever in a position that you have to shoot at a person, aim to kill, Ausley," he had said as he helped guide her arm toward the target. She was uncomfortable with the gun and squirmed under Daddy's instruction.

"But Daddy, I couldn't kill anybody. If it came down to it, I would just try to shoot them in the shoulder like the hog or something like that," Ausley had said, with sincere distress. Even then I knew it was true, and so did Daddy. Ausley was too kind for her own good sometimes.

Daddy had straightened her arm again and focused her weapon on the target, "Ausley, listen to me. I don't want you to ever have to use a gun, *ever*. But if you are ever in a situation where you have to pick up a gun as a weapon of defense, then it better be bad enough that you have to shoot to kill."

"Especially with your aim," I called from her right side. Ausley couldn't hit the broad side of a barn.

Daddy ignored my teasing banter, and Ausley looked like the gun was going to bite her arm off. "Stay calm, breathe, and relax your shoulders. The gun will kick a little, but it won't hurt you."

Bang! The gun had fired, and the sound ricocheted across the sky. Daddy walked down to check the target, which I was sure was still intact, without a single bullet hole.

I looked at Ausley, "You have to know how to protect yourself," I had said.

Ausley placed the gun down on the table and turned away from me to hide her tears, "What if I don't want to protect myself. What if I think the other person's life is more important than my own?"

"Even the Friguscor?" I asked to prove my point.

She turned and looked at me with her blue, blue eyes. "Even the Friguscor, Veralee." Then she had walked back towards the house.

I shook the memory from my mind. "Daddy, I need to talk to you," I repeated with more strength this time. "It's serious. I've done something that I didn't mean to do... I didn't mean for it to go this far..." I trailed off, and on hearing my voice cracked and he jerked his head up.

"What's wrong Little Bird? What did you do that has you so upset?" He stopped what he was doing and looked at me, his eyes full of concern and compassion.

I hated to tell him this. *What had I done?* The fire popped and settled again. I sat down on the end of the wing-back chair feeling like the edge would give me a way out. It didn't.

"A couple of weeks ago, before the 175th Ausley and I were delivering dresses and uniforms for Mother. Something happened in Montgomery that day." I swallowed and then pushed the words out of my mouth. *I would not be a coward, I would not stop now.* I retold the day's events of the protest march downtown, the bookstore and the little family talking behind us. I told him how the boy had fallen and the chaos that surrounded his parents. "I don't know why...but I," my chest felt heavy, like the story was weighing me down, "I gave the boy my blood."

There. It was done, I could not take it back; it was out there, floating between us.

Daddy sat frozen in his chair; pure horror painted on his face. His mouth hung open, and he stared, unseeing into the space between us. Suddenly he jumped up and shut the door to his study with a bang. He started pacing. "What? Veralee...what are you saying?" He rubbed his head with both hands as he tried to keep his voice calm.

"I have no explanation, I know I owe you more, but I don't have one. I panicked, the child was dying, and somehow the idea came that I could save him. I could help him, and I acted before I could even talk myself out of it." I blurted out.

"You have put this entire family in danger! I don't even know where to start. You know the rules, Veralee. We taught you the rules." His voice gained volume with each word.

"There's more," I said flatly, forcing myself to tell him everything.

He looked at me incredulously, "More?! How could there be more? What has happened to the boy?"

I told him about the visit to the house and then the phone call in the middle of the night. "Atticus went with you on this? What was he thinking? I don't know what to say." He looked like his mind was racing around the tracks of the Talladega Speedway. I sat still, on the edge of the chair.

"Let me finish. I need to tell you....everything."

He looked like a brick had hit him in the face. "Everything? What happened last night, Veralee?" he said, visibly shaken. Then I told him. I told him about the father sitting in the chair. How he had attacked me and how he had said he wanted my blood. Then I told him about how Atticus had saved my life, and Nathan's life. I told him about Nathan's mother, who would never be coming back for her little boy again.

Daddy sat hard into his chair and let the weight of the news wash over him completely. He put his head in his hands for a long time and then looked out the window for even longer. The grandfather clock was the only one to speak in the room as he ticked away the passing of time. I stared at the fire and replayed the horror of the night before in my mind. A single tear came down my cheek, but I did not wipe it away.

"Veralee, you know the law! How could you? This is why we have rules. You have never had any respect for rules! Two people are dead because of your... you have always done exactly what you wanted to do, regardless of the consequences... but this, this..."

"He was dying Daddy!" I said hotly, with tears rolling. "A little boy, a child. I know it was wrong, I know...but I couldn't let him die." The anger, frustration, grief, and horror I felt bubbled out and erupted all over the library. I railed further, "The law is great to know, but when I am standing there on the street, watching an innocent child bleed to death, the law doesn't help me. His blood was pooling, red and thick all over the ground. Something snapped in me. I couldn't just stand there and talk about the law. The law would have let him die, but I chose to give him life."

Daddy shot back, "That was not your decision to make Veralee, don't you understand? You always think you know the right way to do everything, the best path for yourself, without asking for advice. This time you have decided for all of us; your decision exposes us all. Was it right for this child's father and mother, both dead as a direct result of your action? That was not your right to decide. The law protects us, all of us, Friguscor as well as Simulacrum. The law keeps us alive. You have no idea what you could unleash. You have never seen war, Veralee!" His eyes burned with anger.

War. The vision of my dream flashed in front of my eyes. I saw Red Oaks blazing with a destructive fire, while the Friguscor tore her from limb to limb. He was right.

I dissolved into unbidden tears, "I know, I know, I'm so sorry... I'm so sorry," my voice groaned in anguish.

Daddy dropped his hands and his head before making his decision. He came close and stood in front of me as I cried into my hands. His muscled but gentle arms wrapped around my small frame. I bit my lip hard, but still the tears came, unwanted and full of shame. He exhaled long and hard, as if releasing his anger to the air, one breath at a time. We stood together while the clock chattered away.

Pulling me close he bent down to look in my eyes. "Veralee, I can't believe you've done this thing. I can't." He shook me slightly by the shoulders. "I am so angry with you... but, I understand your heart, Little Bird, I do. What is done is done; I cannot pour water back into the bucket that has been spilled onto the ground. I wish I could, Little Bird, but I can't. We will figure this out. I don't know what this means right now. I don't know how far the repercussions of your actions will go." He sat down hard. He looked more worried and tired than I had ever seen him. It was as if this news had aged him by ten years in only a matter of minutes. I wiped my face and forced my eyes to dry in the heat of the fire.

"The boy is at the cottage with Atticus," I said into the fire.

"How much does Atticus have to do with this?" he asked pointedly.

Suddenly I felt the need to protect him. "No... I did it before Atticus came. It was me; he had nothing to do with it, besides going with me to the house. I told you that already."

He rubbed his jaw, which was covered in a morning beard. He was deciding something. "It seems about time that I speak with Atticus as well."

"What do you need to talk to Atticus about?" I pushed. I dried my eyes on Daddy's offered handkerchief.

"Veralee, you know who he is, *what* he is. Guard your heart. He cannot be what you are looking for. It's impossible."

The tears were gone, burned away by a new fire inside of me. I opened my mouth to argue, but someone knocked hard on the door as it swung open. Adair stood in a striking yellow dress that made her look like she was born of the sun.

"I think I see Issachar and Naphtali arriving," she announced with a warm smile.

Daddy rose in one breath and removed his hunting vest. I saw his Army training kick in, and he immediately folded his emotions behind a poker face. "Oh, guess I won't have time for target practice. Thank you for letting me know, Adair." He looked at me, and I saw the pain flicker behind his eyes; then he smiled softly and walked out of room to greet the guests.

"The Caterpillar has arrived," said Adair as we walked into the hall to greet the arriving guests.

I looked at her, confused, trying to hide the stress in

my eyes. "Who are you calling the Caterpillar?"

Adair gave me a knowing look and then with great exaggeration recited, "Who... are...you?" while she pretended to smoke on a pipe. We had both read *Alice in Wonderland* countless times as children, and even more now, since Mattie came along.

I laughed, needing a moment's release from the noose around my neck. I knew the words by heart, so in my best Alice voice I added, "Why, I hardly know, sir. I've changed so much since this morning, you see."

Adair puffed her face like the blue caterpillar, "No, I do...not...see, explain yourself."

I explained, "I'm afraid I can't explain myself, you see, because I'm not myself, you know."

"No, I do not know," said Adair, still playing along. It was so rare to see Adair's playful side. I missed her even though we lived so close.

"I can't put it any more clear, sir, because it isn't clear to me," I finished triumphantly as Alice just as Mother came down the steps to open the door.

"What isn't clear, Veralee?" Mother asked before she swung the door wide open.

"Nothing," we chirped in unison.

"Welcome, Issachar. Welcome, Naphtali. Lignum Vitae," Mother extended her hands out warmly to her old friends and ushered us all out to the porch to greet them.

"Issachar," she said as she kissed his cheek. "How does the forest treat you in Oregon?"

"Et Sanguis est essentia. Oh, she gives me a wide berth," he said, in a rustic voice. Issachar had been old before I was born, and I did not have any idea how many days he had lived. He still looked extremely handsome, with a shock of lustrous white hair that shined like moonlight. He was short and stocky, like a well-aged whiskey barrel. He wore a herringbone brown jacket with patches on the elbows that fit a little big and smelled like pine-blossom honey fresh off of the comb. It had been seven years since I had seen him. I liked him immediately.

Naphtali was the color of onyx, and her skin was so smooth that it almost seemed to shimmer, like she was wearing lip-gloss all over her body. She was tall and stately, standing eye to eye with most men. She was dressed simply in black riding pants and a maroon wrapped sweater. She was not overdone, not over-tailored in anyway, but still looked like she belonged more in Paris than Samson, Alabama.

"Ahh, Gail Lynn, so wonderful to see you." Naphtali hugged mother tightly, like she could squeeze away the years that had separated them.

"How is it in New York these days? Much colder than it is here, I'm sure," Mother said as Naphtali slowly released her hold on Mother's arms. Naphtali laughed as she nodded, and they started a conversation about autumn in the Big Apple.

Issachar turned his smile to Adair. "Hello again,

Adair. Lignum Vitae. I trust you have been well?" She replied in kind, but something about Issachar's eyes caught my eye as Adair spoke. I could not put my finger on what I saw there until he turned his gaze on me.

"And who... are... you?" He said the words slowly and then laughed his cavernous barrel laugh.

Adair raised her eyebrows in a "see-what-I-mean" gesture.

I couldn't help but laugh, Adair had been right on the mark with this one. I opened my mouth to tell him that I was Veralee, but just before I spoke, I looked into his golden eyes. There the question seemed deeper than porch-talk made by friends in Alabama, much truer than simple idle talk, and harder than a four-word question. Then the words from Alice sprang to my tongue without a hint of mockery.

"I've changed so much since yesterday, that I'm afraid I can't explain myself, because I'm not sure who I was is still who I am."

Issachar nodded stoically while a deeper recognition flickered in his eyes. I blinked, and then like coming out of a short dream, I was back to the greetings and chatter on the porch.

"Well, there he is! Good to see you Edwin, my friend," Issachar said as he embraced Daddy with two handshakes in one.

Daddy looked his normal self and was the perfect Southern host. I wondered if I was hiding my emotions as well as he was, but no other person on the porch seemed to notice my odd behavior. Ausley came out holding Mattie on her hip and passed Adair the child whose greedy fingers were calling for mommy.

Throughout the day the doorbell rang and greetings and warm embraces were exchanged with smiling hearts. Other Simulacrum from Florida, Georgia, Texas, Nebraska, Maine, and Canada arrived. Last but not least, was Meridee of Colorado. Even as a child I had loved Meridee, it was almost impossible not to. She was the embodiment of a gentle mother. Her long, auburn curls flowed freely at all times, and I think it was because no part of her could be ruled. She always wore a scarf even when it was hot out, giving her the look of an eccentric landscape artist. She lived a couple of hours from Denver, but I had never seen her home or talked for any length of time with her husband. He was a quiet man, who talked mainly to Meridee. So in my mind, she was simply Meridee of the forest.

When we would sit around the big table and eat with the Council members, Meridee would not join in the conversation often, which could make her seem cold or aloof if you did not pay attention. But if you watched her for even a moment you would see that she listened to everything. Nothing eluded Meridee's notice. When friendly banter or heated debate arose, she would sit so quietly that one could forget that she was in the room. Her peaceful expression never left her face nor showed what was truly happening behind her eyes. Then, when most had expended their word banks and exhausted their passions, she would interject a comment that would inevitably shift the entire argument into focus and clarity. Her words were round, with no sharp-edges or angles. Such was the way of Meridee. Her restraint fascinated me.

Maybe I could learn a bit of that from her.

I slipped out the door the first chance I got, which was not until the middle of the morning when Mother started lunch. The house was so busy with the new guests and the preparations for the Council Meeting that I knew I would not be missed.

Rap, rap, rap. Gently, I knocked on the cottage door. Inside I could hear the complex harmonies of Chopin's *Revolutionary Etude* playing. *Appropriate,* I thought wryly. Atticus answered the door with a guarded look on his face. The relief of being near him washed over me, like balm on a raw wound. I smiled at him, trying to bridge the awkwardness between us. Seeing him this time seemed different than any other. I studied his face for a long moment, trying to grasp what made it seem so rich, so intimate. Then the words came to give my mind its answer. I *knew* him now.

Last night, amidst the fury of panic, terror, fear and compassion, Atticus had saved my life. And then, he had told me his story. Knowing where he had come from, what had happened to him, his purpose in this big picture of life, they all worked like superglue bonding my heart to him. He looked relieved and smiled back at me. He felt it as well. The freedom of being completely open, completely truthful with another person. No hidden skeletons or shadows that lurked in the corners, but the true beauty of wanting to be known and having another know you. With my right hand I let my fingers brush his as I stepped into the cottage. He gripped my hand

and squeezed it before returning it back to me.

Inside, Nathan sat at the small wooden table with a pen and several sheets of paper before him. He looked so very tired but still smiled when I came to sit beside him. I studied his artwork for a moment.

"Is that your mother, Nathan?" I asked as I pointed to the drawing, which was good for a six-year old. Too good, actually.

He hunched his shoulders slightly and did not stop drawing as he spoke, "Uh-huh. That's what she looks like now." She was lovely.

"Nathan, why did you draw your mother like this?" I used a gentle voice to hide my shock.

He fingered the portrait fondly, "'Cause this is what she is like now."

"Why do you think she looks like this now?" I asked out of pure fascination.

He smiled that smile that only a small child can give you when you have asked a question that seems so obvious to them.

"Cause I saw her." He gave me a look of satisfaction.

"You saw her? Where did you see your mommy, Nathan?" I asked this carefully not wanting to push him too far, but curious to find out what he knew.

His mouth quivered a little and turned down, "She

went behind the curtain, I saw her last night, but I couldn't touch her." His face brightened, "She was sleeping."

He pointed to the woman lying in the boat that he had drawn. Atticus sat across from me and our eyes met. He did not doubt the boy, and neither did I. How would a boy who was Friguscor for most of his life know what happened to the Simulacrum when their bodies died in this world? We did not even truly know what happened to them. Most did not wait for their bodies to give out in this world, but left willingly for the Alabaster City in the Terebinths, before they had to endure the pain of withering away. But how would he know what had happened to his mother? She would not be at the Alabaster City since she had actually died in this world. The answer to my question seemed simple when I looked at his little face. His mother had told him.

Nathan continued to draw but spoke up, "She can't take me to school anymore, or make country-fried steak on my birthday." His lips quivered and tears rolled down his cheeks, but he did not stop drawing. "Can you make me country-fried steak, Vewalee?" Without pause, I wrapped my arms around this small, brave boy with sandy blond hair that fell over his ears and eyes and I kissed his face.

"Yes, I can make country-fried steak, Nathan. Don't cry. We will love you, Nathan. You are safe here with us. Atticus and I will keep you safe." He did not push away or arch his back against my arms, but fell into them like he had been waiting to be held. I folded him into my lap and sat rocking him as I pushed the hair back from his forehead like my mother had always done for me. There was a weight on my chest that longed to protect this little boy, to hold him and rock him back and forth until all of his troubles were gone. His body relaxed, but he kept his right hand on my arm. "And plus," I whispered to him, "I make a mean gravy to go with it."

After some time, Nathan fell asleep on my lap, and Atticus helped me move him onto the bed. I covered his frail body with a warm blanket and watched him sleep before I headed back to the kitchen.

"Has he been talking a lot this morning?" I asked Atticus as he started to unload sandwich makings from the fridge. Just being in the room with him sent an electrical current running up my right arm. I saw him touch his arm, and I knew he felt it, too.

"No, not much. We didn't mind the silence. It was nice to spend the morning with each other without being bothered by words," Atticus answered.

Atticus enjoyed silence. Even when we did talk, he was not a man of many words. He put a plate of saltine crackers on the table with a block of cheese and offered me a glass of sweet tea. I grinned, realizing this was his attempt at hospitality.

He noticed. "What?"

I laughed, needing it more than I realized. "Nothing, you're being hospitable, it's cute."

He arched his eyebrows, which made him look young. "Cute? Does that mean nice? Or does that mean childish?" He was toying with me.

"Cute, it means....nice...and like you're trying at something you are not used to doing."

He grabbed a cracker. "Well, I'll enjoy my crackers and cheese, and you can just go hungry." He smiled widely and almost lost half of his cracker out of the side of his mouth. We both laughed.

"Atticus, Nathan is already talking about his dreams," I said, thinking out loud.

"Don't you believe in dreaming, Veralee? I happen to remember you telling your father at the dinner table that you dreamt of me before I came." He shoved another cheese cracker into his mouth.

"Yes, I do." It was awkward to talk to someone outside of the family about my dreams. "My mother and grandmother knew then that I could ' hear' as they called it. People that do not understand the gift will tell you that they can ' see.' But my mother has always insisted that it is not seeing, but hearing that is important. Throughout my childhood I would hear through dreams things that were happening, things that had already happened or things that were going to happen. I learned to differentiate them from other dreams. It was the reality of those dreams that made me know when I was hearing. Normal dreams are just watching a movie play out. They are silly and make no sense, or scary and easily shaken off by the morning light or inconsequential and forgotten by the time you reach the shower. Hearing is not like that at all. When you hear, you have been there; you have tasted and smelled, and you have heard the message. You cannot forget those messages. They stay in you and prepare you for things that are to come." I surprised myself with how much I told him.

My mind flashed back to myself at nine. I was in the sewing room and playing with my mother's seam ripper when I asked her why we hear through dreams and others do not.

"Oh, I don't know exactly, Veralee, but every person has a different gift. Some are great at speaking to crowds, and they end up on the radio or television. Some people are compassionate and they serve as counselors or work at halfway houses. Some are strongly analytical and very good at reasoning and they work as engineers or architects, so I guess some people have the gift of hearing, and they listen well." She spoke with a needle sticking out of the side of her mouth, and her head buried in her seams. Sounding a bit like Reba McIntyre with the needles on one side of her mouth, she twanged, "but we seem to be gifted with hearing. You hear, I hear, your grandmother can hear, and her mother did, too."

"How do you know when to talk about what you hear, when to tell someone about what you hear or how to understand what you hear?" I asked too many things at once.

Smiling with her eyes and one side of her mouth she laughed. "Those are good questions. You will grow into most of those answers."

Turning back to her machine she spread her hands out across her newest project and looked down at her work. "You know, Veralee, when I am working on a sewing project, I have no idea how it will eventually end up. I start with a plan, but it almost always develops a life of its own, as if the fabric is telling me to add this, subtract that. Sometimes it comes out totally different than what I thought at the beginning. I think that is way of our dreams and our lives. We think we have a plan, that we understand what we are looking at, but life most often turns in directions we never expected. It's only in the end that we look back and see the design in the quilt. These fabrics were created to become something of use or beauty, so I give my hands to the cause and see what comes of the thing at the end of the day." I set the seam ripper down softly and turned to leave as I heard her mumble something about it becoming a dress, or an apron, or a purse, or a quilt. Endless possibilities.

The first time Mother remembers me dreaming was around the age of two and a half, the same year that my grandmother went away. The gift was not an anomaly among the Simulacrum, but the talent didn't seem to manifest as much as it did at one time.

"Just old enough to talk in full sentences," my mother had explained. My grandmother was still living with us then at Red Oaks. She came in to help my mother get me up and dressed for the morning.

"Good morning, Veralee," she had said in her wise voice. She picked me up from bed and held me on her shoulder. She softly pushed the hair from my face and kissed each cheek tenderly. She forever smelled of Chanel No 9 that came in a purple cylinder. Ausley and I had a dozen used bottles that we played with in the bath.

"Veelee, do you want to get dressed? What should we wear today?" Mother called out from the closet.

Mother walked out with a pink dress that had watermelon pockets she had hand stitched to the front. She laid out the matching fancy panties, which every good Southern girl wore, so not to show her underwear when she is twirling around and flipping upside down. Mother had made Ausley a matching version of the dress. So, wherever we went, Ausley and I looked like twins.

Grandmother put me down and began to pull my pajamas over my head.

"There was blood ewerywhere, all over Veelee, got blood all ower!" I stated with the certainty of a two-year-old.

My grandmother looked at me confused, "Veralee there's no blood. Are you bleeding? Did you scratch a mosquito bite open?"

"No, no right here on the flo', there blood here and here and ewerywhere. Veelee make big mess all ower. It fom me nose," I insisted.

Mother stopped searching for the matching socks to my watermelon dress and looked at me. She would later tell me that she remembered the certainty in my face.

"Veelee, did you have a nose bleed in the middle of the night?" She questioned as she searched over my bed sheets and the floor around my bed.

"Yes, Veelee nose bleed all ower the floor. Veelee makes big mess."

Seeing nothing my mother turned to pick up my

dress, just as my grandmother gasped. My nose began to bleed then, all over the floor.

Atticus waved his hand in front of my face with a look of amusement. "Veralee? You still here?" he asked playfully. I snapped back into the room and looked down at my hands, embarrassed at the amount of spacing I had been doing today.

"So why is your dreaming so different than Nathan's?" Atticus pulled me back to the conversation at hand.

"I guess it's not. I just didn't realize he could do it," I explained.

"I'm sure he didn't either, until he had your blood in his veins. If you think about it, it's probably from you, seeing as he is from your bloodline." Atticus started to make a sandwich.

My bloodline? I had never thought about that before. Nathan was from my bloodline? I tipped my chair back so that I could just see my bloodline sleeping soundly on the bed.

"Because I gave him my blood, he is now my bloodline...like a...like," the thought was so new, I struggled to make it into a sentence.

"Veralee, sometimes I wonder if they *taught* you about being Simulacrum at all. Yes, he is your bloodline now, just the same as if he had been born of your body. Haven't you noticed the connection Nathan feels for you? The first day we went to the house, he could barely hide his love for you then, his need to be around you and to touch you. Just like a child with his mother. You have created a blood bond with the boy that will not be severed."

"So what you're saying is... I have a six-year-old?!" My world tilted slightly, but as I spoke the words out loud it seemed to come right again. I knew that Atticus was right because even as he said the words I felt them in me. There was a deep bond that had formed between Nathan and me. He was not like a boy adopted into my family through the courts, something deeper had occurred here, something even more powerful. Nathan had my blood running through his veins, changing him even as he slept in the next room, more and more into Simulacrum. I looked back at Atticus for confirmation.

"He looks different today. Did you notice it? It's subtle, but still there. His skin has healed even more, and his eyes are changing color. This is all from the blood, I assume," I stated, seeking confirmation.

Atticus looked toward the bedroom as well, "Yes, Veralee. He will continue to change until the blood has completely healed what was broken. He won't look like the child he did before when he was Friguscor. He will still be himself, still have those features, but he will also be more like you. He will even come to look like you a little bit. This morning, his eyes even look more silver, just like yours. I can't say how much, just like I couldn't say how much a child between any man and woman would look." He stopped talking abruptly and looked away.

A child. I imagined what a child between Atticus and me would look like. In my mind I let the words form a little baby girl with a pink blanket and Roman eyes. Then, to help

the Oaks Remain

overcome the uncomfortable silence I chimed in, "That will work in our favor, I guess. The police will be looking for Nathan; they probably already are. I didn't get a chance to read the paper this morning to even see what they are saying."

As I finished talking, Atticus went to the small table beside the door and picked up a small AR screen.

He slid the screen in front of me and activated the screen as he spoke, "I picked this up this morning from the Big House. I'm sorry, but I knew that the news came in this paper, and I thought I would get it before your family did. I didn't know what, or if, you had told them." He dropped his eyes looking a bit ashamed. The shock of seeing Atticus operate an AR screen dissipated with his words.

"I told Daddy this morning," I said as the knot tied back inside my stomach. "He was upset; he didn't know what all of this would mean, particularly to the Council. I don't know what they will do to me for breaking the law."

I activated the screen and saw a large story about the Mad Dog Disease. Scanning quickly over our economic problems, promises from State Representatives, and then, there it was. On the third page of the paper: *"Police Officer and Wife Found Dead"* stared at me as plain as day with black and white boldness.

Two people are dead, a wife and husband after what police are calling a grisly and bizarre ritual murder. Police Officer Jeffery Waters 39, and his wife, Linda-Faye Waters 35, apparently died shortly after midnight on Saturday morning. It appears that Waters killed his wife, though the police will not release the cause of death, and then a few hours later, Waters is believed to be murdered by an unknown assailant. Their son, Nathan Waters, is missing and feared dead by police. Chief King stated that Waters had been working undercover on a drug case with a local gang, and feels the murder is most likely drug or gang related.

A coworker, who asked to remain anonymous, reported that Waters had become increasingly agitated over the past few weeks and had been put on a leave of absence from the force after experiencing hallucinations at work. Several believed that Waters had become involved with the use of the illegal drugs.

"He kept saying that his boy was not his boy anymore, and that his wife was a monster. He had some crazy theory about them being aliens or something like that. The chief couldn't keep him in a patrol car and sent him home without his weapon. He was supposed to see a shrink, but I don't think he ever went," a fellow officer stated. Chief King would not confirm or deny this.

Police will continue their search for Nathan Waters, 6 years of age. If you have any information about the whereabouts of the child or of any next of kin, please contact the Montgomery Police Department.

That was it. No picture of the scene, no more explanation.

I looked up at Atticus, "They believe it was gang related? That Nathan's father was on drugs?" I could hardly believe what I was reading.

Atticus watched my face for any fear, "Through my years of experience with the Friguscor, I have often found that the intricacies of their own lives usually provide the greatest solutions for covering, shall we say, unpleasant circumstances."

"Like covering up a dead body? That kind of unpleasant circumstance?" I asked with frost in my voice. How could he be so casual about killing someone? How could he be so cold?

Atticus did not look apologetic, but unemotionally calm. I looked at him. He was a soldier who had seen too much death and had been trained to control his emotions. Even though I knew his story, I still found it somewhat unsettling. "Veralee, I understand that you have grown up here at Red Oaks, and that much of the world outside is somewhat foreign to you, but as I told you last night, I was not given the same ease of life as you. I have always, and will always do what is necessary to complete the mission."

"This is life, Atticus; it's not a mission," I said, exasperated by his oversimplification of what I had witnessed last night. Even though I didn't want it to, self-pity dangerously resounded in my voice, "And you don't have to be a warrior all of the time."

Atticus cocked his head without changing his expression at all. But he could not hide the fire I saw ignite behind his eyes. I had hit a nerve. "*That* is what you still do not understand Veralee. This life, *my life*, is a mission. Without the mission, I have no life. I cannot separate the mission from myself. I will always be the warrior, and I will always do what I have been called to do." His calm was shaking. I saw it cracking at the outer edges.

"But what if you wanted a different life? What if *I* wanted a different life?" I asked, pushing at the thin ice. I didn't know if I was trying to drown him or myself with this questioning.

He looked annoyed with me, "It is not about what I *want*. It is bigger than my personal desires. I gave my life to this mission, and I could not stop now even if I wanted to. The truth is, neither can you. And that is what you are really afraid of. You have already chosen a path Veralee, now you will have to walk it."

I set my mouth firmly, and decided to change the subject, rather than walk another step through a conversation I was too tired to have. I didn't even really know what it was that I was trying to get to with him. What was it that I really wanted to hear from him? Maybe it was not my exhaustion that made me back away from the conversation; maybe I was scared to find out that I could not fit into the life of an Ayindalet. Or maybe I was afraid of what my life was going to look like from now on, either way...better to not know, at least then I still had hope.

"What about Nathan? Someone could track him to us," I said, my voice trembling with fear before I could stop it. Atticus changed his military stance and leaned across the table taking my hand in his. Maybe he wanted to hope as much as I did.

"You stayed off of those roads that their government uses to track the vehicles?" he questioned.

"Yes," I said, reassuring us both. "I made sure we avoided the street cameras and I used only the rural roads. They don't have systems in place to track vehicle movement on the old country roads yet." I bit my lower lip and thought through our drive home last night like a mental checklist. The house had no neighbors close by but…we had forgotten about their chips. My stomach turned again.

"Oh, no! Atticus! The chips in their arms! They will find my cell phone number!" I almost tipped over the chair as I stood up, shaking with realization.

Atticus reached for my hand and pulled me down into the chair again. "Veralee, they will not find those chips."

I looked at him with crazed eyes, "How do you know that?"

"I saw to it, after you told me about the chips in their arms." He tapped his fingers on the top of the table several times, "They will not find those chips."

I nodded and bit my lip. "How?" I began but stopped just as quickly. I decided then that I did not want to know anything more. Besides, if they found anything that led them to Atticus, it would be a dead end. How would they trace him? Where would they look? In their files from the Roman era?

"Veralee, what you said to Nathan will be true. He will be safe. This is not the first, nor the last time something like this has happened. The Council has ways of making "new" people. Even though it is very rare, they can make their old lives disappear when they come over. Don't worry; I will protect you as long as I can. I promise you that."

"Protect me? The man who wanted to hurt me is already…" I could not bring myself to finish my own sentence. Atticus noticed and kindly cut me off, "Not from him."

"Then who?"

"Veralee, you could be in trouble with the Council," Atticus said simply.

"Oh them...yeah, I know."

Atticus watched my nonchalant response and leaned in close. "Veralee...you do realize that what you did will not be a small thing to the Council, do you not?" I knew that it was a big deal. But the truth was I did not know how big of a deal it was, or what they would do to me, so it seemed easier to not think about it. So, I didn't.

"So, you've changed your mind. You are going to the Council meeting now?" I asked with a smug smile.

Atticus shook his head a little in disbelief of my denial. "I think you need me to be there. You need someone to be there to keep you from self-destruction."

"Oh you're attempting humor now." I put my elbow on the table and leaned toward him. "You should keep your day job....whatever that is," I replied.

Atticus smiled for a minute while he studied my face. Then he turned more serious, "Veralee, I will not speak at the Council meeting. I do not need them to know that I am there. But, I will protect you as long as I can."

His eyes were so intense; I didn't know how he would protect me, but I couldn't doubt him for a second. His hand slowly rose to my face, and he allowed his finger to trace my cheekbone. The feeling of his touch was so solid, so durable.

It was not simply lightweight romance, it felt like more, like it held longevity.

Before the moment could fly away, I pushed myself up, armed with courage, and closed the space that had lain between us for too long. Atticus stood, like a good Southern gentleman did whenever a woman stood up from a table. If I had slowed to think about what I was doing I would have talked myself out of it, so I didn't. Purposely, I closed the part of my mind that objected and slid my hand up to his face. He did not jerk away, but flinched slightly with surprise.

"Veralee?" He asked just before I placed my lips on his mouth. His lips responded immediately, and I felt the desire in them. He kissed me with intensity, and I let him. His hands were in my hair, and I stood on my tiptoes to wrap one arm around his neck while my other hand twisted the front of his shirt into a ball. The room spun around us. The chair Atticus had been sitting in knocked over and slammed onto the floor, but the sound seemed a million miles away. Gently, he lifted me onto the edge of the table without releasing my mouth. I felt lost in him, realizing that the current of electricity forming between us was pounding in my head and circulating my body. Through him and into me and back again. A circle of oneness was closing in around us. There was desperation in his kiss, as if time was running out like sand, and life itself was pouring through a broken hourglass.

But then, he stopped. He pulled back from my mouth and placed his forehead to mine. His breath was ragged. I loved that sound instantly.

He kept his right hand on my collarbone, tracing its

defined lines back and forth. I closed my eyes and let his touch warm my entire body. He traced my collarbone and then ran his hand down my arm and closed his grasp around my tseeyen. He lifted my hand and inspected my mark. "A little bird?" he asked, smiling in a way that made me want to kiss him again.

"Mmhmm. It looks like a sparrow made out of clock...a little bird," I added.

Atticus traced the lines of my tseeyen with his warm finger. I felt every moment of his touch, every heartbeat that pulsed through my veins as his finger lingered on my skin.

"A sparrow... interesting. She is a small bird, but a determined bird. She is bound by no rules, she is free...but, she is tethered all the same, to her mate. Loyal to one single other." His fingers felt like fire on my skin. "And yet, the pieces of time are here." He pointed. "Time is a boundary in and of itself."

I swallowed and bit my lower lip, "Maybe freedom is never truly free, as they say," I said into his green eyes, "it comes with a price, and sooner or later, time will come to collect its toll."

Tenderly, he put my arm down, and pulled up his sleeve to show me his own mark. I followed the white lines that looked as if they had been tattooed into the skin with white ink. The lines wrapped around each other like a never-ending rope. It looked almost Gaelic in nature. But in the center was the back of a mighty bird with its wings spread wide.

"Is that an eagle?" I asked, looking up into those amazingly green eyes.

"I guess we are birds of a feather, Miss Veralee."

{ 16 }

Ancient Voices

Another couple of days ticked by, and I had returned to a sliver of my regular life. Most of the North American Council members had arrived and were preparing for the meeting at the Terebinths of Mamre.

Daddy had not yet publicly acknowledged the arrival of the Archaon to the Council members. *The Council meeting, he must be waiting for the Council meeting.* Council meetings opened with the first light of the morning sun. It reminded us of coming from the darkness into the light, awakening from the slow, sure death of the Friguscor to the warm, forever life of the Simulacrum. So the next morning, while most of the world slept, we would enter the Terebinths of Mamre. And then, the Archaon would come. "*We will come with the last light of the blood moon,*" Achiel had said.

The last light of the blood moon. I let the words roam through my mind as I sat in Daddy's wooden chair staring up at the Histories on the top shelf. The house was quiet now.

The sound of the grandfather clock soothed me like the presence of an old friend. Everyone must have been out, walking the trails of Red Oaks.

Atticus had not yet ventured to the Big House; there were too many Council members around. Last night, we had lain together in the cool wet grass, on top of an old quilt I found in the cottage. The thought of him made my heart beat faster. We had spent hours wrapped in each other's arms, and I reveled in the pure bliss of his skin next to mine. Even now, I could smell his sweet scent on my skin. I leaned down and breathed in his smell that hung on my arms. My body responded immediately, and I shivered from the memory.

Softly, he had told me stories about his life growing up, of the kindness and tutelage of Pallos, of how much he had loved his mother, of when he had first learned to ride a horse, and how he had learned to read in multiple languages. Then he spoke of the wars he had seen throughout time. He told me about life as a soldier and the horrible acts that he had committed that were considered normal during that time. They still slept with him. I told him that he was not that man anymore, that those things happened another lifetime ago, so long ago that they did not have to define him anymore.

"No, he had said, "they are a part of me, and I keep them on purpose. If I forget them, if I try to pretend that they do not matter anymore...then I have not changed at all. I think it is important to renounce of those things, to admit that I behaved like an animal. Remaining accountable for my actions keeps me under control in some way. It is, in some way, my own personal atonement. The Eiani changed me, but I do not want to forget what it changed me *from*, any more than I would forget what it has changed me into," he had said.

I told him about life at Red Oaks with my sisters. About Jackson, and how I always seemed to buck the simple paths in life. I spent a lot of time explaining things that he had never heard of or seen before, but he spent just as much time explaining things from his place in time.

Phineas had shown Atticus the Internet, and he pored over summaries of history and articles about the modern world. I was not surprised to hear how much he already knew, or how quickly he had learned and adapted to each age that he traveled through. He told me how long it had been since he felt he had a home and how lonely his years had been. "I guess the last time I felt like I was home was the day I left my mother and Pallos. But now…now there is you," he said, stealing a glance at me and then looking up at the stars.

Lying beside him on that blanket, I felt like ice slowly dissolving down the neck of a longneck bottle, melting deeper and deeper into him. Each moment with him hastened the cascade so that soon, like the ice, I would be forever changed to fit the new form of the bottle. But the part that thrilled me the most was that I didn't want to be poured back out. Never before had I felt the intensity of these emotions, this longing. I wanted him. I wanted to bond myself to him for all of time. But more than that, something that was hard to express, was the feeling or the knowledge that we were created for each other.

"Do you believe that we are created with our match in mind, or do you believe we should simply match with the best bond we find in another Simulacrum?" I asked him nervously.

He pulled himself up onto one elbow and hovered closely over my face. His finger slowly traced the edge of my jawline and down my neck. I swallowed hard, and let the pleasure of his touch burn through me.

"Before knowing you, I would have laughed at the thought that one person could be created or formed with another in mind, like two halves of the same apple. I have not seen many great matches anyway; they were rare in Rome. Mostly, they were created for political gain. I have been moving down the River for so long that I had come to believe that being alone was part of my calling. But now...now, I do not know what to tell you."

He felt the edge of my cheekbone with his fingers, "From the first moment I saw your face, something came alive in me. It was as if all of the places I have been, all of the time I have lived...it was not just to watch for the Door, but it was also to find you. Like I had been searching for you all this time, even though I did not know you were lost."

He dropped his mouth to mine, and then showed me all of the things he could not tell me. I had never been truly kissed, not like this. This types of kiss started with your lips but burned down so low that it seemed to settle into your core, changing your nucleus, your DNA, like you were not the same once you came up for air. Like the world had shifted focus while you kissed, and now everything looked new and different, brighter, more colorful, more worth living.

His hands had trembled slightly over my neck before he allowed them to explore my skin. He had pressed his forehead hard against my chest and then pulled back and flung himself onto the blanket.

"Veralee...it's time for you to go back to the Big House. I should go in and check on Nathan," he said, resolved, but still lingering tantalizingly close to me. I understood his request. He was asking me to make the decision; he was asking me to make the *right* decision. For him, I did. After one more moment of feeling his lips against mine, I forced myself to stand and walk back to the house. But I already knew I did not want to make the right decision again. Because I knew that *he* might be the wrong decision for me, and I didn't care.

Sitting in the library didn't stifle one bit of memory of the night before. I ran my fingers over my slightly swollen lips. I could still hear his ragged breathing; I still felt the soft touch of his rugged hands on my back. Last night was like standing on the edge, if I were going to turn back, it was too late. I had stared into his eyes, into his soul, and found the place for me. Then, without thinking, without fearing, without looking back...I jumped.

The old clock ticked and bonged from the foyer. Time was so bossy. Atticus had talked so much about his purpose last night. He would not stop until he found the Door. "The time has been determined long ago, it was written with the words that bring life," he had said.

I turned the chair around. So much was happening at once, so many moving pieces. Leaning forward, I dragged my fingers across the bindings of the books, letting their backs prick interest into my spirit. Could I find the answers in these books? I climbed the ladder and reached for the Histories, taking three large, black leather volumes down with me. These books had always been a comfort to me, words that explained things and gave meaning to the world around me. Now more than ever, I desperately wanted explanations. I flipped the ancient pages over, as if they themselves could speak to me. These books *were* ancient voices, speaking across the eras...voices of my people, Simulacrum, who had long ago left this place to live forever. Wise souls filled with ancient knowledge, housed within the yellowed pages and still living within the black ink.

Hadn't I always known that these words contained the mysteries of life? Had I done to our Histories what the Friguscor had done to us, relegated them to the domain of children's fairytales?

I reflected on the past several weeks. My world had changing so quickly. The pages fell open to a picture of a great warrior of the Archaon. These stories that I had loved as a child were not just stories, they were part of *my* story. They were truer than mere ink or paper that could burn or disintegrate. They had now come alive before my very eyes: I had seen a Friguscor become Simulacrum, I had held the hand and kissed the lips of an Ayindalet, I had heard cumulative voices of the mighty Archaon float on the wind, I had seen my dreams step into reality, and I had been healed by marvelous light and marked by its presence. No, the words in these stories were not just ink on a page; these words brought forth life, and not the other way around. What was written was happening, and I was a part of it.

A voice floated peacefully through the silence of the room. "Yes, Veralee. Those words are alive, though you still do not fully understand them." I did not jump back or flinch. I was too shocked to do that. I simply stopped breathing until my body forced air through my lungs.

Achiel sat, as best a creature of his size could, in the wingback chair by the fireplace. He made it look like it was made for a child. My mouth went dry. "Do not be afraid, Veralee, it is I, Achiel. We have met before, have we not?" The voice of many spoke through the singsong cadence. I sat, practically hypnotized by the legato sound. Every word seemed to be connected to the one before and the one after it.

Achiel's large presence made the room feel small, but I liked being near him. He smelled like another world, one that didn't fit in this one, like days long passed or cultures long forgotten. His silver hair glimmered, as though illuminated, even though there was no sunlight in the room. His eyes dazzled with color and clarity, green and blue in the center and then a starburst of purple and yellows dancing to the edges, like crystallized gems reaching to the surface. He redirected me with a question, as if he knew that his beauty was distracting me. "Veralee?"

When the door to my mouth unlocked, I could speak again. "Yes, I remember you. How could I forget you?" I stumbled over the words like they were blocks in the floor. He sat comfortably, glancing around the room.

"Ernest built this house with the Red Oaks. We can feel them here, it is a comfort," he said.

"Ernest? Oh, my great-great-grandfather. Yes, I suppose he did," I answered watching the cat-like creature.

"We enjoyed him. His humor... it was always so clever and pleasant," Achiel added, as if this conversation were completely normal.

"You knew him? You knew Ernest Weekes?" I asked.

Achiel smiled brilliantly. "Yes, Daughter of the Blood. We led him to the Red Oaks." He looked at me fully with those feral eyes that seemed to pierce much deeper than my skin.

"*You* led him here? Is that why the trees are always red? Because of you? I mean, all of you, the Archaon?" I had simply accepted that the trees had always been red because of us, but maybe there was more to the oaks than I realized.

Achiel studied the chessboard, which sat on the round table beside his chair. He moved a knight and then lifted his long fingers from the board like he had just injected a new element into the game.

"No, we do not make the trees red, though we might add to their richness, for we visit this land often. The trees are older than you or we. Their memory is long and their roots deep." He finished speaking as if he had explained something to me, but I felt as though he had told a joke I didn't understand.

"So the trees are not red because of you, or the...Archaon, but because of...?" I raised my eyebrows questioningly.

Cutting his head slightly to the right, he pursed his lips and blinked slowly. "Could your oral history have been lost in so few years? The Red Oaks, the trees of this land, were born in the first of days in order to usher in the last of days. The Terebinths of Mamre are connected—have been connected, throughout time—to the One Tree. It is the Eiani in you, and the Eiani in them, which burns red with life. You have been to the Terebinths of Mamre, have you not?"

I shifted in my seat leaning closer to the beautiful creature, smelling the freshly cut wood and earth mist that surrounded him, "No. Before now I was too young to attend the Council meetings; tomorrow will be my first time to see the Terebinths of Mamre."

His eyes opened a bit wider. Was that a look of surprise in his face? I could not be sure. "Too young?" he asked, as if he did not understand the words.

"Well, you have to be sixteen to attend, and I was only twelve the last time the Council met, so this will be my first meeting," I explained.

His inhuman eyes twitched slightly as he digested my words as one would digest rocks. He did not move, but sat perfectly still, chewing mentally. I did not know why, but I had the feeling he was listening to something that I could not hear, or maybe speaking to someone I could not see. What was it that made me know this? Was it the vibration in the air or the tilt of his cat-like face, as if an invisible mouth whispered into his ear? I was sure that all of the Archaon were in the room with us. The more I thought about it, the more I could sense a wavering of the walls. They were there, but only Achiel was visible.

"The rules and laws of the Simulacrum are foreign to us. Does entrance to the Terebinths of Mamre come with a price paid through age? Was the way to the trees not shown to all Simulacrum? Why do your people weigh themselves down with heavy yokes, like oxen in the heat of summer? It has always been this way for your kind. We have never understood your need to build walls to contain the things that have been revealed."

I retorted, "But we don't need to enter the Terebinths until after the age of sixteen. That is when we begin needing to drink from the river and eat of the Basar tree."

"Your kind develops rules to protect things you do not fully understand. The things unknown belong to the mysteries, but the things that have been revealed belong to the ones who hear. Who among you decides to hold the things revealed from some and yet gives it too freely to ones who do not hear?" His voice held much wisdom, yet it did not condemn me. But through him, I saw a grave error in our thinking.

"Our rules..." I said slowly, thinking about his point.

"Rules not required, but created from ignorance or pride. They will choke your people and steal life from them," Achiel expounded.

"I've never been one for rules anyway. Rules are made for bending, in my book." I said it a little too flippantly, before I remembered to whom I was speaking.

Achiel did not miss my slip of the tongue, "Do not despise instruction, Daughter of the Blood, for Wisdom comes only to those who seek her." He watched me, and I thought for a brief moment I saw amusement in his eyes. "And, do not mistake rebellion for righteousness because of your youthful passion."

That hit hard. I sat still for a moment feeling like he had read my diary. My entire family had been saying this to me all of my life. Was he also implying that I was one of those who couldn't hear the truth?

"Who are the ones who can hear, and who are the ones who cannot?" I asked, tilting closer to the edges of his mind.

"You, Daughter of the Blood, are one who hears; we have showed you many things while you slept, and you have heard our voice."

Yes, I had. I had heard their voice in my dreams. Achiel continued, "But there are some who sit in authority, who have seen many of the mysteries revealed, and yet they no longer hear the way of the Simulacrum or the way of the One Tree."

Some who sit in authority? The Council? Who on the Council can no longer hear the way of the Simulacrum?

Achiel unfolded his giant hand and pointed his long fingers toward the books piled high on the desk that lay under my hands, "*They* are not new to you, we hope. The Simulacrum still honor their word and at least teach the ancient ways to their children, even if they do not *show* them the ancient ways...do they not?" I followed his long fingers down to the pile of books. The Histories of my people.

"No, these stories are not new to me. I was taught about the Histories all of my life. The Simulacrum still honor the ancient ways." I proudly defended this part of our life, at least. The stories were taught at the dinner table and read to children beside warm fires and cozy beds. To know them was an essential part of the Simulacrum life. But somewhere along the way, I had nurtured a seed of doubt. I might have known the stories, but until recent events, my simple life at Red Oaks seemed more real to me than the words on the pages of the Histories.

Again I felt the presence of more beings than I could see.

"Taught about the stories? But, Daughter of the Blood, you do not *know* them, do you? You read as one who has not seen." He cocked his head to the side and focused on some unseen sound. "No. You know in part, but you do not yet know in full."

He moved forward much too quickly to the edge of his seat without stirring the air around him, threatening the balance of the much too-small chair. His relaxed stance was gone and instantly replaced by the warrior within him.

"You will, Daughter of the Blood. Soon, you will know them through sweat and blood. It will be asked of you, required of you. Only then will the words of life birth truth in you. For those who do not give their own tears and blood, these are only words in an old book for children to read at bedtime. But you, Veralee, Daughter of the Blood you will be asked to give all. I wonder, will you be willing? Or will you be like so many before you, so many who simply could not let the words in those books germinate new life within them."

His words, sharper than a two-edged sword, sliced deeply into my spirit, slashing through the parasitic fear that had gripped my soul for weeks now. I could feel them beginning to release me from the specter of the unknown and the fear of what was coming. In his words I felt what I could not grasp...the courage to overcome, to rise to the occasion and to do what I have always known I would be asked to do...to give it all. Deep in the secret places of my mind, I felt the wheels turn, oiled with words that I had heard spoken to me before time began. Achiel spoke the truth. What was happening to my life was no accident; I was not a feather floating on the wind, waiting for the next gust to tumble me hither and yon to the four corners of the earth. No, I was born for this life.

The great creature watched as the revelation stirred inside of me, and then they spoke as one, "We are here now to walk with you, Daughter of the Blood. Long have we waited for this time to come; long have we waited for these days to begin." Achiel stretched out his arm and put his hand on my heart. I felt light radiate from his palm and pour inside me like water rushing from a pitcher.

"Seal up these words so that you can stand when you fall, run when you are weary, and hold fast against the nefarious days which come. I will watch you, Daughter of the Blood; I will help you when I can. But it is your burden to carry, and I am sorry for that, Little Bird. This you must do...alone." Air rushed into my lungs, and I collapsed back into the hard wooden chair as if I had been pushed. And then, he was gone.

Tears fell into my hands, not from fear, but for the loss. "But the Simulacrum are never alone," I whispered into the silence. Something in me broke, and the dam of emotions came flowing out and over my face. I wept. I wept, for the life that I would never have. For the dream of growing old at Red Oaks with my family while watching my children and grandchildren play underneath the great canopies of red. My dream was vanishing like the morning mist in the sunlight, and I mourned its leaving. I cried for the events of the past two days, for the death of two people that I had catalyzed, and for a little boy who was now an orphan.

But as I remembered Achiel and my purpose, I felt my courage rise. I would not allow fear or the need for stability—or even grief for a dying dream—stop me now. I glanced down at my arm. The bird on my wrist seemed to stir slightly, as if it wanted to take flight off of my arm.

I looked up with new resolve and spoke into the empty room, "If I stopped here, I would never know how far I could really go."

{ 17 }

Eyes like a Snake

"Well, look at you, Veralee! You've grown up, Little Bird. I believe you are even more striking than your mother, if that is even possible." Uncle Austin's voice snatched me from my daydream and deposited me back on solid ground in the library. How long had I been sitting there? I glanced through the large windows and saw that the sun hung low in the afternoon sky.

He stood in the doorway with a bag on his shoulder, which he quickly let fall to the floor as he opened his arms to me.

"Uncle Austin! You've come! I'm so glad to see you!" I said, running to hug my favorite uncle's neck. Austin lived in California, and we did not see him often. When we were young, he would come to Red Oaks often, to play with us and to visit Daddy and Mother. But then something had started to change, and we saw him less and less. He brought us the best presents and spent hours playing games and walking with us through the woods. Uncle Austin always had a way of listening to me—even when I was a child—that made me feel I was just as important as an adult. He did not casually listen while looking around for something else to do, or ask me to hurry my stories. No, Uncle Austin had *really* listened to me, as far back as I could remember.

But something, like the slow erosion of a rock in the waves of the ocean, had changed. Not so much in his demeanor towards me, but more in his character. Red Oaks seemed less like a respite for him and more like an irritant. The tension began to mount considerably around the dinner table when he would discuss what he called the *politics of the Simulacrum* with Daddy. Years ago, those dinners had just been good conversations over mashed potatoes and red wine. But as more distance and time grew between his visits to Red Oaks, those conversations would end with Uncle Austin pushing away from the table, still chewing on his bitter words, as he packed his bags to leave again. He hadn't been here since the last Council meeting.

Uncle Austin sat on the edge of the desk with his hands folded into his lap. In his green cargo jacket and dark-washed jeans, he looked full of energy even though he had traveled all day. "Where is everybody?" he asked timidly, with a smile that did not completely hide the unease behind his eyes.

"I'm not sure. What time is it?" I asked, more to myself than to him. The clock said 3:15. I had lost most of the day.

"Well, it's good to be back here at Red Oaks. Since we have this time together, let's not waste it! Tell me what you're up to these days, and how you've been doing. Taking classes now?" There in his face was that look that had always drawn me into talking. The look of true interest, true concern... it was worth its weight in gold to me.

"Right now it's our fall break, but I am taking classes. It's not exactly riveting, but I do enjoy it. Being on campus is interesting; I get to see what the professors are teaching and what the newest issues of concern for the Friguscor are. There is no better place than a college campus to find out the newest reckless causes and harebrained ideas. That part I do enjoy."

Austin's smile stayed in place, and he nodded in agreement, "You've got that right. It was like that when I went to school as well. But don't discount what they are saying before you have heard them out completely. Think of the great teachings, the great philosophers that have come out of university settings. It often takes the youth of society to see dreams that the old can no longer imagine. For that reason alone, you must value their ideals." Austin picked up a round glass paperweight and flipped it in his hand.

"But what about the extremists, who prey upon the inexperience and idealism of youth, manipulating them into becoming robotic clones of their own ideals? Don't they implant their own personal dreams into the minds of the youth, like a usurper who sees the weakness in the very thing that makes them valuable?" I asked, truly interested.

"What weakness makes them valuable?" he retorted, smoothly.

"The ability to see the dream. It's like you said, it's what makes our vitality as youth so valuable. We can dream because life's experiences have not yet pushed us down and blotted out our hopes, but at the same time it can leave us exposed to the wolves who want to use us, manipulate us and prey on our dreams for their own personal desires. This has occurred over and over in history. The dreams of youth can be a great strength when used correctly, but the dreams of youth can also be a Trojan horse....can't they?"

A satisfied smirk crossed his entire face, but I don't know what had amused him so. "Ah, Little Bird, you *are* growing up. Good for you. It is wise to think through such things, to ask many questions and to doubt everything around you. This is how you grow, change, and even how you find purpose in life. I'm glad to see that you have your father's ability to see through the grey in life, but your mother's ability to value the grey.

It was an odd compliment, but I nodded more to myself than to him as I tried to put my finger on the uneasy feeling that had descended on the room. The round glass paperweight rolled out of his hand, and he stretched across the desk to grab it before it shattered on the floor. As he reached, his jacket bunched up around his elbow, causing his forearm to stick out. Then I saw them. He had scars up and down his arm. Scars. Simulacrum do not ordinarily have scars, and if they do, they are only caused by extreme injury.

A memory rushed to mind, of Mother and Daddy speaking in hushed voices in the library early one morning. I remembered how Mother's worried voice trembled when she said, *"Have you told Austin, he must know that they are watching him."*

"Good catch," I said, masking the growing anxiety.

The smell of fermented honey wafted in as Absalom drifted through the door. "Here we are...." he smiled and raised his talon-like hands. As if he were making an announcement he said, in his slow, guttural tone, "Ah, it is the Little Bird." Absalom stood in his long, scarlet robe. It belled around his hands and pooled around his feet when he walked. He wore the robe of the Council Seer all of the time, whereas all of the other Council members only wore their robes during Council meetings. But Absalom had always been...eccentric. He was like a storybook character that had lost his place in time. Maybe he had hopped right out of the pages of his story into another one, and he couldn't get back home again. Absalom was a seer. Actually he was *the* Seer for the Council.

Daddy had told me that Absalom had been elected to the Council because he was more gifted than any seer the Council had ever met, but he feared that Absalom's gifting outweighed his character.

"Veralee and I were just discussing the dreams of youth," Uncle Austin said with a smile and a wink. The same wink that I gave Adair when we were playing with Mattie.

"Ah, yes," Absalom said in his abrupt staccato tone, without taking his eyes off of me. His accent was old European, with harsh articulation. "And what have you been dreaming of these days, Veralee? What secrets have been whispered to you in the dark of night?"

Maybe it was because I had recently been in this very

room with Achiel, or maybe it was because I had never really looked before now, but for the first time I noticed that Absalom's eyes were not at all like mine. They were much too slanted, the pupils too vertical; they were much too…too what? It was odd, because Simulacrum eyes, no matter what race or ethnicity, always looked alike to me. All of a sudden I had a flash of the diamondback rattler Daddy had killed in the back last year. Absalom had eyes like a snake.

"Hmm, Veralee?" asked Uncle Austin.

I thought about the question. So Absalom knew I dreamed, but how much did he actually know? This was the problem with a seer. You never knew how much they really knew. Did he know just enough information in order to gather more from me? By the hungry look on his face, he was used to gathering knowledge like a farmer gathers eggs for breakfast. I drew a veil over myself and masked any transparency.

"I cannot control my dreams; they come and go as they please." There was no point in denying that I could dream, he could see that. But still, I thought it safer to err on the side of caution.

He smiled and clapped his long, bony fingers together into a steeple and then patted them on his red lips. "Of course, my dear girl, of course. That is how dreaming goes. But what," he stretched his long arm out and placed it on my shoulder, "what have you been dreaming lately?" His eyes fluttered slightly and then jerked wide open. "Afraid of something that is coming? Something large that you have been running from?" Then he licked his lips and peered into my eyes, "Veralee, what have you seen in your dreams?" I felt the vibration of his mark run down my spine where he touched my shoulder. Something was wrong. Something was different. I tried to remember Absalom the last time I saw him. It would have been almost seven years ago, but still I could remember him.

Then, he had worn his robe over grey wool slacks and black leather shoes. I remembered him pulling a Hershey's kiss from behind my ear and touching it to my nose playfully before placing it in the palm of my hand. He had sat for long hours in the library, reading through the Histories and making notes on a yellow legal pad.

Uncle Austin pretended to play with the glass paperweight in his hand, but obviously he was listening intently.

"Oh you know, just normal dreams that kids have. I'm at a crossroads in my studies, and I know I have to decide what I am going to do next. Thinking about the next move in my life and career just makes me a bit anxious...there are so many possibilities," I tried to devalue myself with youth.

Uncle Austin flipped the paperweight up high in the air and caught it, "But Veralee, didn't you just tell me that the dreams of kids can be their greatest strength?" he said, pressing down on me. What did they want? What were they getting at here?

"Or their greatest weakness," I said flatly. I was done playing this game. I looked at the two men. They had me cornered between them. Whether or not they meant to, they were making me feel like a caged bird. And I hated, more than anything else, the feeling of bars around me.

I stood up a little taller. I did not know what was going on or why they were asking me these questions. But I knew I didn't play well when cornered. I touched my tseeyen; it was beginning to burn.

"Well, I guess it's about time to get ready for the bonfire tonight. It's going to be pretty chilly. So if ya'll will excuse me," I jerked Absalom's hand from my shoulder and started to the door. "I'm going to see where everyone has gone."

Uncle Austin spoke first, "I've been talking with Ausley today. She told me about the boy." I froze with my hand on the doorknob. Every nerve in my body came to life. *The boy!* I stared out into the foyer, keeping my back to them long enough to compose my face into a hard wall. What had Ausley told them? They knew about Nathan. Turning around, I closed the door behind me and leaned against it, keeping a hand on the doorknob just in case.

"What boy?" I asked, defiantly.

"The child that you saved, Veralee. I'm sorry that I didn't just come right out and ask you, it's just so amazing to me. I want to know everything." Uncle Austin looked like a child himself all of a sudden. His baby face was always soft and round, and his eyes still held the excitement of youth. "Veelee, seriously, I'm sorry if I was acting strange, I just have to know...did you really save that boy? Because I would have done the same thing." His words were a dangerous confession. He would have done the same thing? A short beat of relief pulsed through me. Then he continued, "I know it was your last resort; I know that the boy was dying. I know you were trying to save his life." He paused, then continued slower, quieter, "You see, Veelee, I *have* done the same thing." I looked over at Absalom who had sat himself in the winged chair by the fire. He was calm. This was not new information for him; he knew all of it.

"*What* have you done?" I asked. The possibility that I was not alone in my act of defiance against the Simulacrum gave me a thrill of comfort like eating chicken and dumplings when you'd been sick.

Austin sighed deeply and gazed out the window, "Veralee, I...several years ago, I met a woman named Caraway. She was an artist who painted the most beautiful portraits you have ever seen. When she painted it looked like the people in her pictures could reach out and touch you, they were so lifelike. She lived in the apartment next to mine, and we became friends. It was so nice to have a friend out there, someone to watch a movie with, someone to laugh with and someone to share the day's events with. We decided to commit ourselves to each other completely," he said.

"You never told us that you—" I cut in, shocked by his words.

He used his words like a shoulder and pushed back into the conversation, "My life is my own. I may be Simulacrum, but they do not own me body and soul. Caraway and I loved each other, and I knew that I could not live without her anymore." He looked out the windows again, like the dirt road would take him far away from his own story. "She had the most beautiful hands," he said, in a faraway voice. I watched the tears spill over his cheeks and felt the burn of them in my heart. This time I allowed the silence to wrap him in her arms and comfort him.

"But...after a while," he continued with trembling lips, "she got sick. Really sick. The doctors didn't find it until it had spread to her lymph nodes. The cancer....it was everywhere." I froze. Sick? Cancer? The room spun a little as I tried to make sense of his words. Caraway was not Simulacrum? She was....? Austin was so wrapped up in the pain of his memory that he did not see me nearly swoon, but Absalom did. Absalom met my eyes, and I knew he had been watching me the entire time.

"Have you ever seen someone you love die of pain and sickness?" Austin laughed a harsh, cynical laugh, "No, of course not. We do not see such horrors. We are like the rich living among the poor. We are the have's while they are the have not's." His voice was hard now, angry. "According to our rules and our laws, we are supposed to watch the people around us die of sickness, disease and poverty while we sit fat and happy as kings. Let them eat cake, we say!" his voice rose with each word.

Absalom sat silently in the chair with his hands folded in his lap, but his eyes never missed a thing. I could feel him from across the room, like he had tentacles that prodded my mind for every thought, every reaction, and every emotion. Breathing deliberately, I controlled my face and made myself a statue, refusing to give him the show he clearly wanted from me. Austin continued, "I refused to let her die, she was the most magnificent thing I had ever seen, she was good and pure and mine. She was mine...so I did what you did, Veralee. I made the choice to save life instead of ignoring it, like it didn't even matter. I had spent too many years of walking by these people like they had no value. I believed for far too long that they didn't matter because my blood was different from theirs. Who decided that mine was better and theirs was worth less? Who decided that?" he held his open palms out to me, gesturing for an answer. I had none.

My gaze drifted to the floor. His were words I had thought many times, but they still seemed wrong somehow. Absalom spoke now, "It is hard for the deer to realize that the hunter needs meat to live, fur to stay warm, and food for their children. The deer wants to believe that the hunter is a monster, not a man trying to survive the best he knows how. The hunter has no more choice in being the stalker than the deer has in being the prey."

Had I not done the same thing with Nathan? Had I not chosen to give him life, even though our laws forbade it? And now, he was Simulacrum, full of possibility. Did he deserve to die, simply because he was born Friguscor? Then the question slipped into my mind like a back door had been cracked open, *What if we helped the Friguscor instead of leaving them to die? What if we gave them our blood…the blood that changes, that transforms, that heals and gives life…instead of letting them die? How could it be bad to help those who are in such need?*

I looked directly at Absalom and saw the question on his face, as if it was he who had spoken into my mind. Even Achiel had said we made rules that we should not. What other rules did we not need? What if our rules, which were crucial to our survival at one time, were now are keeping us from fulfilling our purpose? I felt confused, like I didn't know my own thoughts from alien thoughts that seemed to be circling inside my head. It was hard for me to think clearly.

Absalom and Austin both started to speak at the same time, but Austin acquiesced to Absalom with a hand gesturing for him to continue. "What has happened to the boy, Veralee?" Absalom watched me entirely, like my body language spoke as loud as my words.

I didn't want to talk about Nathan. I didn't want to bring him into this, not before I knew what this conversation was about.

So I didn't. "What happened to Caraway? Where is she now?" I directed my question to Uncle Austin. I knew the answer, or at least part of it, before he answered it by the look in his eyes. She was dead, as dead as the hope in Austin's eyes. He swallowed down a lump in his throat, "That is part of the reason I am telling you this story, Veralee. Caraway, she...after I gave her my blood she seemed like she was getting better, at least at first, for a while. You see, I waited too long maybe, but I knew the rules of our people and it wasn't until she was taking her last breath that I cut my wrist. I sat and let my blood drip down into her mouth slowly as the tears dripped down my face. Then the color returned to her face as I held her hand, and she started to stir. Her eyes opened, and she sat up. You can't imagine how happy I was. She did well for two days; it was quite remarkable. I thought I had done it; I thought she was changing, but then...then the hunger began. Caraway came down with what I thought was the flu, and then she started to do crazy things...she begged me for more blood. She said she was hurting, that she knew she would die without it...and so I started...feeding her." He stopped speaking abruptly and I felt as if his words had slapped me hard with terror. *Feeding her.*

"How did she die?" I asked slowly, not wanting to know, but needing to know.

His eyes looked wild with passion, "I...killed her. These hands, that promised to love her...that touched her face and held her each night, these hands," he said holding them up like they were traitors who did not belong to him. Then he dropped them down to his lap again, "It took a while, but she finally came for me. It wasn't really her anymore, but something else altogether, something I had created in her." He stopped then and wiped his face. I didn't need to know anymore. I had seen this already, in the little house where Nathan had lived. I never wanted to see it again.

"So it doesn't work," I said softly. But Austin jerked his head up and said, "No, that's not true at all. I didn't do it right, I didn't know what I was doing, and there is still hope for the Friguscor. Don't you see, Veralee? Caraway, she was so full of life and she was...mine. I can't stop trying. I see her in all of them now."

I looked hard at him, searching for the rational man I knew, but finding a stranger sitting in front of me. "Uncle Austin....our blood killed her...it changed into a cold-blooded killer...and you had to kill her!" I all but shouted at him.

He jumped up from the desk. "And what about the boy? What about the boy, Veralee?" he said, with venom in his voice. I set my mouth in a hard line as he continued, "I think he is alive... not only alive, I think he has changed! I think he is Simulacrum! Am I right?" How did he know this? I felt a strong need to protect Nathan rise inside of me, to hide him from them for a reason I could not completely understand.

Absalom calmly spoke, "Veralee, we will not harm the boy. Please do not think such a thing. The boy is amazing. He is the proof, the miracle we have been looking for. We want to help the Friguscor. We cannot leave them to die, alone and wounded as they are. We can offer them life, and I think you know that. You have seen the power that our blood has to transform. You yourself have seen it change the boy, have you not?" He knew.

Quickly I nodded once in confirmation but kept my lips sealed, not trusting what they would say. Absalom breathed deeply and leaned in, letting his seductive passion leak out through his voice, "Veralee...Veralee..." I hated how he rolled my name around in his mouth. "Don't you see? *You* have the gift to change them. Your blood is transformational, it is strong and pure. Not all of the Simulacrum can change them, but you can. You can give life where death is trying to steal it."

"What do you mean, my blood can change them? We all have the same blood," I asked, confused. I had never heard of this before.

Austin laughed again, and it was an unnerving sound, "No, no Veralee. That we do not. If I had had your blood, well then, Caraway would still be alive. But I do not have blood that changes them as you do. I do not have that gift. Ironically, I would give all of my gifts away to have the one you do not even know you have." He smiled at me, and I saw that the pain of loss was like a destructive drug to him. It was controlling him, driving him to act and not think. My heart hurt for him, and I pitied him then.

Absalom looked from Austin to me, "Veralee, the ability to change, to transform is only given to certain Simulacrum. You have that gift. I can smell it in your blood, and it is strong in you. You can help us. You can help them," he said. Help them?

"What do you mean... help them?" I asked, feeling like the statement held a much deeper meaning than it seemed on the surface.

Absalom stood up, "Why, help us change the Friguscor, of course. Veralee, it has already begun....we just need the Council to agree." His cutting tone was undergirded with obsession.

"We are going to ask the Council to amend the law that says we cannot share our blood with the Friguscor," Austin said feverishly.

Amend the law; share our blood; change them now.

"But they haven't changed that law in a thousand years....they aren't going to change it now," I said, incredulously.

"So your reasoning is that we don't try because it has always been a certain way, so it always *should* be a certain way? Where is your belief in fighting for what is right? We don't fight for what is right because it is easy; we fight because it is the RIGHT thing to do!" Uncle Austin looked like a man in the middle of a marathon who still had 13 miles to go, exhausted but determined to cross the finish line.

"But what about the reason they made it a law to begin with? We don't know what will happen if we begin to share our blood. Every time the Simulacrum have tried that, we have ended up running for our lives. Look at the results with Caraway! You had to kill the very one you hoped to save! And anyway, how would I help you with the Council? I'm not even on the Council," I almost yelled at them.

Absalom spoke quietly, "You can help us...by showing the boy. Show the boy to the Council, show that he has changed. Then they will see." Show Nathan? I read through his words quickly. Use Nathan. Use him to stand against the Council for a testimony. The problem was that we didn't even know what had really happened with Nathan. He must be Boged for the blood to have changed him, but that was all we knew. We didn't know if it would happen the same way again, or if it would be catastrophic the next time. Nathan was a child, not a pawn in whatever game these men were playing.

Absalom continued slowly, as if walking over a rickety bridge. "We know this is all new for you right now, and we have given you much to think about today. All I ask of you is that you do *think* about it. Really *think* about that fact that you have in your veins the ability to give life, to help the helpless and to change the world. And you have evidence in the boy of what can be done...and what can be undone."

With that I turned and walked out of the room. But I did not close the door on my way out. I did not know what to think or believe, so I left the door wide open.

{ 18 }

the Seer

I slipped through hidden trails, carrying food from the kitchen and clothes I had picked up for Nathan. As I approached the backside of the cottage, I could tell Atticus and Nathan were outside. Their voices, carried by the wind, found me as I rounded the corner to the house. I stopped for a second, eager to hear the way Atticus spoke to Nathan when I wasn't around. Fleetingly, I was transported and saw him standing with a knife in his hand in the living room of that small, dim house. There was a part of him that I could not fully understand, a part that I never would be able to be completely comfortable with. But it was a part of who he was, and I could not change that. I heard Nathan ask Atticus something under the muffled sounds of the swing swaying back and forth.

His voice was quieter, but it seemed to hold within it the character of a grown man, more than a simple boy of six years. "But, my hands," Nathan marveled, "they look so different." He held them high, letting the waning sunlight slip between his fingers.

Atticus chuckled softly. "Yes, I remember my hands looking different when I became Simulacrum as well. Even though you have changed, you are still you, but you are no longer a cold-heart, or Friguscor."

"But I'm still a people? I'm still a people like you, right?" asked Nathan.

Atticus smiled. "You are still a ' people;' you are still human. But a very long time ago, there was just one kind of ' people.' Then something happened and people split into two types: some are cold hearts, we call them Friguscor, and some are Simulacrum, like you and me. We still look similar, like different types of dogs do. We Simulacrum have two legs, two arms, and a head, just like the Friguscor. But things about our insides are different," Atticus explained.

"People come in different colors. My friend Mack was black here and here," Nathan pointed to his face and arms, "but I don't think he was different. He was just the same as me. I liked him a lot. We had lots of fun together. Was Mack's insides different?" Nathan asked with what sounded like a mouth full of food.

"No, not at all. That is not what I meant. This does not have anything to do with the color of our skin, or our hair, or anything like that. Those things are just how we look to other people. It would be like...if you took a piece of white paper and colored it green. It would still be paper, just a different color. It would be a very dull place if we all had the same color hair and skin and eyes, don't you think?

Nathan nodded his head, thinking. "Yeah, I like red. I color with it a lot. I like fire trucks. They're red."

"Fire trucks? Atticus was obviously trying to figure out what a fire truck was. "These are vehicles which carry fire, or these are vehicles which are burning with fire?"

Nathan chuckled. "You're silly, Atticus! Fire trucks don't carry fire, they put *out* fires! Whooosh!" Nathan made the sound and motion of a fire hose spraying.

"Ah, of course. They put *out* fires," Atticus responded, obviously not exactly sure, but he went on. "No, this is much deeper than outside things. You can feel many of the differences. The special part of our blood, the Eiani, makes things warm and alive, but the blood of the Friguscor is different. It takes life away from them, little by little bit. From the moment they are born they begin to die. Do you remember the color of your skin, and how it was starting to crack and itch?"

"Yes. I know about blood, too. Sometimes if you scratch too hard, the blood comes out... Mommy always said, ' Don't scratch, Nathan, you'll make it bleed.'"

Atticus continued, "Right. The others, the Friguscor, they know something is not right about their way of life, but they just don't know what. Some get sick and die from disease."

Nathan interjected, "Like Nana and Pops? Pops just died one day. He wasn't sick; he just fell over, Nana said. I asked her to be careful so she didn't fall over. She gave me a big hug and said that Pops was sick on the inside where we couldn't see. Then Nana got sick and came to stay with us. I loved her; she read me stories at night. But she couldn't breathe good, and she had this tube sticking in her nose and it went to a big tank next to her, and it helped her breathe. Then she just didn't breathe anymore. I was sad when those men came and got her. I thought it would be fun for her to ride in the am-boo-lance with all the si-reens going, ' woo,woo,woo,' but she never came back. Mommy said Nana's heart was sick and quit working."

"Did you have other grandparents?" Atticus asked.

"Do I have some other ones? I don't think so, because Daddy never had a Mommy or Daddy. He grew up in a house with lots of kids, but they weren't his brothers or sisters. He didn't have any of those either, like me. Neither did Mommy. It was just Mommy and Daddy and me." That answered the question of other relatives, then.

Atticus gave Nathan an affectionate swipe across his blonde head, "Well, you have me now, and Veralee, too."

Nathan nodded and smiled. "I still miss my mommy sometimes, but Miss Veralee is so nice. I like her a lot." Then his face clouded. "Did my mommy get sick like that, like you said? My daddy was so mean. I don't know why he got so mean, was he sick, too? Why did Daddy hurt Mommy?"

Atticus thought for a minute and then started to explain. "Well, you said you remember how your skin itched and burned sometimes. And we talked about how our blood is different from the blood of the Friguscor."

Nathan nodded, "Yes, Daddy wanted Mommy's blood. She gave him some, but it made him sick and then he got meaner. He was not sharing; he wanted all of Mommy's blood. And he wanted mine, too. And then...then...why did Daddy get so mean? Mommy was sharing with him."

Atticus sadly tried to make some sense of it for the child. "Yes, if the Friguscor do get some of the *good* blood, they want more and more. It is like being so hungry that you would do anything for it. It is like a mean lion that wakes up so hungry that it kills everything it sees to get something to eat. When the *Esurio* awakens in them, it will be fed." Atticus became quiet then.

Nathan put down his cup slowly. "The ee...shur....e,i,ei,o?"

Atticus's words felt far away, like he was remembering another time. "Esurio," he corrected, "it is a name we gave to the *hunger.*"

"Yes, that thing. It's always in them? Was it in me?"

Atticus looked at the small boy. "Yes, it was in you. It is in all the cold-hearts. You are young, but you began to feel the *Esurio* with your first breath. It drives them forward, always searching, always wanting more, never satisfied, never content. It is the Esurio that causes war, and it is the drive of Esurio that causes the murder of innocent people. It is the Esurio that causes a thief to steal. The Esurio is always with them, and it drives them to evil."

"Because they want life? Because they know only death? But what they really want...is life?" Nathan asked, sounding once again like a grown man instead of a small child.

Atticus looked at Nathan, as if he were determining that the child was wiser than his years and added, "Yes. That is it exactly. They want life; everything in them longs for life, but all they have is the death they are born with. So they seek to fill the void—the gaping wound in their innermost being—with anything that satisfies their flesh in the moment."

Atticus knew I was there. I felt his tseeyen greet me with vibration. Stepping onto the porch, I felt his eyes follow my every move. "I think that is enough talk about the *Esurio*, Atticus," I said, chiding him with a smile.

Nathan's little eyes had grown wide and his mouth had fallen open at Atticus' grim words, but when he saw me, he grinned, showing his square little teeth. I sat down beside him on the swing and pulled his tiny frame to me. Atticus put his arm around Nathan and rested his hand on my shoulders.

"I suppose you are correct. I forget sometimes. I am a soldier, and not cunarius....hmm....babysitter, yes that is it. I have never had a child of my own." He looked at me for a long moment and then let a soft smile spread across his lips. His lips stretched into a full smile as our eyes met and then my cheeks blushed red. We sat there together, swinging rhythmically, while the sun hovered above Red Oaks. Nathan put his hand in mine, and I felt his contentment spread through me. His emotions were becoming easier to read the more time I spent with him. The bond was deepening between us, and we both felt the light weight of love building.

"I have another question." Nathan piped up after some

time of silence.

"Oh, do you now? Have you been asking questions all day?" I asked, in the same voice I used for little Mattie.

"Yes, Atticus said I could ask as many as I wanted today. This morning at breakfast, he said it was a great day for questions.

"Well, sounds like y'all have been busy today," I said winking at Atticus. Mattie had taught me what it was like to spend the day with a child full of questions: it is exhausting, but also pretty entertaining.

"Just one more," added Atticus, "we don't want to use them all up in one day."

"Well, the Friguscor...they die right?" Nathan said. Atticus nodded. "Well, then...what about the Sim-ya-cooms...what about us?" Nathan asked.

"Well, you know about your mother...you said you saw her on a boat, that she was still alive," I said.

"Yes, but...but so do the Sim-ya-cooms *ever* die?" he asked sheepishly, like he was trying to connect the numbered dots in a coloring book to see the full picture.

I put my other hand over his and then flipped his palm over so that I could trace the long line in his hand. "No, we do not die in the same way that the Friguscor do. The Eiani in us is immortal, that means it lives forever, and it changes us so that we are immortal, too. We can be hurt, and this body can be broken to the point that it can no longer live, but otherwise, we live much, much longer than the Friguscor. When it is time for us to enter the deep sleep, we simply close our eyes on this world and on this body and wake up on the boats to the new world...just like your Mommy showed you. Death for the Friguscor is permanent. But for us...death is simply a door."

"A door...to the new place?" inquired the little curious six-year-old with eyes as big as saucers. I smiled, seeing the innocence in him again.

Atticus continued where I had left off, "The new world is where we are meant to live. It's where we are always trying to get back to, in one way or another. There, our lives truly begin, and not just simply continue. All Simulacrum are gathered there to live for all of time once the Door opens, but until that time, we live either here or in the Terebinths of Mamre."

"I've heard of this before. It's like in the stories Atticus told me," Nathan said.

"Yes, long ago, Simulacrum wrote the secrets about their real lives into stories to protect us all," I said. "Most believe that these are simply fairytales, but we know they are real. They are the truths that this world is founded upon," I said with a new understanding, surprising even myself. "They *are* real." Atticus noticed my intonation. He nodded at me with approval in his eyes, but said nothing more.

How long had it taken for the truth of the legends to seep into *his* bones and become his waking life? Maybe when he first saw the Man of Words? Or when he plunged into the River that first time? The past several weeks had taken me on this journey of finding myself—maybe I was rediscovering the truth in the legends of the Eiani that ran through me. Maybe it was more about finding who I was in relation to the Simulacrum—to the blood inside of me—and less about finding myself in relation to who I *wanted* to be. Maybe I had gotten those two things mixed up along the way.

Nathan scrunched up his nose, "But...what do you mean? Who chooses to go across on the boats? Who has too many years and who lives on like long days, or with days that are long or, or..?" He did not miss a beat.

I looked quickly toward Atticus. What did Atticus want to tell him? How much did he want Nathan to know? This was Atticus's story to tell, not mine. Atticus, always weighing his words, spoke candidly with Nathan.

"Each of us has a different part to play in this world, Nathan. We are all pieces of a giant mosaic, or a puzzle, and we all have to do our part to see that the picture is completed. Some of the Simulacrum live many, many years."

Nathan blurted out, "How many years?"

Atticus shrugged, "I do not know. I have met some who have walked this earth for the better part of a century or more. But a decision was made, long ago that in order to protect our people, in order to hide us better, that all but a select few would leave this land at a certain age."

Atticus abruptly stopped talking and went rigid. He must have smelled him before I saw him, for he stood and protectively tried to hide Nathan behind his body.

"Well, hello," Absalom whined. He looked through Atticus. "You are the child we have been waiting for, young Nathan." Absalom kept his steady gaze on Nathan. The smell of stale honey rolled off of him and spoiled the air around us. It conjured the image of finding an old jar of honey that had been left open, letting moisture in. Absalom's scent was like fermented honey I remembered tasting before. The taste was off, stronger, with the bite of alcohol.

Quickly I spoke to Atticus, "This is Absalom, the Council Seer."

Absalom's head jerked toward Atticus, and he smiled brightly. "Atticus, that is not a name you hear every day...or every year, for that matter."

Atticus's tension was palpable, and Absalom's excitement undeniable. "Long ago I heard that name, but it has been," he thought for a moment, "well, it has been too long for me to remember when, I guess. I am an old man now, and sometimes these things just slip from my mind." Absalom smiled feebly and folded his hands together. Atticus remained alert, standing with his hand on Nathan.

"Can I help you, Absalom? We were just about to go in," I said. I knew he was here to see Nathan. He had undoubtedly followed me here. How long had he been listening to us talk? Unease crept into my mind.

"I had to see the boy. He truly is amazing, Veralee. This is what your blood can do!" he said, extending his hands toward Nathan. "A miracle. This is what I am asking to show the Council. They will not be able to deny the power of change once they see him."

Atticus stole a hard look at me, and then he inched away from Nathan, leaning on the porch railing and directing the rest of the conversation to follow. He addressed Absalom, "What are you talking about?"

I spoke quickly, trying to catch him up to speed, "Absalom and my Uncle Austin spoke with me earlier. They want to speak with the Council and ask for the law to be changed, for an allowance to be made to change the Friguscor. They believe they can be changed, and they want to ask for permission to try."

Atticus blurted out, "Are you mad? Do you know what you would do?"

Absalom stayed calm and rubbed his hands together, as if to warm them. "We will give them the chance at life, to live and not to die. Look at the boy; he has been given a chance at life, to live for all of time. Do you not think all deserve that right?"

Atticus looked as if he was talking to a living nightmare. "You are ignorant of the workings of our blood on the Friguscor. We do not know why some turn and why some do not."

Absalom pushed back in, like a foot catching a closing door. "We believe in giving them a chance. What they do with that chance is up to them, but we have to believe it is worth saving a few," Absalom's words were full of passion, though they sounded devoid of wisdom.

I broke through their standoff, "You say that as if the Friguscor have a choice. It is not up to them at all, Absalom. Some will turn yes, but the rest...the rest will turn into monsters."

Atticus followed me, "Monsters who will stop at nothing, who will kill their own children for the blood, who will destroy everything in order to hunt us down and devour each and every one of us."

The ice in Absalom's eyes cut as he spoke. "A price must always be paid, boy." He said with venom, "the price to find the Boged is to be paid by the rest of the Friguscor."

I spoke louder than I intended, "Who are you to decide the price for life?"

Atticus spoke so low that I almost did not hear him at first, "You have no idea what you speak of; you have not seen the horrors that this would unleash on the world. The price would be on all of us; the cost would be our existence on this earth."

Absalom matched Atticus's level when he spoke. "It is part of the plan; I assume you have read the Histories. It is part of the end of days. You cannot stop it, nor can I. We can only do our part."

"I do not believe that forcing these events to happen, that forcing your own personal plans and costing the Simulacrum their very existence, is a part of the plan," I said, attempting to fathom the gravity of Absalom's words.

"Then you choose to do nothing? That is your answer? To let them die out there on the streets? Look at him," Absalom said, pointing his long fingers at Nathan, still sitting on the swing. "Can you really tell me that he didn't deserve the chance to change? Can you tell me you regret changing him? I can see that you are already bonded to the boy, and it was compassion for his life that caused you to act, to change him. If you choose to sit by and do nothing, then you are still choosing. You are choosing to let them all die."

His words cut through and hit me hard. He was right in so many ways. I did not regret changing Nathan. I looked over at his soft blond hair that even now seemed darker than it did yesterday. He was changing so much. His eyes looked like mine, they had the light of life burning behind them and the Eiani running through his veins made his tiny hands warm. *Didn't he deserve the right to live?* Absalom was right, and yet...something about it was all wrong.

He watched me, knowing he had spoken the exact words that would entangle me. Even that seemed wrong. *Why should he use words to entangle me into his web of plans? Why did he need Nathan or me? Couldn't he leave us out of this?*

"You are right," I said cautiously, "I do not regret changing him, and I would do it again if I had to. They, the Friguscor, they should have life as well, and I do not know why I was chosen to live this life, and they were chosen to live theirs. But, to do something so hastily, so rash because we do not have the discipline to wait, to keep our hands still long enough to see a clear way through this issue...that is just as wrong."

Absalom looked directly at me and bent his ear toward me, "Veralee, I am not asking you to be quick at your decision or to follow me just because I have asked. I am asking you not to be complacent, not to sit by while the world dies. I saw the horrors of complacency in Germany long ago, and it is as cruel a murder as vengeance can be." His words were quiet and convicting.

Atticus broke through their spell, "Your hastiness, your form of a solution, will bring our downfall."

Absalom pressed his lips hard and then smiled slightly. "It comes whether you will it or not. You have read the words in our Histories. You grant me too much credit, young Atticus. My hands cannot bring our downfall. It is the words that have already been spoken into existence that has done this thing to us. I am not opening a door; I am merely looking for a key to unlock it. The words alone can open the Door," he stepped back and inclined his head slightly and said, "as you should well know, Ayindalet."

Atticus did not move; he did not flinch or show any surprise that Absalom knew who and what he was. After all, Absalom was a seer, and it was a seer's gift to see. Absalom focused back on me, "Veralee, I will not ask you now, but please think on the things we have talked about. Think about Nathan. And when you have to come to the conclusion that I can already see is in you, stand with us at the Council meeting and lend your voice to change the world."

"And just how are you going to change the world today, Veralee?" Mother's voice rang out from the path in front of the house. My heart skipped a beat when I saw her standing there, holding the floral bag she used to carry casseroles. We all froze like an ice storm had suddenly hit us.

"Gail, it really is a wonderful day out," Absalom said. "I was out walking and found these three enjoying their day on the porch. Well, now that you have come to chaperone," he said winking and grinning much too broadly, "I will be on my way to enjoy the trees." He walked down the steps and waved goodbye. Mother waved and said something pleasant, but she seemed very aware of the hostile dynamic in the air. I couldn't hear her over the sound of my beating heart. There was no time to put Nathan inside. I looked at her as she walked up the porch steps. She knew. Her face was heavy, her eyes focused on Nathan.

She came up the steps and dropped the bag as her hands flew up to cover her mouth. "So it is true," she said in a whisper. I did not respond. She came close to Nathan and bent down to meet his eyes. He looked nervous for a moment, but then Mother reached out her hand and touched his cheek gently. Without saying a word, she placed her tseeyen on his. Their eyes met, and they both smiled warmly.

"Hello. I'm Gail, but you can call me Grandmother if you would like," she said with the same voice she used to comfort me as a child in her dark brown rocking chair.

All caution left Nathan's face. "I'm Nathan. I'm six years old, and I would like to call you Grandmother. You're warm, and I like your eyes. They look like Veralee's."

"What a fitting name for such a boy. Do you know what your name means in the ancient language?" she asked kindly.

Nathan's eyes got big and he shook his head vigorously, "No...do you know?"

"Mmmhmm," Mother's delicate hands touched both sides of his cheeks as she spoke, "I do. Your name means ' to give' or ' gift.' Like giving a gift, or it means you *are* a gift." Then she tapped his nose, "I wonder...what have you been given or what might you have to give?" She looked directly at me, and I knew she meant the question for me as well.

She sighed and looked down at her feet for a long moment, like she was an egg shattered on the floor and needed time to pull herself back together. I hated it, and I wished I could make her see that we were going to be all right. But I knew she deserved the time and opportunity to work this out for herself, just as I had done. Then, as if she had decided to overcome her grief, she looked up at me, "Veralee, I can see you in him already," was all that she said.

Atticus stepped back, giving her room to sit on the swing with Nathan. She sat for a time with Nathan on the swing, holding his hand and allowing the weight of the situation to fully fall onto her lap. I stood by the door and let the time work its way through us. All the while Atticus stood leaning on a rail. He did not look directly at me, but I felt him the entire time. My arm buzzed with the familiar feeling of him, and I knew that he was comforting me. I let it wash over me and wrap me like a warm coat.

"I'm very hungry," Nathan said in a tiny voice, "could I please have something to eat?"

He looked toward me, but Mother answered first. "Why, yes. Do you see that brown bag? I brought you something special to eat." She turned and spoke to Atticus, "Atticus could you help him inside with the bag?"

Atticus agreed quickly and led Nathan through the door. His hand briefly touched mine, telling me without words that he was near.

"You spoke with Daddy," I stated as soon as the door closed.

She looked at me with eyes full of pain. "Yes, Veralee. He told me." Her shoulders dropped, and she sighed. "Oh, my Little Bird."

"I'm sorry, Mother. I am so sorry...I just couldn't let him die. I—" my voice broke, and I shut my mouth hard.

Mother gently pulled me onto the swing and touched her tseeyen to mine. "Little Bird, I know. I know...truly I do. It was your heart that led you to do what has been done. He is a beautiful boy. He is, I see he has you in him; already he has begun to resemble you. I do not fault you or your decision really, but I fear that it will bring you great heartache." She pushed the hair back behind my ear. "Veralee, the Council...you know that you have broken our law." Her voice shook slightly as she spoke.

I nodded. "Yes, Daddy said he would see what he could do."

She bit her bottom lip. "They will not take this as a light violation of our laws; they will not let this be borne easily.

If they did, then you could see the repercussions that it could create. They are not cruel, and they will not wish for you to endure any hardship, but you understand why their hands will be tied." I knew. If we did not follow our laws, then the laws would become meaningless. If we did not have consequences, then what would keep them intact?

"I know, Mother. I have been thinking about it. I am prepared for what they will give me as a penalty for my crime," I said, squaring my shoulders. She looked fearful for a moment, and then swallowed it down.

Her hands covered mine, and she rubbed my skin with her thumb, "I know you will. You are strong, Veralee. You always have been. I just wish... I wish that I could make it easy for you. I wish I could take it from you." No truer words had ever been spoken. I knew that this came from the depth of her heart. She would have taken every scraped knee for me, every hard turn in life, if she could. "You know that I will stand with you," she affirmed. She would walk to the ends of the earth for me and back.

"Yes, I know that." I leaned into her shoulder. "Sometimes, I wish that I could have stayed little, that I could have stayed a child underneath these trees. It would have been a great place to stay forever... and it would have made my life so much easier," I added jokingly.

"If I could have found a way, I would have kept you little. But in spite of my best efforts, you continued to grow," she said with a sad smile in her voice.

"Veralee, I need you to listen to me. Let your father

and me help you at the Council meeting. Let us lead the way for you. We know the laws much better than you. Let your father speak for you, and hold your tongue until they ask for your input." The disciplinarian entered her voice. This was the firm voice she used when she was laying down the law. There was no use arguing with her. She had already decided.

"Um, okay," I said.

"No, I mean it, Veralee. Hold your tongue. Do not speak until you are asked for your input. Let your father and me handle this," she reiterated. I saw then that she was pleading with me. Her hands trembled slightly, and her lip quivered. I did not know how, but I knew I had to give this to her. I had to agree.

"I will," I said. She searched my face, "I promise," I finally acquiesced. Only then did she breathe deeply and let her body relax against the back of the swing.

Then we spoke at the same time.
"I think it's time for me to tell you—" She said as I said, "We should check on the boys."

We both smiled.

"Well, should we see how Nathan is doing? What did you make him anyways? Homemade macaroni and cheese?" I asked as I started to stand. She pulled me back down with a thud.

"Veralee, I must speak to you about one more matter," her voice was grave. "You know his purpose as an Ayindalet." She tilted her head toward the door. She was speaking of Atticus. I felt the heat rise in my body,

"Yes. I know," I said, matter-of-factly.

"Veralee, I know you decided to turn Jackson down, and I understand why you did, but this..." she pointed to the door, "this cannot fill your void."

"This?" I asked, feeling the anger rising. "You mean Atticus?"

She put a hand on my leg, trying to calm me. "Honey, listen to me. I know. I can see how you look at him, and how he looks at you. I can see it in both of you. It's not that."

"Then what are you talking about?" I asked, frustrated.

"Veralee, listen to me. He will leave; maybe soon, maybe later, maybe even today. He is pulled down the River of Time, and he does not control it. He cannot promise you a second of his *day*, much less the years of his life. His time is not his own; he cannot promise you a future." My fingers trembled with anger, but I knew her words were true so I listened as she continued.

"I do not say these things to hurt you, but this," she pointed again, "this will end in heartbreak. It has nowhere else to go." Her eyes were soft and sympathetic. I wanted to argue. I wanted to scream that she was wrong, that she didn't understand. But it wasn't true. The same fears had been circling my mind like turkey vultures above a possum carcass on the side of the road.

"I know." I felt bile rise up in my throat. "Don't you think I've thought about these things? I'm not a silly girl who runs after every guy she meets. I know what you say it true, but I can't stop what has already been started. I can't change the way I feel," I said with desperation. Having these things said out loud made them feel more real, more painful even. When they were left unspoken, they seemed to have less power over me.

Mother looked at me with wise eyes, full of understanding. "No, I guess you are right. You cannot stop what has already been started, but you can protect your heart, Veralee. For your own sake, and his, try to cut the bond that is being tied between you. I want you to find a match you can bond yourself to wholeheartedly. I want you to be happy with a man who loves you fiercely. But in this I see only a hard road that leads you to a broken heart. Are you ready to walk that alone? Because he will not be able to walk it with you. You do know that, my darling? His purpose is not to stay with you, but to continue down the River until the Door appears."

Her words stung; they seared like hot coals against my skin. She put her arms gently around me and held me to her on the swing. "My Little Bird, I am so sorry. I do not want your path to be hard. But I'm afraid, as the days come to pass, that you will walk a hard road, and I know that I cannot save you from it. I just don't want you to make it harder than it has to be, if that is at all possible. Use the strength in your blood to stay focused, to stay the course."

"But Mother, the course has already been put before me. I cannot control where it takes me now. It has already begun. I love him, Mother. I love Atticus." Her eyes met mine and were full of hot tears, mirroring my own. She did not speak, but kissed my forehead like it would erase the stubbornness from my mind...or maybe it was her blessing. Maybe it was both. Then she touched my cheek with her gentle hand, like she always did, and stood to leave with trembling lips. A lone tear escaped her control and ran unhindered down her cheek. She wiped it from her jaw.

"Just make sure that you don't make it harder than it has to be, Little Bird. No matter what, you must be strong enough to walk your path all the way to the end. Never stop; never give up, for it is for this purpose that you were born." Turning from me, she walked down the path towards home.

I sat on the small white porch alone. It seemed even smaller without Mother there. Tears pooled in my eyes. Suddenly I was very tired. Curling up on the swing, I closed my eyes, begging for sleep to come. I could sleep until the struggles of the day washed away into distant memory. Too much information swirled in my head, too many decisions and too much responsibility lay on my shoulders.

Then I thought of Nathan—of his bright face. I thought of Atticus and my dreams of running with him right beside me. *I love him.* I did not know where I was going, but now I knew... *I would go where he goes.*

I sat straight up and put my feet solidly on the ground. I would not cry. I would not sleep away the hard. There was more in me than that. The Eiani flowed through my veins, and it called me forward, even now. My course has already been put before me, and now, there could be no turning back.

{ 19 }

the Edge of Dark

The sun set slowly on the edge of darkness that night, lingering above the trees and creating a magical dome around us within the little cottage. Up at the Big House, they would be sitting under lanterns that hung from the giant oaks, enjoying dinner under the stars. Ausley would help mother set the table, with Vera's beautiful china. Daddy would share the best wine to celebrate the occasion, and Ausley would sit beside Uncle Austin. PH would present the ribs he had worked on all day, and Adair would serve a cake fit for a wedding. After dinner, they would sit around the bonfire and tell stories about life. Those stories had always been my favorite part of a gathering.

I should have been there with my family, but something had changed inside of me. My place was here now, with Atticus and Nathan. Tucked securely within the old walls of the cottage, we created a world of pretend between the tiny stove and the simple wooden table. The warmth of the cottage, the fire burning steadily, little Nathan's laughter, and Atticus' touch molded into an intoxicating feeling of home.

Nathan sat on my lap as I read him books and rocked him back and forth, back and forth. Atticus stoked the fire, and I bathed Nathan and dressed him in his dinosaur pajamas. Atticus stayed close to us, as if he was afraid that, at any minute, we would vanish. I touched his arm, or his back, or his hand every time I could, feeling the same fear swirling in me as our happiness grew in each other.

In his eyes I saw longing for the family he might never have and the yearning for more, more of this, more of now. Like children so often did, we pushed away the heaviness of reality and let ourselves breathe deeply in the simplicity of the night. This was a game I knew well: How to evade reality by pretending that it did not exist.

But the edge of our dream cracked slightly when Nathan began to cry. He whimpered for his mother while he lay in my arms, and my heart ached for the pain of loss within him. He called into the night for her, but no one answered. It was an empty plea that echoed in the hollow of his soul. Sometimes he seemed so grown up for his age that I forgot he was merely a six-year-old little boy who had lost his mother in a most horrible way and with her, the only life he had ever known. This is the type of pain that never fully heals, but reshapes you as you grow.

It reminded me of a picture I'd once seen of a tree that had grown through a bicycle, twisting and turning around the carriage until the bike was an integral part of the tree. There was no separating the two; they had grown into a single entity. The tree grew and changed, but it was permanently and irrevocably marked by the bike.

My eyes filled with tears, for Nathan, for his mother, for the past several days, and for Atticus. Mothers were meant to last forever in a six-year-old's mind. They were meant to protect, to hold, to rock and to love. They were never meant to die. Their hands steadied the tilting earth. When those hands were gone, could anything stop the spinning? Did we ever truly outgrow the need for those steady, unbending, gentle hands that brought comfort, even in the dead of night?

I thought of my mother. Even after all these years, she had never stopped talking to my grandmother. She would see a floral arrangement and say, "Oh, Mama, you would have loved this," or after a compliment would come on her cooking or sewing, she would sigh and with eyes very far away say, "Thank you, I learned from the best. Mama had the most talented hands."

I bent down and kissed Nathan's soft, chubby cheek as he drifted to sleep in my arms. I held him close as my tears found their way to his cherubic face. He was hurting without even understanding what had happened. What if the wounds in him were too deep to heal by the time he was old enough to really understand them? Did a child need to understand in order to hurt? No. Pain so often precedes understanding. I understood better than Nathan, and still my heart beat a broken rhythm. In the morning, we would walk to the Council meeting. I did not know what awaited me there, so I held him tighter. So much had happened, so much that he did not ask for, that he did not cause. And yet, it was just beginning for him and for me.

With tears fresh on my cheeks, I looked up. Atticus stood across the room with his arms dangling helplessly by his sides. He did not move towards me but stayed, with great restraint, at a distance. His face looked pained, like something heavy was breaking him.

"What's wrong?" I whispered, but it was not really a question. I knew what was wrong. If only this were real; if only tonight were not two people playing house. If only. He put a finger to his lips and motioned towards the sleeping boy in my arms. Walking on eggs shells, I tiptoed to the bedroom and reluctantly laid Nathan down. He hugged a pillow to himself, trying to fill the hole in him, and then exhaled noisily before settling back down where sleep would numb his pain. I hovered over him until Atticus softly laced his fingers with mine. The tears continued to stream down my face as he led me from the room, closing the door behind us.

We stood face to face while the rain beat down on the tin-roof. It felt like the world was coming down around us. He looked down at his hands and then up at me again, and I saw the distance in his eyes. Like he was already leaving me

"Don't look at me like that." The sound from my throat was broken and breaking even more.

"How?" he began.

"Like you agree with her, like you're already saying goodbye. Like you are resigned to leaving....to leaving me." I put the back of my hand up to my mouth to stop the tears and trembling, but it didn't help. It hurt so far down that I didn't know where it began or where it was going or where it ended. So much was happening, so much was changing, and now...now I saw in his eyes the goodbye that he did not want to say.

"I'm going to lose you, and I've barely found you," I said, lips quivering. I bit down hard, determined to keep my dignity intact.

He put his hands through his hair in frustration, "Veralee, I heard what your Mother said to you on the porch. She's right. I don't control what happens to me. I do not choose when to leave or when to stay. If it were that easy, if things were different, maybe. I would promise you my hours, my days, my life if I could, but I can't. It's not mine to give. I am not in charge of my own life. What can I give you? Only heartache...only the promise that, at some point...maybe tomorrow, maybe tonight, maybe in a year...you will live a life without me and without love. What kind of man would I be to do that to you? You deserve so much more."

"You're wrong," I said, shaking my head, "you can give me the chance...the chance to love you." Then out of desperation I asked what was burning in my chest, "Do you love me?" He looked at me like I had just hit him with both fists. "I have to know; I have to hear you say it," I said, tears cascading down my cheeks.

"It will only hurt more if we say those words. They are useless words for us; they do not come with the promise of forever like they should...they come only with the promise of heartache when I am gone."

"They come with the promise of now," I said, too loudly. "I have to know, I can't—" my voice broke, but I pushed on, "I can't just move on and pretend this isn't happening. I have to know. Because the not knowing—the pain of not knowing—will make my heart break." I spoke as if the words themselves would keep me from falling off a cliff. He grabbed my chin in his strong hands and the world tilted on its axis, as his lips hit mine, smooth and gentle. In that moment, I untied any doubt that kept me clinging to the cliff, and I fell into him, not knowing how long it would last, not knowing when it would end, but desperate to feel as much as I could, to touch the place in him that he hid from the rest of the world.

"I love you, Veralee," his fingers knotted into my hair as his hot breath warmed my lips. "I love you more than I have ever loved anyone in all of my years, and I know just as I know my own name, that I will love you until the end of my days." He buried his head into my hair and wrapped his tense arms around me, groaning slightly.

"But how can I do this to you; how can I ask you to share this life with me? I would not put that on you...I couldn't." He touched my cheek and then traced a line down to the hollow of my neck. There his thumb lingered while his fingers cupped the back of my neck.

"When I leave, I will not even know if you cry. I will not know if you stay at the last place you saw me and wait for hours or days, or if you will simply turn and forget me. I will not be able to protect you, to keep you warm or to shield you from the darkness. You will be alone, Veralee. You do not understand how hard that road is. I do, and I could not do that to you. I will not let you—"

"Atticus, I will never bond myself to another. It is you that I want; it's you that I have been waiting for. I don't know how long I have with you, but I want *you*, Atticus. If you say no now, or if you leave tomorrow, it is the same for me," I gestured to him and back to me, "This...this is already done for me. I can't go back now. Don't try to decide what I am capable of. That is my decision, mine to make and discover. It's not yours, or Mother's or Daddy's, but mine alone. And, I choose you. I choose you, Atticus."

His eyes glimmered slightly, but they did not spill over. He was still in control, still commanding even his tears to obey his wishes. He rested his forehead on mine, "Veralee...I will love you for all of time. I want you," his hand moved down my side and along my hips. Forcefully, he pulled me against him. "I want you to be mine, but I do not want to hurt you. I know I will have to leave you." He said it painfully, like a Roman knife was slowly but steadily piecing his heart, and with his words, I felt it passing through mine, pinning us together.

"Then don't walk away from me," I whispered.

He groaned again. "I don't know when I will leave; it could be tonight or tomorrow. What will you do then?" he whispered back, his lips dangerously close to mine.

"Then I will wait for you here or in the Terebinths of Mamre. I will wait until this life is over, and we have done what we have been called to do....then I will have you back again. Then you will forever be by my side, and I will be by yours...forever."

Something broke. Maybe it was his resolve or maybe it was his heart, but I saw the wall crash down in his eyes. He kissed me then, freely, like all of the locks had been blown off of his restraint. Together as we kissed, we jumped, letting go of reason and holding fast to each other. Time was not ours to control. We did not number our days, and we did not decide our hours. And eventually our time together would run out. Pain was inevitable, but completely worth the risk of loving him.

"Veralee, bond yourself to me. I will love you even if I am not here beside you. I will love you." His voice was airy, like he had been running, "Will you bond yourself to me?" he said hoarsely, as he dropped down onto both of his knees in front of me.

My hands were in his. Hands that felt fresh from war, and yet still soft, still tender. His green eyes softened in the firelight. Sliding down onto my knees beside him, I said yes as his eyes said please. His welcoming mouth met mine, and he pulled me into his arms.

He pulled back and held my face in his hands. "When I first heard your voice, something awakened in me. Something I thought had died a long time ago. You brought a piece of me back, Veralee," he said, with a rough edge in his voice that pushed me closer to the edge of my restraint.

Still on our knees, I put my hands on his chest where I could feel the beating of his heart through his shirt. My heart pounded painfully in my chest. He took a deep breath as I boldly undid the top button to his flannel shirt. His hand ran up my spine and brushed down my back. I arched toward him, wanting more as my breathing became more uneven.

"We have to make it legal, before the morning, before the Council meeting." he said with resolve...he was not going to budge on this one. I looked into his eyes and knew he was right. Tomorrow was a mystery, a Damoclean sword that should not be left to determine our path.

"We can go to Issachar," I said, without taking my hands away from his chest, where my hands felt secure. Issachar would stand as a witness for many bonding ceremonies during our time in the Terebinths.

Before I could stand, Atticus was on his feet, pulling me toward the door. "Hold on," I laughed, "my boots." A euphoric thrill filled the little cottage.

"Yes, of course," he said, slightly embarrassed but chuckling. I sat at the kitchen table and tried to get my boots on. My hands trembled, and my fingers felt stiff as I fumbled with the boots. Atticus pointed towards the bedroom. "What about Nathan? Can we leave him here?" he asked, with the concern of a father as he bent to help me zip my boot. His hand rested on my thigh, and I was more than just a little aware of it.

"Issachar's cottage is just across the field. I can feel Nathan from that far. I'll know if he stirs or wakes. The bond...it's so strong now."

We crossed the moonlit field hand in hand, and I felt the enchantment of the silvery, velvet night. A cold, misting rain fell around us as a ghostly fog blanketed the ground. The trees stood as witnesses and seemed to glow in the moonlight. Did they agree with this...with us? Did they know already what would become of this night?

I thought of Mother and Daddy, and Adair and Ausley. Mother would be heartbroken when she learned about this. She had spent years dreaming of this moment for all of us girls. My feet slowed briefly as I thought about the pain this might bring her. Atticus felt it instantly, "Veralee?" he asked. I looked at him in the moonlight, as the rain dripped down onto his coatless frame. The intensity of his emotion rolled off of him and rushed over me like a train. Everything else vanished, like it had been wiped off a dry-erase board. It was him that I wanted. I saw our lives merging together, the hope of forever blending into the pain of the unknown, and it was all I could see. Gripping his hand as tight as I could, I kissed his warm lips against the cold of the rain. Our breath swirled around us as we hurried through the night, the hazy fog rising higher in the night.

Issachar was slow to open the door. Old, knowing eyes watched us on the wet front porch. Atticus held my hand and spoke clearly, "Issachar, will you stand as a witness for us. Will you speak the words over us...now?" Issachar looked at each of us and then he looked over our heads, into the dark of the night, and sighed heavily into the cool night air. "We do not want to wait until tomorrow," Atticus said, overriding Issachar's private thoughts, "we want to be bonded to one another tonight."

Issachar looked at me then. "Is this what you want, Veralee? Is this the life you have chosen...to bond yourself to an Ayindalet?" He looked concerned and rubbed his long, white beard. His question was filled with warning and his tone with caution.

"What is done cannot be undone. Issachar, a Timekeeper knows that better than I do. I cannot take back my heart once I have given it. The truth is it was gone before I realized it was missing. I love him, Issachar, I will not bond myself to another; it is him...it will always be him," I said looking straight into the green eyes that seemed to disarm any fear in me.

"What will your father and mother say?" he questioned me, knowing me better than I realized.

"Issachar, I am of age to choose for myself whom I will bond my life to, and I have chosen Atticus," I said, tearing my eyes from Atticus to meet Issachar's gaze.

He nodded and grinned to himself, "That you are, my dear girl." He crossed the room and sat in an old grey chair as Atticus shut the door. "So this is the path you have decided to walk," he said as I steadily held his gaze as he looked for any reservation in my face. Of course he knew more than I did, for he had lived so much longer. He had seen more, read more, known more and watched more than I had, and I admired him for it. But I would not back down. Issachar may have known a lot of things, but he could not know my heart.

After a long moment he shook his head. "Well, I cannot stop the sun from setting or the moon from rising, that I can see clearly in your face." He rubbed his beard again and looked into the fire. I didn't know what he saw in those flames, but in them he found his answer. "Yes, I will stand as a witness for you," he said finally. "I do not know exactly what is happening, but I believe you are right. This is the path you are meant to walk. Things that were started so long ago, things which were put into motion, things which have been kept hidden are coming together in the most interesting ways as they come closer to the light. This....this I did not see. But in some way, it seems so very...fitting."

Then he smiled ruefully, and I saw a young man surface in his eyes as he mused, "So the hopeless wanderer has found at last the light in the window that draws him home?"

Issachar went to his room and returned to stand in front us. In his hand was a single silver dagger. The hilt of the dagger was shaped to resemble a great oak tree. He held it by the handle, and I noticed that the silver branches curved around his hand. In his other hand he held a long, 3-stranded scarlet cord, which gleamed, even in the dull light of the fire. The cord was made of some kind of metal that had the flexibility of rope but the strength of iron.

Atticus led me to stand in front of the fire, and we turned to face Issachar together. The heat on my back did not compare to the fire burning in my chest as I waited for Issachar's words to begin. My heart raced. Atticus settled a steadying gaze on me and calmed me. He was always so calm, so controlled, so entirely confident. He was safe, and yet danger lay just behind his eyes, like a wild thing that could not be tamed. He was a warrior in his core, but I did not fear even that part of him, because, I knew he would do anything to keep me safe. I had felt it in my dreams before I even knew his name. He felt the vibration of my mark and smiled knowingly at me.

Then as if I was standing in the middle of a dream, Issachar took the dagger and spoke the Words of Life over it, calling it to awaken. The dagger stirred and waves of heat waffled across it. He handed the living blade to Atticus. Atticus turned to face me. I knew this part. I opened my right hand to him.

"Blood of my blood, flesh of my flesh, bone of my bone," he said, as the knife sliced across my palm. I winced as it cut, but I kept my eyes on him. This was a good pain, the pain of joining my life to Atticus. We both knew this would not be the last time that we would know pain because of each other. So I kept my eyes on him, as I felt the burn, and he kept his on mine. This pain was beautiful.

Then, I, in turn, sliced his palm with a little more trepidation, but it cut just as deep. I slid my hand up his palm and forearm. My blood spread across his wrist. We stood facing one another as Issachar tied our arms together with the metal scarlet cord. It began to wrap itself, unassisted, around our wrists.

Issachar's voice was low and ancient as he spoke the words into the stillness of the night:

"As you are bonded to the blood within so you are bonded to the blood in him.

From two, there will be one."

Time seemed to move slowly. The very air around us froze and stiffened as he spoke. He looped the cord around our hands and tied the first knot. The metal rope began to glow. It was warm, like it had been held over a hot fire. I knew it was our blood that set it ablaze.

Ancient are the roads, sacred are the ways,

That which is obscure to the eye, lies open to the heart

Consecrated to the journey

From two, there will be one.

He looped the cord around our wrists and tied the second knot. As it heated, the metal rope turned from a rustic iron color to cherry. Then it glowed a progressively brighter orange, until it was as brilliant as the morning sun. The light flowed through the cord like an electric current. Starlight bent around our arms and wrists, bonding them together.

"Under the watchful eyes of the trees of old,

Upon the sacred paths

Sanctified in the journey

Let the bond of blood seal forever;

Behold the ageless mystery

From two, there is now one."

Finally, the shining cord tied the third knot itself. It was tied by no human hand, so that no human hand could undo it within us. The light gliding along the rope sped up until an intense blur surrounded our arms. The rope was so hot it turned cold like fiery ice around us. Then the light burst, and the debris from the metal rope fell around us like stardust. All that was left was a faint scar, which started on Atticus and ended on me. With our arms together, the circle of the rope was complete. I knew from my parents' arms that this would never fade; it was the permanent reminder of the bond we had made. *Flesh of my flesh,* I thought. It was finished. We were bonded for life, or as much of it as we had together.

Atticus walked me back to the small cottage, across the field where we had pretended, like children that we could live forever as a family. The moon lit our path and the wet grass soaked our boots. He walked backwards, slowly pulling me towards him. I felt the power in him as he led me to the door and then inside. The cottage was still, except for the low crackling of the smoldering fire. My lips trembled slightly, and I told myself it was because of the cold night's air and not because of him. The cottage seemed to be filled with him, his broad shoulders, smiling lips and green eyes.

We stood once again in front of the fire as he fingered the freshly burned scar on his arm and followed it to mine. We had already begun to heal, the blood was dry, the cut almost gone, but the burn of the metallic rope would last forever. He ran his hand over the cut, now a pink line, in my palm. Wordlessly, he lifted me without effort and carried me, as I had carried Nathan to the second bedroom. I laid my head on his shoulder and, for a moment, let the exhaustion of the day fall on me. I was safe in his arms. I bent my head and kissed his neck before he lowered me down onto the old quilted bed.

He bent his body over mine, and caressed the back of my neck with warm fingers. Then his lips grazed over mine, "Blood of my blood...." He said so softly that it felt like someone speaking from a dream. I reached up and pulled his shirt from his body. I sucked in a gasp of air when I saw him. He was chiseled as if out of marble. Years of battle scars from wounds suffered before he had the Eiani that healed still showed on his olive skin. I lightly traced a deep cut that ran across his abdomen with my finger.

He pulled my shirt over my head and kissed my collarbone, "Bone of my bone..." he whispered again. His voice was raspy, and his breath became more labored. For a second his fingers lingered around my hips, tracing the invisible line between them, across my stomach. My skin electrified and burned where he touched. Every nerve in my body was suddenly alive where flesh met flesh. In one quick motion, he pulled my jeans and everything else onto the floor, and I was laid bare in front of him. Blood rushed into my cheeks but he pulled me into his arms quickly, "Flesh of my flesh" he said as he covered my mouth with his.

His hands ran down my back and over my hips. And I grasped him as I arched up at his touch, shivering as his hands explored my skin. "You are faultless, Veralee, perfect like a carved Roman goddess," he whispered into my ear. Slowly, deliberately, he laid his body down on mine and said, "And you are mine." The fierceness in his voice and his touch ignited my entire body. I was on fire. I twisted and bent to his hands' command. He pulled me into the innermost chambers of his heart. I felt the beat of his wild rhythm as he pushed forward. And I saw a tear slip down his face before he buried me under his lips. The blood of life, the blood that bonds flowed between us, and I felt a burning sensation run up and down my right arm. Then I felt like my entire body was on fire as he claimed me for himself. Breathless, I let go of everything in that moment. I felt the electrical current run between us, and I lost my space and time. I no longer knew where he began and I ended. We blended and stirred into one another and molded like two colors of clay being pressed into one. Once upon a time, there was a boy named Atticus and a girl called Veralee. But now...now there was one being, with one mind, one body, one soul, bonded together through the Eiani that bonds forever.

The alarm on my phone beeped in the night, calling me awake. I opened my eyes and immediately felt his arms around me. His grip had not lessened in his sleep. He held me like someone might come and take me from him while he slept. I loved it and sat for another minute to soak in his smell and smooth skin. Then my phone beeped again, and I reached to silence its hateful alarm. It was 2:00 in the morning. Atticus felt me shift and pulled me closer to his naked body.

"Mmmm," he said sleepily, "Let's stay here, just like this, for the rest of our days."

"You would get hungry eventually," I said with a smile. "Oh, I can go a long time on an empty stomach, if you are willing to keep me occupied." He said and then started to kiss down my neck again. "Atticus, we have to be ready in two hours to walk to the Council Meeting." With the mention of the Council Meeting he stiffened and tightened his grip on me.

"Listen to me, Veralee. Let your parents help you. Your Father will have pull with the Council members. And remember that no matter what happens, I will stay with you for as long as I am able."

A shiver of fear ran down my spine. What was going to happen at the Council Meeting? The night suddenly felt darker. I put my head on Atticus's chest and let his warmth flow through me again. "I have to go now." I said sadly.

He pulled me up and kissed me. "Yes, I know," he said, matching my tone. He flipped on the lamp by the bed, so that we could find my clothes. Even though the light was soft from the lamp, it felt harsh against my eyes. I reached down to grab my shirt when I saw it. I stopped and held my right arm to the light. Atticus did the same. "It is already changed," I said, tracing the thin white lines with my finger.

"Once the blood bond is made, it changes instantly. Did you not feel it burning through your arm?" he asked.

I blushed and looked at his green eyes which were filled with me, "I...felt the burning...but, well, I felt a lot of things at that same moment." My arm was still my arm, and the mark of a swirling sparrow could still be seen clearly, but a woven pattern encircled the bird that had not been there that morning. Atticus put his arm against mine and I saw that the pattern, which started on my arm, was completed on his. The swirls and coils of movement ran from him to me and back to him again. We smiled at each other.

"You are mine," he said again.

I felt those words settle inside of me before I spoke, "And *you* are mine, Atticus." He pulled me into him again and showed me that I was indeed his.

By the time I left the cottage I knew it was time to run. I only had 55 minutes before I was supposed to be dressed and ready. Waving at his silhouette standing in the door, I turned towards the house before I heard him. "Thank you, Veralee," he called. "You've given me the one thing I never thought I would find."

I smiled as I ran through the trees, marked forever by the man of my dreams.

{ 20 }

Terebinths of Mamre

In the darkness I reached out and felt the rich, silk dress. Once it had belonged to Vera, and now it belonged to me. It was kept under lock and key in the closet on the third floor, with all of our Council clothing. Vera was the last to wear the dress. Adair had been too tall and Ausley too young, so the dress had lingered on its velvet-covered hanger, waiting for me to come of age. I smiled to myself at the thought: when I stepped onto the path to my first Council meeting, I would actually be wrapped in the fabric of my history.

As I dressed in the luxurious silk, I brushed my swollen lips and the memory of Atticus flooded my mind. So many beginnings...this would be my first time walking the lighted path with the Simulacrum. As a child, I had pressed my nose and palms against the panes of the upstairs window, watching as they left and dreaming of the day I would join the procession. Holding small lanterns to light the way in the pre-dawn dark, the column snaked steadily through the woods like elves in a Tolkien novel, each beautifully dressed in deep hues of scarlet and crimson. As the dawn drew near on this new day, I would, for the first time, walk into the Council side by side with my family, my people. No longer would I watch longingly from behind the window. It was my time now.

Quickly I dressed and stood before the long mirror in my room. I searched for my face in the woman who looked back at me. The girl I was so used to seeing...the girl who looked out from the recesses of the mirror with a bit of uncertainty...was no longer there. Now, to my utter surprise, a woman gazed back at me. She had the slightest air of wisdom around her eyes, and a small mouth that looked stronger than it should. Her eyes were filled with determination, and her chest faced the world like nothing could stop her. The woman in the mirror was striking, much more so than the girl who watched from behind my eyes, and in the period dress, that woman looked out of place in this world. She opened her mouth as if to say something to me, to impart some pearl of wisdom or profound truth that would reveal her to me, but no words came. I looked at her in her world, which looked so much like my own, only slightly altered by the mirror. The crimson of the dress, rich as an imperial ruby, rippled and reflected in the folds of the fluid silk like a bottle of expensive Bordeaux. The jewel-toned hue brought out the woman's silver-grey eyes and highlighted her olive skin. That skin, flawless and smooth, like the sculpted women idealized in marble on the floor of the Louvre, showcased the soft mahogany waves that shimmered as it gently fell around her shoulders. That was the woman in the mirror, but I was not her, I was not that beautiful or that confident. *Was this what they saw? Was this how others saw me?* The woman in the mirror offered no answer. But I knew that she was the woman Atticus loved... *this woman* and the girl inside of me.

Thoughts of Atticus's body ran through my mind, and I touched my neck where he had laid his head. Memories engulfed me, and then the girl inside of me surfaced in the mirror as I blushed the color of the dress.

The long skirt fanned slightly around me on the floor, with layers of chiffon overlay coiling around itself. Vera must have been a little taller than me, like everyone else in this family.

A flash of red caught my eye from the mirror. Turning, I saw one of Mother's famous red boxes sitting on my desk. A small note was scrawled on top:

For my Little Bird,

From the first time I set eyes on you, I knew you were too wild a thing to be caged. Too beautiful, too strong, too determined. So, the door has always been open. Still, life here in the trees would have been so silent without your song.

With all my love,

Mother

Carefully, I pulled the white ribbon and opened the box. Mother's sweet scent, like expensive perfume, drifted from the layers of tissue paper. The comforting aroma of jasmine honey settled over me. Trembling, I opened the tissue. Folded inside by careful hands, lay a cloak made of a million red feathers. I pulled the long cloak from the box and gasped. The feathers were such rich claret that they almost appeared purple in the low light. Swiftly I draped the cloak over my shoulders and clasped the golden oak which dipped like a necklace on my bare chest. The feathers lay flat, giving it the appearance of velvet, but it moved so easily that it mimicked small ripples of water with the slightest shift of my arms.

I looked at my reflection once more. Priceless art, made by Mother's own hands, draped around me. Reaching up slowly, I touched the woman's face in the mirror, testing to see if she was real. I caressed the intricate weaving of gold and silver that laced up the long flowing sleeves of the dress and stopped just above her elbow. My dress, Vera's dress, fit like a glove, even though it was a little long. It had not lost one bit of its vibrant scarlet color or its plush nap. The alarm on my phone jolted me back to the here and now. It was time.

I left the uncomfortable looking black shoes that came with the dress where they sat and grabbed my brown riding boots instead. No one would see them anyhow. And it felt better having a piece of me inside this dress, something that was mine, something that I recognized.

I stepped out the back door and quickly donned my hood against the chill. My breath swirled around my face in short puffs and dancing ribbons. My eyes searched the crowd, but I did not find what I wanted. The thought of Atticus made my pulse quicken. I swallowed hard and smoothed my dress.

"It will be your first time to walk into the Terebinths of Mamre," Issachar spoke quietly as he approached me, not wanting to break the silence. His white beard hung down to his chest and came to a point just over the place where his cloak was snapped closed by silver buttons. His hood hid most of his face, but I could still see the dimples in his cheeks as he spoke.

"Yes, I really can't believe it's time... I've watched the Council leave so many times, and now I get to walk with them at last," I said, with the thrill of a small child. "Thank you for your help last night," I added, with a touch of embarrassment.

"Many things hidden in the dark of night will shine in the light of day," he said, like the caterpillar again. "Hmmm, yes, it is a great time in a young person's life. Now you stand for yourself, now you are a part of the Simulacrum Council as an adult. No longer are you under the authority of your parents. You have a voice that is your own now. It is a rite of passage, which should not be taken lightly, for with it comes great responsibility and great accountability," he said like an old man in a rocking chair. I wondered then how old Issachar really was. How long had he been on the Council?

"When did you take your first walk into the Terebinths of Mamre?" I asked curiously.

He lifted his hood slightly so that I could see the twinkle still in his eyes as he said:

"An old man stirs the fire to a blaze,

In the house of a child, of a friend,

of a brother. He has over-lingered

his welcome; the days,

Grown desolate, whisper and

sigh to each other; He hears the

storm in the chimney above,

And bends to the fire and shakes

with the cold, While his heart still

dreams of battle and love,

And the cry of the hounds on the hills of old,"

Issachar quoted with the wisdom of age in his voice. I smiled at the smoothness that made the words spread easily in my mind, like butter over warm toast. He smiled then, "Forgive the ramblings of an old man, my sweet Veralee. I took my first walk into the Oaks of Mamre, long ago, when the courts of Spain still sat as a mighty power above the world."

"I don't think you ramble at all," I said. "I have always loved Yeats. The Wanderings of Oisin, right?" I asked.

His eyes twinkled again, "Why yes, that is exactly right. And I love Yeats as well. A good Irish man he was," he said, with an air of surprised satisfaction in his voice. "Well, I need to see that we are ready to cast off on this journey," he said, bowing slightly and turning to leave.

"Issachar," I said quickly, as he turned to face me again. "You are not as old as you think. I can see that you still have the strength for battle left in you. Don't discount yourself yet," then my face colored slightly. It was a little forward of me to speak to him like this. But, as was my custom, I spoke before thinking. He studied my face for a moment.

"You may just be right, Veralee. Time will tell if you are true," then he winked at me, "Better a wise youth than an old king who no longer knows how to take advice," he said, then blended into the blur of crimson and scarlet robes. I stood for a moment looking at the crowd as I thought of his slip of the tongue. Didn't he mean, "Time would tell if your *words* are true?" Then I shook my head, remembering Adair's words; "The caterpillar always speaks in riddles." Once again, she was right.

Mother waded through the crowd, splitting them like a red sea. She was stunning. Her red cape, made of heavy silk and lined with rich black velvet, looked fit for a queen. Her deep, mahogany hair framed her face, and instantly I saw Ausley there in the crook of her chin and the delicate bend of her nose. "This is a wonderful day; all of my girls will come with us for the first time. I am so proud to have you with us, Veralee," she said and then kissed my cheek with her warm lips. Ausley and Adair approached with Daddy and Phineas. Daddy smiled, but behind his eyes, I saw something else. He looked like the Cheshire cat, smiling at me like there was a message hidden there.

"My girls," he said proudly. "I've waited a long time for this day. Finally, we will go to the Council, as a complete family. I could not be more proud of you three girls." Phineas pulled Adair close and kissed her cheek while Ausley hugged Daddy. I hid my marked arm in my cloak. I would not tell them here, in the midst of such a crowd.

Daddy looked over at me across the semicircle we had created. "Veralee, remember your promise to your mother," he said without letting my eyes go.

"Yes sir, I remember," I said, trying to reassure him. Maybe he was just tired from entertaining so many people, but he looked weary.

"Good, don't forget, Little Bird," he said, and then he moved closer to me. "I have spoken to Naphtali, and she has arranged to deal with your infraction in a private meeting with the Council. It will go much better if it is not addressed at the General Session with everyone present. Keep still through the meeting, and then after the gathering meal, we will meet in executive session with the Council."

"Oh!" I gasped. Relief flooded me. "Thank you, Daddy!" The cloud of anxiety that had hung over me suddenly dissipated, like mist in the sunlight. I threw my arms around him, hugging him with all my might. My lip trembled, but I held the tears in check as I choked out against his chest. "Thank you so much."

He tipped my head up and winked at me, "It will be okay, but you will still have to face some consequences." He held my chin in his hand, "You are my strong girl; you can do that, right?" I nodded boldly at him. "That's my girl. Now we've got to get ready to go." He kissed my forehead, and I released him from my bear hug.

"Okay, Gail, let's go," he said, leading Mother away.

Ausley turned around toward Daddy and scanned the crowd. "'Where's Uncle Austin?" she asked.

the Oaks Remain

Daddy looked around," I'm not sure." He smiled. "You know Austin. I'm sure he's busy working the crowd, saying hello to old friends. He'll be there; he knows the way."

Ausley nodded, but I could tell she was a little disappointed. Uncle Austin had always doted on her when we were little, and Ausley loved it. He would pick her up and spin her around, dance the waltz with her little feet on top of his, and even let her put barrettes and ribbons in his straight, silky strands. She was excited to have him home, and now she had expected him to walk beside the family at the front of the procession.

From across the small courtyard where we stood, I caught Jackson's eye. He stood with his family, and he looked handsome in his Council clothing. He waved to me, and I smiled back. He motioned to my dress and gave me a thumbs-up. It was his first time to walk with the Simulacrum to the Terebinths of Mamre too. We had talked and swapped information about what we knew about the Council Meetings many times as children. Jackson was just as excited as I was. He came over quickly and stopped in front of me. "Nice dress, Little Bird," he said from under his crimson hood. He grabbed for my hand, and I reluctantly spun around, guided by his arm.

"Very nice dress. You look amazing, Veralee...I don't think I have ever seen you look so...womanly." His voice sounded hoarse.

"It was my great-grandmother's dress," I said, trying to avoid his eyes. He knew me too well. I knew he would be able to tell how different I was. Last night had changed me.

Atticus had changed me.

"Well, your great-grandmother had great taste, and so do you." He reached for my hand to twirl me again like I was a small child, but stopped abruptly. I tried to hide my arm into the deep folds of my cloak, but he gasped. Without asking, he grabbed my arm and turned it from side to side. His eyes said enough. He knew. He saw the deep burn marks that the bonding rope had permanently left on my arm.

"Jackson, I..." I bit my lip and looked around nervously. This was not the time to have this conversation.

I was saved by the clarion blast of the silver ceremonial trumpet soaring through the air, signaling the beginning of the proceedings. Immediately, the energy level of the group climbed to a frenzy. It was time. Everyone moved to line up in family groups. We would walk with our families, together making one body.

"I have to go," I said apologetically. "We can talk soon; I'll explain everything."

As if he had finally found his tongue he blurted out, "You don't even know him, Veralee! You barely know his name." He was astonished. Truly shocked and truly hurt.

"Jackson, it's Atticus. It's always going to be Atticus...for me, there is only him. I'm so sorry, Jackson, but you have to understand; I love him. I love Atticus."

The light-givers proceeded down the rows, handing lanterns to each of us. The outside house lights extinguished as the candles were lit.

the Oaks Remain

"You could at least have told me, Veralee. We've always been honest with each other, and I thought...I guess I was wrong. About a lot of things." Jackson dropped my hand, turned and walked away.

"Jackson, wait!" I wanted to run after to him, to explain everything, to fix it somehow. But Jackson never even acknowledged that he heard me, and I was out of time. Besides, what could I say? I had no words to mend his heart. But, he was Jackson. He'd been mad at me before, plenty of times. When he'd had time to think about it, to process it, he'd see it differently. He'd come around; I knew he would. Wouldn't he?

As I watched Jackson go, I realized I had just cut a tether from my childhood and released what I had once thought would be my future. I turned from him to find Adair and Ausley, who stood with Daddy and Mother at the very front of the line of Simulacrum.

In Simulacrum tradition, each father, grandfather or husband would light the candles in the dark lanterns of their family members. Daddy would light Mother's and then Phineas' candle. Then Phineas would light Adair's while Daddy lit mine and Ausley's. As head of our family, Daddy had the responsibility of passing the light to each of us. As the Guardian of the Gate, he had the responsibility of leading the Simulacrum to the Terebinths of Mamre. But the truth was, after last night, Daddy was no longer supposed to light my lantern. A new flame burned in me, lit by a new man. But where *was* Atticus?

Nervously, I watched Daddy light Mother's candle.

Where was he? His hand touched my shoulder. Spinning on my heels, I saw Atticus standing before me. He was wickedly handsome. Not boyish, but dangerously beautiful. He wore black pants and black, knee-high leather riding boots, and a rich scarlet vest over a tailored black shirt. His coat was embroidered elegantly in gold, with branches of the great trees overlapping, forming a brilliant pattern. A crimson hood covered his face, until he raised his black lashes to me, revealing the green of his eyes. I sucked in a short breath in appreciation, and then I breathed a heart-felt sigh of relief at his presence. He reached for my free hand and rubbed his thumb across it.

"You are the most beautiful woman I have ever seen," he said, without any sense of mockery. He stared at me, his emerald eyes full of intensity, which made my eyes water. He was here, with me.

"And you...are mine. I have thought of the way you looked last night in the moonlight over and over since you left my bed," his eyes lingered on my mouth, "and I will need to have you back there very soon."

Why did we have to be around so many people? I wanted to talk to him privately, to hear his soft voice against my chest. I wanted to lie beside him again and feel his lips on mine, and tell him that I wanted him forever. A shiver ran down my spine, and I longed to kiss him. Not sweetly, but hard and feral. But there was no time for that. "Atticus, I love you," I said with heat in my breath that radiated through my body and escaped through my eyes.

His lips brushed mine, and I smelled his sweet breath.

"And I love you," he answered as he leaned in so that only I could hear his whisper.

"You look completely medieval," I said, breaking the tension with a smile. Otherwise, I might have just grabbed his hand and dragged him away to the cottage right then. It didn't quite work; I still felt the heat of desire rising.

He shrugged and pushed his hair back from his smoldering eyes, which never left mine. "Yes, in fact, I do. Maybe later I can educate you on what the medieval knights wore under their leather and chain-mail. After all, I did live there for a time," he smiled, with restrained longing undergirding the tease.

We both looked at each other, feeling the fervor of last night course through our bodies. Then he smiled for real and held up his lantern, which was alight with fire. I looked at him and anxiously agreed. Daddy approached, with Mother at his side, to light my candle. He stopped when he saw Atticus standing in front of me, holding out his fire.

"What are you..." his voice fell flat as I motioned to my arm. Daddy followed my gesture, and then his eyes grew big with understanding. Mother drew in a sharp breath.

"Veralee...you didn't," Daddy stammered. I opened my mouth to speak, but Atticus spoke first.

"We are bonded to one another. And I will keep her safe now," Atticus said.

Daddy looked stricken and grabbed at Atticus's shirt, "And how will you do that? You know what you are." Atticus did not fight back, but looked calmly in the face of the storm before him. The sound of the horn wedged itself between the two men, insisting they stay on task. It was time to go.

Mother put a strong hand on Daddy's shoulder, gesturing him back. "She has chosen for herself, Edwin; we cannot change this. It was hers to choose."

Daddy's anger did not abate, but slipped behind a trained curtain of control. His face went blank. They both gave a resigned nod of their heads, but Mother's eyes brimmed with fresh tears. She gave me a half smile as she turned away.

Atticus stood before me, holding his flaming candle. Standing by my family, standing with him, a million emotions collided within me. But my decision had already been made. I was his; I belonged to him.

I held my lantern out to him, and to my surprise it felt lighter than I thought it would. Without taking his eyes off me, his hand covered mine, and he gave me the light I needed to see through the darkness. This was what I couldn't explain to Jackson or to Daddy or to Mother. Atticus was the one I had been waiting for. It didn't matter whether I knew the way; I could follow him because together we would find our way through the darkness. The trumpet rang out again, and it was time to begin the journey through the woods to the Terebinths of Mamre.

With a long line of Simulacrum behind us, we weaved our way down one of my favorite running paths toward the woods. We walked, following my father's lead, with the stillness of the coming dawn wrapping us into a cocoon of tranquility.

I remembered sitting with Daddy in the wingback chair in the library as a child after a Council Meeting. I must have been about four years old, because I had been small enough to tuck my legs up into his lap and lie comfortably in his arms. "But, why don't you use a flashlight? You don't have to light them, and they are lots of fun to play with, like when we hunt sand crabs at the beach in the dark," I had philosophized.

Daddy gave me a little hug and explained. "Well, that would certainly provide us with light, but it's not just the light that we need. It's what the light means to us. The fire that we hold in the lantern reminds us that we were once in the dark, that once we were all one in death, as the Friguscor are now. But then the Primogenes, the Firstborns, found the One Tree, the Tree of Eiani. Through the flame and the blood, they came back into the light, and the Simulacrum were born. They showed us the path. We came out of death and walked into life through the living fire of the blood. So, we use a living flame–candlelight–to remind us of all of that."

"Oh," I had said, though lanterns still hadn't seemed as fun as my Barbie flashlight. But as I got older, I understood. And today, in particular, I needed the light.

Daddy, with Mother on his arm, led the procession into the forest. He was the Guardian of the Gate. He knew the way. Mother held onto Daddy's arm and pulled him closer still. They walked in step and seemed to be having an unspoken conversation. He kissed her cloaked head. She walked forward with her head on his shoulder.

After a short distance, maybe a little over a mile into one of my running trails, we stopped. I knew this place well. I had followed Daddy down this trail more times than I could count. The path turned hard to the right, but we were facing straight, where no path led. A set of worn stone steps lay before us. Those six wide limestone steps had stood there, leading to nowhere, for as long as I could remember. They looked like steps that would lead to a Greek temple, so Ausley, Jackson, and I had played Helen of Troy here many times over the years. When I had asked Daddy, he had jokingly told me that they were made by the hands of giants. Now they were cracked in places and pitted from the elements.

Issachar and Naphtali stepped out from the crowd and stood by Daddy in front of the steps. Mother took a noticeable step back, joining Adair and Ausley. No one spoke. Even the trees seemed to be holding their breath.

Daddy took a dagger from his sheath. With a quick motion he cut his palm and made a fist. The droplets of blood coagulated in midair before falling slowly to the dirt.

"Out of the ground came flesh." Daddy clenched his fist firmer and the blood flowed quicker as he spoke, "And from the ground, the voice of the blood cries out."

The smell of the blood of the Guardian mixed with the sound of Naphtali's voice as she sang...

"The way paved in blood,

Wrought by Sacred Words,

Founded upon roots of old,

Guarded by Great Trees of oak,

Breached by fire and light,

Open to the blood-born this hallowed night,

The way paved in blood."

Three times she sang into the dark of the night while Daddy's blood called to the earth. Nothing moved, nothing stirred on the first two recitations. But on the third, something began, far away, that I could not see. It pushed forward through the trees, like a wave rushing the shore. With the sound of a mighty wind, the trees before us shifted and creaked as they folded to each side, as if someone were walking through them as easily as a child would walk through tall grass.

At the top of the stairs, a woman, or the outline of a woman, appeared. She did not have a physical body, but was formed of natural materials from the forest blown by the wind into the shape of a woman. Her long tresses, made of wild flowers and verdant grasses, moved constantly, as if it drifting in water. Her hair floated and danced with an ethereal light around her head.

Naphtali stepped forward and spoke, "We seek counsel with you, Wisdom. Long life lies in your right hand, and in your left, riches and honor. Your ways are pleasant, and your paths are peace. Your words are truth; to the discerning, they are right. When the world was formless and void, you were brought forth; before the mountains were born, you were begotten. You were the first of the *Acts of Old*. Blessed are those who hold fast to you, you, who delight in the Children of Man."

The form of the woman turned her face slightly to acknowledge Naphtali's words.

"Who comes to walk the ancient paths?" the form asked.

"The Simulacrum, the Image-Bearers of the Ancient One," Naphtali announced. The form looked out across the crowd of Image-Bearers and considered us with discerning eyes. Her words were sharp, but beautiful, like the razor edge of a diamond blade.

"Is the time nigh?" asked the formless woman.

Issachar lifted his wise voice, "That which is, already has been, and that which will be is done forever so now we seek that which has been driven away."

"Hear my words, Children of Man, and do not neglect me. Choose my instruction instead of silver, my knowledge instead of gold. Hear my words and walk in the way of the ancient path. Step forward and leave your simple ways behind. For those who do not hear my words, walk the path of desolation to enter the House of Destruction."

A rumbling moved through the forest. Like watching a movie in fast forward, the trees, which had been scattered randomly throughout the woods, now stood side by side. Their great white branches stretched to make a canopy above the stone path that lay between them. The stairs no longer climbed without purpose into the forested hill, but now led up to a stone path between the red-leafed trees.

The woman without form opened her arms wide. "Come and let your days be multiplied, and let years be added to your life." Then she stood to the side, ushering us in. Issachar joined Naphtali, and they walked arm-in-arm up the stone stairs into the new world that miraculously appeared before us. Daddy returned to stand by Mother. I held my breath in awe.

Atticus came closer to me. "This is the way to the Terebinths of Mamre. One cannot find the way without first finding Wisdom," he whispered.

"Oh," I nodded, "of course." *She was Wisdom herself, the one who was first formed before the creation of time or space.* Atticus stayed by my side as we climbed the great stairs and stepped out onto the stone path. I watched the formless woman as we passed her. She moved like the wind or the waves in the sea and held the path open until every Simulacrum had passed through. It was she who opened and shut the way to the Terebinths of Mamre. To enter without her would be impossible.

Red leaves slowly bled into white as we walked further. Suddenly, we seemed to be walking through a snowstorm of white leaves. A distant song pricked my ears. Groups of people, strangers, dressed in shades of red moved all around us through the heavy foliage. The stark contrast of the red cloaks against the white forest created a dream-like world.

I looked to the right and left, and then questioningly at Atticus, "Are these Simulacrum from other places?" I knew the Simulacrum from all over the world would gather, but how could they be here with us, right now? "Where did they come from?" I asked, while curiously pointing to the people walking through the woods toward the path.

"Yes, they are the Simulacrum from other parts of the world," he said, his lips so close to my ear that I could feel his warm breath on my skin. It sent electric waves of heat through my body, and I wanted to touch his face, but I knew it was not the time.

"They are from the other Gateways...throughout the world?"

"Yes," he explained, "there are at least twelve Gateways scattered across the earth where the Simulacrum may enter, but all of those lead to the same place. To the Terebinths of Mamre. Those people are probably from the Gateways closest to the one on Red Oaks. But, remember, there is only one Door," he said softly, careful not to break the beauty of the moment.

"You mean the trees from the Histories that are connected by the same root system under the earth? Is that it?" I asked as I put together what I was seeing with the stories I had been told.

"Yes, Veralee. The different entry points all lead to these Terebinths of Mamre. Every seven years, the Simulacrum come together as one people here underneath these ancient branches. But remember, there is only one Door.

There are many entrances to the Terebinths of Mamre, those were created so that all Simulacrum from around the world would have access, but as for *the* Door, there is only one. It is *that* Door that I am waiting for, in fact that we are all waiting for," he said. I couldn't tell if he was talking more to me or to himself.

The music grew louder and clearer, and I heard the song in the air. The song was not new to me; I had heard it since the crib in the house at Red Oaks. We sang with one voice, in one accord. The music soared with a beauty and majesty that would have made Fauré jealous. It was ethereal—otherworldly—and so pure. I looked behind me; we had not come so far, but Red Oaks seemed a world away now. Atticus clasped my hand and held me firmly. It centered me again.

The song filled my lungs and my mouth and, along with Atticus, I joined the voices of our people. Each of the groups was unique, diverse, and yet the song cascaded and reverberated through us all, sine and co-sine, until it resonated in perfect harmonics. It was the song that called to be sung:

"Let all the earth keep silent

Let the Stars refuse to Shine

Let the River cease its harmony

Let the four winds refuge find.

For we, the Children of Blood,

Triumphant o'er the darkness

Sanctified by water and light

Called from death into promise

Sing we all as one,

Creation adds it voice.

Sing we to the

Ancient One.

Selah, Selah

Selah.

Selah, Selah

To the giver of all good things,

Selah."

The euphoria of unity soared through me, e pluribus unum: out of many, one. *These are the people of my blood. Blood of my blood, bone of my bone, flesh of my flesh.* This was where I belonged.

For hours we walked, but I was not tired. The ecstasy of the moment invigorated me; the energy coursed through me, pushing me on toward the oaks that I could feel calling us home. Then the sun broke free of the darkness and warmed the velvet sky with swirls of deepening violet, fuchsia, and gold. Slowly, the hues of pinks and yellows warmed to brilliant canary as the light pierced the last remaining dark edges of night. A misty fog settled around our feet and gave the appearance that we walked among the clouds.

"Atticus, it's beautiful!" I breathed out, as I grasped his hand tighter.

He watched my face and mirrored my excitement, "Just wait...we have not yet reached the Sacred Oaks."

A colossal tree—larger than anything I had ever seen—stood in the middle of the path. Its crown stretched as high as the stars in the sky, and I could not see the edge of its breadth. Three other trees of the same size created a fortified wall around the Sacred Oaks. Tunnels had been carved through the center of each tree, each one wide enough for a superhighway to fit through. These were the entrances to the Sacred Oaks, and I was sure these trees must be Originals.

As we entered the long tunnel, I marveled at the scenery on the walls. Elaborate motifs, intricate patterns, and detailed scenes wove a tapestry of wooden illustrations on all surfaces of the tunnel. They were so much a part of the wood I wondered how they had been created; surely no human hand could have created such pictures. The tableaus depicted the history of time and mankind. The pictures held a familiarity to those in the Histories.

The sound of rushing water grew louder as we neared the other side of the tunnel. At the end of the tunnel stood a cascading waterfall, closing off the exit. But it did not stop our advance. Most of the Simulacrum did not hesitate, but stepped into the powerful water, disappearing immediately. Some stopped, obviously to explain the process to others who were there for the first time. But no one held hands as they stepped into the torrent. Each one stepped in alone.

In front of me, Daddy and Mother stopped and turned to say something to Ausley. Then they dropped hands, smiled and walked into the water. Ausley followed right behind without a moment's hesitation. Phineas turned to Adair. Adair stopped for a second; I knew Adair was calculating the risk in this, but then she and Phineas, one by one, stepped forward into the unknown.

"You must go alone through the water." Atticus said with his warm breath on my ear.

I nodded, feeling both the nervous exhilaration of his touch and of the unknown at the same time. "What about my dress?" I asked, fingering the broach of my cloak.

"You cannot take clothes or anything else from the outside world into the Sacred Oaks. They will be gone as soon as you reach the water."

We stepped to the edge of the waterfall. I had waited all my life to get here, and I was ready for whatever awaited me on the other side. This was my moment to walk through the waters and join my people on the other side. Whatever I was, whatever I was meant for, I was not completely sure. But I knew where I belonged.

Motionless, I stood, waiting for the white noise around me to dissipate into nothingness. The sound of my breath and the beat of my heart against the roar of the water echoed through the cave, creating a cadence that I was sure was the rhythm of creation, of nature and the earth. I raised my face up and held my palms flat out. With eyes closed, I followed the beat of my heart and stepped into the water. It drenched me instantly, soaking down much further than my bones. It was not a soft summer rain. It was the ocean being poured from a bowl. Cool water, refreshing streams. Bitter at first, but somehow sweet as wine as I drank it down. In the midst of the roaring water, I heard a voice. A voice that did not speak, that did not break my solitude but a voice nonetheless:

> *You are part of the plan; you are part of the water, the tree, the road, the path, and the light. Jars of clay, formed and filled to the brim, are meant to be poured out once they are broken and shattered.*

The voice swirled like wind and then echoed off of the water as light on a crystal. Naked, I stood, letting the words resonate while the water cleansed. There in the middle of the downpour I was alone, and yet...I had never felt so much at home in my entire life.

The waters pushed me out, and I found myself on dry ground, clothed in a white gown. My skin had a translucent quality. Clean. The fabric of my dress touched the ground around me. IT was softer than Alpaca, smoother than Thai silk, and more comfortable than Egyptian cotton. With all of Mother's sewing, I thought I had seen and felt every fabric known to man, but I had never seen or felt anything like this. A golden belt with some kind of inscription on the buckle lay across my hips. I gingerly fingered the metal medallion at the center of the belt. A wheel within a wheel, a world within a world, time within time.

I felt him before I saw him, and my head jerked up as

Atticus stepped through. Atticus, I breathed his name in and it filled my lungs. No words could fill this moment. He glimmered in the fresh light. He walked toward me, and pulled me behind a recess in the cave, concealing us from the others. His strong hand slid under my chin and lifted my face to his. His eyes were brighter, changed somehow. Here they were unguarded; here he was safe. His hand sketched the outline of my jaw and I felt his heartbeat quicken. He slid his fingers down my neck. "I see you," I said, under my breath. It was as if I were seeing him for the first time. Completely him.

"Your skin, it's glowing." I whispered. He nodded. His hand followed down and curved with my body until he rested both hands on my hips.

He put his lips on the indentation of my collarbone and whispered into my skin, "And I see you, Veralee" he slid his lips along the bone, "you are beautiful." A shudder ran down my spine. "You are stronger than you know." After the water, after the voice...I believed him. "Did you hear?" I said, distracted as his mouth worked its way up my neck.

"Did I hear what?" he whispered.

He made my mind unravel.

The water roared, and the cave told no secrets. I lifted my dress and he smiled knowingly at me. Could I love him more? Could I freeze time, and freeze this moment?

Wrinkling his eyebrows together, his face pained, he said, "It is best that we keep moving, but—"

"No," I whispered forcefully, "let's stay here, just like

the Oaks Remain

this."

"Veralee, you will be my undoing." He said as he kissed my mouth, pulled up my gown... and made me see the stars even inside of the cave.

Once we were put back together, he motioned to the crowd of people milling around us. He was playful, not embarrassed.

But, my cheeks burned as I became suddenly aware of the people around us. I looked back to see where we had emerged from the cave, in order to cover my embarrassment. On each side of the tunnel exit stood two enormous marble statues of the Archaon. They stood guard, watching the comings and goings of all. More and more Simulacrum emerged in all types of white garments, no two exactly the same. Each seemed to be designed and fitted just for them.

"Atticus," I whispered in awe, "it's them." I pointed to the carved images, "It's a statue of the Archaon isn't it?" They stood thirty feet tall with gleaming swords hanging from the belt of each warrior.

Atticus intertwined his fingers with mine and nodded, "That one is. But that one," he said, pointing to the other statue, "is an Original Man."

The water from the cascade swept over the side of the path and created a river teeming with brilliantly-hued fish of all kinds and sizes, most of which I had never seen before. It was a sanctuary with forests, rivers and life within its walls.

Ausley ran to us, holding the hem of her skirt in her

hand like a small girl playing in the fields at Red Oaks. To me, she was still that small girl. Her golden curls and white robe gave her an ethereal shine. "Oh, Veralee, I cannot believe we are finally here," she said breathlessly, then scurried away again.

Beside us the river ran farther than I could follow. Leaning over the edge I mused, "I wonder how deep it is." I picked up a pebble and dropped it in. The pebble drifted down, down, down; the river was unfathomable, but the water so clear that it looked like I could wade in it. A sleek porpoise swam by with her calf, and I couldn't help but smile in amazement as they breached the surface in a graceful leap.

Atticus pulled me forward. He knew the way. Intricately carved wood and stone bridges crisscrossed at various points along the pathway, allowing access to indescribable gardens and blossoming orchards on either side. I heard water from all sides and realized there were three other entry tunnels and waterfalls, each creating a river, making four rivers in all. The river veered from the path and trees of all types grew along the banks. I picked a low-hanging yellow pear and tasted it. It exploded in my mouth. Its sweetness coursed through my veins and sent a shock wave of pleasure through my system.

"It's better than anything I have ever tasted... I don't know what to say. I am at a complete loss for words."

"*You* are at a loss for words?" Atticus raised a mocking eyebrow at me. "Well, I guess this place *is* magical.'"

Adair came up from behind us with brisk steps,

"Come on, Veralee. Stop messing around. We can't be late." I could tell from her wide eyes that she was overwhelmed, too, but Adair was still Adair, even here. The rule keeper. It made her feel more secure in all of this newness, I guessed. She had been here once before, but looking around, I could see that a thousand years would not suffice in order to take it all in.

As Atticus began walking on, I grasped his hand and followed dutifully.

A white wolf crossed before us. The wolf stopped beneath a tree by the river. I had never seen a tree like it before. Its three-pronged silver-gray leaves hung on the branches in groups of three and seven. The tree was laden with large, egg-shaped fruit that glistened like abalone. The wolf jumped and grabbed one with his teeth, then settled down with the fruit between its front paws. It broke into the fruit and started eating. A rabbit hopped over and a fruit dropped in front of it. The wolf briefly looked up at the distraction, and then went back to its meal. The rabbit gnawed delicately at its fruit.

"Atticus, that wolf is eating...fruit or something."

"That is the Basar tree; grown from the seeds of the fruit of the One Tree. All the beasts here eat its fruit. And so will we, tonight, at the gathering meal," he said. It was there that I would, for the first time, drink from the river and eat the fruit from Basar tree. The fruit of the Basar is what renewed and rejuvenated our bodies for life in the natural world. It healed any imperfections and slowed the aging processes. Without it, our bodies would be subject to disease, decay, and death just like the Friguscor. The river contained Eiani from the One Tree, and drinking from it renewed our blood and our minds. It was this meal that ensured our longevity until the Door appeared.

"Look, Edwin, have you ever seen such purple orchids? Look at those brilliant yellow phalaenopsis hanging from that giant chaste tree! And look at the birds of paradise! Oh, look at those fields of tulips, blooming at the same time as the dahlias and the hydrangeas!" Mother was as excited as a two-year-old at her first visit to a toy store. It made my heart glad to see her happy.

Daddy grinned at Mother. "Yes, I know. And I know what this means for me when we get back: new flowerbeds and more gardening… my back is aching just thinking about it! You can be some taskmaster, Gail Harper!"

I watched them and hoped they would forgive me for bonding myself to Atticus without their presence. They had to.

The panorama inside the Sacred Oaks looked like a global reunion of long-lost family. Simulacrum laughed and greeted each other with kisses, tears, and warm embraces, as the four paths merged around a crystal pool of water.

"That's where the rivers end," I realized aloud.

The vast lake, spread out with elegant curves, shone an emerald hue that I had only seen in paintings from the German Alps. White swans, gray herons, teal-headed ducks and myriad other water birds swam peacefully along the banks. The heads of graceful black anhingas stuck up like walking sticks as they waded across the bottom. Red-winged blackbirds and purple martins darted and dipped, drinking

the Oaks Remain

from the clear waters. At one far side, something like an alabaster grotto glowed in the morning sun.

I froze, as what looked like a Bengal tiger slinked lazily to where the swans were feeding on some leaves on the shore. But instead of attacking, he pawed at one playfully, and then walked on.

I whispered to Atticus, "Did you see that?"

He nodded, "Yes, there is no death here."

"Incredible. No wonder everyone wants to stay here," I answered longingly.

"But remember, there is no birth here either. Life cannot be created here in the Terebinths. That can only happen outside of these woods. That is why life outside is just as important as life inside," Atticus explained.

"Or maybe life outside is *even more* important." It was Uncle Austin.

Ausley hugged him. "Uncle Austin, I was hoping we could walk in together!" she squealed.

He touched her cheek with fatherly affection, "Me too, Ausley. I was hoping to have a lovely girl on my arm as I entered the gathering, and now I shall have one." His eyes cut sharply over to me.

With Ausley on his arm, he stepped closer and kissed my cheek. He looked at me for a long moment and then quietly said, "Veralee, there is so much in you. So much you are capable of. Don't be afraid, and remember I will always be on your side."

His words felt wrong. They held an edge to them that cut at my throat. "I didn't know we were choosing sides. Regardless, I told Absalom, I do not want to be involved with your agenda."

His animated face flashed with sudden anger. "Veralee, you have no idea what you are capable of, what could be accomplished through you!"

Atticus wedged his words between Uncle Austin and myself; "She wants no part of this. Leave her out of whatever you are doing, Austin." There was a frightening calmness to Atticus's stance as he watched Uncle Austin.

Ausley looked wide-eyed at all of us and then pulled at Austin's arm. "Come on Uncle Austin! I can't wait any longer!" He looked into Atticus's truculent eyes and reconsidered any further discussion. Quickly he turned, feigning a jubilant demeanor, "Yes, let's not wait a moment more for what lies inside. I have been waiting for years for this meeting." His words held a threat.

Atticus watched after Uncle Austin. "What is that man going to do?"

"Nothing. He's harmless, really. He's my uncle. He may have lost all reason, but he's still my uncle." I said, trying to convince myself.

"I will not let him drown you in his madness, Veralee," Atticus said.

the Oaks Remain

"I know." I pulled him toward the coliseum. "He won't. In the end, he is family. He won't do anything to hurt me."

The coliseum was breathtaking to behold. Standing on an elliptical base just above the river, it had five floors of arched, open arcades and a sixth floor with rectangular windows, that soared into the clouds above. There were approximately eighty arches on each of the lower floors, which were divided by pillars of stone and massive columns. The main entrance, supported by four pillars on the axis of the building, was etched with patterns that swirled and domed around it. Thick vines of almond blossoms and pomegranates grew over the arches with flowers that made the stone look alive. At the ground level, the river poured out from each arch.

We entered into the center of the crescent-shaped coliseum. On each side, the cavea, which had four horizontal sections, was made of travertine stone and grass. The richly colored grass filled in, making a comfortable seating area. In the center of the coliseum was a vast lake.

The shore around the lake was floored with white oak, and at the east end, an ornate, carved platform rose of the same oak. A long, beautifully carved, stone bridge led from the west edge of the lake almost to the other side. It ended in a round stage formation that faced the platform. On the platform stood a long table made of the red oak. It was bent and curved in odd places, making it look like the natural bend in a trunk of a tree more than a flat table. Behind the table stood a tree so large and imposing that I was sure it was an Original Terebinth from the time of Original Man. But behind that, on either side of the tree, all you could see was the sky, for we were high on top of a mountain here at the Sacred Oaks.

Mother and Adair sat on my right, Atticus sat on my left. I felt his presence in the vibration of my tseeyen. I knew I should say something to Mother, but I didn't know what. Another horn blasted a clarion call across the gathering and brought order to the crowd. As the crowd grew quiet and took their seats, I noticed that Atticus was no longer as calm as he had just been. The conversation with Uncle Austin was visibly bothering him. The Council began to walk up the stone steps that led to the great table.

I felt Attiucus's heart quicken as the Council members took their places at the oak table. Some of the Council I knew, but other Council members had clearly come through one of the other paths from another part of the world. Issachar, the Timekeeper, sat all the way to the left of the table, followed by Naphtali the Wisdom, and then Absalom the Seer. I did not recognize the next man on the Council, though I could assume that he was Sonith the Lawkeeper, who was followed by Meridee the Discerner. I did not know the next two men. Atticus leaned into my ear. "They are Eliezer and Joab, the Chief Warriors," he said so softly that I had to strain to hear him.

"Who is that?" I asked, nodding toward another man I did not know.

"That is Larius the Historian." Larius was a small man, who looked like he had spent his life in a library. "And that," Atticus pointed to a robust man with a square jaw and kind eyes, "is Hayden the Healer." Just beyond his seat, where the table curved outward, a deep creviced staircase, large enough for six men and women to stand on either side, flowed out from both sides of the center table. These twelve were the Guardians. I beamed with pride to see Daddy take his place as Guardian of Red Oaks.

Twelve gates to the Terebinths existed around the world, and each was protected by its Guardian. These men and women were sworn by blood to fulfill the duties and responsibilities of their positions, among which were protecting the secrets of the Simulacrum and the land upon which the gate was located. It was a great honor among the Simulacrum to be a Guardian, but it also carried a grave responsibility. The men and women who performed these duties must have unquestioned integrity and loyalty to the Simulacrum. They were duty-bound to put the needs, safety and lives of the Simulacrum as a whole above their families, if required, and certainly above their own. The survival of the entire race in the natural world depended upon their faithful and discreet service.

The twelve Council members took their seats and the twelve Guardians stood in place, so a small, dark woman with silver-white hair rapped a gavel down upon the table, opening the Council. Mother leaned into me then and spoke quietly, pointing at the tiny Indian woman who was wrapped in a white robe, "She is Deena the Judge."

Deena's voice was fuller than I expected from her tiny-framed body. With great authority she spoke to us in the old language that had long been forgotten among most of the world. The vast pool of water and the surrounding landscape created a natural amphitheater. "Welcome from the four ends of the earth. Welcome my brothers and sisters to the Council of the Simulacrum. Seven years have we waited to stand together again in the Sacred Oaks. Long have the days grown and dark have the nights become. Again, we call upon you to lay before us the path of the Simulacrum for the next seven years. Again, we, your Council Elders, will serve you and help to guide you through this time of uncertainty and change. We have much to discuss, and much will be decided in the coming days. So let us not tarry any longer."

Then she slammed the wooden gavel onto the table. "Let the Council of the Simulacrum, the True Image-Bearers of the One Tree...begin!" The sound of the gavel ricocheted across the water, creating a wave on the surface of the smooth pond. The trees shook with a small earthquake, and the warrior statues snapped to action. Their long swords crossed, barring the way in and the way out. And then the whole earth cheered.

… 21 …

It Begins

The Council met over a period of three days within the coliseum of the Sacred Oaks. I wondered briefly, painfully, how Nathan was doing and whether he was still asleep. Mattie and Nathan had stayed with Phineas's younger sister, Morgan, who was just two months shy of being able to attend the Council meeting herself. He would not have to miss me long since time in the Terebinths did not pass in the same way as it did in the natural world. But the bond between us grew stronger with each passing day. Even now, even so far away, I felt the beat of his little heart as if he were here himself. My mind traced his soft, rounded cheeks and listened for his infectious laughter. But he was not here, and I forced myself to focus on the Council meeting.

Deena the Judge had opened the floor for several discussion topics, and men and women from all over stepped forward to tell the news from their side of the world or to give an opinion on this subject or that issue. Hours passed, but we listened intently to every word. Every Simulacrum who attended the Council meeting was eligible to speak. Every voice mattered, but the responsibility of a vote lay in the hands of the Council members themselves. There was one Council seat for each of the twelve Simulacrum tribes, and the Council member who filled that seat was selected by his or her tribe. Officers of the Council, selected by the Council members, comprised the Executive Council. In matters requiring a vote, each Council member cast a single vote, while two votes were cast by the consensus of the twelve Guardians of the Gate. Matters were decided by a majority of the fourteen votes; the Council Judge would break any tie vote.

New and old business continued as expected on a pleasant and amiable level for some time. But then the tone changed. There seemed to be growing anxiety among the Simulacrum, and it all swirled around the same problem: the epidemic.

"It spreads like fire through our country even now," said a man from China. Everyone spoke in the old language, which was not used at all, except at the Council meeting. I cannot explain how we knew this language, but it was not learned. It was given to us through the Eiani, and used only when we met together as a unified race. As a child, I knew that the Simulacrum spoke in this mysterious language, so Ausley and I had spent hours making up a pretend language of our own. Our "language" was just gibberish, but now the words came to me clearly, like a pure line of thought.

Another stepped forward. "In our village," said the slight Kuna woman with a square jaw and rings through her brown nose and ears, "they came for us during the night, a mob of angry men, women and children. They moved like jaguars, sniffing the air. They were as swift as harpy eagles. We had no time...no time. They smelled the Eiani, and they came to drink us dry." Her eyes were filled with sorrow, and her words reminded me of the madness in Nathan's father. The memory sent a shiver through my bones. I had heard these words before. Atticus shifted his weight behind me, and I felt his heart begin to race, but when I turned to look at him, it did not show. He was as calm as ever, intently watching the Council.

Absalom rose from his seat and held out his bird-claw hands to calm the crowd. "Listen, my brothers and sisters. Let us not be consumed with fear. For we are not a people without hope. We are the Children of the Blood, and we have no reason to dread the night." He looked compassionately at the woman. "I am truly sorry for your loss, but I see no pattern in this. These things have always erupted in small, isolated incidents here or there. But we must not give in to the terror that will try to smother and paralyze us."

A young man with flaming red hair spoke up. "We've run this course more times than I can count, and you say we will be fine. Why then is it showing up in every country, every major city?" The crowd standing around the pool of water agreed with the man. Naphtali narrowed her eyes and watched every movement like a hawk scanning its surroundings. She didn't miss a thing.

Eliezer, the warrior, spoke, "Are we going to look the other way, to put our faces in the sand and pretend that the *Esurio* is not awakening among the Friguscor?"

Joab stepped forward in agreement with Eliezer, "We will not be like sheep led to slaughter! Our warriors are ready," he thundered, with a voice that echoed through the trees. The warriors were, of course, always ready. It had been their job for centuries to contain the small fires started by the Friguscor around the world, but with Eliezer's comment, soldiers stood at attention all through the coliseum, hands on shining swords. Ceremonial swords I assumed, but still, it did not feel right. Suddenly the tension felt like a noose around my neck.

Naphtali raised her hands. "My friends, we must not allow fear to determine our path. Take caution with your words, young Joab, those who live by the sword will most likely die by it. The time for the sword has not come. Hasty decisions made in the heat of emotion often lead to regret." Everyone quieted with her words, and an anxious calm returned the meeting to order.

Meridee looked to Absalom. "Seer, what do you see in this madness with the Friguscor?" she asked, with a voice of authority.

Absalom smoothed his hair back and replied, "I have indeed peered squarely into this madness, and you must hear my words. This is not the great beginning to the end. The Awakening will come as prophesied, and we must stand ready. But this is not that day. This beast always awakens with voracious hunger. It bares its fearsome teeth, growls, and devours many, but then it curls up to sleep again. This disease will run its course, and sadly, kill many of the Friguscor, but then, my friends," he paused for effect, "it will sleep again. So has been its pattern time and time again."

He held out his thin palms in a conciliatory gesture to the crowd, "Many of us have seen the Esurio awaken in the Friguscor. There are brothers and sisters who now reside in the Alabaster City who witnessed the horrors of Athens, Milan, Rome, London, China, and the Americas," he gestured in a circle around him, "and yet Simulacrum still live within the world of the Friguscor."

He turned to face the Council. "The members of this Council have seen outbreaks of the hunger wax and wane and still we live among the Friguscor. The Esurio always comes with deadly vengeance, but then it slowly recedes back into the shadows. This phenomenon will be similar to the bubonic plague in the Middle Ages or the Spanish flu in the early twentieth century. We even saw the Friguscor come to power in Germany and the murder and destruction that ensued there, but the monsters were, in the end, subdued." His words flowed smoothly, like molasses, coating the crowd's fear. I could feel Atticus, still on alert.

Deena the Judge and Naphtali the Wisdom inclined their heads to agree with Absalom. Meridee the Discerner looked momentarily confused by something that he had said, but then straightened her face again. Many of the people in the crowd agreed with Absalom, though there were some who clearly did not.

Atticus whispered something meant only for himself, but I heard it. "I know you," he said. I turned and raised my eyebrows at him, but he was not looking at me at all. He was staring at Absalom who was busily placating the crowd with words of encouragement for the future of our people.

"You know *whom?*" I asked.

Atticus tightened his jaw in deep concentration and looked so hard at Absalom that I was sure it would hurt. Then he whispered, "I know him...but I just cannot place him."

I leaned into him more, enjoying the excuse to be near his sculpted body, "You met him at the cottage...on the porch."

He immediately looked at me and raised one eyebrow. "Yes," he said slowly like I was a small child who didn't quite have a grasp on the bigger picture, "I know that, Veralee. I mean I know him from...from long ago, from a different time."

I pursed my lips and shrugged my shoulders, "Oh yeah, of course." Then he smiled at me, and I tried, almost unsuccessfully, to stifle a giggle.

Mother whispered, "Quiet," with a finger to her mouth. Adair glared at me as if to say "*Why can't you ever follow the rules?*"

From the edge of the crowd, Uncle Austin stepped forward and stood at the beginning of the stone walkway. Ausley whispered excitedly, "There's Uncle Austin! He is so brave!"

"Brave?" I said a little too loudly.

"Hush," Adair growled.

Mother's eyes pleaded with Austin to stop. Her mouth was firmly set in a thin line to hide the fact that she was biting her lower lip. Uncle Austin did not even notice. She glanced at Daddy who was already looking at her. I watched

Daddy, but I could not read him completely, for his military poker-face covered his true feelings.

Deena the Judge spoke, "Do you wish to address the Council, Austin Harper?"

Uncle Austin wrung his hands twice and then looked up from his feet. "Yes," he said, as if a bit unsure of himself. "I wish to address the Council... and the entire General Assembly."

Deena considered him with steely eyes. "Austin Harper, I believe your request would be better suited for the cell meetings. Let me remind you that the General Assembly is for business that affects us as an entire people, not for personal debate."

"I have the right to address the General Assembly," he said, raising his chin in defiance.

Deena granted his request with the wave of her hand, gesturing for him to come to the center of the stone stage in the lake. Eliezer and Joab looked hard at one another and then at Austin. Something about the way they looked at each other brought me back to the morning I had overheard Mother speaking with Daddy in the library. Those words, "They are watching him," rang through my ears. I looked from Eliezer back to Uncle Austin. Daddy shook his head, already knowing what must be coming, and Mother closed her eyes for a moment and caught her breath as Austin began.

"I have come, as many have come before me. I have come to open the discussion—about change—that was tabled at the last Council meeting." The crowd erupted into a cacophony of voices, but then quieted again with Naphtali's outstretched hand. Austin continued, "Seven years ago, we tabled that discussion for this meeting. We all agreed that we could not live as we had a hundred years ago, and that we could not ignore the change around us anymore." Uncle Austin turned and addressed the crowd behind him as well, "We must evolve with the world around us in order to survive."

Joab looked incredulous. "You are asking that we change our law again? You are asking for the right to change them?"

Eliezer had heard this argument before and barked out, "In the wake of the disease that is spreading, you are asking to change the law that protects our people? Have you heard nothing at this meeting, Austin Harper?" he asked in amazement and bitter frustration.

Austin eyed the two warriors, and then squared his shoulders, standing up taller. But it didn't matter, he still looked weak. The strength in his voice returned. "At the last meeting, we agreed that the Friguscor deserved the right to life, just as we do. Long ago we too were once Friguscor and deserved the right to life. Once again, I am opening the discussion of the *Boged*." The word rang out in the echo that was naturally created by the small stone platform in the middle of the vast lake.

His raised his voice even louder. "Can we, those who have been given the gift of life in our blood, lower our eyes and ignore their deaths? The Boged can change; they have the ability to change and to come to life. They can become as we are," he said, raising his voice with each sentence until he was almost shouting by the end.

I looked at Absalom who sat, curiously, as quiet and still as a mouse. They had said they were going to do this, and they were. Then he looked directly at me and I saw the question in his eyes: *Will you stand with us, Veralee?* I *heard* his voice in my mind. *Choose the path before you.*

Sonith the Lawkeeper spoke with a thin, wiry voice that floated across the air. "The law was given in order to preserve our people. The law was passed in order to protect our lives. No Simulacrum is allowed to give their blood to the Friguscor. It awakens the *Esurio*, the hunger in them that turns to madness. You know this. It is not possible to do what you ask."

His words clicked on a light in my mind. *It awakens the Esurio, the hunger in them that turns to madness.* The epidemic. I looked from Austin to Absalom, but they did not flinch. But then Austin's eyes cut over to mine for one second too long. I remembered the scars stretching up his arm that I saw in the library. He was not just looking for my help to start changing them. In that moment I knew: He had not only tried to change Caraway; he was still trying to change them now. To be Simulacrum and have scars like that—scars that would not heal—meant that he was depleting most of the blood that would have rejuvenated and healed such marks.

I gasped as I thought of Mr. Hinsley. *Mr. Hinsley had said that he had seen Uncle Austin...that he had visited during chemo. But why would he travel all the way to Alabama to see Mr. Hinsley?* Mr. Hinsley's words came back to me: "Hadn't seen him in ages; I guess he heard about my cancer." Austin had said that Caraway had been sick with cancer before he tried to change her. What if he had tried on Mr. Hinsley as well? What if he was trying all over the country? That night by the fire, what had Daddy said? His words came rushing back: *"If they haven't already found us, it won't be long now. There is something more to this than I can put my finger on. It's like someone is helping them find us, like someone has told them that we are here."*

I gasped and looked straight into Absalom's eyes. They were doing it already. They were breaking the law already, and now they were trying to make it legal with the Council. Could they have a hand in spreading the disease? *No...no...Uncle Austin could not do this. He couldn't! He wouldn't! Everything they said in the library......but why? Why would they do this? Was this why Daddy told Mother that someone was looking for Austin, because they suspected he was doing this? But whom? Someone on the Council?*

"Help us change the Friguscor, Veralee. It has already begun...we just need the Council to agree," Absalom had said in the library. It had already begun. They had already begun attempting to change them, and the epidemic was the result. My eyes locked onto Uncle Austin's. "Why?" I breathed out the word slowly, more condemnation than question.

Suddenly, I was no longer standing at the Terebinths of Mamre. I was on the porch of the little white cottage back at Red Oaks. Except everything seemed like it was inside of a shell, the sound was mixed with a rushing of wind and my vision seemed blurred. I saw myself, Nathan, Atticus and Absalom speaking. I walked closer to hear through the sound of rushing wind.

"A price must always be paid, boy." Absalom had said, "The price to find the Boged is to be paid by the rest of the Friguscor."

Then I watched myself challenge Absalom, "Who are you to decide the price for life?"

Atticus had yelled, "You have no idea what you are doing! You have not seen the horrors that this would unleash on the world. The price will be on all of us, the cost will be our existence on this earth!"

Absalom the Seer, who sat on the Council, had grinned wickedly at Atticus and me and said, "It is part of the plan; I assume you have read the Histories. It is part of the end of days."

Atticus put his hand on my shoulder from where he stood behind me. This gesture pulled me back through the tunnel to the Terebinths of Mamre. Absalom glared at me. He released my gaze, and I felt his mental hook being pulled from my mind. Atticus pulled me closer, feeling my anxiety grow. As I turned back to look at him, he looked curiously into my eyes. I did not have time to tell him everything, but whatever he saw in my face was enough. "It's them, Atticus... they are the ones spreading the disease. I think it's them," I breathed out. His eyes shot up to Absalom who watched us as we spoke.

Ausley moved near me, "Veralee, give him a chance to speak. Uncle Austin wants to give them a chance at life. If you only knew his story, Veralee, you would agree with him. He lost the love of his life." My mouth fell open and almost hit the ground, but she continued, "Veralee, he is so brave to put his reputation on the line for what is right...for what is true." They had gotten to Ausley. They had been trying to convince me to join, but I never thought they would try to convince Ausley. By the look on her innocent face there was no way she really knew what they were doing. She did not know about Caraway. Atticus heard her words as well but did not speak.

I started to tell Ausley, but then I heard my name, and everyone looked toward me. "We have proof that it works!" cried Uncle Austin. "I ask Veralee Harper of Red Oaks to come forward."

"Veralee Harper of Red Oaks, you have been called," said Deena the Judge. I was completely confused. I had not been listening. Why was I being called? A lump started to grow in my throat. What had he said? All around me, the crowd looked horrified, like I bore a disease myself. My arm began to burn. Atticus moved along the edge of the crowd, paralleling me like a string was attached between us, as I inched my way down the stone walkway to the center of the stage, where Austin stood. With each step, I felt like I was walking the plank rather than simply being called for questioning. Uncle Austin gave me a pleading look as I came to stand by him, but I scowled back at him with horror and disgust. He had pushed me into this; he had not allowed me to choose at all; he had chosen for me. I hated feeling like a captured and caged animal, and now I felt the doors clink shut around me.

Meridee looked concerned as she spoke. "What does this woman have to do with your request? Leave her alone, look at her face; she has not volunteered to speak on your behalf!"

Uncle Austin put a hand on my shoulder, and I shrugged it off. He smiled down at me like we were the best of friends. "Council, they *can* be changed, their lives *can* be saved. I have seen it with my own eyes." The Council looked at each other anxiously. Daddy looked as though he were ready to jump across the water that separated them and strangle Austin. His teeth were set on edge, and his jaw trembled with rage.

He interjected, "Council of the Simulacrum, Veralee is my daughter, and she is under my protection. She should not be called to speak."

Deena looked at Daddy and answered with sympathy in her voice, "Edwin, she is a full member of the Simulacrum Council this day, with all the rights...and with all the responsibilities. She has been called, and she must speak for herself."

Daddy closed his eyes slowly; Mother began to tremble.

Deena turned back to Austin, "Why do you call Veralee Harper to speak at her first meeting of the Council? What could this young woman possibly add to this unpleasant business? I warn you that the Council will not tolerate more of your nonsensical rants regarding your personal philosophies."

"Veralee, my own niece, has bravely done what none of you have dared to do before. She believed that a small boy's life was worth more than our laws. That giving him the chance to live was more important than saving her own skin. She is the bravest of us all."

My chest exploded, and my heart skipped several

beats before it began drumming as though to escape the ribs that imprisoned it. Then the fear was overtaken by anger boiling to the surface. *He was using me*–sacrificing me! And if he could, he would use Nathan too.

"Today I have brought for you the boy." As he said this, the crowd behind us split and Nathan, being led by a man I had never seen before, came walking down the stone aisle.

When he saw me, his eyes came alive, and he ran as fast as he could to get to me. "Vewalee!" he cried excitedly, "They said I could come and see you and Atticus!"

I caught him and pulled his head to my chest. "Oh, Nathan," I said as the nausea rose.

Sonith stood up. "What is this? The law states that no child is allowed to enter the Terebinths or the Council meeting! You are out of order, Austin Harper! Who is this boy, and why have you brought him here today?"

Austin raised both hands triumphantly. "This is the proof we have been waiting for!" he turned in a full circle as he talked, to address the entire audience, "This boy was Friguscor, but through the power of the blood that runs in our veins, he is now Simulacrum! Look at him, and you will see the truth!" The crowd erupted like a volcano, and I instinctively held Nathan closer as I looked for Atticus in the crowd.

Deena, the Judge, slammed her gavel down on the Council table. "Quiet!" She demanded; she looked stricken but set her face on continuing. "Quiet, I say. Come to order!" The crowd started to settle a bit, so she continued, "Is this true, Veralee Harper of Red Oaks? Are the charges brought against you true?"

Daddy raged, "Charges?! Who has brought charges?!"

Deena raised her hand to silence him. "Answer, Veralee, who is this boy, and is this account true?"

I held on tightly to Nathan's tiny hand. It seemed even smaller here, in this great, big place. Then I raised my chin high and gathered all of my courage so that my voice would not shake. "Yes," I said resolutely, and the crowd erupted again.

I heard shouts of, "She has broken the law! She must be punished!"

"No, they deserve to live!"

"She has started Esurio, she will get us all killed!"

"Give them a chance!"

"This is madness!"

"This must be stopped!"

"This will be the end of all of us!"

Meridee's measured voice rose above the chaos: "Let. Her. Speak."

Thousands of eyes turned to watch me as I retold the story of Nathan, but I was afraid that many of their ears were already closed even before I began. "He is Simulacrum, as you can see; he is bonded to me, and I to him." I shot a look at

Daddy who looked like he was going to be sick. Then he set his jaw in the Harper way, and nodded at me in encouragement. Even though he stood beside the Council, with that look, I felt he was right beside me.

I looked back to Deena the Judge who spoke swiftly to Sonith. Sonith exhaled and turned to me. "Do you know our law?" he said, out of protocol.

"Yes," I replied again.

Sonith continued like he was reading my Miranda Rights. "You gave your blood, which you know is against our laws, and changed a Friguscor. You have put all of our people in jeopardy. You have broken the law. Do you deny these charges?"

I looked down at Nathan, and then immediately back at Sonith. But I could not look at Mother. "I did give this child my blood. He was Friguscor, and now he is Simulacrum. But, I do not believe this put all of our people in jeopardy," I said, refusing to cry or to tremble.

Uncle Austin alleged again, "This is the proof we have been waiting for...the proof that the Boged are out there." Austin reached toward Nathan's head, as if to comfort the child. I pulled Nathan back like it was a tiger about to pounce instead of Austin's hand. Austin pretended not to notice as he continued, "They can be changed. Look at the boy! You cannot deny that he was worth it, that his life was worth the cost of a small amount of her blood!"

He was right about that. Nathan *was* proof that the Boged were out there, and in that moment, standing with his tiny hand in mine, I knew that he was worth it. I knew that the cost of my blood was worth the price of his life. My back straightened then, and I felt strength rise within me. I would fight for Nathan...for my child...with every last breath in my body.

Eliezer shot back at Austin, "Does she know how?"

Austin looked quickly at Absalom, who did not move. "How what?" he asked, confused.

It was Joab that answered him. "Does she know *how* she changed him? Does she know *how* to identify the Boged from the Friguscor?" He turned his heated question to me. "Do you, Veralee Harper of Red Oaks, do you know how to distinguish the Boged from the Friguscor?"

No. No, I hadn't *known* whether Nathan would turn. I had acted out of a rash emotion that had changed my entire life. It was a decision that I did not regret, but also one I did not fully understand. "No," I admitted.

Sonith clapped his hands together. "Then you do not deny that you have no more knowledge than we do. You do not know how to identify the Boged from the Friguscor any more than any of us do. *That* is why the law was passed so long ago. There is no way to know which will turn to Simulacrum and which will turn into blood-seeking monsters with the *Esurio*."

The crowd of Simulacrum around me agreed with Sonith's words, and so did I.

Uncle Austin jumped in, hot and angry. "That is no

reason to keep an old law, just because our knowledge is limited! We cannot allow lack of knowledge to determine our actions! These are *people* we are talking about, and they deserve the right to life," he shouted at the Council.

Naphtali spoke slowly. "The law protects our people, our children, and our way of life. We do not wish ill on the Friguscor, nor do we take joy in their deaths. All here live among them. All here have met and even made a friend among the Friguscor. But, what you are suggesting is too dangerous. To open ourselves up to this would hasten our demise. The law was made to protect us, not to limit us."

"But what about *them*? What about the ones who are dying? Do we just build up walls around ourselves and continue to live like we don't inhabit the same world with them? Like we don't see them dying day after day, because we are afraid of what will happen to *us*? Is that the kind of people we have become? People who make rules out of fear and not out of love?" Austin yelled back.

I looked at Naphtali, hoping she had an answer to his very valid question. A small number of people seemed to agree with Austin's question. A small earthquake rumbled in my epicenter; something in me, some foundational truth that I had always known and trusted, suddenly began to fracture under the pressure of the shock waves. The law was to protect us, but had we misused the law? Had we allowed fear to warp the law and our hearts into an iron fortress while people died outside our gates?

The Simulacrum raised their voices:

"Yes, are we to only care about ourselves?"

"The blood is a gift, should we not try to save them?"

But other voices countered,

"The law was made to protect us. We have to think about our children, about their safety!"

"You do not know what you are asking for! This would be a disaster!"

"Changing the law will destroy us! It would be the end of the Simulacrum way of life as we know it!"

It was getting intense, so I leaned down to Nathan, "Nathan, go stand with Atticus until I finish." I watched as he ran back along the bridge and Atticus took his hand.

Deena the Judge addressed the crowd, "The Friguscor are not our concern. We do not govern them, and we cannot protect them." And then she folded her hands. Uncle Austin looked at the Council and saw what was becoming more and more apparent. He had already lost this battle. He had lost it before it had even begun.

"Besides," added Eliezer with a hard edge to his voice, "only we are called to protect the Simulacrum. Each of us must remember our purpose, our responsibilities. We warriors are the only ones protecting the Simulacrum." He sat back, satisfied with his knowledge of the word. Even though I knew what Uncle Austin was doing was wrong, I began to feel his sympathy for the Boged.

"But we are no longer alone," I said quietly.

"What?" Meridee had heard me.

I looked up at her, realizing I must have spoken too loudly. "I...I was just saying that we are not alone anymore." I nervously looked at Daddy. He nodded for me to continue, and then I remembered the message I was to give to the Simulacrum. The dramatic turn of events had almost made me forget what Achiel had asked me to do. "I said," my voice was stronger and more confident again, "We are no longer alone."

"What do you mean, Veralee?" asked Deena the Judge.

I spoke loud enough so that everyone could hear. "The Archaon have returned. They walk among men again." My voice carried over the people and reached through the empty spaces.

Absalom moved for the first time since Austin first spoke. "What madness are you speaking, girl?" I saw Issachar's eyes. His mouth opened, and he looked at Daddy who nodded, verifying what I had said. Then Issachar sat back hard in his seat like a blow had pushed him.

Daddy spoke fiercely, "No madness, Absalom. She speaks the truth. Listen to her." He nodded at me and opened his palms, gesturing for me to continue.

"They came, ten of them, and spoke to me in the woods at Red Oaks. They asked for a meeting with the Simulacrum. They said that they would meet us at the Terebinths of Mamre with the last light of the blood moon," I said, loudly, for all to hear. Hushed murmurs spread through the audience. The Council looked shocked, like a rug had just been pulled from under them. All sat silently, blinking in my direction.

Then they turned, one by one, to look at Issachar, the Timekeeper. He leaned forward.

"Do you know the name of the one you spoke with?" Issachar asked, his tone colored with more than a little bit of doubt.

"Achiel of Paraclete, Lord of the Archaon," I announced confidently. Issachar's eyes widened with the mention of Achiel's name.

"Achiel. You spoke with Achiel?" he questioned in astonishment. I nodded. "Then yes, you are right," he said, satisfied that I was telling the truth.

Sonith gasped. Meridee's face shone with excitement, and the warriors stood speechless with their hands on their swords.

Issachar said, "The next blood moon shines this very night. If the Archaon have come, as she says, to walk again with men, then they will be here with the first light of day tomorrow." A gasp rippled across the crowd.

Absalom stood, "What news of joy this would be! But does anyone have the courage to ask the question that is on everyone's lips?" He spoke with an air of vague disdain. "Why would the Archaon come to a young girl? Why would they not come to the one of the *Council* to ask for a meeting?" He said, as if to remind the people of the importance of their governing body. "And more importantly, why would they come at such a *convenient* time to a girl who had betrayed our most important law?" I felt the emotions shift in the people around me as their eyes turned to search my face.

Daddy walked around the other Guardians, toward the Council's table as he spoke. "She speaks the truth. She did not try to hide from you what she had done. When asked, she freely told you of her actions. Why would you question her honesty now?" His voice was clothed in reason.

Meridee agreed, "Yes, Veralee has not been dishonest with the Council when it concerned her guilt, why would she now be dishonest to us?"

Absalom pushed harder. His tone was like silk, smooth and slippery, "Can you not see?" He raised his long arms up like he was ushering a chorus of responses from the audience before him. "This girl is a dreamer. She has confused her dramatic dreams with reality...or..." He looked derisively at me and hardened his voice for effect, "This is merely a tale to distract us; a smoky mirage to convince us that the age of the Simulacrum is coming to an end." He gestured with his hands and continued, "An elaborate ploy to turn our attention from the gravity of her actions, and a desperate stratagem devised by her family to release her from the consequences of her crime."

I stared at Absalom. *What was he doing? Why was he doing this? He must know that the Archaon had come; if he was a true Seer, he must know.* "That is not true!" I yelled back at him, too passionately, as anger's flames erupted from my core and poured over the surface.

"I have not seen the coming of the Archaon, nor have I heard the whispers of the signs pointing us to that time," continued Absalom the Seer, as smoothly and as deadly as a diamondback rattlesnake slithering through a peanut field.

Then he spoke to me. "Did you think that I, Absalom, Seer of the Simulacrum, would not see this coming if it were true? Do you forget the Office of Seer? Who are you, Veralee Harper, that they would come to you instead?"

I lost control of my tongue, "No, because I see now that you are selfishly blind. You cannot see the nose in front of your face, unless it benefits you to do so!"

The crowd gasped and stepped back from me. Then I felt him; Atticus stood in the crowd across from me. He had been there the whole time. I looked at him with pleading eyes, and he comforted me with a look. He was standing beside me. I was not alone.

Naphtali spoke, "I see no reason for the child to speak falsely. If the time for the Archaon to walk with men has come, we do not want to miss it because we fixed our gaze elsewhere and refused to see. Wisdom calls for us to wait and see if the Archaon arrive before we make a decision. What is one more day? If it does not come to pass, then the Council will know that her words are false, but if they do arrive as she has said, we will know the truth is in her." She did not look over at Absalom but looked straight ahead.

Deena the Judge stepped in, "We will meet in executive session with the Council members to decide how to proceed. There are serious issues before us. Emotions are high, and I believe Naphtali speaks truth. We must not decide before we have examined and contemplated all of the evidence. Larius, I believe it is time that we break for the first meal, is it not?" she said, directing him to give her the right answer.

Larius pushed his shaggy hair away from this face and looked up from the giant book where he was fervently writing down each word spoken. "Yes...yes it is time," he said looking at his round silver stopwatch that he pulled out of his vest pocket.

Deena the Judge continued, "Then I believe we will adjourn for—"

Sonith raised his hand. "Yes, Sonith?" Deena said.

"I am so sorry," he began, "but we still have the crime at hand to address. The law *has* been broken," he added with the conviction of one who sees the world in black and white.

Deena pursed her lips and blinked her dark brown eyes slowly. "Yes, you are correct, Lawkeeper," she said, as if the words themselves might choke her.

Daddy tensed up and looked at Naphtali, who sat watching Deena and Sonith. I looked over at Mother, who stood like a statue, holding onto Adair's hand. Ausley looked back and forth between us. And the world seemed to stand still for a moment before Deena the Judge spoke again. "Sonith, what is the consequence for the law that has been broken?" She said this out of respect for the crowd of people, for I was sure that she already knew.

Sonith cleared his throat. "For those who break the law of the blood...." he grew poignant, as if the reality had just dawned upon him. "They will forfeit their years here. For endangering the people, they shall be banished from the Simulacrum and the Terebinths of Mamre, forced to walk alone, without fellowship, in the land of the Friguscor, until death claims them or, if they still live, until the time when the Door opens." A stunned silence filled the assembly.

Forfeit their years? In the land of the Friguscor... without the protection of the Simulacrum? I let the words crash against me over and over, like a wrecking ball bringing a building down. I would have to leave? I wasn't ready. I was so young. I looked at Nathan, held securely in Atticus's arms, but clearly crying.

Then the crowd erupted into chaos. Tears rolled down Adair's face, her mouth twisted into a horrified gape. Ausley sobbed hysterically, "Veralee, no, no, no... Veralee!"

Uncle Austin looked frantically around like someone would come to his aid at any moment, and started mumbling, "What is happening? This is not what we agreed upon." His voice got louder and more insistent, "This is not what they told me. This is not supposed to happen! No, no, no!" he shouted.

Daddy, the soldier, the engineer, the problem solver, my protector all my life, grabbed the edge of the stone partition in front of him. He yelled at the Council, "NO, you cannot do this! She is so young! It was just a foolish mistake! Issachar, Naphtali, do something... stop this!"

Deena raised her hand again and bellowed, "Silence!"

Issachar spoke, trying to inject some reason into the spiraling chaos, "Is this what is best for the girl, for us, for the Simulacrum? Is this what the Council is going to require of one so young? Is this truly justice?"

Sonith looked resigned, but justified. "It is the law. We cannot choose to ignore the law. It is written."

Naphtali spoke, "The law was written in order to protect and to have order. Do we abandon reason in regard to the law? Do we not consider circumstances as well, when we interpret the law? To banish one so young to walk without the protection of the Simulacrum in the world of the Friguscor, and then to keep her from entering the Terebinths—what purpose would this serve?"

Sonith looked scandalized, "We do not *interpret* the law; we merely see that it is followed. If we do not follow the law, then how shall we have any order among us?"

I heard Adair as she spoke, but it felt like she was down a long tunnel, already far away from me, "How will she drink from the river and eat from the Basar tree? She has to come every seven years to rejuvenate the Eiani in her blood. Without it..." her voice cracked and quivered.

I finished her sentence in a whisper, "I will die."

Sonith scratched at his mustache nervously, and I noticed that the eyes of those in the gathering began to dart anxiously. But no one spoke for a long moment.

Meridee interjected, "Sonith, I believe we, as the Council, should vote on how best to decide a course of action."

Eliezer spoke directly to Meridee, "We will stand with the law. It is our job as Council members to stand with the law." Joab backed Eliezer's words with a sturdy nod of his head.

"Yes, the law is clear. But, the law does not have eyes, ears, a conscience or an intellect. People must interpret the law. It is our moral responsibility to do so," Hayden the Healer spoke for the first time. He was a man motivated by compassion, but tempered with reason.

Sonith reiterated, "It is the law. No one wants to be unkind or cruel, but it is the law. We must follow our law, even when it is unpleasant or difficult to do so."

Mother stepped forward and silenced the argument with a question, "Is this what you will speak over my daughter?" Her tone was fierce. Her long, red cloak flowed behind her, and her striking beauty enveloped her. She looked at Deena the Judge and did not break her gaze.

Deena looked heartbroken as she spoke. "It is the law. We cannot choose which laws we will enforce and which we will ignore. We, as the Elders, are tasked with upholding and enforcing the law."

Mother narrowed her eyes onto Deena and raised her voice so that it echoed across the coliseum. "Then I invoke my right to *Padhah*. She is blood of my blood, bone of my bone, flesh of my flesh. I invoke my right to pay the price for what she has done."

Deena dropped her head. Daddy yelled, "Gail!" and then stopped abruptly.

I screeched, "What are you doing? What is Padhah?!"

Sonith spoke into the chaos in my head and to the crowd. "Padhah is the right of any blood-bond carrier to pay the price for another of the blood-bond. For one to redeem or purchase another by offering their own life as payment." The words cut through my entire body and left me naked to the pain.

Ausley began sobbing again, and Adair dropped to her knees screaming, "Mother!" Both brought their hands to their mouths, dissolving into fits of sobbing.

"She can't do that!" I yelled out. Daddy shot me a hard look warning me to stop. But I didn't care; I could not let her do this. "You can't do that, Mother! You can't! I won't let you."

She turned quickly, "Hush, child! You know nothing." Her harsh words hurt.

Sonith raised his hands to quiet the crowd again. "Is this your decision, Gail Harper of Red Oaks? It is within your right to invoke Padhah, but think long and hard before you answer."

Meridee looked at me with tears in her eyes. We both knew Mother's answer before it left her lips. "Yes," she said, as if she was spitting glass from her mouth.

"NO!" I screamed. Mother stood strong, at the edge of the water, in front of the Council.

Absalom clicked his tongue several times and held out his long boney finger, "Sonith," he said in a sickeningly slow voice. "Am I wrong in remembering that the right to Padhah only applies to the innocent?" Sonith looked confused, so Absalom continued. "Is it not written that only the innocent may stand in for the guilty? The guilty cannot stand for the guilty. Am I correct in this?" Sonith looked around to the other Council members; he sensed a trap was being laid, but he did not know where.

Sonith answered as slowly, "You are correct, it takes the innocence of one person to erase the guilt of the other when invoking Padhah. You must be innocent to take the consequence for another. But, I fail to see what that—"

Absalom clapped his hands together again, "Well, is my memory the only one that goes back long enough to remember why Edwin Harper sits as the Guardian of the Red Oaks and not Gail Harper of Red Oaks? Is it not *her* family's lineage to protect the land? Have we so easily forgotten why Edwin Harper fills the position instead of his lovely wife?"

Daddy snarled, "Absalom, you—" Deena silenced him with a look and an outstretched hand. Mother's gaze turned icy as she watched Absalom continue his measured speech. I looked back and forth trying to make sense of what was being said.

Austin dropped his shoulders and rubbed his face with his hand. "I didn't mean for this to happen, Veralee. I'm so sorry, so sorry..." Austin whimpered like a whipped dog.

Absalom took advantage of his lead and continued, "Or are we to ignore deals that were made in secret, as if they do not pertain to the light of day?"

Sonith looked absolutely lost as he said, "What are you

talking about, Absalom?"

Deena the Judge turned on him, "I do not see how that relates right now, Absalom. Let the past alone and deal with the living," she pronounced.

Absalom looked at Sonith the Lawkeeper, "Oh, I think it has great weight to the present situation, and I am most certain that Sonith would agree. For he himself has already said, and rightly so, as the law goes, that the guilty cannot stand in place of the guilty."

Deena the Judge looked at him hard. "But she is no longer guilty, for her crime was absolved by her mother's sacrifice." She narrowed her eyes at Absalom, "Or have you forgotten that?"

Absalom smiled meekly and spoke softly, opening his hands. "Madam, please, I am not trying to cause more hardship for this dear family, but as Sonith said, we are to uphold the law, not to interpret it. And if my memory serves me right, and, as Seer, it always does, her crime was not *pardoned*; it was not *abolished* by the Council. Her mother paid the price for Gail's crime, but Gail was forever to live with the weight of her crime on her shoulders. Is that not why she still cannot fill her family's position on the Council? If I am wrong then we need to reinstate our sweet Gail to the Council at once!"

Sonith exhaled loudly, "What is this? I do not know what you are talking about! What secret meetings? What is Gail Harper of Red Oaks guilty of?"

Absalom looked at Deena. Deena studied Absalom for such a long time that it became uncomfortable to everyone

the Oaks Remain

around, and then, reluctantly, she turned to face the people. She gave Mother an apologetic look as she began speaking, "Long ago," then she stopped. The words came slowly and were clearly hard for her to speak when she started again, "Years have passed since Richard Wilson sat as Judge over the Council, may he be remembered well. Now, he sleeps until the Door opens, may the time come quickly. But his wife Sarah does not sleep, nor is she residing within the Alabaster City."

My heart beat faster. *My grandparents. She was talking about my grandparents.* I was so small when they left. It was so long ago, but the pain of separation was still so fresh for my Mother that even to this day she never speaks of them. And we, in return, never asked questions and never brought up raw memories for her. Silence became a tacit understanding in our home. But if my grandfather was asleep...that could only mean one thing; he had been killed outside of the Terebinths of Mamre. And why would my Grandmother not be in the Alabaster City? I looked at Mother who was staring directly at Deena with her strong jaw tightly closed and pointed defiantly toward the Council.

Deena continued with a professional demeanor, "It was discovered that a certain child in their family was not Simulacrum by birth, but in fact had been...changed. That child was...Boged." The people around me gasped audibly, and I tried to process her words.

What was she talking about? What child? Deena looked like the pain of telling the story made it difficult to continue, but she pulled herself together and looked stalwartly towards the audience.

Mother moved onto the stone aisle so forcefully that her long scarlet robe swayed around her and dramatically fell at her feet. "I request to address the Assembly."

"Yes, of course," Deena responded with a heavy sigh and empathy in her voice.

"I will speak on my own behalf, if that is acceptable, Judge." Deena's mouth turned down, and she gestured for Mother to continue.

Mother breathed in to steady herself. And with that one action, I saw that her creative side, the one I loved...the side of her that always had pencils stuck behind her ears and threads clinging to her shirt and swatches of fabric in her hand...was set aside. What was left was raw. It was my Mother when no one was around but us, when she was sitting at the table and telling us the truth about our lives as the Simulacrum, when she was giving me the words that changed how I saw the world, and when she was quiet and thoughtful sitting by the fire at night. She spoke directly to me as she walked down the stone path, like the rest of the world did not exist around us. And the crowd around her seemed to disappear, for I saw only her face, the face that I loved fiercely, as she spoke.

"Many years ago I was in Montgomery, visiting my favorite bookstore after a long day. I stayed longer than I had planned, and when I left the bookstore, it was late and cold. As I stepped onto the sidewalk I heard a soft, stifled sound floating on the wind. It was so faint that I had to stop and stand still to really hear it. It was a baby's cry." My breath caught in my throat.

Mother inhaled deeply and went on, "I followed the sound—and my life's destiny—to the alley beside the store... to the dumpster. The high-pitched cry grew weaker with every breath. When I reached in, I found a tiny baby in a cardboard box. She had been discarded carelessly in the pile of wretched garbage, like her life didn't matter, like her ten fingers and ten toes didn't count. I put my arms around the baby. She was beautiful: she had such soft skin, such big eyes that begged for love and comfort, with depth that touched a part of my soul. She had been there for some time, and she was so... cold... and blue. I could feel death on her skin. Those big eyes closed shut, and her mouth sagged as her cries went silent. I felt the life seeping out her. She was dying as I held her."

My pulse quickened. *What was she saying?*

"Something in me screamed, even though my mouth did not make a sound. She was a baby; innocent of wrong. She did not choose this life or this death. She had been left to die alone, abandoned to a dumpster, never to be known, never to know anyone......never to have a name of her own. I made a decision that I have never regretted for a day in my life, nor do I now. As the Eiani filled her mouth, she began to suck hungrily, and I watched as the blood dripped down her throat. She stirred and color began to return to her pale face."

My heart beat so loudly I could hardly hear her. *Who had Mother saved?*

"Later, as she changed... when the Eiani forced open her little veins and pumped through her tiny body, I feared that I had made the wrong decision... that I had created a monster from our Histories, but instead...she lived. Within three days she was alive for the first time in her young life. She was alive, and she was mine. My daughter, blood of my blood, flesh of my flesh, bone of my bone."

Me?

Mother continued, "I have never regretted that decision, and I am proud to this day of the woman she has become. Veralee, my precious baby, with eyes of grey that shine like the moon, do not ever doubt that you are loved. For we would give it all again to save you, if that is what it took." And then she smiled at me, her face shining with a mother's wholehearted love.

I reeled as she turned and faced the Council. "And now... now I will give it all again if that is what you require." Mother turned and looked at me again, and I saw myself in her eyes. The dark hair, the grey eyes. But I was short, the shortest of all my family. And the bond was so strong with Mother, but not so with my sisters...

"No..." I said softly.

Her eyes brimmed with tears as she continued, "I came, with my mother, to the Council and admitted my crime. They gave me the same sentence that you now give Veralee. But my Mother," her voice cracked and she bit down hard on her lip that quivered with memory, a memory that still cut like a knife left in the victim. She looked to Daddy for strength. He stood on the edge of the platform, willing his arms to reach to her. The lake was too large for him to physically reach us; it would have taken too long for him to make his way down from his place by the Council and all the way around the large lake.

He was trapped, forced to stand apart from us, separated by water. But blood was thicker than water, and Mother still drew her strength from him. He did not have to touch her with his arms to hold her up, for the bond between them was too strong. They could have been across the world from each other and still would have been united. Mother cleared her throat and pushed on.

"But my Mother refused to let me go. She had lost my father that year, and she could not...she said that she could not bear the pain of losing me," Mother stopped speaking and wrung her hands. Silence hung around the assembly. "And so... she chose to go in my stead. I was informed that I could never serve as the Guardian of Red Oaks, due to the nature of my crime, so Edwin volunteered to continue the family purpose. The Council accepted. " Heavy tears flowed down her cheeks but she stood tall...taller than any woman at the Council Meeting that day, held up by her backbone of steel. That woman would not bend, for unlike most, she did not know how, when it came to doing what was right.

The Council sat silently, and Meridee wiped her eyes several times. My mother looked like a beacon of light, standing brave against the wind as her cloak flapped around her legs. I reached out and grasped her hand. Her strong hands, which had made me strong, trembled slightly but did not give. Together, standing side by side, we faced the Council like an iron curtain, refusing to waver. Then, without being asked or cued, Adair and Ausley stepped out and walked to the water's edge to stand with us, even from there. Nathan pulled free of Atticus and came running down the walkway. He hit me at full speed, almost knocking me over. I grabbed him and held him close. "Vewalee....Vewalee," he began to sob.

"Hush...hush little one. You are safe. Don't worry Nathan. Don't worry. I'm here." I whispered into his ear, pained at the realization that I would not be able to comfort him for long.

I looked toward Daddy. He swallowed hard and nodded his head in agreement with his family. He lifted his chin high and set his eyes on us. Though we all stood apart, we still stood together.

Absalom's voice slithered into the silence, "Here it is, the revelation of Veralee Harper. The truth was made to set us free." He leaned over the table before him and craned his neck toward Deena and Sonith, "So what does the Lawkeeper have to say now? What does the law say?"

Sonith rubbed his forehead and then spoke. "The law is clear. You cannot invoke Padhah. I am...so sorry." His words were not formal, but personal, as if he were talking to an old friend. "I hear your request, but you are not qualified under the law."

Daddy's jaw went rigid, and he started to speak. I knew I had to cut him off. If I let them, they would all sacrifice themselves for me. So much had already been given for me; so much had already been lost. How could I ever ask for more? It was time for me to sacrifice for them, time for me to stand in the gap for those I loved. The truth felt harsh as I realized he could not stand in for me even if he wanted to because, I was not blood-bonded to him. The thought felt like a lie, but still it came...the only daddy I had ever known was not my biological father. My consequences had to be my own.

"Then I will go with her." The voice I would know even in the blackest part of night called out over the crowd and wrapped its arms around me. Atticus.

He walked with so much resolve in his gait that he commanded the attention of the entire assembly as he came to stand by my side. "I will go with Veralee, for she is bonded to me," he said with a terrible, possessive wildness in his eyes.

Deena looked hard at him, like she was trying to remember something from a dream. "Who…can it be…Atticus?" She said with a girlish smile. Atticus bowed his head respectfully.

Absalom looked at Atticus with new eyes, which stirred with the beginnings of a storm behind them. "So, the reclusive wanderer has returned to the Council meetings. One must wonder why you have decided to grace us with your presence now…after so much time has passed," his words slithered as he spoke.

Joab asked, "Who…are you?"

"I am Ayindalet, Atticus the Watcher." Atticus spoke with cool resolve, "And I will go with Veralee."

Sonith blurted out, "You cannot. You are Ayindalet. You have a purpose for the Simulacrum people, and that does not include this girl's punishment. You have to fulfill your purpose to us; it is the law."

Atticus cut his eyes and steadied his jaw, "Sonith, I will tell you again. I am not under your law. I go where the River pulls me, not where you tell me to go. I go and come as the River pleases. I am no puppet to your theater."

Naphtali spoke with a calming voice, "He is right. We cannot decide the way for an Ayindalet. Let the River decide his path, as it always has and it always will."

Absalom looked greedily at Atticus and his lower lip quivered with lust as he spoke, "You have bonded yourself to this girl? You, who have no say over your days or nights? Go with her; it is only a matter of time before you are taken away, and she will be left alone again." His words hit me with both fists, slamming into my chest. But Atticus did not waver and neither could I. Mother, Daddy, Ausley, Adair and now Atticus. They would all give their lives for mine.

"I accept the consequence of my actions" I yelled out with a fierceness spouting from my core, "and I alone will serve it. I am guilty. No other but me."

Daddy yelled across the water, "Veralee! Do not do this!"

Mother jerked my hand, pulling me closer to her, "No...no!" She gasped in shock and agony.

I turned to her. "Mother, my path has already been laid before me. You gave me life, but you cannot rewrite it. You cannot change or determine it. You must let me do this. You must let me go the way I am supposed to go. Remember, we are Simulacrum. I will never be alone because, as you have always taught me, we...are never alone. Whatever comes, I will know in my heart that you and Daddy and Adair and Ausley love me, and that will give me strength."

"But...one thing," I called out loudly.

Deena, answered with tired eyes, "Yes, Veralee?"

"What about Nathan? Is he banished as well? It was not his fault; it was not his choice. I did this to him. He had no choice. Will you banish him as well?"

Deena slumped slightly in her chair and did not look at Sonith but looked straight at me, "We will not punish Nathan. He has committed no crime in the eyes of this Council."

But he can't go with me, I thought. I had no idea where I was going, what would happen or what was coming. I could not take a child with me. My stomach churned and I willed myself not to vomit.

Mother grabbed my hand. "I will take him, Veralee." Her beautiful eyes, that matched my own, were full of compassion and tears. "I will keep him safe, until you return."

I felt her resolve quiver and shake for a moment, and I put my arms around her to steady her. She wrapped her arm within mine, and our tseeyens burned with the love that ached inside of each of us. Tears streamed down her face, and I looked up to the sky to gather my courage.

Then, I turned to face them again with iron in my voice, "I may have to walk the path that you have laid out before me. But," I turned and looked at Absalom and then Uncle Austin with my teeth clenched tightly together, "But, you will *not* determine my way, for *my* way, has already been written in my blood, and *none* of you—nor your laws or politics—can change that," I cried out rebelliously.

Me, Veralee of Red Oaks... of the Simulacrum and of the... Boged. Boged. I am Boged! My world tilted, reshaped, reorganized within the walls of that one word. *Boged.*

The Council looked grief-stricken, but then after a long moment, Daddy tried to stop the decision by bellowing out, "Do not do this to her; show mercy with justice! Do not do this!"

With the full weight of the Council and a nod of her head, Deena the Judge accepted my confession. And the weight of the gavel on the old oak table condemned me. "Let it be known, that Veralee Harper of the Simulacrum is hereby banished, set apart from our people, to walk alone for the rest of her days. No Simulacrum will harbor her; no bed will give her rest. She is condemned to live apart for her crime against our people."

I was guilty. Guilty of changing a Boged child, and of breaking our law. But I was guilty of so much more. I was guilty of being Boged myself.

I looked defiantly towards the Council. Tears rolled down my face. I was not sure, but through my blurred vision, I thought I saw Absalom smile with satisfaction.

And then in the distance, something began. "Do you hear it?" I asked.

Mother looked perplexed, "Hear what, Veralee?"

"Drums" I said, "I hear the beating of drums."

Mother tilted her head and looked toward the horizon.

Atticus said, "Those are the war drums." His voice crashed into the silence that had formed all around us as we listened and something...maybe it was our sense of security... shattered like glass around us.

"Something has happened outside," Mother said with a gasp of shock that rippled through the crowd around us.

And then Atticus turned to face me and spoke as if I were the only one in the world, as if he saw me and only me while the world began to spin faster around us. I clung to his green eyes, to the one thing I could rely upon now.

"War is upon us."

It begins at the end, for it is the end that begins it all...

Coming Soon:

Book Two of the Simulacrum Saga.

For more information go to:
www.theoaksremain.com

Julia J. Gibbs

GLOSSARY

Simulacrum (simyə¹ lākrəm**):** Latin. Image or representation of something; Image-bearer

Friguscor: Latin. Cold-heart

Veralee: Truth or Faith; Shelter from the Wind

Absalom: Hebrew. First meaning my father is peace, grew to mean the usurper.

Achiel: Hebrew. My brother

Archaon: Ancient Ones

Ayindalet: Hebrew for the year 5774 or 2014. Ayin means eye; to see-and by extension, to understand and to obey. Dalet means hanging tent door; also can mean the movement of one coming in or going out of a tent door.

Basar: Hebrew; body

Chaim Arukim: Simulacrum chosen to live years past the normal 110 in this world.

Et Sanguis est essentia: Latin; And the blood is the essence

Golah (go-law') Hebrew: remove, away into Exile, carried away into captivity

Issachar: Hebrew. One of the twelve tribes of Israel. Book of Chronicles, *men who understood time and what Israel ought to do.*

Lignum Vitae: Latin; The Tree is Life

Naphtali: Hebrew. My struggle; One of the twelve tribes of

Israel. Genesis, *Naphtali is a doe set free who bears beautiful fawns.*

Padhah: Hebrew; To rescue, buy back or ransom

Paraclete: Latin. Advocate or Helper

Primogenes: Latin; first-borns.

Terebinths of Mamre: Where God appeared to Abraham. Genesis 18:1

Tseeyen: Hebrew. Marked or noted.

Wakeful Ones: Aramaic term for messengers. Occurs only in Daniel 4:13,17,23. Messenger or one who is awake, while Nebuchadnezzar sleeps.

Woman without Form; Wisdom: Proverbs 7